PRAISE FOR HEIKKI H

"This is a thoroughly enjoyable read and a 'must' for any fan of military aviation."

—M Howard Morgan, author of *First Fleet*

"Adventure, excitement, tragedy, romance and engaging characters, this novel has it all."

—Susanne O'Leary, author of *Fresh Powder* and *Finding Margo*

"The location is beautiful, the hotel well worth a visit, and the lives of the guests are intriguing... A great read."

—Historical Novels Review

"… gives you excitement, pathos, tenderness, love, nostalgia, beauty and a set of characters that, even in the sadness of some of the episodes, convey the essential resilience and value of human beings."

—Bill Kirton, author of *The Figurehead* and *The Sparrow Conundrum*

"… thoroughly in command of a setting half a world away and 65 years in the past. I can't imagine how he did it."

—Stephen E. Gallup

"… beyond the technical details lies a wonderful story with beautifully written characters full of personality and charm."

—Raven Dane

Also by Heikki Hietala, available from Fingerpress.co.uk

Filtered Light & Other Stories—The Complete Collection

"Breathtaking, outstanding, complete."—Aison Wells

"…an ineradicable sense of dark chill lurking."—Dan Holloway

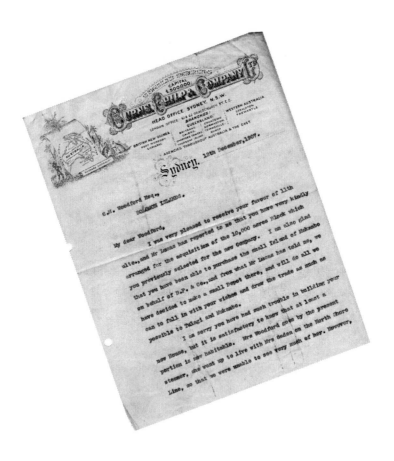

Tulagi Hotel

Heikki Hietala

FINGERPRESS LTD
LONDON

Tulagi Hotel

ISBN (pbk): 978-1-908824-16-5

Published by Fingerpress Ltd
This book was previously published by Diiarts (UK) and Pfoxmoor
(US). All English-language publication rights now reside with
Fingerpress.

Production Editor: Matt Stephens
Production Manager: Michelle Stephens
Copy Editor: Madeleine Horobin
Editorial Assistant: Artica Ham

www.fingerpress.co.uk

To Leena-Mari, Ossi and Paavo
and
to Wells Norris, who flew those skies.

HMAS Canberra underway off Tulagi, during the landings there, 7-8 August 1942. Three transports are among the ships visible in the distance, with Tulagi and Florida Islands beyond.

Tulagi Hotel

A U.S. Navy Vought OS2U-2 Kingfisher seaplane in flight in early 1942.

1

"Jack! Hey, Jack! Wake up, there's someone to see you."

"Ohhhh ... go away, Martin. I'm dead."

The man on the bed didn't bother to face Martin in the doorway or even open his eyes. Instead, he rolled to his left and curled up. Undeterred, Martin rushed to the bed and shook Jack with vigor, then bounced back to the doorway and swayed hanging on the doorframe, knees bent.

"Jack!" Martin wasn't about to give up so easily. "I think you want to see who came in today."

"No one's coming today. Not that I know of at least. Go away and fix my funeral." He curled up even tighter and pulled the covers over his head.

Martin let out an exasperated sigh and returned to the task at hand. "Jack—she flew in on the Trans-Oceanic last night, and now she's here. She stayed at Sir Randolph's guest house overnight at Tulagi and they brought her here just now. She says she knew Don. She wants to talk to you about Don Wheeler."

Martin pulled the covers off Jack's head to reveal an un-kempt, unshaven man in his early thirties, hangover incarnate. Martin shook his head. "You should know better, Jack. Never ever drink with the Headmen. Their beer is not of this world. Besides, you need to get up anyway. No time to sleep all day."

Jack tried to force his eyelids open, but now Martin was standing against the bright morning light flooding the hut from the open doorway. The blacksmiths in Jack's head accelerated to full speed. The blood rushing between his ears sounded like a mighty furnace bellows, driven on by a feverish pulse.

"Come on, you want to see this lady. She's not here for a holiday."

Pushing himself up, Jack sat upright on the bed. With unfocused eyes, he tried to stand but fell back on the mattress instead, hitting his head on the curve of the corrugated iron wall. With a strained effort Jack finally stood up and managed to train his eyes on the porch bathing in the brilliant Solomon Islands sun.

A lady in a light dress with flowers stood there, on the porch. In her hand she held a purse and beside her was a leather Gladstone valise. Pushing Martin's extended arm away, Jack dragged his feet to the door, painfully aware of the finesse his appearance lacked this morning.

"Jack McGuire?" The lady smiled. "So nice to finally meet you. I'm Kay Wheeler."

The lady held out her hand. Jack took it and felt her firm grip. He tried to fix the name with someone Don might have mentioned when they flew together way back when, but his brain flashed *"No Match"*. But then, that morning, even his mother's name might have pressed him hard.

Eventually the lady's surname registered. A relation of Don's? A sister or something?

"Hello," he managed. "Have a seat."

Martin stepped in, sparing a disgusted glance for Jack. "Would you like something to drink? All we have is gin and tonic, and some local beer, I'm afraid, but I think the gin would be safer."

Kay nodded. "That would be great, thank you. It's so hot

already. It's not like this in Boston." She sat down on a rickety director's chair on the porch. Martin nodded and went inside to the small wooden cabinet to make her a drink.

By now Jack had his head a bit clearer, and he was running it double time. Boston? Don had never mentioned Boston. Meanwhile Martin had returned to the porch and had passed the drink to the lady, who smiled her thanks and had a sip.

"I always thought Don was from Washington," Jack ventured.

"Yes, he was born in Seattle, but I met him in New Mexico in 1939. We married in 1940, and you sailed out with him in July 1942."

Jack was stunned. Don was married? As far as he knew, Don Wheeler was the archetype of the womanizing fighter pilot. Indeed, his wallet was among the thickest Jack had seen, not because of greenbacks but because of phone numbers hastily scribbled on the backs of restaurant bills, napkins and any other stationery available on the move.

So how come Don had married this lady, was living with her in Boston, and yet had collected such a walletful of acquaintances? He'd been even faster than Jack had imagined. Besides, it was not possible to be a married aviation cadet, at least assuming regulations were followed.

A response of some sort was in order. "Ah. Well, yes. Right. Ummm... How did you find me? Can I help you with something?" Stupid, Jack thought, but he could not help it.

"Well, that's why I came, you see. Don used to talk about you when he was on leave, telling me how you always flew together." A brief shadow crossed the woman's face. "And when the official letter came, just saying he was killed in action, I needed to know more of his death. But I couldn't get started. It took me years to get to this point." She paused for a

3

moment.

"So last year, when I finally decided to do something about this, I went through his letters again. I found some names and tracked down John Radner. He said that you were with Don on his last flight and I should try to find you."

"Bunny Radner? Is he still in the Marines?" Hearing his squadron commander's name felt odd to Jack, like an echo in a corridor of closed doors.

"No, he's out on a...medical discharge due to an accident he had in '45. He has an office supplies shop in Manhattan now. But he thought you could help me—he sent his very best regards to you. It so happens he had a newspaper clipping on his office wall, *New York Times*? It or some other paper sent a reporter here."

Jack tried to remember a reporter visiting the area, but could not. He merely nodded in agreement because he found no useful comment, and let Kay go on.

"...and he passed through the Solomons on his way to Japan to see how the South Pacific was recovering and stayed with you. Now I knew the part of the world you were in. The rest was easy—I just wrote to the British authorities here and they knew you." Kay's face had returned to normal.

Jack's head felt like a vacuum. "How did you get here? Sit on a copra ship for a week?"

"No, actually I flew to Sydney and went to the harbor to find a ship for the last leg. I was told that besides ships, I could try and see if the Trans-Oceanic Airways was headed this way soon. I was in luck, and only waited three days for a flight. A cruise would have been just as fine though," Kay added with her head held high, looking every bit the adventuress.

She looked around. "And now I'm here. Is this place Tulagi? I thought I'd stayed overnight at Tulagi—the British administrator was very kind and offered me the guest house. The boatman talked of Hale ... Halava? Something like that?"

"Halavo Bay, that's the bay down there," said Jack, pointing west down the gently sloping hill towards the deep-blue waters gleaming between the trees. "Tulagi is where you landed. I just thought to call my place Tulagi Hotel because nobody would know Halavo, but someone may know Tulagi, at least those who were here in the war."

Jack studied her face intensely, trying to remember her from somewhere, to pin a label on her, but gradually felt ashamed of scrutinizing her. Kay was not a stunning beauty, but her delicate eyes glinting with intellect and curiosity and high-angled eyebrows caught Jack's gaze, and for a brief moment he felt he had achieved complete contact with her.

He decided to return to the original conversation. "And yes, I flew with Don. I mean, I was his wingman. And he was my wingman. Always. We never flew with anybody else."

Jack sounded stupid to himself, but Kay encouraged him with her eyes, so he went on.

"I was his wingman when he died. It was an even day. On an odd day he'd have been on my wing. It's a long story, really." Jack looked over Kay's shoulder into the bay, where his OS2U Kingfisher floatplane was moored, aligning itself with the light wind.

Kay settled to a more pleasant posture in her chair, which let out snapping sounds of imminent structural failure, a counterpoint of suspense to Jack's prologue.

"I'm not sure you want to hear it all," Jack said, hoping she'd agree.

"I would very much like to hear that story, if you'd tell me, please. I need to know how it all happened. I've spent so much time wondering if he suffered much." Kay let her gaze traverse the lush surroundings and paused a moment on the beautiful woodwork decorating the window of the hut. Then she fixed her light-blue eyes on Jack's bloodshot and black-rimmed ones.

Jack's head swung as if he'd been hit.

"No, I don't think he knew a thing. It was a routine mission from Munda to Bougainville, nothing special." He picked up a half-empty beer bottle from the floor, had a sip of the stale contents, flicking the loose and torn label with his thumb. He needed a tangential focal point to recall that single mission which had become an almost unreachable part of his memory, fossilized by the sediment of dead emotion.

He was about to embark on a voyage to dark waters.

2

With a roving gaze across the bay, Jack started his story. "We took off from Munda Field at daybreak, eight Corsairs in two flights of four planes each. We were to cover the landings on Bougainville which were in a dangerous phase, so we headed northwest, climbing and forming up on the way. There had been little opposition in the air lately, so we didn't expect much of that day's mission. Over Kahili we settled into a routine of flying lazy circles above the beachhead at seventeen thousand feet."

"We didn't see any air action until about an hour later when a formation of nine Val dive-bombers and six Zero fighters appeared from the northwest. Vals were slow and not that dangerous, but the fighters were bad." Jack leaned back in his chair for a moment but soon returned to a forward crouch: the pilot position.

"Don called them out, bellowing into the radio: 'Got 'em! Bandits at eleven o'clock, four miles, slightly high!' We all dropped our belly tanks, pushed the throttles wide open and went to meet the enemy planes. I could see that Don's tank didn't fall off, and I called him to tell him that, but I only got a 'Yeah, yeah, don't worry' in response. The fight was on already and he didn't want to miss a second trying to get the tank to drop by diving and then pulling hard up."

By now, there were drops of sweat on his brow, and Jack was growing restless in his chair. "I was still in a shallow

7

climbing turn when Don opened up on the lead Zero. I must say he got lucky, he was still far but the Zero flamed immediately and the plane went down. Don pulled up and left to get behind the Vals, and I cut my climb short and managed to join him. The Vals were firing like crazy but the gunners were not of the top stock we had seen."

Not noticing he was doing so, Jack performed the choreography of combat with his hands. "Soon Don was able to fire on the nearest Val. His bullets killed the gunner first, and then he must have hit the bomb as the plane exploded in a ball of flame. I had by this time closed in on another Val, and I downed him. Jones and Becker, the other two pilots on our flight, each bagged a Zero."

Jack scanned the sky just as he had done in the cockpit.

"The eight of us now fought three Zeros and seven Vals. One of the Zeros just exploded in midair, without any of us firing at it, and I really can't say why. By this time the fight was pretty one-sided, as Vals are no match to Corsairs and the two remaining Zeros were busy saving their own necks, unable to protect the bombers."

With associated hand movements, Jack was more reliving the battle than conveying it to Kay. "I had lost sight of Don for a while, but I could hear him shout on the radio: 'Splash Zero three!' I asked him where he was and he said he was currently chasing three Vals. I glanced around and saw such a formation on my right and below me. I could see he had a Zero on his tail. Becker fell on the Zero like a hawk for a pigeon and saved Don's feathers that time. He had an hour to live at that point, but of course we didn't know that."

Kay was also leaning forward, intent, as Jack returned to the combat which had been branded in his memory, every last jerking turn and hasty evasive move. Still unaware of his movements, Jack leaned forward in his chair as if to grab hold of the plane controls once again, to try and fight again, only this time to save Don.

"I joined Don's wing to get to the dive-bombers, but the Vals had ejected their bomb load without any effect and split up for turning home. Don still had that tank hanging from his plane. We patrolled the beachhead for another hour, after which we were relieved by eight Army P-38 fighters and started home towards Munda."

Jack wore a ghost of a smile with the post-battle adrenalin surging through him once again. "Don was jubilant. He had downed three Zeros and a Val, and his total tally was now thirteen and a half kills. I could see him rejoicing in the cockpit, letting off the steam of the battle. Jones and Becker joined up and we settled down. Only dead pilots ever let their vigilance wear off, so we did the usual routine of glancing at the instruments and scanning the whole sky."

Kay understood the inside joke and smiled, but Jack didn't see it.

He went on. "Just about halfway back to Munda Jones shouted: 'Betty at two o'clock low, heading north!' And there it was, a lone Betty twin-engine medium bomber, probably on a reconnaissance mission. Don called the flight and said, 'I'll splash that one—just watch me!'"

Another cloud of worry formed in Jack's eyes. "We tried to talk him out of it, but he peeled off and I followed him. The Betty's pilot started looking for cover. There was a light cloud below him and he started down towards it. When the Betty reached the cloud, Don throttled back, playing cat and mouse. He was going to let the Betty emerge from the north edge of the cloud, which was visible to us about a mile away and get it. I was a few hundred feet above and to his right. It all depended on the Betty maintaining course and altitude, but we'd done this before."

Still fighting demons, Jack tried to concentrate. "All of a sudden I could see the bomber lunging up from the cloud like a rattlesnake, with its engines roaring and the tail gunner firing. Don had crept too close to the Betty, he had not throttled back enough, so his engine covered the Betty. The gunner must have seen his shadow on the cloud cover and told the pilot what to do."

Having arrived at the decisive point, Jack squirmed in his seat. "As soon as the gunner got a fix on Don, I could see pieces of Don's engine cowling flying off. Within seconds the Jap had Don's engine on fire, and when one bullet hit his spent auxiliary tank, it was all over."

His voice had become monochrome and hard, like lacquer on wood.

"With just the fumes in the tank, it was as lethal as a bomb. Don's plane went to pieces at the explosion—the engine tore off and went down trailing smoke, and both wings were wrenched off from the fuselage. Don went down like a dart in the fuselage, straight down, but the wings took a long time to fall into the ocean. I remember thinking of autumn leaves, red and yellow maple leaves, when I watched those wings floating down."

A long pause followed, which Kay dared not break. Jack closed his eyes and took a deep breath, as he had done when he realized his friend was gone.

Finally he spoke again. There was more to the story.

"I had to pull myself into action, as the Betty again dove for the cloud cover. Both Jones and Becker had come down too to watch Don's attack, and they happened to be in a good position to fire. The Betty made it for one more minute after

Don had gone down, but it never stood a chance. Jones finished the Betty off and it fell into the sea, unguided. Another oil slick marked the spot where Don had hit the ocean. Nothing else was visible on the surface."

Jack looked across the porch at Kay. Her eyebrows were notched all the way up. He had to keep the story going.

"All three of us were in a daze and I can't say I remember anything of the trip back. All I remember is that I just went in and taxied off the strip into the parking area, and then the engine died, no fuel. When I exited the plane Don's crew chief came up and looked at me. 'Don's gone,' I said to him. The plane captain walked away. He said nothing, but then, we never did say much in those moments. There were just too many of them."

At that, Jack leaned against the wall and put his hands in his lap. Though he was nearly as exhausted as he was after a flight, the last bit of the story would take even more energy. "I sat down on my parachute and buried my head in my hands. I had lost my best friend, my section leader. I had seen it coming but I was not in a position to help him. I could not do anything but watch my friend die."

Kay fumbled in her purse for a handkerchief. It was plainly tormenting her to hear Jack's story, and yet as she'd said, it was just what she had waited for all these years.

Jack paused until she seemed ready to listen further. "I think I sat there for an hour, or maybe more, but I really only thought about losing Don. Nothing was bringing him back, but I tried to think of him sitting next to me, like he used to do. And for a moment I thought he was there, but that feeling faded the next second, and then it was just me and my plane."

Jack briefly studied the beer label, ripped it off the bottle to roll it up in a ball, and looked back out to the indifferent sea. "After that, flying lost its charm for a long time. I did fly, I gained kills steadily, but my heart was not in it anymore." He shot the label off his curved index finger with a flick of the thumb.

Silently Kay was weeping, her teardrops gathering volume and weight and then rolling down her cheeks to disappear into her collar. After what seemed to Jack an arduous wait, she dabbed her cheeks dry, looked into the horizon for just a second more, and then faced Jack again.

"Thank you for sharing that," she said with a firm voice. "It matters so much to me that he didn't suffer. He's dead, but it helps to hear he died like that, doing what he loved best. He loved me very much, I know, but flying was his greatest love." She managed a faint smile. "Now I know he died happy," she said.

Jack felt at a loss, and tried to console Kay by mumbling a few platitudes about life in general.

Kay looked straight into his eyes, and it was clear to Jack she was beyond mere platitudes now. "It's time to go on," she declared. "I am no longer going to think about the past. For all this time I've been wondering, about Don, about his death, but now I'll start again. Thanks to you, I can do that. It's been too many years already. Six years is a long time."

And with that she stood up and offered her hand to Jack, who also rose to his feet. "The flying boat will head south on Friday, right? I'd need to stay for one night then, if you have vacancies. And if you don't happen to have any, can I stay over there where the plane landed?"

Jack shook her hand and then scratched his head, trying to remember the schedule. "Yes, it'll leave on Friday, early in the morning. I think it was 6 o'clock. Let's just confirm that. I think I have the schedules here somewhere." With a nod Jack stepped into the hut to try and locate the paper. "There's always the odd plane passing by Guadalcanal, too," he called back to her. "Not much comfort on those, mainly they run cargo, and that can be anything from fuel to fowl. It will be an early morning for you tomorrow in any case."

After a few minutes of shuffling stacks of coffee-soiled papers he eventually admitted to Kay that his filing system was a bit messy for a hotel owner.

Putting her hand on the war-weary typewriter, Kay pulled out a ribbon with a knot in it. She smiled and said she could live with just the knowledge that it would be possible to leave for the United States again soon.

"We'll have to get you settled down for the night," Jack said. "I have three cabins available. One is up here, another's over there on that knoll, and the third one stands there overlooking the harbor." Jack pointed this way and that, providing no sense at all of direction, and hid the fact that he had nine other cabins clear of lodgers as well.

"I'd love a view to the sea," Kay said.

At her cue, Jack picked up her leather bag. "Then follow me, please, and watch your feet—the trails are not exactly paved." He led her down the trail winding between the palms and wide swaths of lawn to a hut resembling a huge barrel half-buried in the ground along its length. Though it had been adapted from a Nissen hut, its military origins were cleverly concealed by woodwork, added windows, and paint. The result was a fairly comfortable-looking dwelling.

On the top of the hut, at the apex of the semicircle, was a double row of open ventilation hatches, like a backbone with stubby little wings. The view from the hut's porch was truly glorious, with lush palm trees framing the deep blue ocean.

Jack handed her the key, which had a heavy wooden tag

bearing the number 9. "I'll leave you here. If you want to have a dip, the path to the sea starts from there. We've installed sweet water showers at the beach. Dinner will be ready in about an hour, so just come back to my hut and we'll hop up to the lunch room."

He left Kay to settle down and made his way back to his hut up on the hillside.

"Martin! Where are you, you old rat? Martin!" Jack shouted, and soon Martin's smiling face appeared at the doorway.

"Yes, Master?" he said, knowing full well how it irritated Jack beyond all other taunts to be called 'Master'.

"Martin, I need you to go up to Wilma and have her spruce up lunch a little bit. Tell her to cook for lunch whatever she was thinking to do for dinner, or maybe that great stuff we had last week, when we had the Resident Commissioner over for dinner…I can't remember what it was exactly, but it was so good. She'll know."

Martin was already on his way there as he shouted, "Yes, Master, right away, Master, immediately, sir" and whistled his way uphill. Jack shook his head, freshened himself up somewhat, and then turned his attention to sorting out the abominable pile of paper on his desk.

Half an hour later Jack could look back on his desk with great satisfaction. Where tattered piles of assorted papers had been, there was now a neat and organized desk with all paperwork placed in manila folders, and newly-excavated office tools, such as the typewriter and a fountain pen with a stand, laid out in a workable arrangement. "If only I could have this setup last for a week…" Jack muttered to himself, but his thought was interrupted by a cheery voice from the doorway.

He turned to face Kay, a glowing aura of sunlight pulsing around her. "Hi, Jack—I know I'm early, but what if we went for a stroll before lunch?"

"Sure, just a second," Jack agreed, casting a final look at the desk. He went out to meet a radiant Kay who had changed into a most appropriate, light and colorful summer dress.

Jack had to remind himself not to ogle her, and tried his best to treat her like just another guest.

"My guests usually take that trail down to the water, and then they take a sweeping round walk that way, and they then arrive back at the hotel from there, where you can't see from here," Jack explained, accompanying his directions with broad, if nondescript, sweeps of his right hand.

"Sounds fine to me!" Kay said, starting swiftly down the hill. Jack took a few long strides to reach her. "Isn't it odd that it's just a few years since the war ended and the place looks this good already?" Kay asked when he pulled up alongside.

Jack had to agree. "Tulagi itself was defended to the last man by the Japanese—we had to fight real hard to wrest the place from them. We had a seaplane base later on this island and that's why the Japanese did try and target this too. This place is actually called Halavo Bay, and it wasn't hit as hard as Tulagi. It's a pity about the palms though," he added, pointing to stumps of palms that had been severed by heavy projectiles.

"Yes, I guess they'll take years to grow back," Kay said. "Lucky some of them survived."

"Exactly. On some islands, like Tarawa, the bombardment before invasion was so thorough that no trees were left standing. It was called a Spruance haircut with Mitscher shampoo—you remember the admirals?" He immediately regretted staying on the subject of war.

But it seemed okay. "Yes, I do," Kay said, stopping and looking Jack in the face. "I guess there was a lighter side to the war as well,"

With that, Jack sensed a go-ahead in her voice.

"There was, Kay, especially when Don was still around. We horsed so much and had a ball practically all the time…but it was all necessary. The business of war is not a nice one, and without some laughter it's nigh unbearable. We used to joke about the clouds having the Pearly Gates, complete with St Peter managing the flow of lodgers.

"Really?"

"That's right. We even called out promising cloud formations to each other while on combat missions," Jack added. "And out here you're never short of clouds which could pass for the Pearly Gates," he said and pointed to a particularly massive and beautiful cumulus cloud above the sea.

"So, you adapt to the situation as best you can," Kay said, her springy gait taking her downhill at an even faster pace. Jack followed her, alternating between glancing at her small frame and making certain he didn't trip over rocks or tree roots on the uneven path.

He reached her by the waterside and pointed to the sea-front. "The natives rebounded really fast out of the war," he said, and indicated a market flourishing right by the sea, which they reached in a few further steps.

"They certainly seem to have it worked out all right," Kay said, picking up some form of marine life from a stall. "What's this?" she asked.

"Your guess is just as good as mine," Jack said with a smile, "but when Wilma gets it into her pot, it'll taste just great."

"Who's Wilma?"

"Wilma is my ace up the sleeve. When I have the hotel running at full speed, and competition starts to arrive in the area, none of them will be able to serve food as great as that at

16

the Tulagi Hotel."

It struck Jack that fierce competition in hospitality was not very probable, but he decided to press further.

"Wilma is the best chef in the islands. She is Martin's relative somehow, like a fifteenth cousin, but when I got here, needing a chef, Martin said there's only one person to consider. She works for me, but she also cooks for the entire family every day. I pay her enough so she can do just that, and everyone is happy. In return she makes sure no one leaves my hotel feeling they've been served bad food."

"Sounds like a winning arrangement," Kay said with a short sparkle of laughter.

"It is. And to keep it that way, I also make it a point to stay out of the kitchen. I can't name any of the ingredients or identify any of the courses, but my guests always ask for seconds. Besides, last year I brought her some macaroni from Australia, just to see if she had any use for it, but I got my cue when I began to see all the kids on the island wearing matching bracelets and necklaces."

Kay's giggle filled his head like confetti. He was thrilled by the feeling, something he'd not felt in ages.

Their stroll was soon approaching the point where they had to decide to take either take one of the upward traveling trails or to venture out to the main harbor. "Can't we have a peek at the harbor too?" Kay pleaded.

Jack nodded. "Well, let's do that, but not for too long— already I can see Wilma at the main hut, looking down at us. You see, there's only you and me for lunch today."

Kay was genuinely surprised. "What—don't you have any other guests?"

Reddening, Jack was digging a hole in the ground with his left foot. "Well, no—not just now, not today. But there'll be more once the travel to these parts begins for real," he added cheerfully.

Kay turned away from him and raced to the main pier jutting out of the shoreline about fifty yards into the ocean whose color went from light to a dark opaque blue. "Isn't this just great!" she exclaimed, looking down at the ocean. "The ocean is so clear that I can see the bottom—I can't even tell how deep the water is!"

"It's about fifteen feet right there," Jack said. "I've seen lodgers jump in from that point, but please don't do that right now!"

"Right, we can't keep Wilma waiting." With another spark of tee-heeing, Kay ran further out to see the plane Jack had tethered to a buoy, some fifty feet from the pier. "Is that your plane?" Kay wondered. "It doesn't look at all like a fighter plane to me!"

Jack stepped up to Kay. "Well, your judgment is right— it's a scouting and observation plane. Fighters are no fun in peacetime—you need something more useful than six machine guns and bad fuel economy.

"It's an OS2U Kingfisher, built by Vought, and flown by the US Navy as a reconnaissance and rescue plane. After the war, when I made the decision to come here, I went up to a Navy surplus auction and bought two of those for peanuts. I stored the other plane down in Sydney for spare parts—they'll last for a good while. I also have a working maintenance agreement with the airfield on the big island. And that's the big idea behind my air force of one," Jack concluded.

"It's a beautiful plane," Kay said, tilting her head.

"It sure is, and it flies like a butterfly compared to any other plane I've flown. In fact, I think I'd have enjoyed the war better in a rescue plane than in fighters, but that's said with the benefit of hindsight. There's no match for the thrill of flying fighters, but these days I much prefer this one."

Now, above, Wilma was on the porch of the main hut and the ringing of the iron triangle made it clear enough it was time to speed uphill for lunch. "Come, Kay, let's get going. Wilma's getting irritated by our lollygagging," Jack said, and escorted Kay off the pier. He briefly wondered to himself how such a lovely creature could allow him to touch her as he briefly guided her by the arm off the pier.

They made the trip back up the hill in little time and apparently had not incurred Wilma's wrath, because the lunch was a true feast of tastes. Having no other guests at the meal meant that Jack had Kay's undivided attention, and in her gaze he reveled, feeling refreshed and alive, something he hadn't experienced in a long while.

Afterwards Kay went to the porch, but by that time the day had become very hot. She stayed out of the sun's reach and sat down on a chair, watching the golden afternoon sunlight glimmering on the bay. "This is life...I haven't felt this good in ages. This place is heavenly!"

Jack came out just in time to hear her compliment. "Glad you like it—that's what got me here in the first place." He offered Kay one of the tall ice teas he was holding.

"Ice cubes in the Solomons?" she said, taking the glass with a thankful nod.

"US Army. They wouldn't fight without some perks, you know. The operation over here was really critical for a long time, and supplies were hard to come by, but later on they had refrigerators and even ice cube machines brought here through the supply system. I bought my fridges, aggregators, and these huts, and lots more from the Army over there on Guadalcanal."

19

Jack clinked the ice in his glass. "They were stored at the end of the war, and the ice cube machine was a bonus, as it was not in much demand by the natives. I guess the stuff was already struck off the books and nobody wanted them back. Too much red tape, transport, and other hassles. Nowadays they still have some surplus there and they just want to get rid of it."

Kay looked back at the main hut. "So this was an army hut?"

"Yes, this is a Nissen hut, or Quonset hut, as they sometimes were called. Prefabricated, easy to pitch, easy to strike, sold as surplus once the American troops left. You'd be amazed at the number of these huts still here when the war ended. Some of them were still in their crates, and I got eighteen of them. I haven't assembled more than ten so far—no, eleven, one is my hangar down there by the pier—but I believe I will have to put up more later on."

Jack slid his hand down the woodwork which a local carpenter had put on the edge of the roof. "I am also trying to rebuild the old plantation lodge, but it's taking up more time and effort than I thought it would. So, till it gets finished, I'm using this hut as my lodge."

They continued to discuss Jack's hotel business. As they talked, Jack once more tried to remember where he had seen Kay before, but with no luck. He knew he recognized her, but for the life of him, he still could not recall details. At some length he decided to put it to his subconscious to come up with the answer, and he was then better able to join the conversation.

He found that Kay was interested in anything he could tell her. There was no end to her curiosity, and he felt valued in her company. All his anecdotes as an expatriate in the Solomons elicited giggles and occasionally outright laughter, and he found himself addicted to all the sweet little sounds she made.

They talked until the sun was well out west, and then further into the warm dark night. It seemed to both of them that they would never run out of things to discuss, and they both welcomed that feeling, albeit to themselves only.

As the sounds of birds descended around them, Jack brought up an unpleasant subject which seemed to hang in the humid, fragrant air. "It's really too bad the Trans-Oceanic will fly south again so soon, tomorrow morning already. I would have liked you to stay for a while."

"Actually, Jack, that's something I wanted to talk you about. You seem to have space right now. I mean, I'm on holiday right now for three weeks anyway, and first I thought I'd spend some time with my aunt in Santa Barbara on my way back to Boston, but what I'd actually like to do is to stay here until the flying boat returns, maybe see some sights and get to know the place a bit better—if that's okay with you?" Kay blurted out this last bit as if it had been percolating for a while.

Jack looked at her and smiled.

"Well, we're not exactly booked full, never yet have been. You're free to stay as long as you like. In fact, I'd like to take you around for some of the flight routes we run for sightseeing. There's a great run we do to Bougainville and back, and with the Kingfisher we could go on a day trip to some of the small islands in The Slot, if that'd interest you. The Slot is the waterway between the two strings of the Solomon Islands. Besides, if you leave word with Bill Peet on Guadalcanal, you may be able to hitch a ride to Sydney with some cargo plane that passes this place, if and when you get itchy."

Kay beamed. "Excellent! I'll just cable my aunt and tell her I missed the plane and got stuck here for a while. In fact I'd like to skip seeing her altogether, as she is as big a bore as there ever was." Her face fell a little. "Umm ... how do I cable someone from here?"

Jack instructed her to write the message on a sheet of paper and give it to Martin, who'd see it was sent from the British District Officer's wireless station. Kay could not stop smiling all evening, and every time Jack saw her smile, he felt a jolt in his heart.

*

Kay retired to her hut, but only after Jack had shown her all the constellations that he knew in the southern sky. As, by nature if not desire, he had always been a loner, it was such a pleasant feeling for him to have someone reserve all her attention for what he was saying, and especially to smile at him so warmly, as Kay did frequently.

Back at his hut, Jack found his copy of Norton's Star Atlas which he had bought back in Sydney years ago, to brush up on his stars. When he fell asleep on the book which he took to bed that night, Kay's eyes shone in his dreams like Sirius and Canopus, and the southern sky had received a bright new constellation.

As for Kay, it proved to be an even later night. Now, alone, she had time to assemble her image of Jack. She had immediately liked the resolute gaze of his gray eyes, and the nose which had been broken somewhere in his past provided some pugnacious realism and a mystery to solve, eventually. She wondered how he could look so much like Don from behind; both had a muscular frame without any hint of having built it

22

on purpose. Jack was slightly taller than Don had been, though, maybe six foot two.

From the front, Jack's high and receding hairline and mouse-colored short hair was very different from Don's mop of unruly curls, which brought to mind an excitable Irish setter. Also from the front, Jack's shy smile melted its way to her heart. But Jack's stories had brought the two men—one dead, one living—together in her mind, and Kay found she could not think of one without the other now.

Having pondered upon these observations for a good while she fell asleep, expecting her stay at Tulagi Hotel to prove quite memorable indeed.

3

Jack McGuire was not built of the same stock as most pre-war Navy aviators, but for the wartime Navy he was typical. The McGuire family home was some five miles from Winton, Nebraska. The family had moved to Winton in 1923, when Jack and his twin brother Tony were two. Sisters Anna and Emily soon followed, in 1924 and 1926. At first his family had little in the way of earthly fortune, but his parents were quick to see that Jack and Tony worked hard at school, and stayed at the top of their class at all grades. They also diligently tended to their animals, and more often than not brought home blue ribbons from the county fairs. The family's hard work earned them a farm that produced more than most, and steadily they expanded it.

What separated Winton from many small rural towns was that it had an airfield. It was a field in the strictest sense of the word, with all of seven hundred feet of dusty runway. It was not used much as a regular destination or departure point, but as an emergency field it did have some visitors, such as barnstormers and mail planes with engine trouble. And it was Old Joe Selig's home field. Joe had a battered Avro 504 two-seat biplane he had acquired at the end of the World War One and shipped home from England, though nobody knew with what money, or how.

Joe spent all his money on that plane, patching it up, reinforcing the worn airframe, and maintaining the engine as best he could. He lived on a small farm close to the airfield, but his heart never was in farming. He was an aviator. He could tell stories from the Western Front like no one, and in boys like Jack and Tony he had a grateful audience, ready to hear every air battle over and over again, as Joe would spice his stories up every time a little differently. Some adults would venture to say that Old Joe rarely let the truth interfere with a good story, but to the boys, his words were legend.

On Sundays after church he would gather the boys of Winton together inside the hangar. He'd let some kid sit in the cockpit and wiggle the stick to see the elevator and ailerons move, and try to reach the pedals with his feet. Every boy in strict rotation had his shot at the pilot's seat, and every boy would watch Joe take off for his Sunday evening hop, vowing to become a pilot someday.

But before they could fly themselves, they built model airplanes. Jack could always beat Tony at that. His fingers had the gift of feeling the form of the wings, and his eyes could see just when a propeller was perfect. His planes were of varied types—some gliders and many with rubber-band engines.

Tony, on the other hand, focused more on sports than Jack. They both were very good in baseball, but Tony was the better runner. Consequently, when he was too annoyed with Jack nibbling away at him for building such crude planes, Tony would grab Jack's latest creation and outrun him to the fields to fly the plane himself until late in the evening. To his credit, he never broke a plane, and in his heart Jack was not at all annoyed by Tony. Rather, he built some planes for the express purpose of letting Tony fly them. They were a close pair, all through the years.

Tony would coach Jack for hours on his baseball pitch behind the barn, until Jack had it all together and could throw anybody in the school off his swing. Tony had his revenge for the modeling gap when he would taunt his twin until Jack threw his cap on the ground and walked away, sulking, vowing never to pitch again. But by nightfall they would always be back in line, talking about flying, baseball, fishing, and (later on) girls.

When they turned eighteen, Tony came home with a letter. He hid it from everybody, or so he'd thought, but twins have a hard time hiding things from each other. When Jack picked up the letter from its hideout in the barn, he saw the emblem on the cover: "United States Army Air Corps".

Jack placed the letter back in its cache in the wall and immediately went to Tony.

"You're going to run away, aren't you? Joining the Air Corps, eh? Oh boy, are you serious?"

Tony grabbed his arm and without a word dragged Jack into the barn.

"Don't you tell anyone, you hear! You tell anybody and I'll break your arm!" Tony blurted, once they were inside.

"C'mon, Tony, what're you thinking of doing? Dad reckons we'll take over the farm in a few years!" Jack reminded him.

Tony was silent for a long time, staring into a hole in the wall. Then he said: "Look, Jack, if I stay here, I'll die. I'm not cut out to be a farmer. And neither are you. Just admit that to yourself and you'll see. We're made for flying, can't you see?"

"But how'd you afford that kind of fun? There's no way Dad will put up the price of flight lessons. And you only have eighteen dollars yourself!" Jack pointed out.

"I'll join the Army and work my way up to Flight School," Tony said confidently.

"That'll take you years, and there's no guarantee you'll get in! You might as well waste your time right here," Jack said.

"For Chrissake, Jack, I've made up my mind, and no one will change it. And as for you, just take a long hard look at this farm, at Winton, and at all Nebraska, and then come back and tell me you want to stay here and farm right here for the rest of your life! This isn't for me! I want to see what's past the fields, just like the way we could see it when Old Joe took us up for a spin. There's lots out there, and I want to see and know it all. And say ... how'd you know I only have eighteen dollars, anyway?" Tony asked, squinting.

"Come on, we don't have secrets. You know where my money is, too, and I've seen your eighteen dollars *and* Nellie's picture in the hole in the wall of the barn," Jack explained. "Don't blow it all on her present—you'll need money if you do join the Army."

"My money'll be spent the way I see fit," Tony said, and left the barn in a huff. Jack stayed there for a while, trying to keep his mind off the question about his future Tony had just put to him, and then with a shrug he went to supper.

During supper the boys' father figured out something was brewing. He couldn't put his finger on it, but something was definitely in the works between the two lads, and John McGuire was not one to let secrets be kept within the family.

"How's school, Tony?" he asked, splatting a mound of mashed potatoes onto his plate and then balancing it with a generous helping of green peas.

"Okay, I guess. Lately I've been working hard on math." Tony answered, wary. A long silence ensued, and it brought a sort of static electricity to the air around the family dinner, the folks around the table just waiting to zap fingers when discharged.

"What was that letter you got today, son?" John prompted

Tony.

"What letter?" The boy tried in vain to dodge the question.

"Come on, now, the manila envelope you brought in from the post office. We usually let the postman deliver, so it must have been something special. Out with it!" The father's usually even voice raised in tone, slightly annoyed.

Tony shrugged. "I just ordered a few brochures, that's all, and since I happened to be at the post office before Bernie left for his round, I picked up the letter, the only one that was coming to us, so Bernie was spared from coming round here just for that."

"And which brochures were they, if I may ask?" John continued. "Show them to me."

Tony saw that the time for hedging was over. "They're Army brochures. I want to join the Army Air Corps and become an Army fighter pilot."

Suddenly John McGuire brought his fist down on the table, a violent gesture quite unusual for him. "A pilot, for the Army? Are you mad, son? Are you willing to sacrifice all we have here for some flimsy kite someone wants to shoot down from the sky?"

"But, Dad, I'm not a farmer! I like animals and I like to work hard but I want to see the world, too! I can't stand the thought of having to sit here all my life, while there's places to go and things to see out there! I'm willing to do it the hard way, to enlist in the army and then work it on into the Flight School. I know I can do it, and Old Joe says so too!"

John McGuire's face showed a steely determination. "No son of mine will desert this farm for a career in flying. You have a choice: work your way into college, or work this farm. There's no third option. You might as well burn those brochures, since you won't be needing them."

As Tony opened his mouth to protest, John cut him off with a commanding wave of his hand. "Now, that's final, Tony, and if you're entertaining similar thoughts, Jack, consider that plan banned from now on. And as for Old Joe, remember his experience in flying for the Army is twenty years back and has no connection with the modern world. He's an old owl, perched in that shabby, shot-up plane of his, dreaming of past brave deeds, either real, imagined or acquired from someone else for all I know. You shouldn't take his words to heart, or he'll make you believe it's all true."

He folded his hands. "And now we'll have dessert and talk about something else. This conversation ends here."

With some measure of relief, Jack reached out to have another helping of apple pie. But Tony glanced over at Jack with an iron stare, and it was clear to both brothers the conversation was far from over.

In bed that night, Jack dared to ask Tony whether he was still going to go ahead with the plan of joining the Army. Tony, his hands under his head, looked at the ceiling, and said, "Yep—my mind's made up and it's not going to be changed by Dad or Mom or anybody. I'm going to be a pilot and I'm going to be the best of them all."

"Well, send me a postcard then when you get there." Jack turned to face the wall and fell asleep in a few minutes as usual.

Tony, meanwhile, lay awake for a long time, looking overhead at the cracks in the plaster and thinking about all the hops he'd flown with Old Joe Selig, and how much faster the modern planes were. It was well into the wee hours of the morning before he finally dozed off and slept, dreaming of all-metal monoplanes with large engines and an on-board arsenal of big guns.

One morning three months later, Jack woke up alone. There was no trace of Tony to be found. With a measured excitement, Jack got dressed and went downstairs, where clearly the news had already broken. Mr. McGuire sat at the end of the table, stirring his eggs and bacon with his fork, looking at a point in the distance; Mrs. McGuire tried to act normal, but her nervous fuddling with the dishes at the cupboard was not customary for her. The girls were playing outside, having sensed the uncomfortable atmosphere. Jack, however, saw no chance of escape, so he thought he'd brace himself and sit it out.

Jack's mother set him a plate heavily laden with eggs and bacon, poured him a glass of milk, and returned to her aimless activity at the cupboard.

Jack's father moved his gaze from the horizon to Jack, but did not focus on him, until he began to talk.

"How much did you know, Jack? Did you know he was going?"

Jack took a deep breath, but did not even get started before his father again addressed him. "Did you know he was going *now*? Do you know *where* he went? Does he ever plan to come back? Talk to me, son!"

Swallowing, Jack decided to go for it.

"All I know is that a few months ago, right after the time he got the brochures—remember?—well, he said he was going to do it somehow, and some day, but he never told me when. Or where. Heck, there must be hundreds of bases in the country, and he could've gone to any one of them!"

Jack's mother winced at his talking like that, but Jack went on, heedless. "Actually, Dad, I think he did the right thing. He was never going to work the farm. Look at it any way you want, but it's the truth. And now it's happened, and he's gone, and he's not coming back until he has those silver wings on him."

Jack had never been this bold with his father and already he could feel his spine chill as his father looked at him, sterner than ever. "You say he did the right thing? *The right thing?* To go out in a plane and get shot down in flames? If he had to go, why not join the Army and at least have a fighting chance, not to be blown out of the sky where Man has no business in any case." Having finished his argument, Mr. McGuire again fixed his eyes on the far edge of the field.

"Dad," Jack tried to start again, but his father hushed him with a swing of his calloused hand.

"Jack, there's no excusing his actions. I forbade him from doing what he wanted but he went off anyhow. No words of support from you will ever make him my son again—and let this be a warning to you, too. I told you boys what your options are—either college or the farm—and for you, there's no third option. That's the way it is. And as for Tony, he's gone, and gone forever for all I care."

With that he stormed out of the kitchen, grabbing his hat on the way, and continued on out to the yard from where the girls fled in the direction of the river. Jack's mother could no longer hide her tears, but started to cry silently, only her twitching shoulders betraying her pain.

Standing up and going to his mother, Jack held her in a consoling bear-hug. She clung to him, sobbing in his chest, and asked him after a few moments, "Jack—surely you won't ever leave us like that, promise me! It'd kill me if you did that to us, after what Tony did!"

Jack tried to tell her what she wanted to hear, but he could not. He was completely unable to promise she wouldn't see another son leaving the way of the first, but he knew he had to reserve that option for himself. Tony's leaving home had already started to erode the foundation his life was built on, and he knew in his heart that there was no turning back. Sensing this, his mother suffered a new surge of sobs, this time out loud. Jack had never felt so terrible in his life.

The next four weeks were absolute hell. No word was spoken that was not necessary for some practical purpose. All social interaction between family members ceased. Jack's mother tried her best to bring the family life back to normal, but her brave attempts failed. Mr. McGuire stayed outside from dawn till dusk, hiding his feelings in working like a horse. The downside of his plan was that since he had worked hard all his life, his body was unable to take that kind of punishment any longer, and taking breaks was completely new to him. This aggravated him even more, and he didn't utter a word to anyone he met, whether family or friend.

The town came to know that Tony's leaving had cut a deep wound through the McGuire family, and everyone let them be; about the only person who tried to make contact with them was Old Joe, since he'd worked as a farmhand for the McGuires on and off for years. He was again in need of some work, but there was no way John McGuire would hire him now, given his part in Tony's plan.

As for Jack, he did exactly what his father did. He kept to himself, excelled at school even more than before, and stayed alone for the most part. He did, however, become better friends with Nellie. Although Jack knew she was Tony's sweetheart, his actual contact with her had been minimal. In fact, Jack had had his eye on Nellie's cousin, Amy, but as a painfully timid boy of seventeen, he had never been able to get anywhere with her.

He had listened to Tony's braggadocio about his exploits

with Nellie, most of which he suspected were much inflated—as they were—but in any case he had envied Tony having a girlfriend in the first place. Now with Tony gone, Nellie often sought out Jack at school lunchtime to chat with him, while trying to learn about Tony. Amazingly he had not shared his plan even with Nellie, which was a cause of distress to her.

One morning, three and a half months after Tony had left, Nellie ran up to Jack before school. "Jack! You won't believe it! I've got a letter from Tony, and it's addressed to you!" She quickly closed the distance between them and frantically waved the letter, which Jack snagged from her and opened in a hurry. He glanced through the short letter and related the highlights to Nellie as he did so.

"He's in Texas … somewhere near San Antonio … he's on a plane mechanic course which ends in eight months … he wants to become a pilot but had to take the course because he … he'd have needed two years of college to make pilot now … all's well and he send his regards to you…"

"Regards?" Nellie was indignant. "Is that all? Regards!"

Jack went on. "There's more; he wants me to tell Dad he's fine and he's going to make it to piloting later…" Jack folded the letter and stuck it in his pocket. "Mechanic, hell … that's a far cry from what he really wants to do." Falling into his thoughts, Jack started to walk away from Nellie.

"Jack!" she said sharply. "Don't you dare leave me here after I took all the trouble to deliver that letter to you!"

Walking back to her, Jack shook her hand in gratitude, then turned again and went up the schoolhouse stairs. Nellie was left standing at the foot of the steps, unable to believe that someone could be so rude, until she remembered how clumsy Jack was with people.

During the school day Jack was unable to concentrate at

all, and he was relieved when the final bell rang. He took his book bag and walked home across the field, via the fastest route. When he got home he was happy to see his father aboard the tractor, headed for the more distant fields of the farm, because he wanted to talk alone with his mother. He found her in the kitchen as usual, peeling potatoes. "Mom, I got to have a word with you." Jack thought that there was no need for beating about the bush. "I have a letter from Tony".

Jack's mother sat down with a light in her eyes Jack had not seen in a good while. She folded her hands in her flowery apron in anticipation of the long-awaited news. "Tell me how he is? Is he all right? Is he happy?"

Jack took the letter from his pocket and gave it to her with a smile.

She read it as fast as her eyes could move, from as far as her arms could hold it, what with her glasses again on the table near the fireplace. "Mechanic?" she asked Jack with a cocked eyebrow.

"I think that's the best he could do right now, Mom. After all, he's a high-school drop-out, not a college graduate, and I think there's just no way around it right now. To be a pilot you've got to have a degree, or at least some time in college, I guess."

"But he's not flying, is he?"

Jack shrugged. "No, Mom. I don't think he will fly for some time now. But it's a good trade he's learning and he gets to tinker with planes, which must be good for him." Jack saw mixed feelings run through his mother as she fumbled with kitchen utensils. On the one hand she was overjoyed to hear his son was safe and happy; on the other he was not doing the thing which had caused the breach in the family—becoming a pilot. Worse, apparently it was not even possible for him to become one right now.

She had pinned her hopes on healing the breach once Tony returned home with his silver wings proudly pinned on his chest, because even though forbidden, becoming a pilot would still be an achievement and such achievements meant a lot to her husband. She could anticipate more trouble if John McGuire learned Tony was actually learning how to change the oil in an engine; he would say that even his tractor needed that done every now and again and that skill could have been learned right on the farm.

And so she said, "Jack, I think we had better keep this between ourselves. It won't please Dad to hear that Tony's not in pilot school."

Jack felt happy to have the burden placed between the two of them, shared, so no longer as heavy. "I thought so too, Mom. It's our secret. But I'll ask Nellie to relay any more letters she gets, so we can keep up with his progress in getting greasy."

With that, he hugged her. She smiled and they both felt a faint but definite sense of relief.

In the morning Jack met Nellie again as usual, near the school. She was eager to know what he had told his mother about Tony, and Jack decided it was best to make her an accomplice. "Umm, Nellie, about the letter—do you think you could be quiet about the whole thing? Who did you tell yesterday?"

"Why, no one! I thought it was not my place to tell anyone, although I must say a fair number of folks asked me about Tony right after he went away, and even now."

"Nellie, I reckon it's for the best if it's only you, and Mom, and me who know about Tony's business. Let's keep this under wraps. He'd like it that way, I think."

35

"Well, what do you know—I got a letter of my own from him yesterday!" Nellie said, pulling another letter out of her blouse pocket that looked just like the one she had given to Jack yesterday. "And what's in this letter, Jack, I won't tell even *you*!" she added, placing the letter on her heart with an impish look.

"Sure, Nellie, that's your right, for being in this with me. But please tell Tony when you answer that letter that you'll act as postmaster here, that the messages are safe, and that he can write us."

"It's a deal then!" Nellie said with a grin, and ran up the stairs.

Over the next eight months there were a total of thirteen more letters to Jack, now that the channel was open and secure. In them, Tony extolled the virtues of Army life up to the point of sounding completely ridiculous. There apparently was no other occupation in the world worth considering. Tony only complained about the pay. Jack was sure there was more to the matter than what Tony wrote, and that most of the things he discussed were not quite that glamorous after all. Still, he had to admit he was fascinated by Tony's pages-long descriptions of the Army's planes, and what all the pilots put them through.

He read about the thick and stubby Boeing P-26 Peashooter, and the two new monoplanes entering service, the Bell P-39 Airacobra and the P-40 Warhawk. Apparently Tony was on good terms with the pilots, since he could relate conversations where they discussed the virtues and vices of each plane. His letters made it hard for Jack to forget the dizzying flights with Old Joe Selig in his Avro, and the as-yet improbable future of Tony as an Army fighter pilot filled him with a feeling of distant envy.

Eventually, though, Tony had to confess he had no way to become a pilot. Even his base commander had tried to speak up for him, impressed as he was with his eagerness, but to no avail; there had to be two years of college studies behind all prospective pilots. So Tony bit the bullet and entered a multiengine plane crew course, with the position of a bomber ground crew chief in his sights.

He did well, and eventually when the first American bomber squadron left to fight for Europe, Tony was on the boat. His convoy successfully dodged German submarines and landed in Liverpool. The squadron found itself in the thick of the effort to bomb Hitler, and Tony was immensely proud in his letters about how his plane had been there with the first to hit the enemy.

By this time Mr. McGuire had come to know Tony wasn't a pilot but was still a crew chief and a master mechanic, and gradually he'd changed his attitude towards Tony. He even sent him regards in the letters Jack wrote to him. The McGuires thought that pilots and air crew flew and ground crews were safe on the ground. What they didn't know was that Tony and the other ground crewmen often doubled as gunners on the bombers, and that casualties were high. Jack did not share this information, reasoning that what they didn't know couldn't hurt them.

It was not until after December 6, 1942, that he had to tell his father that Tony was hitching rides on the bombers. Tony's plane, a B-17 of the 8th Air Force, failed to return from a bombing mission to France; there were no survivors. The official telegram arrived late in the day a week after the event, but all in the household figured out the contents without opening it.

It was a long and somber evening. Mr. McGuire felt guilty

for having let his son leave without ever having come to terms with his departure, and the rest of the family languished in the fact that he wasn't coming back from the war. Anna or Emily would start to tell a story involving Tony and then finish in mid-sentence when the grief gripped her throat.

Jack was notified of Tony's death by a letter from his mother. By this time in Pre-Flight training, he had been called up right after Pearl Harbor, because in the university he had completed sixty hours of Civilian Pilot Training and was now a certified pilot. He had been very happy to receive orders to report to Pre-Flight, as it promised he had at least a shot at becoming a real pilot.

Though he felt the loss of Tony very keenly, the busy days and demanding schedule left little time for grieving. Actually it was only on his home leave that he had time to mourn his brother, which he did with great sorrow. He was able to convince the entire family, though, that Tony had died happy, doing what he loved best; still it pained him to see the profile of his father in the sunset, watching the sun go down, silently weeping.

When his brief leave ended, Jack went back to the hectic pace of training, running full-bore, determined to fight for the memory of his brother.

4

When Kay woke up, it was already well past eight o'clock. She considered herself an early riser, but the cabin had proved an unusually good place for sleep. She put on her bathing suit, shorts, and a loose shirt, and went down to the beach for a dip. After a swim and a shower (a sun-heated rainwater shower crafted from an oil barrel with a stand and some black paint), she was ready to return to her cabin to dress for breakfast. But then she noticed Jack and Martin coming toward her down the trail from Jack's cabin.

"Morning, Kay—sleep well?" Jack asked.

"Why, yes, better than in a long while!" Kay responded with a bright smile.

Martin bid her good morning as well and, with a half-bow, started to the pier towards the Kingfisher.

Jack pushed his sunglasses to his forehead. He liked to see the dimples form on her cheeks when she smiled. It was the first time in a long while that he'd noticed such minute details on a woman's face. He found himself wondering what to do next. He was very unaccustomed to being alone with women, and he feared his uneasiness showed.

Kay settled the matter by starting back towards her cabin. "Well, if you'll excuse me, I should change." She half-turned back towards him. "Say, is there any breakfast available for late risers, or will I be punished for oversleeping?"

"No punishment. There's breakfast for you at the main

lodge. Just ask Wilma for some!" Jack said as he walked towards the pier, where Martin had already opened the engine cowling of the Kingfisher. Jack could not help looking back over his shoulder as Kay bounced up the trail at her usual swift pace, disappearing into the trees. Only then did Jack face forward.

When Jack reached the plane, Martin was already elbow-deep into the engine.

"Well, Jack, looks like you finally found someone to your liking?" Martin was loosening a bolt in the bowels of the engine.

"Get off it," Jack answered. "She's an Eastern gal, way out of my waters. Besides, I'm never going back to the States, and she's leaving in a couple of days, so I'm not going to do anything about it. And even more besides, it's none of your business!" Beads of sweat broke out along his brow as he talked.

Martin grinned. He knew he was the only one with whom Jack would have such conversations, and he enjoyed pushing his buttons once in a while.

They had met during the tempestuous days of the air war over Guadalcanal. Martin, fifteen at the time, had become the errand runner of the pilots. Jack came to like the boy, who seemed utterly fearless and oblivious to the falling bombs. When Jack's squadron departed Guadalcanal for the last time in 1943, he pinned his golden wings on the boy's tattered shirt and said, "Keep these for me."

Since Jack's return to the islands, Martin had seen him at his most vulnerable: homesick, lovesick, drunk, and ill with malaria. He tended to Jack every time, and because of this Jack had opened himself up to Martin more than he had to anybody in his entire life. They were close friends, much like

Jack and Tony had been in their boyhood. For half an hour they worked in silence.

"Pass me that number thirteen, will you?" Martin asked, to no reply. "Jack! I need that thirteen!" he said again more forcefully.

"Huh? Right, here," Jack said, peering up into the hills as he handed Martin the tool.

Martin sighed and wiped his hands. "Look, Jack, why not just go and ask her out for a flight or something? You're of little use here, and I can do this myself anyway. I'll have it ready for you within an hour and then you can go off to see Gula Island."

"Y'know, Martin, you may be right. Sorry for being such a dummy. I just feel like I need to ask her something." Jack started towards Kay's hut. "Do you think Wilma might furnish us with a lunch basket, or is she already preparing something for lunch?" he asked sheepishly.

"Just go, Jack, and ask Wilma on the way up. Boy, you're all screwed up when something like this happens. Now get going!"

Jack muttered something out of Martin's earshot, and briskly went on his way.

As Martin had suggested, Jack arranged for a basket of food with Wilma and then went up to see Kay. She was in her hut, the door open, moving her clothes from the Gladstone to the wardrobe, when Jack knocked on the doorframe. "Umm, I was just wondering, if you're not busy, we could perhaps go for a flight and ...see some islands here nearby, that is, if you're not doing anything more important, or if you're interested."

That sparkle in her eyes. "I'd love to! When do we go?"

"Martin said he'd finish the spark plugs in half an hour, so we could start at twelve noon."

"Suits me just fine," Kay nodded, and after hanging up the last of her outfits, came out to the porch. She sat down on the railing. "This place is more beautiful than I could have ever imagined. I went to Honolulu with some friends last year, and back then I thought that nowhere could be more beautiful than that, but this place certainly beats Hawaii."

She leaned against the roof post, looked at Jack for a long time, and ventured a question:

"Tell me, Jack, why are you here? I don't mean to be intrusive or anything, but what brought you *here* of all places?"

Jack briefly met her eyes before letting his gaze drift into the bay, its blue waves rolling in the light southeasterly wind. "Um, I really don't know. Honest. I thought I knew, but I really don't. I just didn't feel like staying in the States after the war. This place appeals a lot more to me than, well, Nebraska, for example. Or any city, for that matter."

They could hear Martin starting the Kingfisher engine and leaving it idling, its throaty sound reverberating from the hills. The sound made Jack antsy, ready to fly, as it always did. "Well then, why not see you on the pier in ten minutes? Can you manage?" Jack said quickly, and started towards his hut.

Kay smiled at his back and hurried to pack her small bag.

In his hut, Jack tried to concentrate on something useful, but found it impossible. He sat down, only to bolt back up and peek at the pier to see if Kay was already there. He then thought he might just as well go to the beach and do the pre-flight check of the Kingfisher so they could then take off right away when Kay got there.

But Kay was already at the pier talking with Martin, apparently about the OS2U scout plane, because she was pointing to parts of the plane and Martin was explaining something to her, also using his hands. When Jack met them on the pier, Martin gave him the brief on the plane. "She's topped off, and the ignition is back in place. Should run smooth now."

"Thanks, buddy," Jack said. "I think we'll take it nice and easy on this one. OK, let's go then," he said, and climbed up onto the wing and stuck out his hand. Kay grabbed it, and when she jumped off the pier Jack marveled at how light she felt. She climbed into the second of three seats Jack had installed in the plane. He had upholstered them much more elegantly than the Navy Bureau of Aeronautics had specified, and had added panes of Plexiglas to the fuselage for better viewing. The seats were cushioned and the seat harnesses had also been upgraded to more comfortable ones.

Jack hoisted himself onto the pilot's seat and turned back to monitor Kay as she tried to put on the harness.

"I take it you've never been in a military plane before?" he asked.

Kay laughed. "Heavens, no!"

"Well, it's safe to say this is the most unmilitary military plane ever," Jack said, and finished strapping Kay in. When all the arranging of belts and communication systems was done, Jack belted himself in and gave Martin a thumbs-up. He replied in kind and turned to walk up the pier with his determined gait as Jack throttled up the engine, and soon the plane was sliding out towards the shiny sea.

From the swaying of the plane as it lumbered along in the little waves, Kay had an amusing thought of riding piggyback on a whale. A few more RPMs from the engine, and Kay could feel the drumming of the waves against the main float accelerating below her. A bit more speed, a slightly more agitated sound of the engine, and they glided along the surface seemingly without effort.

Suddenly Jack pulled the stick, and the Kingfisher popped out of the water, leaving behind an abruptly-ending wake, and started climbing in a left turn. The ride on the back of a whale became the heady sensation of flight, which Kay had always enjoyed, and the lush islands and the deepening sea receded below her. Taking in all the sights and sensations, she giggled to herself like a little girl in a porch swing.

The plane continued to climb in a slight left turn, affording Kay a wonderful view of the Tulagi harbor, Jack's hotel on Halavo across the bay from Tulagi, and the lush island below them. He set a north-northwesterly course, and adjusted the controls to steady the plane at 2000 feet at a comfortable cruising speed. Via the microphone, Jack pointed out the sights to Kay: Savo Island, the site of fierce naval battles in 1942-43; Guadalcanal, the kidney-shaped island for which the Americans and the Japanese had fought so bitterly over a course of five months; and all the islets in the Indispensable Strait and the body of water now known as Ironbottom Sound due to all the ships that had succumbed to bombs, torpedoes and artillery shells during the war. He also mentioned how the waters between the two parallel island chains were often called The Slot.

Kay marveled at the sea—a hue which she had never seen before, with the shadows of clouds specking the glimmering deep blue water, its color gradually blending into the white sand beaches on the rims of the islands. She felt close to something for which she had no words as yet, but which she was sure would reveal itself at a later time.

For now she concentrated on enjoying the flight, which was not hard, given the environment, the weather, and Jack's company. He could constantly be heard explaining something, and Kay knew it was mostly to keep his façade up. But gradually she found herself enjoying listening to the sound of Jack's voice. She wondered if the picnic could top the flight to get there.

After about twenty-five minutes of flight, Jack told Kay, "There's the target—sorry, picnic island!" and he led the Kingfisher into a slight descent, throttling back the engine. At first Kay didn't see anything, but then the island popped into view from below the wing. It was like a tiny green diamond set on a thick velvet pillow whose color blended from deep blue through pale blue into the white sand of the beaches.

It looked perfect, and Jack executed a 180 degree turn into the wind to touch down on the sea close by the beach. As he cut the throttle and the plane set down on the small waves, Kay admired the flawless beauty of the palm-rimmed beach, maybe a hundred yards wide. Jack pointed the plane towards the beach, and with care he edged the main float onto it. Then he shut the engine down altogether, and after a few moments of ringing ears, Kay again became aware of the gentle sound of the ocean and the rustling of the palms.

"Here we are then…just unbuckle the seat belt—turn the buckle like so." Jack again nervously tried to be useful, while Kay just smiled at him and told him she'd manage.

Leaving her to it, Jack got out onto the wing and jumped down to the shallow water. He got out a rope and fastened the plane's pontoon onto the trunk of a fallen palm tree protruding from the soft white sand. "No need to tie this down too hard. The wind is so light it won't move the plane," Jack said, and waded back to the water to accept the picnic basket from Kay, who had made it out to the wing. After taking the basket out to the beach, he returned for Kay, who clambered down from the wing.

Jack grabbed her before she was even close to the water and

lowered her gently into it. He loved the feeling of her lithe body in his hands; it created a happy burn inside him. She smiled her thanks, and Jack felt his heart miss a few beats. Then he reminded himself not to fall for this lady, or any lady for that matter, and put the kibosh on.

Meanwhile, Kay waded onto the beach, splattering far more water than necessary in the process. "Isn't this simply paradise!" she called out to Jack, who was busy checking the tether of the plane. She took a few more steps in the soft sand, digging her small feet ankle-deep into it.

Jack cast sidelong glances at her, trying to appear nonchalant but failing miserably. Kay could sense his infatuation, but given her looks and her open nature, it was nothing new to her. She suddenly realized that for the first time in a long while, she felt good about someone looking at her like that.

"Paradise? Well, yes, none of my guests I've brought here have complained…they've all liked it here. The beach is easy to reach, there's sand far into the sea, and for some reason, there's no hostile fish around here."

"Hostile fish?" She wrinkled her nose.

"Sharks."

"Oh, I see!"

Kay's laughter filled Jack's head and he had to fight it hard to keep his staid demeanor together.

Mentally Jack delivered a kick to his stupid ass for lapsing back to military slang again. "It's a phrase that stuck to us pilots over here. One of us was shot down, and he floated around in his rubber dinghy for four days. In his action report he said he'd met seagulls which he tried to catch, fish he did catch, and hostile fish that tried to catch him."

To move on to something different, Jack took the basket, opened it, and spread the blanket onto the sand. There was

46

something else...

"Hey—I almost forgot," he said suddenly, and waded back to the plane. Attached to the side of the strut of the main float was a perforated metal tube, and as Kay watched, Jack pulled out a bottle of white wine.

"Properly chilled; see, that tube is lined with thick cotton. As the tube gets wet during takeoff, the water evaporating during the flight cools the bottle, and when we land, it's chilled. Brilliant, no?" Jack handed the bottle to Kay so she could feel the bottle was indeed cool. Jack took back the bottle and opened it with a corkscrew, while Kay dug around in the basket to find two glasses. These he filled, and Kay handed him one.

"What shall we drink to?" she asked, smiling that dangerous smile of hers.

Jack was on the verge of saying "To you," but managed instead to suggest the day.

"To a glorious day then," Kay said, and sipped. Jack, too, had a sip, and their eyes met for a long while, just watching one another.

Neither of them seemed to want to lose eye contact, but finally Jack looked out to the sea. "What say we have a swim and then have some lunch? I'd like to dip in first, since my mother always said I should never eat before swimming."

In solidarity, Kay set her glass down to the blanket against the basket and had stripped off her shirt and shorts within seconds.

Jack was still removing his bermudas when Kay called to him from the water already: "Come on Jack, don't be so slow! The water's lovely!" Her voice instantly transported Jack into distant memory. As a kid, his father had taken him to see a freak show, the outing a freak occurrence in itself, considering how stern his father was. In the show, Jack had seen his five cents' worth of hairy ladies and other oddities, but the thing that had really caught his eye was a reproduction of the famous Cottingley fairy photographs. He had fallen under their spell instantly, and his father had had to drag him out by the ear. And the question that had stuck with him was, what do fairies *sound* like?

Now he knew.

After a clumsy struggle Jack finally got rid of his clothes and jumped in the ocean, diving in the surf to swim to Kay under the water. He ran into her underwater, toppling her over, and after that there was nothing that distinguished them from a couple of ten year-olds frolicking in the water.

After a good ten minutes of horsing around, Kay dragged herself onto the beach, exhausted, and lay prone on the hot white sand beside the basket. Jack followed her up and put up a large sun shade he had carried from the plane. Then he sat down on the other side of the basket. He poured her another glass of wine and took out of the basket the lunch Wilma had packed.

"Chicken or tuna?" he asked, passing out silverware.

"Chicken, please," Kay said, accepting a bowl of salad. They ate in silence, admiring the sea and beach, and watching the Kingfisher's wings waggle lightly in the moderate surf.

"Wait, wait! I almost forgot!" Kay started fumbling with her canvas bag. "I need to document that I've been to paradise!" she explained, ejecting components of feminine necessity onto the blanket. She reached the bottom of the bag, and the discovery of the Kodak Retina II camera she withdrew resulted in a triumphal shout. "Now you can picture me in it!"

As she opened the camera, Jack held up his hands. "Whoa, all I've ever operated was a Brownie. You'll need to teach me first."

Even so, Kay thrust the camera into his hands. "There's nothing to it. Just look through this little window and fiddle with this thing here until the little image matches the other one, then press this button. Wind up for next shot—like so. I pose—you shoot. Easy as that."

And then she struck a most delectable pose. Jack hoped the rangefinder wouldn't steam up when he saw her through the small lens. He shot four frames with a fervent hope that he understood the focusing business. Kay wanted poses against the plane too, so he shot a few with her and the Kingfisher. Then a few with both of them using the self-timer, with the canvas bag serving as a tripod on the sand.

When the film ran out, a smiling Kay packed the camera and reassembled half her life into the bag. "Now I know why you're out here," Kay said. "It's the sheer beauty of the place, isn't it?"

Jack thought for a second. "Well, the place in itself *is* one of the reasons. But the main reason is really hidden from me—I guess I could just as well have returned back home and started farming or some other business over there too."

Then he considered again. "No, that's not entirely true. Ever since my brother left home to join the Army Air Corps I knew I was not going to become a farmer, even if I was planning to study agronomy in college. And then, when it was all over and I found I'd survived the war, I went to college on the GI Bill. But then I just needed to go away to think and figure it all out, and this is where it got me. And I'm still figuring."

Kay nodded in agreement. "I know how you feel. I mean, the turning point in my life was when I met Don. It was just that everything before then was somehow reduced to just memories and plans which didn't happen, and I felt my life take on a new direction—his."

"And with Don, I bet it wasn't exactly a boring way to go, was it now?"

The result was just what he wanted, a sparkling laugh.

"No, it sure wasn't boring! He was a riot when he wanted to be fun, and to me it was the best show to watch him work over my mother. You know, she's a fussy, prim lady trying to pass herself off as something really fine. But Don figured her out in two minutes flat. Him having a pedigree which my mother appreciated gave him certain liberties, you see."

Kay smiled at the sea, and Jack admired her profile. "It's just that we didn't have too much time together." She went silent.

Inside, Jack panicked. What should he do now, to try to get the mood back up? His experience of these situations was severely limited. So he thought of Don and just started talking.

"Don sure was something all right…he was well-liked by the crew chiefs and mechanics too, since he could talk to them in their own lingo. I fell off the conversation real fast when they started discussing the finer points of engine maintenance, but ol' Don could go on for hours." He shook his head, remembering, reliving the conversations in his memory. "I've taught myself a lot about maintenance lately, but Don was from a whole other planet in that sense."

Kay brightened up. "Funny. That's exactly what made him friends with my father! He made his business from a car mechanic shop into a dealership in Pittsburgh, and he just loved talking cars with Don. My mother could be put on hold for hours with dinner on the table if Don went out to the garage with my father, and when they got back they were greased up all the way to their ears."

Kay lay on the blanket, stretching out her body at full-length and looking to Jack like a mischievous cat. "One thing does make me wonder, though. Do you have any idea why Don never told you about me? I mean, when he received his commission, I expected to get invited to the ceremony, but no—he just turned up at my doorstep in a new uniform with the golden wings and took me out to dinner afterwards. I was a bit sour on him for that, but as you know, it was too hard to be mad at Don for more than a moment."

Jack sweated over the right reply. Of course no mention of Don's womanizing would be appropriate, and he knew of no other thing that would have excluded Kay from Don's life so completely, until he remembered. "As cadets, we were not allowed to marry. The few cadets who were married kept it dark from the Navy, because they'd be washed out from flight training and sent to the Great Lakes for some other duty. We were deathly afraid of the words 'Great Lakes', as it implied descending from the air into some unknown depth and alien duty. I have no clue what they did to the ones that were sent there, but the word on the corridor was that they became proficient foxhole diggers."

Kay nodded. "Yes, that must have been it. He didn't talk anything about the training except how much flight time he had and how much he enjoyed flying with you. Maybe he wanted to steer clear of the system when he was on leave."

Jack felt like the big one that got away. He lowered his Ray-Bans from his forehead to his eyes and used the shades to admire Kay. But soon he felt ashamed for being a Peeping Tom, and rolled to his left to reach into the basket.

He poured some more wine and lay back down on the blanket. "It's been a great day, but I think there may be a change of weather in the offing." He pointed to the northwest.

Behind the towering cumulus clouds there were darker, more solid cloud formations.

Kay also looked that way. "A storm?"

Jack nodded. "Probably tonight, maybe tomorrow."

"I love storms! Don and I went up to the hills sometimes to watch the lightning strikes, though we knew the place was dangerous in a storm. I bet the storms out here are even more powerful than in the States, no?"

"They sure are, and if that one goes the way I think it will, we're in for a show all right. But that's not until tonight, or tomorrow, so let's make the most of this day…who's last in the water?"

And he bolted up towards the sea, leaving Kay behind, crying: "Hey! Not fair!"

After the second round of swimming, they sat back down on the blanket. Though the wine bottle was all but empty, Jack's canteen was full of spring water. After refreshing themselves, they collected the silverware, bowls and glasses into the picnic basket, and Kay darted into the bushes to change back into her clothes for the return flight. Jack donned his clothes and packed the plane.

By the time she returned to the plane, Jack had already loosened the rope and tied it onto the central float. "Now, Kay, this is a bit trickier than at the other end," he told her. "You'll have to let me push you up on to the edge of the wing, and from there you can climb on to the fuselage and get in the plane. Otherwise you can clamber up on the trailing edge of the wing, but this is probably easier."

Kay smiled. "Fine by me!"

Jack carefully grabbed Kay by the thighs, like a cartoon caveman transporting his sweetheart, and carried her to the plane while she giggled and pounded on his back with her fists. She was such a light load that it was not too hard a task. Standing by the wing's leading edge, Jack pushed Kay up until she was able to pull herself up onto the wing. He took great care to act like a gentleman, and treated her as if she were made of porcelain. Jack grabbed the basket off the sand and carried it to Kay, who was waiting for it on the wing. Then, inside the plane, they readied for the return.

The flight back, although by no means a dud, lacked the magic of the outbound trip. Not much was said outside a few disjointed questions and answers.

After a smooth landing, Martin was on hand at the pier and helped Kay out of the plane. Then he assisted Jack in getting the plane moored on the buoy.

"There's some bad weather coming up. We better make sure the ropes are tightened well," Jack said to Martin. "Kay, if you want to freshen up for dinner ... this will take us some time."

Kay took the hint, flashed her dazzling smile, and darted uphill.

"Well?" said Martin.

"Well, *what*?" Jack snapped.

"Is she the woman you'd always wanted?" Martin asked in all sincerity.

Jack thought a while, allowing: "She's a lot better than any of our guests so far."

Martin could tell that there would be no point in continuing to press Jack just now, so he left it at that. They discussed where to moor the plane, mostly because of the heavy wind that was building from the northwest, and decided it would be safest by the shoreline. When they had progressed to a point where Martin could manage alone, he sent Jack to go and prepare for dinner. Jack was silently grateful for Martin's courteous offer. He practically ran to his cabin and changed clothes, then sped to the main hut.

Jack was happy to see Kay had not come up yet. When he tried to be helpful in the kitchen, Wilma ushered him out with a meat cleaver. In the dining room, the table by the main window had already been set for the two of them.

Desperate for something to do, Jack wound up the gramophone and put on the only classical album he owned, even though he knew how introspective it always turned him, even gloomy. Eh, anything to class the joint up a little. It was also his only record that would play through without getting stuck. As the first dark chords spread through the room, Kay opened the door and walked over to Jack. He stood up and admired her black dress ornamented by a white flower print. Jack felt himself warm up as he took in her beauty and confident air. Her slim but shapely body was outlined by the tight-fitting dress, and her sling back heels were the first he'd seen on the island.

"Now, that's pretty gloomy music to have dinner with after such a great day!" she said as she clung to his arm.

Jack—electrified and feeling lucky—had to agree. "Well, now that you mention it, you're right. The reason I play it is actually that I have only one classical record. Then I have some Japanese music, left by the previous owner of the gramophone, I guess. Every time I go to Australia, I always forget to stock up on music."

Kay followed the record with her head as it turned on the gramophone and tried to read the label. "It's torn. It only says 'elius 4th Sym' and 'Ormandy'. I wonder who wrote it?"

"I seem to remember Ormandy is a violinist, but of the 'Elius' character I have no clue."

For a while they were tantalized by the music. As they listened, clouds rolled in from the northwest, and the wind blew through the doorway and fluttered Kay's light cotton dress. "In any case, it suits the weather," Kay said, and went out to the porch.

The clouds had blocked the sky altogether, and since the sun was already down, the island was dark. Gusts of wind rattled the corrugated iron on one of the huts, and Jack made a mental note to fix them tighter. The wind brought in the lush scents of the jungle, myriad flowers sending their greetings. Kay shuddered when the first mighty lightning bolt ripped across Halavo Bay, and as the thunder crash arrived only seconds later, they knew the storm was upon them.

The rain began, first a drizzle, but within minutes it roared down, a true force of nature. Grabbing his arm, Kay led him off the porch.

"What? You want to go out *there?*" Jack managed, but already Kay was running down the path to the pier. In the torrential downpour she slipped once but Jack grabbed her just in time, whereas she could not stop him from falling over a slippery root. After the delay in regaining his balance they made it to the pier soaked, and Kay ran all the way out to the end of the pier. Jack followed her close enough to catch her if she slipped, and half hoped she would.

"Isn't this wonderful?" she exclaimed, holding out her arms as if to embrace the water as it gushed down in sheets. Jack couldn't exactly relate as he had always hated being wet, but went along to indulge her. He went out to her and before he knew it, she had wrapped her arms around his neck and kissed him on the lips. Water slithered down their faces during their kiss, which lasted a good while. Then she let go and pushed herself away from Jack.

The wind was now howling, but underneath it Jack could

still hear her say softly, "Sorry..." as she turned away and started up the path to her cabin. Jack stood out there for some time, inside as calm as a cauldron. He went to his cabin, changed his soaked clothes, and went to bed for a sleepless night.

That night, Kay couldn't sleep either. She listened to the rain until it stopped around three in the morning, and then she decided she wanted a sip of water. She went to the lunch hut and opened the door, but as it was dark inside, she needed to light a candle. The logical place for matches was the mantelpiece of the big fireplace, so she fumbled about up there until she found a short, thick candle and matches in a curious matchbox holder. Lighting the candle, she had a look at this artifact.

It was an enameled piece of brass, with a motif of a mill house by a river and the word "Sverige" imprinted on it. Kay smiled, replaced it on the mantelpiece and went to fetch her drink. Coming back, she blew out the candle, but before she left, she grabbed the matchbox, wondering as she did so why she was taking it. Perhaps she was developing antisocial tendencies, she giggled to herself. Back in her cabin she hid the little thing between her clothes in the suitcase.

In the morning, Kay appeared at the lunch hut for breakfast, nearly her buoyant self again. Jack could feel her trying to find a moment to say something about last night, but it was hard for her.

Finally, with Wilma out of earshot and Martin having gone out to check for storm damage, they had a moment alone. "Look, Jack," she said, "please don't get any ideas. I wasn't out to get you; I'm not that sort of person. It was just that, well, just that the moment seemed right and that, you know, I got carried away and all that. Not that I didn't like it, please don't think that, but could we leave it at that? Please? I'd appreciate it."

At the regret which flowed through him as she spoke, Jack knew it was happening to him once again. "Sure thing," he nodded, nonetheless. "Let's forget about it altogether." Again they went the way of small talk as both knew they should, even though they both longed for more rain, rain which lasted for more than an evening.

All too few days later, it was time for Kay to go. The plane would leave at six in the morning, taking off into the sunrise. By four-thirty she had packed up and stood ready for good-byes at the pier when Jack rushed down the trail in the dark.

Kay smiled at him when he reached her.

"Thank you for everything, Jack. You have no idea how much this has helped me along. There are no words to express it."

Much to his regret or relief, Jack couldn't find a single word himself, so he merely nodded and smiled.

She stood on tiptoe and Jack obligingly bent down for her lips to brush his cheek chastely. They then shook hands and she descended into the Commissioner's speedboat which would take her to the flying boat moored at Tulagi Harbor.

She waved once, in the royal fashion, with upturned palm and a scarcely noticeable rotation of the wrist. "Oh, Jack! One thing I forgot to mention! This place would be great for waterskiing!" she shouted just as the boat started to move.

Jack watched the receding aft of the speedboat disappear into the darkness, when the solution to Kay's identity hit him. Kay's portrait was the only picture in Don's wallet, which contained a plethora of phone numbers for as many women, scribbled on any material imaginable. After Don's death Jack had had the unenviable task of checking through his friend's personal effects. The wallet was thick with the notes, and he'd felt horrible having to sift through them one by one to see if something valuable was stowed in between the notes and cards and slips of paper.

When he'd finally decided that the phone numbers did not need to reach Don's family, the wallet, which had stretched to accommodate the phone directory, looked like he had deprived it of a major part of its rightful content. He did leave the picture in there, not having spent too much time looking even at that—only long enough to decide it was probably all right for it to remain in the wallet. When done, he was glad he was over with prying into Don's private life.

But now, in the present, Jack felt he should get into the Kingfisher and hop over to meet Kay at the Tulagi pier to tell her about this; in fact, he was boarding his plane when Martin strolled up the pier.

Jack explained why he was in a hurry, but arms crossed, Martin provided a reality check.

"Let's see the big picture now. You really want to run up to her and say, 'I know why you looked so familiar! Don had your picture in a stack of about 300 phone numbers from strange women!' Now, how does that sound to anyone, let alone the widow of the guy?"

Jack had to pause to think. Only one answer to Martin's question.

Martin kept going. "Come on, Jack—is it something you really feel you should say up front? You might get a chance to say something like that later, but get real with this one. She's almost off the islands and she's feeling great. She just said goodbye to her husband ... don't go and break it all up for her!"

Jack retied the rope he had nearly finished untying in his

rush to get going, and stood back from the edge of the wing. "Yeah, you're right, Martin, it's better this way. If she doesn't know by now, it's better if she doesn't hear at all, and if she does know, there's no need to open the wounds." He dropped off the wing and into the water feet first, surfaced at a distance and went for a swim, while Martin looked on and shook his head, laughing.

The next day, Jack decided to pay a visit to the American base at Guadalcanal to see if they had one more generator for sale. To conserve fuel, he hopped on a boat going that way instead of flying over. At the depot, he went inside the cavernous storage building full of surplus materiel still lingering, even though four years had passed since the war had effectively ended here. He wound his way to a desk in the front, behind which stood a burly Army sergeant. Jack knew him well by now. The sergeant, fists planted firmly in front of him, was comparing two lists and looked busy, so Jack waited to let him open the conversation.

"Hey Jack, what're you missing *this* time?" Sergeant Baker said, not looking up from his lists.

Jack pushed his skipper cap back and scratched his forehead. "I need one more generator," he said, "if you have one just like the two I already bought. They work just great and I get good electricity, so I thought of wiring up three more cabins."

Baker kept on matching items on his lists and jerked his thumb behind him. "Sure, we got...let me see, eight more. You sure you don't want to buy 'em all? I get to go home as soon as everything here is sold or otherwise struck off the books."

"Sorry, pal, I only need one right now. Actually, make that two. Do you have one that could be used for spares? It doesn't have to work"

"No, they all work fine. Murph checked 'em when he shelved them."

"What the heck, I'll take two anyway. Can you get them to the harbor, when you have any business there?"

"Tell you what. We're kind of busy round here today, so why don't you borrow the truck and get them there yourself? That'd save us some time."

Jack agreed to terms and paid up. "I guess they're back there, eh? Where I found the others?"

Sergeant Baker nodded. "Yep, pick any two. Anything else you want?"

Jack thought a few moments, then chuckled. "I'd take a pair of water-skis, if you got any." He fully expected a sneering gedouddahere with associated laughter.

But no rebuke, no laughter. Sergeant Baker finally looked up from his lists. "Murph?" he bellowed.

From the back of the warehouse came the faint reply. "Yah?"

"Where'd you stash the water-skis? With the tennis stuff?"

Another faint message echoed in. "No, they're with the volleyball nets and badminton gear. Shelf 12-A, all five pairs!"

Sergeant Baker looked at Jack. "We got five. How many you want?"

His bluff thus called, Jack said, "I think just one pair will do for now, and I'll get more later if I need them. 12-A? That way?" With Baker's curt nod, Jack started down a long aisle.

When he found the skis, he selected up the least worn pair and, as an afterthought, picked up a badminton net and six rackets. Shuttlecocks were nowhere to be found, but he was sure the British authorities would have a supply on Tulagi. He returned to Baker and paid up again. "Know what, Baker? I've never done this. Is there an instruction manual or something for pointers?"

Sergeant Baker looked him in the eye. "Look, Jack, we ain't a sports store or your local yacht club. And by the way, I didn't know you got yourself a speedboat."

"Good point. I haven't got one."

Shrugging his massive shoulders, Baker signed the list. "You gotta paddle that canoe awful fast if you want to water-ski. The guys who used these over at the Florida Island Recreation Center had a PT boat for the tow. Good idea, tows five no problem, but it takes a whole navy to supply the gas. We got two PT's left, you wanna buy one?"

Jack decided not to make any hasty decisions. "Tell you what: I'll let you know. Thanks for your help, Baker." Then he carried all his purchases over to the truck and drove down to the harbor with Murph, who'd decided to have his lunch there.

Over the next week Jack experimented with a particularly foolhardy hotel visitor to see whether it was feasible to use the Kingfisher as a towboat. It was, but Jack discontinued the practice after noting how much fuel it took to tow one person. It also helped him to decide when the skier said the experience belonged firmly in the once-in-a-lifetime category.

Thinking it over, Jack decided to see whether Bill Peet could get him a boat for the purpose, and luckily for him, Bill knew some people in Sydney in the business. In due course the boat arrived on a copra ship, and after that Jack enjoyed very much paying a visit to Tulagi.

Instead of the half-hour it might take him to cross over with a fishing boat, with his used but well-maintained Chris Craft, it was a five-minute joy-ride. Not to mention the waterskiing and fishing trips he could also organize now.

Eight weeks later a large box arrived on the Trans-Oceanic. On opening his package, Jack was surprised to find a well-packed stack of gramophone records. On top of the stack was a note from Kay. It read:

"Dearest Jack,
I found out who the mysterious 'Elius' is. He's Jean Sibelius, a Finnish composer. I'm sending you all of his symphonies, so you don't have to listen to that gloomy 4th all the time.
All the best, Kay.
PS—Try the fifth symphony first!"

Underneath the records was a small thick envelope. Impulsively Jack ripped it open before thinking of its contents, and when the photographs fluttered on the floor, Jack realized he didn't want to look at them, afraid of seeing something besides Kay in the photos.

Instead he called out to Martin, who arrived alarmed. "What is it, Jack? There a snake in the room?" he asked.

Jack pointed down at the spilled stack of photos on the floor. "Tell you what, Martin, would you please pick up those pictures Kay sent me and then tell me what's in them?"

"What's that?"

"Just stack them up again and describe to me what you see. Please?"

"Like, why?" Martin looked well and truly mystified. "You got a bad back or something? You can't just pick them up and have a look?"

Jack almost blushed, but fear forced him to press on. "Look, just humor me, okay?"

He turned and looked out to the sea, his back to Martin. He heard shuffling noises as Martin collected the pictures and tried to get some order in the stack.

"Okay, here goes. This is…Rose Bay aerodrome, in Sydney, eh? Never seen it. Then there's an aerial view of some island. Maybe Noumea, don't know. Then…this I know real well, it's Tulagi Bay. She really documented her trip. The next one is from our side, at the main lodge." Martin chattered like a contestant in a radio quiz show.

Jack tried to keep calm and not turn to face Martin and the pictures.

"This is from your trip to Gula. Wow! Hubba hubba! Are you *sure* you don't want to see this picture?" Martin had been peeking through his fingers in an attempt at mock bashfulness, and Jack had to laugh when he saw Martin's reflection in a mirror on the wall. "Your taste is gradually getting better, you know," Martin asserted, "and this one … oh, *man*! She's a knockout!"

Jack tried to get back to business. "Just describe what's in the picture, Martin. You don't have to get all over her case."

"Ah, umm … okay. This is the Kingfisher with her again. Damn, she's hot! And the lady looks nice too. Why don't you want to see these? I mean, you're missing an awful lot here!"

Jack sighed. "Just take my word for it—please!"

Martin shrugged. He stacked the photos, arranging them so that an island landscape was on top.

Jack took the pictures and replaced them in the envelope, then put the envelope on the top shelf of his sorry excuse of a bookcase. Judging from the variety of items in it which could not be classified as books, it was evident to the world that he was not a voracious reader—more of a hunter-gatherer.

After dinner that night, Jack put the fifth symphony on his gramophone. For some reason, he decided to shower and shave before eating. He dressed in his only decent attire—a tuxedo bought from a clerk retiring from the British Resident Commissioner's office, and had his meal alone in silence. After dessert, as the first notes hit him, he sat down on the porch to admire the view. The music and the scene before his eyes melted together with his last image of Kay, with that royal wave in slow motion; he felt the view ebb before his eyes, saw her grow ever smaller, as if he was watching the final moments of a silent movie—iris close—black screen—roll credits—leave theater.

He toasted himself, once more congratulating his timid nature for its victory over his other instincts. Once again, he'd had the chance to extend his heart out and win himself someone to love, but that chance was now gone with little hope of reappearance. He flogged his courage for always failing him when it counted most, and he knew he had to start all over again to rebuild his composure, his ability to survive alone. It hurt; it felt like scar tissue being torn open again in his heart.

And yet, he knew he would make it. As he had in the past, so he would have to now.

5

Jack could still remember when his dreams had started. The first dream had come when he was three weeks away from turning fifteen. Vague and spaced irregularly at first, within a couple of months the dreams had formed a pattern and began to show up about every four weeks. There were always a primary set of objects: a ship, an ocean, sunset followed by a very dark dusk, a huge anchor, and a very uneasy feeling of aloofness. Most nights these swirled into a dream with no beginning or end, just an indeterminate phase inserted into the main feature dream of the night like a stray cel in a film.

All he could do was to bear witness to the events as they unfolded in his mind, in a general mood of restless longing for something he could not name, as a visitor in an alien land, with no point of reference outside himself. In most of the dreams he was an object, not subject, of the dream. He would wake up after these dreams feeling not rested but weary of journeying, as if all his time in sleep had been used up by someone else, doing something to his own detriment.

It was not long before he found the connection between the dreams and his life. Three days before Jack's grandpa passed away, he sailed into the sunset in Jack's dream. Jack's uncle, who had served in the Great War, died when Jack was sixteen, and beforehand Jack saw his uncle's favorite fishing vessel, a small dinghy, being pulled to the bottom by a dispro-portionate anchor. He didn't appreciate these dreams at all as he felt he was being shown something which he shouldn't see, but he learned to stow the dreams away as soon as he woke up.

What bothered him much more was when he saw shadows on photographs of people. When his flight training class was photographed on the tarmac of the Navy training base in Pensacola, Florida, Jack found he was able to single out the men who would die in the near future by the shadows he saw behind them. It was deeply disconcerting for him that he knew weeks in advance which of his pilot buddies would be lost in accidents during the training.

He saw a shadow behind Wallenstern, one of his best friends, in a snapshot of the two of them. Two weeks before the end of the course, Wallenstern crashed while strafing ground targets, a victim of target fixation. When Jack got the class photo in the mail three weeks after the class had graduated, he could see shadows behind three other pilot buddies, and within two months he had received word that all of them were dead. One had crashed when his engine quit during takeoff, another hit the fantail on carrier-landing training, and the third died in a car crash. After that, Jack tried not to look at photographs of his buddies, or of anyone he knew. Most of all, he wondered about whether he would one day see his own shadow in a photo.

When Jack was sixteen, he had the dream which lingered on in his memory for all his life. The setting was his home farm, through which a small river ran. Jack walked along the river, away from home, when the river appeared to widen and widen until he could no longer see the opposite bank. He continued walking down the riverside, but before long he became aware of a gigantic military ship steaming up the river, dark gray with black smokestacks belching clouds of darkness.

Cautiously he approached the ship, listening to the sounds

of the men running about on the decks, pulling cables, tending to machinery, and manning gun stations. As Jack got within a hundred feet away of the side of the ship, he had to bend his neck upward to see the edge of the deck. The eyes in the anchor chain of the ship were taller than Jack himself, made of matte black iron. Jack began to feel fearful awe of the ship, but he stayed there on the riverbank. Again, more due to instinct than for any actual reason, he glanced up to the bow of the ship, and was alarmed to see himself there on the deck, leaning out over the railing, waving slow and silently.

Now Jack was very alarmed, and started to run away from the ship just as it weighed anchor and started to pull in the anchor chain. While he ran, Jack glanced over his shoulder to see the huge anchor pull out mud and silt from the river bottom, along with rib cages, skulls, and assorted bits and pieces of the human skeleton, all of which splashed back into the river. Jack could have sworn he heard muffled cries and moaning as each skull fell, but then he was overcome with the strongest of feelings; he knew he could run for all he was worth, but there was no escape from the ship, his future. Thus resigned, he braced himself and his mind slowly ground to a halt, turning to face the ship. He could still see the tiny other Jack at the bow, waving—first with one hand, now with both hands—until he walked away without turning.

Jack saw the ship pull out down the river, which again began to narrow down until it reduced itself to its original width. He shivered as the wind began to blow from upstream, and he turned to set out for home. Soon after that, the dream dissipated and he woke up exhausted, but feeling strangely sure of direction. He knew now that there was no other thing for him than to go out to find his way.

He had long known the farm would be left to him, as Tony had tended to daydream in a manner not well suited to farming, and his sisters were too young to have fielded an opinion. Now, at sixteen, he was distressed to find himself longing to leave the safety of the farm.

Jack continued to have the dreams at irregular intervals, some very distinct, some less so. In any case he was always able to ascribe the dream to a real-life event. He felt disturbed by the dreams and sought assurance he was not crazy by telling Tony about them. This was clearly a mistake, since Tony laughed him off and once even threatened to tell everyone. Jack was incensed, and after a short fistfight Tony finally pledged to keep Jack's secret.

Still, even with this failed attempt, Jack felt he had to talk to somebody. It occurred to him that his best confidante probably was his maternal grandmother, who always been a person of warm comfort in Jack's life. Missy usually visited the farm early in May and stayed until the end of harvest, spending the rest of the year with Jack's aunt down in Boca Raton.

When she arrived, Jack lost no time in talking with her the first moment he could. He first tried beating about the bush and talking in general, almost vicarious terms, but Missy was no fool. She pressed Jack until he saw there was no way forward but to talk to her straight.

One evening as they sat together on the porch, Jack confessed, "Missy, I've got a problem. I have these dreams, and I'm not too thrilled with them."

"Dreams?" Missy kicked her rocking chair to a comfortable wobble. "What dreams?"

Jack looked at his grandmother. "It's like I can see into the future, and know things before they really happen and all that."

Missy took another sip of her lemonade. "Doesn't surprise

me," she said.

Jack couldn't believe his ears.

"Or actually, yes, it does surprise me on two counts," she continued. "One, it surprises me that *you* got the dreams and not your sisters. They would have told me by now. And two, it also surprises me you come to me only now with these things."

"What do you mean?" Jack asked.

Missy looked at the clouds that the setting sun painted deep orange. "It's been running in the family for ages. They say my mother's grandmother was the first to see, and that all the womenfolk in our family have seen ever since, but you're the first of our men to tell me this. What do you find disturbing in these dreams? Do they scare you, or what?"

"I'm not sure what it is, Missy, but I kinda feel I'm seeing things I shouldn't be seeing. I mean, if I see a dream of someone like Grandpa dying, and then he goes and dies, I don't feel like I should've known."

Missy looked at him with understanding. "Look, Jack, I know what it's like. See, I have them too. It took me some time to learn not to worry about the dreams, but my mother told me you can stop the dreams by yourself if you feel they're too big a burden for you."

"Really?" Jack said. "How?"

"All you have to do to stop them is to stand up in one of the dreams and ask for the dreams to stop. You know how you feel in the dream, you have that feeling like you can do more than just watch it go along. Well, you can. Just do so. They'll cease after that. It's just that I've also been told that if you do stop the dreams, you also stop whatever else was coming up your alley. Sometimes, those who dream like that will also develop other talents, and I think it'd be a shame if there was something useful coming after the dreams and you'd asked them to stop." Her eyes twinkled. "Oh look, the sun has just set. I love the clouds this time of day … they are so pretty."

Missy looked out to the west. "I want to be buried in a sunset cloud when I die. A purple one just like that."

Jack smiled. He'd always liked Missy's perspective on life.

Plus he felt much better after having talked with Missy. She obviously knew what he was feeling and why he found the dreams unpleasant. Arming himself with this knowledge, he went to sleep every night prepared to stop the dreams once and for all.

And yet, every time he had a dream, he did not stand up and give the order to stop. He found himself within the dream, watching the events unfold, fascinated and paralyzed on one hand by the misty, looming atmosphere, and on the other hand, wishing to learn more. He found he could to a degree control the dreams and that gave him confidence. From then on he was able to end any dream by issuing a mental command for the dream to pass, but he did not challenge the dream sequence as a whole.

When Jack was seventeen, he had a couple of very disturbing dreams. A family in the nearby town was lost in a fire during Christmastime, and Jack saw the fire a week before it happened. He was unable to tell which house had burned, but he saw the number of people lost and the ruins of the house. That made him sleep poorly for many nights afterward, until it occurred to him that maybe he was not supposed to be doing anything even if he saw the events beforehand. This comforting thought soothed him well enough for him to catch up slowly on lost sleep.

The other dream concerned his family directly. He saw himself sitting at the kitchen table. It was a fall evening, and it was raining outside. The kitchen stove gave him warmth, and the lamp on the ceiling spread a warm, yellow light across the kitchen. Suddenly Tony burst in, and went to the front door. Opening it he peeked out into the blackness, returned to Jack and asked for a flashlight.

Jack replied, "Find your own flashlight," and Tony rushed out of the door without bothering to find a light of any sort, not saying a word. Jack could see him pass out of the dim sphere of light from the kitchen door, and disappear into the inky night.

Next, Mr. McGuire came into the room. He had an carbide lamp in his hand, and he put on his boots and raincoat and went outside. Jack could hear him curse the weather as he went out of the door to work on the barn door. He had his lamp going, but Jack saw that it was not working properly; the light winked on and off at intervals until it went out completely. Jack did not see his father after that, and the carbide lamp burned itself out too.

The girls came into the room. They both had little storm lights, which they filled from a container. They put on their raincoats and boots, propping themselves up as best they could. Then they went to the stove and took fire out of it on a long chunk of firewood. This they used to light the storm lights, and after confirming the lamps worked, they hugged Jack and went out the door. Jack could see their stormlights swaying as they walked down the road out of sight together. Then one of the lights started back towards the house.

By now Jack was really worried, but he felt compelled to ride it out, to see what came of the dream. He felt a warm hand on his cheek and saw his mother had come to the kitchen. She sat down and watched the fire, which soon reduced itself to glowing red embers. She watched it with her head tilted slightly, as if deep in thought, and Jack did not dare speak to her. Slowly the red of the fire deepened until it was no more than a deep crimson hue on the embers, and still Jack did nothing but watch his mother.

Gradually he became aware of an irresistible urge to leave the house. He went to the door, peered out and saw the rain had ended, but still the darkness prevailed. He wondered why he should feel as if he had to go from the comfort of his home and the company of his mother, but an overpowering urge like a hand in his back forced him out. After fighting the urge with no success, he reminded himself it was only a dream. Then he put on his boots and took his jacket, and was already on the porch when he turned and went back to the house.

He took the matchbox from the stove railing, where everyone knew the matches were kept. It was an enameled matchbox with some Swedish words on it—a gift to his mother from a friend who'd married an expatriate Swede. He felt he wanted to have the matches with him, and his mother waved him goodbye as he pocketed the matchbox and passed silently through the door. No lights were on inside the house.

He awoke as the dream ended. It was 3 AM and he could not make any sense of what he'd just experienced. Nevertheless he went over the events of the dream in his mind and impressed them in his memory many times over, in hopes that the significance of every little detail might someday become clear, and only fell asleep again an hour later.

As Jack grew up, the dreams became less and less frequent. He was no longer troubled by them, and to a certain extent, he was also able to push the shadows of photographs away from his mind.

Still, he never looked at a photo which portrayed people he knew, if he could help it.

6

The carrier *Enterprise* was one day out of Pearl Harbor on its way to the combat zone with the entire air crew of VMF-288 on board. Jack's roommate on the carrier, one 2nd Lieutenant Taylor, was a statistician by training. Somewhat older than the other pilots of the squadron, he already had a steady job in civilian life: he worked for an insurance company, calculating premiums and predicting scenarios. He enjoyed his job very much and took immense pride in his capabilities as an actuary. Some time ago it had occurred to him that the same statistical approach could be employed in identifying the perfect mate.

In his usual methodical way, Taylor had devised a set of 115 questions related to married life, set them up on a huge sheet of paper and created a table of weights for these questions. Having finished his table, he located twenty-two eligible ladies through a wide array of means, and started a large-scale mail operation. Every response to the letters was tabulated in the master sheet, and from the weights and other formulas, he could then rank the ladies. In this way he could easily tell who were the top five applicants of the whole bunch.

When Jack came in from flight practice one Tuesday evening, Taylor had his master sheet spread all across the floor of their stateroom. He also had a stack of fresh mail by his hand. One of the letters was already open and he was in the process of crossing out a girl's entry in the table. "Oh my, oh my, oh my. I just got Dear Johned by Miss Mary Hofsteder, of Secaucus, NJ. Weeeell, no worries, as she wasn't in the top five anyhow."

Jack smiled. "Do you really believe it's possible to marry by numbers? What about love, and emotions, and all that?"

"It all depends on how you set up the questions. And don't forget I allocated up to 30% of the total value any girl can have to this variable here, 'Arbitrary'. With this I can discern, for example, cases like this: Miss Myrna Beck has a body like a Greek goddess, but intellectually she could be happy living in a chicken coop. Her score is only 5 here, because I do value brains over boobies, whereas my foxy friend Lucy Lander can rank a 15 here, to be upgraded to 25 after losing a few extra pounds."

Jack couldn't help smiling, but even so he found Taylor's approach cynical in the extreme, and said as much.

Taylor shook his head. "You know, McGuire, leaving something like this to your balls alone will get you in trouble. When I publish my book on this, you'll be sorry you didn't get on the program when it started, because you'll be spending money on the book later!"

"I'll take my chances," Jack declared, leaving the stateroom for a walk on the flight deck. Taylor voiced some objections but Jack couldn't hear them too well through the door.

Outside he enjoyed the warm Pacific breeze over the flight deck. He could see the last rays of the sun as it set in the west, and he admired the colors it painted on the clouds in the east. Every cloud in the Pacific seemed so different from the ones he knew in Nebraska, and he loved the sunsets out here. He walked along the port side of the ship from the bow stern-ward, but he stopped after a second, because he thought he heard music.

It stopped, but as he started walking again, the tune reappeared. It was a lone saxophone, whose player was not in sight. As Jack neared the fantail, he could hear it get louder, until he reached the 40mm antiaircraft gun mount, port stern. There he found 2nd Lieutenant Moreau, a pilot he knew from primary training. Their names had been next to each other alphabetically, so they'd often been grouped together in exercises.

"Moreau?" Jack ventured. "I didn't know you played saxophone! And where did you get that thing anyhow?"

Moreau stopped playing. "This is on loan from the ship's band. And yes, I used to play in New Orleans, with some big bands, although I preferred the clubs." He laid the instrument across his lap. "I just felt like playing a bit for practice, but also because I sometimes think it's easier to play than think."

He picked up the instrument again and let fly with an undulating tune, which was unlike anything Jack had heard before. It was full of longing and drew on Jack's own blue feelings, yet very appealing. "And sitting here I have had some odd thoughts, which I thought would go away if I played a bit," Moreau continued.

"Tell me," Jack offered, "I know a lot about odd thoughts. I often have them myself."

Moreau smiled and let loose with another long tune, clearly different from and yet very similar in tone and feeling to the first one. When he finished, he again laid down the horn and sighed. "OK, here goes. If I die here, I will be the first Moreau to be buried outside my hometown in Alabama. There's only one family member buried elsewhere, but he was an uncle of my mother's mother who went and fought for the Confederacy in the Civil War, so he doesn't count."

Jack smiled.

"And odd thought number two," Moreau continued. "I've

always been afraid of swimming in water deeper than five feet. And here I am on a ship in the middle of the Pacific, where there's no place less deep than five thousand feet anywhere."

He looked out to the darkening sea. "It's gotta come from my childhood when once I almost drowned in our river, and only just reached the bank—but this is ridiculous! You get shot down in Germany or Italy or anywhere over the ground, right, and they can identify you in all cases, even if nothing else is left but the plane's serial plate. Over here, you bail out or ditch and you're all outta luck, unless you do it close to the destroyers around the carrier. So I kind of see the game's lost, in any case. It also makes me wonder why I didn't sign up for the Army Air Forces—they asked me once but I thought I'd want to fight with the Marines for some godforsaken reason."

"There's Army units out here too," Jack said, "and they fly across the ocean just like us—but I think our navigation training is way better than theirs." Still, Jack assured him he empathized; joining the Marines had gotten them both out of their usual depth. And death in combat in the Pacific would surely have them buried far from their home.

"Does it matter to you where you get buried?" Jack asked.

"Very much, because family is very important to me. We've got a large family where everyone knows everyone, and we always have big wedding parties and big funerals. But if I'm shot down here, and go 13,000 feet down to meet Davey Jones, there's nothing left to bury," Moreau said. "And that would just kill my mother. I guess I really have to figure out a way of staying alive. But in any case, anything left to bury for real, in a real grave, would be better than getting slipped into the sea from under the flag," he added. They had yet to witness a burial at sea, but they knew there'd be many to come.

"If you get wise on how to do that staying alive stuff, pass it along," Jack said. "I guess my mother would send your mom a thank-you note." He smiled.

Moreau smiled too. "Oh well, I reckon you can only try not to screw up out here," he said, and let fly a more cheerful tune, which at some point merged into *American Patrol*.

"HEY, YOU FELLAS IN THAT GUN MOUNT," a bullhorn blared suddenly. "WE'RE GOING TO BLACK-OUT SO GET THE HELL OUTTA THERE." The officer of the deck had been watching them. It was time to go under and wait for the nightly sub scare or some other reason for going into General Quarters and full battle readiness.

"See ya later—and thanks for the concert," Jack said.

"Anytime, pal," said Moreau, and they went their separate ways towards their staterooms.

Back in his stateroom Jack found Taylor still enmeshed in his statistics. Jack hopped over his roommate's master plan for post-war bliss and went to sit on his bunk. "You know, I'm fully willing to locate a girl who will have me, statistics or no statistics, as long as we both agree we like each other," he said to Taylor.

"Ah, the amateur's approach to love and marriage. Well, we'll see later who gets the better match."

Finding the battle unwinnable, Jack decided to retire.

Two days later, a group of eight Wildcat fighters the ship had sent out to check a suspicious radar echo, returned one plane shy. The remaining seven planes landed in good order, but the flight leader was not happy to see Moreau was missing. "We had to duck this huge thundercloud and we skirted it a bit too close, we went in it a bit, and apparently not all came out," he said, going to the signal bridge to listen to the radio traffic in case Moreau tried to home in. He was heard a few moments later, saying that his homing device, known as

YE/ZB, was out of whack and he was already low on fuel.

Three minutes later there was another short message in which he said he saw the task group and that he started to approach them from five o'clock of the group, but after that, nothing was heard. All eyes were fixed in the direction he was supposed to be coming from, and the task group sent out a fast ship at full speed to look for him, but he was not found. Jack felt a shiver go through his spine when he thought of Moreau's intention of flying to survive. He was really sorry to think Moreau was now in all probability very deep in the ocean, where no one would ever know where he lay.

Three weeks later, after the *Enterprise* had already been to Fidzi and resupplied to go to combat, Jack's squadron commander, John "Bunny" Radner, called the squadron up to the flight deck. After all hands had assembled, he addressed them.

"As you all know, we lost 2nd Lieutenant Ryan Moreau almost straight out of Pearl. It was a sad occasion, and we all keenly felt his loss. It has now been relayed to us that he did indeed ditch his plane after it ran out of fuel, but it wasn't until now that he was found. He did make it to the life raft, but judging from the state they found him in, he died soon after reaching the raft, and his raft carried him eastward towards Hawaii. Two days ago he was picked up from the raft by a fishing vessel out of Pearl, returned to the authorities there, and identified. His dried-up remains were interred in the Navy graveyard in Pearl, and the next-of-kin were notified."

The lieutenant next to Jack shivered. "Dried-up remains … I'd rather have taken the dip than have my parched corpse picked up at the shore." Jack said nothing, but in his heart he was happy Moreau had been found. At least his wish for a proper burial had been granted.

Afterward Jack continued his habit of cloud watching as long as the ship was sailing. One evening after sunset he saw a luminous cloud on the horizon, and he remembered the only night of liberty they'd had at Pearl Harbor. Sitting on the deck with his legs dangling out, he reached for his wallet and pulled out a photograph. In it was a pretty girl, whose dark hair flowed down in thick, round curves on her shoulders, and sitting on a beach chair her legs looked as if they went on forever. Jack nearly put the picture away lest he see a shadow in it, but his wish to see the girl again overrode the instinct.

Once more Jack felt painfully shy as he remembered how the evening had gone. As usual, Don had found the perfect hunting grounds at some restaurant, and after five minutes flat had introduced himself to a blonde called Phoebe and a dark friend of hers, Claire. Don lost no time in ascertaining Phoebe's availability, and after that, he relegated Claire to Jack.

"Let's make the most of the time we have here at Pearl with these two perfect specimens of pearls, shall we? And lest recreation turn into procreation, here's something for you," Don said, in a much-too-loud voice and slipped a few Trojans to Jack under the table.

Jack's face went from zero to cooked lobster in three seconds, which did not go unnoticed by the girls. He found that Phoebe had a most annoying giggle which reminded him of a dentist's drill, but Claire didn't laugh at his discomfort. Don put on his best show, treated his party to dinner, and after a nice meal, made a quick getaway with Phoebe. Jack was left awkwardly with Claire, who had clearly had better company in her life. Jack fumbled about trying to get a conversation going, but it didn't go well, and he felt desperately inadequate.

Then Claire surprised him. "Let's go for a walk on the beach."

"Sure, that's a great idea," Jack said with much relief. They collected their belongings and strolled across to the beach. Once on the sand, Claire took off her high heels and they began a slow walk along the dry part of the sandy beach. No other people were visible but by the light of the moon, Jack had to admit to himself that he had never been out on a date with anyone as beautiful as Claire. By the time they reached a solitary palm tree, Jack was lost. She sat down under the tree and motioned to Jack to sit down beside her.

"Well?" she asked.

"Well, what?" Jack asked before thinking, once again immediately kicking his own butt mentally.

"Wouldn't you like to kiss me?"

Jack tried his damnedest to remember and employ all the tricks he'd seen in the movies to ramp up his kiss, and to him, it exceeded his wildest expectations.

After a long silence Claire nodded. "Now I've seen it all. A Marine who can't kiss."

Jack went all red again.

"You haven't had too much practice? Just a wild guess." Claire took Jack's arm. Her smile suggested to Jack that maybe the war wasn't lost even if this battle was a rout.

"You're right there … I've been too shy all my life to get anywhere with girls," he assented.

"Aww, poor thing! Well, I can help you along. I'll teach you how it goes. All you need to do is not to think at all." And to make her point, she kissed him lightly but definitively. Suddenly Jack felt hot all over.

But right in the middle, she unexpectedly drew away. "But if I teach you to kiss, you have to teach me something. *Quid pro quo*, that's how it goes. We have to agree on the trade before I start telling you the real secrets. What will you teach me?"

This caught Jack off guard. He tried to rake his brain for a marketable skill. Model-plane making? Flying? Baseball? Nothing comparable to the priceless art of kissing came to his mind. Besides, he had never heard of the *quid* thing. He decided to make a laugh out of it. "Tell you what. I'll teach you a mean baseball pitch that'll knock the socks off anyone." He fully expected a gale of laughter.

But Claire seemed to weigh the proposition before nodding. "Agreed. I teach you to kiss, you teach me how to pitch. It's a fair trade. Here's your first lesson," and she pulled him down on top of her for a very nice sample.

From there on, it was practical tips and tricks, theoretical lessons on the use of lips and tongue, and more practice, and after a couple of hours on the beach she led him to her flat by the bay. In the few hours before the sun came up to heat up the little apartment, the Trojans marched off to give battle, and by the time the flat was unbearably hot, Jack was much better trained in many respects.

He was also alone. Claire had left her picture sticking out of his shirt pocket, and on the back she had scribbled:

"You pass. You also owe me a lesson. XO"

Grinning ear to ear, Jack got dressed, left the flat and found a café to extinguish his ravenous hunger. Before returning to the ship, he sent a couple of postcards home and shopped for some zinc paste, a hot tip from some pilot who was on his second tour. When he met up with Don on the gangway to the ship, Jack tried to play it cool and to his amazement pulled it off. Don figured his hot date at Pearl must have consisted entirely of intense hand-holding. Jack left him with that thought.

Now, with the ship doing good time across some of the

deepest ocean waters on the planet, Claire and the precious hours Jack had spent with her seemed part of another world, and the fact that Jack had failed to check her address even to write to her, placed that world a little further out. He wasn't too worried about it though for two reasons: it was wartime, and probably he wouldn't be on the top of her list after the war. Jack watched the white surf plowed away by the bow, and noticed dolphins racing the ship to starboard. He could not deny that he felt good.

7

Despite the fantastic vistas she could see from the road crossing Arizona, Kay was bored. Her family—father, mother and
little sister—had taken the train out to Tucson, and then
rented a car to drive to the ranch of one of Kay's father's
former business associates. Bill Rivers had relocated to Arizona
and his constant invitations had finally become so persistent
that Mr. and Mrs. Willis had given in and decided to take
their holidays out West this year. Kay, being seventeen and
three quarters, fought long and hard against having to tag
along, but her mother would not have it any other way. Kay
just had to pack for the three-week trip, end of discussion.

Now, as it was a wonderfully cloudless day, Kay sat on the
right side of the back seat of their rented Chevrolet, in the best
vantage point for the unseen scenery. Her sister, thirteen-year
old Elaine, was reading a book. With glazed eye, Kay deigned
to look out the window to see nothing but a landscape that
could have been the far side of the moon for all she cared. She
was bored to the point that she knew she did not even want to
needle her sister for some action.

In the front seat, her parents were deep in a heated discussion over table manners. Mr. Willis had worked his way up
from a mechanic's helper, but somehow he had managed to
marry above his class. Mrs. Willis was keen on never letting
her husband forget this fact, and she went on crusades to keep
her husband within the boundaries of social behavior, espe-

cially before important occasions. It was not in the name of money or prestige that she did this. On the contrary; they'd had plenty of both since Mr. Willis had opened his successful auto dealership back home in Pittsburgh. It was just in her nature to try to mould her husband in the image of old money. Though her family was old money, unfortunately not much was left in the old coffers these days.

In a desperate attempt to change her state of mind, Kay wanted to listen to the car's radio. "Daddy? Can we have the radio on?"

"No."

"Why not?"

"Because."

Disgusted with the level of discourse, Kay shut her ears from the conversation she had heard so many times before. She wished she was back in Pittsburgh, where all her friends were surely having a way better time than whatever fate had in store for her in Tucson. She wished with all her might that something would come up and bring an end to the monotony of seeing thousands of wooden telegraph posts lined up unnaturally straight, just as the road itself was a rigid asphalt ruler someone had dropped onto the landscape.

She again looked out the window and tried to count the poles, but watching them whizzing by soon made her eyes hurt. To relax her eyes, she looked at the horizon far away, and noticed a small speck in the sky. At first she thought it was a bird, a large one like a hawk, or perhaps even an eagle. After a minute the speck had come close enough for her to see that it was really a plane. The plane was apparently on a course that would cross the road from right to left.

Kay began to wonder what it was like to be in that plane and see all this from far above, and to be on the way to somewhere of importance and not just from home to a boring old geezer's even more boring ranch with just a small pool, probably, if even that. She closed her eyes and thought of flying over all this and away from her dull school and the irritating little sister and the parents fighting all the time.

After a while she looked up in the sky again, but the plane was nowhere to be seen. Kay's briefly-lit interest waned and she settled back to her routine of wondering about what to do next. Just then, like a thunderbolt, the plane roared into the space immediately in front of the car, its engine sputtering and coughing badly.

"Je-sus Christ!" exclaimed Mr. Willis as he fought to control the car, brakes slamming shut, the tires leaving a long black skid mark on the hot road. Mrs. Willis was too surprised even to reprimand her husband for the blasphemy. The plane flared a few feet above the road, touched down, and slowly came to a halt by the wayside. Mr. Willis brought his car to the tail of the plane, jumped out, and prepared to give the pilot hell for trying to kill the Willises with his stunts. "Hey you! Get outta that plane and tell me what the hell you were doing just now!" Mr. Willis bellowed, rolling his shirt sleeves up as if he were about to punch the pilot. The door of the plane opened and out jumped a tall, lean fellow in his early twenties. He had a tuft of brown hair on his forehead that insisted on poking out at a rakish angle; the rest of his head was covered by a mop of curly hair, he had mischievous brown eyes and a small smile on his face.

"Sorry, sir, but I had no choice. Come over to the other side of the plane and I'll show you what I mean when I say I just about had to land right here." Smoke from the engine had blackened the cowling. "It's a rear main bearing failure probably. It happens with this type of engine pretty often. It's

85

frozen, no lubrication."

This was all it took to diffuse Mr. Willis's anger and, beyond that, to get under his polished businessman's façade, and he reverted to the mechanic's apprentice he once was.

Mr. Willis glanced over the plane and, having been presented with a vehicle which failed to operate properly, was back on familiar ground. "Well whaddaya know! That sure makes it hard to run an engine, eh? Let's see what's under the cowling! What kind of plane is this anyway?" and soon he was elbow-deep inside the cowling.

"It's a 1932 Waco UEC," the pilot explained. "I'm delivering it to a new owner." The pilot showed Mr. Willis the guts of the engine, but his eyes flipped quick looks in Kay's direction all the time. At first Mrs. Willis patiently stood by, smiling to the pilot with a tiny smile, but watching the young man with suspicion in her eyes. Elaine was admiring the young pilot with her gaze as if he were Clark Gable; in trying to keep her eyes off the pilot, Kay resorted to an examination of the plane.

Then, after ten minutes of watching her husband get greasy before their engagement, Mrs. Willis had had enough. "Dear, we just have to get to the ranch before it gets dark!" she reminded Mr. Willis.

"What's that? Oh yeah…right…well there's not much we can do about this plane at the moment anyway. It needs a complete overhaul. Where were you going?"

"I was delivering this plane to its new owner over in Nogales. But given the circumstances, I'd be just thrilled if you could pick me up and drop me off at the nearest town where I can call the buyer and tell him the plane isn't exactly arriving at Santa Cruz County airport today."

"Sure thing, kid, just hop on. There's bound to be a town

down the road soon. We're going some twenty miles south of here."

Mrs. Willis made sure the young man sat on the far left on the back seat, with Elaine in the middle and Kay at the far right. Elaine was of course overjoyed, and soon had the pilot telling her about the basics of aviation. The pilot gestured with his hands to illustrate the position of the plane in various maneuvers and Elaine was fascinated, never taking her eyes from the pilot.

Kay tried hard not to look to the young man or to encourage him to look at her, but to her dismay, every time she looked up, his eyes were watching her. Kay looked out of the window but she felt his gaze touch her high cheeks, brush her hair off her left ear, and slide down her all the way and back up again. It made her blush.

"Oh, by the way...I never introduced myself. Name's Don Wheeler, from Pittsburgh. Nice to meet you and your family, and nice of you to help me out like this."

"Pittsburgh? No kidding?" Mr. Willis beamed. "We're from Pittsburgh too!"

"Well, well ... what are you doing all the way out here, then?"

"We're going on a vacation to a friend's ranch."

"A chance meeting, then. We must have been meant to meet up, then." And again Kay felt Don's eyes on her cheeks. She looked at him defiantly and knew right away it was a mistake. She saw that he belonged to that dangerous breed of men whose smile could drown a mature woman, let alone a high school senior. Kay decided to keep her eyes well away from the young man, who was about to be dropped off anyway and out of their lives for good.

But Mr. Willis had other ideas. "What the heck, Don,

what if we take you with us to Bill Rivers' ranch? You can call the plane's owner from there, old Bill won't mind. Besides, Bill can help you with the arrangements and you'll get some supper in the bargain."

"Great idea, Dad!" exclaimed Elaine, but she was quickly silenced by an icy look from her mother.

Mrs. Willis was clearly uncomfortable. "Really, dear, I don't think that's such a good idea. Surely Mr. Wheeler here has other plans. And besides, we haven't told Bill we're bringing in another guest!"

"That's right, ma'am, and I don't want to be any more trouble than I've already been, what with the scare I gave you and all," Don added.

"Come on Liz, it's no big problem." Mr. Willis deliberately invoked his wife's nickname to silence her once and for all. "We'll just take him up to the ranch and Bill can help him get the plane to some airfield or engine shop for maintenance. Bill knows everybody around these parts." And with that, Mr. Willis closed the case.

Up at the ranch, Bill Rivers would not have it any other way except for Don to stay at the ranch overnight, and then go after the plane in the morning. Despite Don's protestations, Mr. Rivers just said, "No, son, we'll fix the plane tomorrow. The phone's right here—you just go and call that new owner in Nogales and say he'll get his plane as soon as we get it fixed. Then, you can call the nearest dealer for a new cylinder or head or whatever it is you need. Say, they might be able to help you right here at the airport in Tucson. I know a guy there who runs a charter service. Let me call him. Or better yet, we'll go there in the morning. For now, just call Nogales now and tell what's up."

Don Wheeler could do nothing but nod his head and

thank his generous host.

Servants appeared from the big house and helped the party get their luggage and bags from the car. Don only had a small bag, but Mrs. Willis was apparently equipped with enough trunks and suitcases for a battalion. The servants showed them the rooms; Mr. and Mrs. Willis had one on the second floor, the girls found themselves on the ground floor, and Don was ushered into a room above the spacious garage.

"Dinner is at eight," said the man who looked to be the maitre d' of the ranch. This left the party just an hour to get ready.

Meeting the others at dinner, Don was feeling awkward in his less than formal attire. After all, he had no plans for dinners on this trip, which was to have consisted of the flight to Nogales and a train trip back to Pittsburgh. However, Mr. Rivers' genial hospitality soon made him feel better, especially by seating Don by Kay's side at dinner.

Soon the company was beginning the main course. Mr. Rivers was very interested in Don's piloting activities, and he asked many questions about aviation, which Don answered as best he could. Mr. Willis, too, eagerly participated in the conversation, if mainly on the mechanical side of aviation.

Mrs. Willis was still trying to decide the amount of danger Don Wheeler posed to her daughter, and to do that she watched him on the sly as he talked. To her relief, she seemed to notice Don was no ordinary mechanic from Pittsburgh. He was well aware of table manners, and his participation in the conversation was active but polite. There was more to the story, and she resolved to draw out the true Don Wheeler at the first possible moment.

But at the moment, Don was explaining his raison d'être. "Basically, sir, I fly for the feeling of being airborne. Nothing on earth can match the feeling of touching the clouds, or seeing far beyond what you can see on the ground. I don't fly for money, rather it's the other way around; I work as a mechanic to support my flying. Trips like these, making deliveries across the country, are the best things in life. I've flown from New York to San Francisco and from Seattle to Atlanta, and I'd never give up the moments I spent on those trips." Don took a sip of his wine.

Now this side of the pilot was to Kay's liking. She had dreamed of seeing the whole of the country, although her idea had been to travel by rail from one aunt to another via some second cousins and uncles. Flying would be...heavenly.

"What's San Francisco like?" she heard herself asking. It was the first time she had said anything directly to Don.

The company fell silent, waiting for Don's answer. Don looked into her eyes and liked what he saw a lot.

Kay blushed and turned her head back to her plate. "I've always wanted to see California. That's why I asked."

Her mother was again sure she had to do something before Mr. Wheeler found a way to her daughter's heart.

Don looked up towards the ceiling, but it was clear to everyone he was seeing the sky beyond. "San Francisco is truly the pearl of the Pacific. I've flown out of there on a September morning, starting after the fog cleared just enough for the tower to let me go, and from the skies I watched the fog drift up the hills in Berkeley and Oakland, clearing the Bay enough for me to see. I had to do three lazy circles around the Bay before I'd seen enough of it to be on my way to Nevada. That was one of my most memorable moments in the air."

Don took another sip of wine. "Too bad the three lazy circles made me fall short of my destination. I had to take refuge in a field."

The company laughed politely, but Don was sure he had broken the ice between himself and Kay. Dessert was served, during which the conversation ranged more freely and away from aviation, mostly to news about Pittsburgh and its happenings. During this portion of the evening it finally struck Mrs. Willis why the Wheeler name was so familiar to her, and she had difficulties maintaining her composure until the dinner ended and the company had dispersed into the library and other rooms.

After Don had accepted a glass of fine whiskey from Mr. Rivers, he found himself cornered by a most eager Mrs. Willis. "Don, dear! There's something I'd like to ask you—do you happen to know the Wheelers of Boston, by any chance?"

"Funny you should mention them, ma'am, they're my father's family. Do you happen to know them?" Don was sly as a fox.

No, Mrs. Willis did not know them; her old money was peanuts compared to the old money of the Wheelers, but the riddle of Don's fine manners was solved. She was overjoyed to hear Don belonged to such a prestigious family, although his way of supporting himself as an airplane mechanic did give Mrs. Willis considerable worry. Still, at least she did not have to keep her daughter away from this mechanic from the skies. This was a mechanic with a pedigree.

After 10:30, Elaine was sent to bed after considerable pleading on her part. At a quarter past eleven Don retired to the balcony for a cigarette and to have a look at the stars. Lighting up, he sat on the ledge with one foot propped up on it, puffing away quietly and enjoying the crisp, dark starry skies above him. He was startled when Kay joined him.

"So ... you like the skies in the daytime and in the evening too?" Kay asked him.

"Well, you could say that. I've made myself familiar with the skies of Pittsburgh … all you can see there I mean, what with the clouds and the city lights. I like watching the stars here, the sky's so pitch-black that the stars just look so close. They just pop out at you. See for yourself." Don watched as Kay slowly turned her eyes upwards, and her delicate profile looked very graceful in the dim light coming from the house.

"I can't say I know any stars, either in Pittsburgh or New Mexico. Never did look at them too well. They're beautiful down here all right. What's that deep red star down there?" Kay asked.

"Take this with a grain of salt, but I believe it's Antares of Scorpio. Yes, it has to be, you can see the curve of the scorpion's tail there."

"Do you feel any closer to the stars when you fly?" Kay heard herself ask.

She was studying the distant points of light and Don could see she was relaxing a bit. He knew full well the effect of deep sky-gazing, and he moved a bit closer. Soon he was sitting beside her on the ledge of the terrace.

"Yes, as a matter of fact, it sure does feel like you can reach out and touch them. I like to fly in the deepest night—then you're alone with the stars, with the dark earth far below … it's stunning." This was not true, strictly speaking, as Don had only flown once in the dark, and even then because he had failed to locate the field in time.

"It must be a dream job, being a pilot," Kay said, and looked Don straight in the eyes.

His heart skipped a beat. "If you want, I'll take you up when I get the engine fixed," Don said. "That is, if your parents allow me to… they seem to watch over you pretty carefully."

Kay harrumphed. "My mother's a terrible fuss. If I did everything her way, I'd still be wearing ponytails."

Don saw his opening. "Ponytails? Hmmm—they might suit you real well!" He recoiled under Kay's fast feigned attack. Now he had her, he knew; she had touched his arm lightly for the first time, and he could see she was hooked.

"Don't tease."

Kay could conjure up the funniest of pouts, and he just had to laugh.

"OK then, no ponytails. Come to think of it, I think that hair suits you just fine." He reached out and caressed her hair with a gentle stroke, inching closer to her again. She was also leaning ever so slightly towards him, fully feeling his presence, awash with oncoming feelings the intensity of which were entirely new to her.

She saw he was about to touch her again, and her eyes closed and her lips parted in anticipation when the door to the terrace flew open and Elaine barged in with all the gaiety of a girl her age.

"Ha! Found you two lovebirds! I'll run out to tell Mama!" Elaine shouted. She attempted to tickle Kay, who sprang to her feet with the agility only big sisters possess when they have to show the way of the world to their siblings. After a brief chase Elaine was shoved down the stairs and off the terrace, but both Don and Kay knew the risk of exposure by Kay's mother was now too great for them to continue their evening.

After a few words of convention they both retreated down the stairs to the company of the others, of whom at least Kay's mother cast a good few suspicious glances at Don. Kay reassured her that nothing untoward had happened, even as she flashed a fast smile across the room.

After an hour more of chitchat, everyone began to seek the

way to bed. It had been a long day, and even Kay, against her expectations, fell asleep very soon. Her dreams, however, were full of excitement, and a certain man offering the pleasures of flight to her.

Early in the morning, Don was on the phone. A call to Nogales announced the delay to the customer, who was not too worried about it. A second call to Pittsburgh started Don's manager into looking for a replacement part, which he would then forward to Tucson via air freight. With Mr. Rivers's help, Don managed to locate an aircraft mechanic who would be able to fix the plane where it stood in the desert, and nearby there was a good enough runway for takeoff when fixed. All it spelled then was two, maybe three days of waiting, but Mr. Rivers would not hear a word of Don going to a hotel for the stay. He would be lodged at the ranch and that was the end of it.

Don was secretly overjoyed, as was Kay, but neither expressed it beyond Don's many thanks to Mr. Rivers and the party.

Over the course of the day, the weather turned bad. By dinnertime, dark clouds cloaked the sky, the wind picked up with a vicious lashing, and all outdoor activities had to be brought to a halt. Even Elaine was carried indoors from the pool where she had spent the day, refusing to believe she had to go inside.

As dinner was over, Don was nowhere to be found. The storm had gathered its might and started the show, and Don had excused himself right after dessert. Kay wondered where he'd gone, but on a whim she decided to check the roof. At least she could scan the entire ranch from there for him.

When she reached the door to the roof, she could hear thunder and heavy rain hammering down past it. She opened the door and stepped out. There, sitting in a recess, was Don, admiring the pouring rain and lightning flashes from his place of shelter. He seemed to be enjoying himself, and Kay very badly wanted his company. She ran over to him and got soaked in the few seconds it took her to get there.

"Now you've done it," said Don. "Your mother won't approve of your getting wet like that. You'll catch pneumonia or some other terrible disease."

Kay shook her head, sending droplets flying in all directions. "I won't tell her. Besides, I think this'll dry out soon enough, it's still so hot."

Don looked at her. "I think it's rude of me to let you get soaked by yourself." With that he stepped out of the recess and into the downpour.

"Get back here, silly!" Kay shouted, but the call was lost in a tremendous crash of lightning.

Don held out his arms to the sky. Kay went to him and tried to pull him back into the recess, but Don turned around quickly as a fox and grabbed her, and kissed her in the rain. She was too surprised to say anything, but when he finally let her go, she did the same to him. Neither said a word after the two kisses, but they knew they were committed to each other now.

The rain went on, the kissing went on, and nobody thought to look for them at the roof. After all, it was raining so hard it was incomprehensible anyone would want to stay outside, exposed to the elements.

When the thunderstorm finally passed, and rays of the setting sun began to peek through the majestic clouds, the lovers wended their separate ways to their rooms and got changed. Kay lied with big eyes to her mother that she'd been at the stables tending to the horses—this explanation did not ac-

95

count for the soaking set of clothes in the bathroom, which Mrs. Willis luckily didn't catch—while Don had to explain to Mr. Rivers that he'd been at the garage helping the chauffeur do something to one of the cars of the estate. It wasn't until Mr. Rivers caught a glimpse that Kay sent to Don that evening that he understood the truth of the matter, but, having been young himself once, he let it pass with a sympathetic smile and a nod to Kay.

In due time the plane was fixed, Don went his way back home, and the Willis family returned to Pittsburgh the long way, via San Francisco. When they finally got home, Don was already there, waiting at the house with a bouquet for each lady in the family, one of them about twice the size of the others.

He courted Kay eagerly but politely and persistently, and within six months had secured himself a regular seat at the Willises' dinner table. It took a year more to get Mr. and Mrs. Willis to agree to marriage, but even that came through eventually. The young couple settled down in a nice suburban house not too far from Kay's family. Kay flourished in her studies at the University of Pittsburgh, while Don worked days and studied engineering in the evening.

All was well for a stretch of time, which seemed like an enjoyable eternity to Kay, happy as she ever imagine being in her life.

And then Don decided it was necessary to join the Marines

8

During Jack's first three weeks at Guadalcanal, his plane was hit on just about every mission, but he himself escaped the bullets. His luck finally ran out on September 15, 1942, when he was on a CAP mission with his squadron above the fleet of transport ships at the harbor and the fledgling Marine base around Henderson Field. Jack had picked up an incoming torpedo attack, tallyhoed it, and zoomed down to attack the fast and dangerous Japanese torpedo planes, dubbed Kate by the Americans.

On a head-on pass he and Don both managed to get one Kate smoking, and turning as hard as the Wildcats could, they went after the Japanese planes, which were skimming barely above the water. Jack finished his Kate off, and it splashed into the sea without harming anything, but Don's Kate managed to release its torpedo at the ships that were maneuvering furiously to avoid the baneful steel fish.

Seconds after the Kate had turned to escape, Don hit the pilot, and the Kate fell uncontrolled into the sea. Jack in the meantime had picked up another Kate nearing release distance from the ships. Its target was one of the destroyers, which was by no means letting the Kate have an easy run for its money. The destroyer was shooting at the incoming Kate with all it had, and as a result a lot of the ammunition whizzed past Jack too. He pondered his choices: either to let the ship try to hit the Kate, or face both the flak and the rear gunner of the Kate and press on. He decided to continue on his current course, as the flak didn't seem to have much of an effect on the determined Japanese pilot.

Jack did hit the rear gunner, as the steady flow of bullets from the Kate stopped and the gun barrels went pointing up. The next seconds comprised such an action-packed blur that later Jack couldn't say in what order things happened, but the Kate lost its left wing, exploded in the water, Jack pulled hard up, his plane was hit, and his engine started leaking oil and began to miss beats in a percussive sputter. He knew he couldn't make it to Henderson but would have to ditch, and as his plane's belly was shining towards the destroyer, some trigger-happy gunner sent out a last volley of 40mm rounds, which hit Jack's F4F fighter square in the engine. It died instantly. Soon after the blast a piece of shrapnel hit him, slicing a deep wound in the side of his palm. Soon there was blood everywhere in the cockpit. Ditching the plane in the water was no longer an option, so Jack pulled on the stick to get as much altitude as possible before he could jump.

The plane barely made it to 800 feet, at which height Jack opened the canopy, climbed on his seat, and kicked on the stick to cause himself to be thrown clear of the wrecked plane. As he left the plane, he smashed his nose on the open canopy. As soon as he was clear of the plane he pulled the ripcord and was very much relieved to see the parachute blossom up over his head. During the descent he bandaged his hand with his scarf.

When he touched down in the water, he happened to be only fifty yards from a cargo ship, whose sailors lowered a boat and picked him up within a few minutes. Within two hours of his bailing out, Jack was happy to find himself back on Guadalcanal, being patched up by the doctor and patted on the back by assorted Marines.

He was awarded a sure kill for the first Kate and a probable on the second. His hand caused him to be detained at the sick bay for a few days, as he had lost a moderate amount of blood and the doctor wanted to make sure the stitches he sewed into Jack would hold.

Soon Jack found that he actually needed the rest and was not overly concerned with being grounded. On the second evening he was taking a nap on his bed.

"What got you here?" he heard a voice from the next bunk. It was one of the young new Marines, a bunch of which had arrived just a few days ago, oblivious of the brave new world that lay before them now. This kid had been slightly injured in his first bombing by a piece of shrapnel which had sliced into his back, leaving a nasty scar down his spine but doing little actual damage. He was due for release the next day.

Though he usually kept to himself, Jack thought chitchat might help him pass the time. "Well, I'm sort of on vacation here," he replied.

The boy laughed. "Aren't we all—a tropical vacation paid for by Uncle Sam!" Judging from his grin, he'd thought it a great joke, and Jack smiled to oblige him. The boy seemed quite happy for having met one of the pilots, who were very highly thought of among the Marines. He offered Jack a cigarette.

"Tell me, you zoomies feel any fear at all when you meet the Japs head-on?" the boy asked, his eyes alight with the intensity all boys have when they speak with aviators.

Jack took a deep one from his cigarette, and then blew the smoke out in one lingering breath.

"You know what? I really can't say. I mean, you never have the time to think when someone's coming at you in a Zero.

You just try and use your instincts more than your brain."

"I wanted to be a pilot myself, but I failed the medical. I have a crooked spine. Not so crooked though that I wouldn't have made the regular Marines. That was my second ambition, to be a Marine, if I couldn't be a fighter pilot. But for now I'm happy just to be somewhere doing my part," the kid explained in one breath.

Jack just smiled and tried to go back to sleep.

"My fiancée said she thought I'd make a great pilot, but when I couldn't make it, she told me she'd welcome me back from the Marines when this war's done just as glad," the boy went on. "I just miss Pam so much, though I've only been out here for a couple of weeks and the training. We've written letters all through the time, and I'm happy 'cause I know I can trust the girl I left back home."

Jack didn't have the heart to say he would rather sleep than talk.

The boy rotated himself to one buttock. "Here, let me show you her picture!"

Jack tried again to tell the kid that he was very sleepy, but already the boy had his wallet out. He pulled out a worn picture and triumphantly shoved it under Jack's nose.

"Isn't she a beaut? This was taken outside her Pop's gas station just last February."

Jack took one look at the photo before he realized that he'd probably see something he wouldn't like, and so he did. The picture had been taken in a cloudy weather, and the girl only had a faintly visible shadow on the cinderblock wall and on the ground, but the wall behind the boy showed a sharp shadow which was looming over him black as coal.

Jack felt sick. "She sure is something, kid," he managed, turning away feeling very tired.

"When I get out of this war we'll get married first thing, and her old man promised me a job running this new gas station of his he's building in Albuquerque." Tenderly the boy put the picture back into his wallet and then patted his breast pocket once the wallet was safely inside. "When I went away she gave me the longest kiss and told me I'd get out of this war without a scratch just to be her man. Well, she wasn't exactly right on that count, with this wound and all, but hey, I'm doing okay already."

He continued for a while longer in this vein before he realized Jack was facing the canvas of the tent. "Sorry to bother you, Lieutenant," he said, chastened, "I didn't realize you wanted to sleep. I'll be quiet from now on."

"No hassle, son, it's just that I'm pretty worn out after the flight and the swim yesterday." Jack closed his eyes but he could not shake the image of that shadow on the wall of the gas station. He knew he'd have to lose sight of the kid soon or watch him die.

Usually the Japanese raided Henderson around noon. So they did this day too, but when the Marines on the island had returned from their foxholes to normal duty, eight Betty bombers appeared seemingly out of nowhere with no prior warning from coastwatchers and delivered a low-level bombing attack on the field. Once the bombs started falling, all of the soldiers in the hospital scrambled to their foxholes.

Jack too headed for the nearest hole, which actually was a bomb crater from a few days before, and jumped in, strapping on his helmet in the course of his dive. He could hear the sickening sound of bombs falling and the huge explosions, and feel the concussions of the bombs as they demolished aircraft revetments close by the hospital. He ventured up to see if all hospital personnel had made it to the foxholes, but the first thing he saw was the young Marine heading back to the sick tent.

"Get out of there! Get out!" Jack yelled, but the Marine yelled back, "I can't find my helmet! I need my helmet!"

The kid stooped down and picked up a helmet from the ground and started running towards Jack in the hole. He began to strap on the helmet, but Jack shouted, "Forget the helmet! RUN! RUN!"

Just as the Marine was about to reach the relative safety of the crater, the belly-load of bombs from the last Betty began to fall about a hundred yards from them. Jack could see the stick of bombs falling, and before the boy could jump into the crater, the bombs went off. Jack watched as the boy was first hit in the neck with a large piece of shrapnel and then thrown into the air like a scarecrow in a twister. In horror, he watched the kid's head with the helmet still strapped on it fly across the crater, spinning in slow motion as it went, and disappear in the grass some ten yards away

The body of the young Marine landed neck first into the crater, its heart pumping blood for a few frantic seconds, and then the limbs stopped twitching, a pool of blood forming at the crater's bottom.

Jack clawed his way up out of the crater, an inch at a time. He could see the last Bettys retiring north, pursued by a couple of F4Fs out of range. To his surprise, Jack saw Don step to the edge of the crater and look down inside.

"Oh boy. We need to do something about these young-sters. They can't keep calm in battle. Just look at this one, he lost his head completely!"

For a second Jack couldn't move, couldn't feel anything but a primordial rage build up inside of him. Fueled by this, he sprang up from the crater with a single leap.

"You goddamn bastard!" he shouted as he grabbed Don by his jacket and shook him. "That boy is dead and you don't have any damned respect for the fallen! How dead should he be for you to show some *feeling*?" Jack took a swipe at Don, who dodged the punch and pulled himself free.

"Respect for the dead? You want respect? I'll give you respect!" Don started punching Jack in the chest to emphasize his points. "So, Jack, that's the closest you been to death so far, ain't it? You're almost an ace, you got three Japs in their planes, right? Did you fret over them when you shot them down in flames? Did you? No? So what makes this guy any different? He's a corpse, a dead body, a piece of meat! The only difference is that he's not broiled in aviation fuel!"

Don shoved Jack a few feet away from him. "There's a number on him, and on you, and on me, can't you see it? His number was called, and nothing you did could have helped him a bit. If he didn't lose his head, he'd have broken his neck landing in that crater or he'd have been hit tomorrow by a stray shell from the Jap field gun in the hills, for all you know. And as for you, you can never tell if the Japanese version of Rosie the Riveter finished the Zero today that will shoot you down a week from now when they get it ferried out to Rabaul! So why get all emotional over this, kid? There's no way of telling when things will happen and we'll all be dead one of these days, so let's just keep cool and shoot down as many Japs as you possibly can, because one of them just may be carrying the bullet with your number on it. Sheesh!"

Turning away, Don started towards the revetments. Jack watched him go in silence, thinking that Don was wrong in one respect: it was possible to know when people were going to go. That was part of the problem. When Don disappeared from view, Jack moved his eyes to the headless body in the

103

crater, with the pool of blood coagulating in the hot, humid air. A couple of medics came out with stretchers to pull the remains of the young Marine out of the crater, and carry them away.

When Jack had swung at Don, a few of the stitches in his left hand had ripped open, and he came back to his senses when he became aware of the blood dripping from the bandage. He walked slowly back to the sick bay, where Doc patched him up again. Jack felt numb all over and waved away the painkiller—his hand felt no worse than on any other day.

He went back to his sickbed, slumped down on it, and felt a profound sense of loss within him. He knew, of course, that Don was right, that war devours life like a bush fire feasts on dry undergrowth, but even more deeply he felt an animus for his gift of seeing shadows. For the millionth time, he wished it would go away, but he knew it was his to keep.

Jack was released from the sick bay three days later, but still he would be grounded for another five days. He spent his time with the plane crews, helping out as best he could. The crews were a major asset the Allies had on this tenuous foothold in enemy territory. If they couldn't patch up a plane well enough for it to fly again, they scavenged every piece of useful material from it: gauges, engine parts, even whole wings. Jack could well identify with them when a plane did not return from a flight. The plane crew would patiently wait, like a dog waiting for its master, well beyond the time fuel must have run out for certain, and even then they held an eye out for the pilot to return. Some happy reunions were seen as pilots were rescued by coastwatchers, Navy ships, or friendly natives, and these were duly celebrated by the true believers as miracles; everyone knew the sea and the jungle played for keeps.

Jack did see Don when he took off in his Wildcat and

when he landed his bullet-riddled fighter a couple of hours later, but they both avoided meeting one another. This détente went on as long as Jack was grounded, but on the eve of his return to flight status Jack knew they had to talk, because soon enough they'd be flying wing again.

Jack found Don beneath his plane, helping out in fixing the main landing gear, which was leaking oil. As Jack bent down, the plane captain silently excused himself. Don did not greet Jack.

The cold shoulder, not unexpected. Jack offered Don the wrench he knew would fit the nut Don was inspecting. "We need to talk."

"What about? You know what I think." Don kept on working.

Jack knew he had to try and get him to talk. "Look, sorry about the other day. It's just that I was talking to the kid just moments before he died, and all of a sudden he's ten inches shorter. I was just plain off my nuts that moment. I don't think I have the right to ask you to do anything you don't want to do, or feel anything you don't feel. Okay?"

Don sat on the ground and pointed at Jack with the wrench.

"That's right, Jack, you sure as hell don't. And it's not that I don't have respect for the fallen. It's just my way of coping with it all. And besides, if you got to go, that's the way. Or you could sure go a lot worse. No pain, no sense of dying, just a clean-cut exit from this hellhole. Pun intended." He went back to his landing gear.

Jack felt as though he had been absolved.

"I guess the guys in the foxholes have a different view on death," Jack said as he prepared to leave. "Up there it's all so distant."

Don looked at him. "Look, Jack, I know you have your religious beliefs. Don't feel offended if I don't share them with you. I just know we have a time down here and when it's up, it's up. That kid's was now, and ours'll be later. Go get some sleep, it's a deep escort tomorrow."

With that, Jack walked away and nodded at the plane captain who was coming back to the plane with two tin cups of coffee.

As Jack was ten feet from the Wildcat, Don called out: "Jack, never mind the shadows. You won't see your own."

Slightly baffled, Jack continued out towards his tent. Then he remembered that in basic training he'd told Don in uttermost secrecy of his odd skill. Back then Don had just laughed him off, and made Jack feel the same way too of it for a while. But now, Don seemed to take the shadows in the photographs much more seriously.

After a final check-up that evening, Jack made it back to flight status. He was instructed to avoid using the wounded hand, even if everybody knew this was a dead letter. There was no way to avoid using it up in the heat of the battle, and the current situation demanded every pilot half-fit to fly to go up and fight.

The morning started calm, but as soon as the coastwatchers up in the Solomons chain called in and reported an incoming raid, all hell broke loose. Their engines straining, planes clawed their way up into the sky to try and make it above the incoming Japanese. Every hundred feet of altitude advantage was crucial for success, as the deficiencies of the Wildcat had forced the Americans to see. With an altitude advantage, the Wildcat was capable of doing great damage to the lightly-built enemy planes, but being caught below the enemy was seen across the board as an untenable position.

Jack and Don were in the first batch of fighters sent up to meet the enemy. It was clear that Jack had been assigned a plane with a better engine than Don, who was threatening to lag behind. When the flight reached 17,000 feet, the first enemy planes were reported to the north-west and below the defenders, and attacked almost right away.

Don was flying wing on Jack, but it was only moments after the battle began that they became separated. They tried to locate each other again but the battle was too intense; there were planes going every way, shooting most of the time. Jack managed to retain his altitude advantage by employing boom-and-zoom tactics: after every pass made from up high, he pulled up and traded speed for altitude again. Then he heard Don make a radio call which momentarily made his blood run cold:

"Jack—get down here—I am at angels ten and I have five of these Zekes around me!"

"Sorry, I'm at eighteen and already engaged myself!" Jack tried to look down for the gaggle of planes Don was in while continuing to chase a smoking Zeke fighter. He had managed to hit its engine once already and with a clear sky behind himself, he was about to finish it off.

"I don't care if you're fucking married! Get down here NOW!" Jack heard from Don's voice that his presence was really requested eight thousand feet below him, but he couldn't help smiling. He rogered the call, throttled off, left the smoking Zeke to wonder what happened, and flipped his plane over into a corkscrew dive. Looking around all the time, his airspeed reaching almost critical values, he saw a solitary Wildcat harassed by four Japanese fighters. It had to be Don. He was shooting at a Zeke in front of him while trying to duck the ones behind who were taking turns in shooting at

107

him.

Jack adjusted his course so he would cross the path of the bunch and announced his arrival by shooting a short burst into the air in front of the attackers. Two of them turned into Jack as two continued behind Don, but at least it meant that four cannon and four machine guns were now off Don.

Jack's burst of speed surprised the ascending Zekes and they missed him. Kicking left rudder he managed to slow down himself just enough to get a fleeting chance to fire at the leading Zeke, which he hit with all six of his guns. It exploded and with anxious memory of his recent crash, he had to pass through some of the wreckage. Clearing the ruined Zeke, he pushed the throttle wide open again and started after Don, who had managed to hit the Zeke in front of him well enough to get him smoking. After a moment its engine quit and the pilot bailed out, his parachute a white flower blossoming against the deep blue sea below.

The two chasers Don had were by now more determined than before and they renewed their attack on Don, hitting his rudder and wings. Jack was now using the speed from the dive to cut down the distance between him and the Zekes, but it was taking him too long to reach effective range. To make things worse, the wingman of the Zeke he'd shot down was now chasing him. Tracers crossed in front of his plane, and he knew it was just a matter of time before he'd be exactly in the sights of the enemy pilot.

"Don, break left NOW!" he yelled into the radio, shooting a long burst at the planes chasing Don. Kicking rudder, he sprayed lead into the air in the hope of scaring the two off Don too, and apparently they decided that Jack would be able to hit them bad if they didn't get out of the chase. They split and pulled up and started off north, while Don ducked and dived towards Henderson Field. Jack followed the Japanese for a short distance, then turned back to the field.

Don flew a circle to allow Jack to catch up with him. Already the attack was beginning to subside, but Don and Jack sped out together as fast as they could toward the relative safety under the AA umbrella of the field. Other Wildcats were chasing isolated groups of both bombers and fighters, and some falling aircraft were carving trails of inky smoke as they fell to explode on impact. Jack and Don landed as a section, their wingtips only yards apart, and they taxied out to the end of the field. Both of them sat in their planes for a few moments, letting the pressure escape before climbing out to the cheers of the plane crews.

"Well, well, well. I know where I stand. So you don't even care if I'm married," Jack needled Don.

"That's why I selected you at Pensacola. I could tell right away that you'd save my ass one day. Thanks, pal!" said Don, surprisingly solemn.

Jack dropped all mirth as well and shook Don's out-thrust hand. "Nothing to it, you'd have done the same for me, right?" he said, and Don nodded.

The crew chiefs came to the pilots and told them that the planes wouldn't be ready to fly before the morning, but that there were no really bad hits on either plane. Jack and Don went on to find that their services were not needed on the afternoon anymore, so they sauntered over to the canteen and had a bit of fun shooting the breeze with all the other pilots.

Later that week, Jack was passing by Don's plane. He peeked below the fuselage and saw two men kneeling there, but before he had time to go round the nose, he chanced to hear their conversation. Don said to the other man, apparently his crew chief, "So what can possibly be so hard about getting my plane that nose art? You've done more complex ones than this. It's just a finger and a scroll of vellum, that's all."

"Look, I told you a million times already. If I try to paint in a 'Moving Finger' it'll look like a fifty-pound frankfurter with a fingernail on it. I'm no artist. I can just barely put in straight text, that's my limit. Besides, what the hell is a Moving Finger, anyway? And vellum, for that matter?"

Don sounded exasperated. "Okay, okay, forget the finger and the scroll, if it's too hard for you. Get me a number '71' instead, how's that? A plain seven and one."

"Oh great. Now you want to have an extra number on your plane? And just how do you suppose it'll look, since we already have them tactical numbers on the planes? Let's see— yours would be MF-8 on the fuselage and a bright yellow '71' on the cowling? Man, that'd look great. At least it would throw the Japs off their Intelligence on how we number our planes."

Don harrumphed off, but turned back and shouted, "Ahh, go and lick your elbow!" The crew chief bellowed behind him, "And what is '71' anyway? It's code, like a secret handshake between you pilots, right? Okay, so don't tell me—be like that!"

Jack decided to take the other path to the canteen to skirt the battle.

The next morning, the squadron was again on alert, but the weather blocked flying. Jack and Don sat on the ground by the operations hut under the roof eaves. The rain formed puddles on the ground and the heavy drops formed intricate interference patterns on the surface. Don watched one particular puddle for a long while and then spoke more to himself than to Jack.

"Isn't it funny how life is like a bunch of pebbles, like cast-

110

ing stones in a pond? You have a stone in your hand, you heft it and think of how it'll fly when you throw it. In the air, it forms a curve, what was it? Parabolic curve? It flies for a long while, and then it falls in the water, and passes through the surface in an instant. It sinks to the bottom of the pond, never to be seen again, and all that reminds you of the stone is the ripples on the surface…and even they just disappear in a moment." To illustrate his point, Don picked up a little pebble and flipped it into a puddle with his thumb.

Jack shifted his attention from the opaque curtain of rain down to Don's puddle. "You mean the stone is … what? I don't follow you."

"An event." Don took another pebble into his hand. "The stones are events in life. Haven't you ever noticed when you wait for something specific to happen, and after weeks of waiting it happens, taking very little time in the whole scheme of things, and right after it you see that nothing changed, not much remains of the event, and you immediately start waiting for the next one?"

"Now that you mention it, yes … in a way."

Don's pebble followed its precursor with another accurate flip of the thumb. "Take school, for example, back when you were a little kid. You wait and wait and wait to get to first grade. The summer never ends before first grade. Then you get there, and about two weeks later you decide that the thing worth waiting for is not school but the summer holiday, except that then you don't see the pretty teacher you fell in love with straight away." Don grinned and continued his parable. "So even while you wait for school to end, the next stone is already flying."

Jack's bewildered but eager expression egged Don onwards in the story.

"This goes on all through school, waiting for it to start and to end. Just as with a stone, the actual event takes like a fraction of the time it takes to wait for it to happen. At some point, you decide you'd like to get to kiss a girl, so you target one, follow her around, spend hours and hours wondering just how to get to do it, and then, through some fortunate set of circumstances, you get the kiss. How long a kiss? Just a second, maybe two. Is there anything left of it? Ripples… and a memory. The kiss is just a pebble on the bottom of the pond of memories after that. Actually, a kiss would cause two sets of ripples, but even they mingle just for a second and then disappear. Sad, ain't it?"

Jack found the train of thought kind of sad, but the intellectual exercise interesting. "Hmm, that applies to flight school too. The long lessons of ground school before they even let you touch a plane were a pain, but that first flight was over in seconds. But the ripples are there. It's still the biggest thrill of my life so far."

"That's right, pal. Bullseye. And our first combat flight? Took us weeks and months to get to the combat zone and prepare for battle, and then when we got to fight, we climbed for like an hour to get two minutes of gunfight. Come to think of it, the whole war is just rushing about to get to be idle in wait for something to happen. Big bags of pebbles plopping into a gigantic ocean…"

"And now I guess we have the next stone in the air already, for the end of the war?"

Don 'tch-tched.' "Now that one's dangerous. It takes the edge off your fight if you believe the propaganda and tell yourself we're already winning. Even if *Stars and Stripes* says so, we'll still have many more fights to win before the Japs call it a day, believe me. Some of those pebbles are best not thrown at all."

Jack moved his hand to the left to let water flow into it. With a full hand he spoke. "That's a funny way of thinking about life. But it sounds right."

"Yeah. What's funny, too, is this: Most of the stones fly and curve down and hit the water and create a satisfying splash, with water flying out and the ripples are like waves. But some stones, especially those that you think are perfect in shape and size, and you throw real hard so they fly real high, hit the water and go right through. They just go *blup*, and the water sort of collapses on itself. Little ripples, no spray... not much of anything. My experience in college was one of these."

Jack could certainly agree with that when he remembered how his stones had splashed.

Collecting water in his cupped hands and washing his face with it, Don went on with his philosophy. "And the saddest thing is, two people can't cast one stone."

"Come again?"

This one seemed harder to carve from idea into spoken word, so Jack allowed Don a silent while for this synthesis. "You'd think you want to build your life with someone special," he began slowly. "So you get a stone that's, to you, the best stone possible for the two of you, and you throw it as high as you possibly can. But the other person, see, she has a stone of her own, and even if you both agree that these are your common stones, the arcs are not equal; one stone will veer away from the other, or the arc is lower, or it flies out further. And in any case, at the end when the stones hit the water, they do it separately, far away from each other. So the only thing that really meets the other's stone is the ripples...for a sec."

"Did you have that special person, Don?" Jack just had to

113

ask.

Don began, "You know…" but then held his reply and said nothing for a while before starting again. "I have tried to stop casting stones and just live to see what happens, with no expectations. I want to collect the ripples, though, so I have something to remember later on. On the other hand, I don't want to become a old gray man holding his sad remaining pebbles in a shaky hand, by the pool at the sunshine home, waiting for the highlight of the week when someone comes over to pump up the flat tire of my wheelchair. I'd rather collect enough memories, lose all my stones, and just leave. And with the war, leaving is easy. No pale February sky for me, not after seeing this blue Pacific."

Jack didn't know what to say to that.

9

One Tuesday morning Jack, Don, and their plane crews were idling it out on Jack's plane revetment on Munda. The afternoon strike had been called off for no apparent reason, and the pilots and crews found time on their hands. This was such a rare occurrence that they were almost uneasy about it, as if someone had given them a present while planning to take it away only moments later. Somebody produced the inevitable deck of cards and a poker game was soon under way, others just shot the breeze, and the most diligent armorers triple-checked the guns of the plane, knowing full well it was unnecessary.

A sundry bunch of men in non-regulation uniforms with nothing to do was not what a United Press war reporter had signed up for, but the base commander had told him to go find Jack McGuire and Don Wheeler—they'd be full of interesting stories of aerial combat. Anybody within the base would have known, however, that this tip from the commander was actually a sign of intense hatred for that particular reporter. There was nobody harder to interview on the base than Don Wheeler.

"Uh oh, weasel at eleven o'clock, closing fast, time for evasive action," Don said, standing up to leave. He was notorious for his disrespect of the press, and he always referred to them as 'weasels'. Don firmly thought in times of war it was no respectable job to bug honest fighting men into delivering fanciful stories of combat. This time there was no escape, because as the reporter briskly walked in around the F4U Corsair on the left, his photographer blocked the right side. The only avenue of escape was thus to clamber up the revetment wall, which would have looked ridiculous even by Don's standards, so he slid back onto the grassy wall and lay down.

"Hi guys, you wanna tell Mom how you're doing out here?" the reporter greeted them. The photographer had already taken five shots of the team and their charge, which, being a war-weary model 1A, was not entirely photogenic any more.

"Sure, just come on over and we'll tell you all you want to hear," Don said to the intense surprise of the team. "The Old Fud sent you to us, right?" He sat up on the revetment wall and offered his hand to the reporter, who shook it and sat down beside him.

"OK, let's start with the squadron details," the reporter began, his pencil already flying over the notepad. "What's your nickname?"

"We're VMF-288, V for heavier-than-air, M for Marine, and F for Fighting," Don stated with complete confidence, "and we're known far and wide as the Milkmen." There was an instant silence in the team, punctuated only by one startled chuckle of laughter which was quickly masked as a powerful sneeze.

"The Milkmen?" asked the reporter.

"That's right. We tried out many nicknames before finally agreeing on Milkmen, but it was the only one that sounded natural to us. You see, we're proud of having done more milk runs than any other squadron in the history of marine aviation. Isn't that right, guys?" Don, apparently intent on delivering a complete snow job to this reporter, sought collusion.

The team nodded in full accord over the issue.

"What do you mean, milk runs? I always thought milk runs were missions where nothing happens," the reporter commented, his pencil already slowing down on the pad.

"They sure are, and we get plenty. Tons of them, with completely negligible results." Now Don's pals were beginning to get the picture. "We Milkmen have always resented the way many squadrons pride themselves on kills and assign themselves ridiculous nicknames such as *Hellhounds* and *Grim Reapers* and *Jolly Rogers* and whatnot. The names don't resemble the true nature of aerial combat. We, however, have not claimed a single kill for any one pilot; our squadron has claimed one kill to eight pilots, so they all have 0.125 of a kill."

Don was getting warmed up. He could see that the reporter was suspicious but not ready to give up just yet.

Directing the photographer to take pictures of himself and Don, the reporter tried anew. "Give me some details on that name, will you?" he asked.

Don was all too happy to comply. "You see, all the other squadrons on the island do the real interesting bits; they hit the bases, raid the ships and do all the aerial combat. That's why they're called the *Killers* and *Maimers* and the like. We're sent in after the excitement is over to see what all happened. Consequently we've seen a great many burning ships and abandoned bases and smoking wrecks of planes, but we have very limited personal experience of actually meeting them in the air."

Some members of the teams were finding it hard to conceal their amusement, and seeing this fueled Don even further. "We do have some diehard juggernauts however—like Bud Walter here. Hey Bud, you want to tell the good reporter here how you single-handedly took on eight Japs over Rabaul the other day?" Bud was another squadron pilot talented in telling tall tales, and willingly he took the gauntlet.

"That's more like it, Bud, let's have the story!" the reporter egged him on.

Bud stretched in exaggerated slow motion. "Aw heck, t'warn't nuttin', I was just stooging about Rabaul at 25,000 feet the other day when I happened to see about eight specks in the distance. I was pretty darn sure they were Japs, since it's their base and everything, but I decided to wait it out to see for sure. In about three minutes it was crystal clear they were Zekes all right, so I thought it best to lure them into the trap of the rest of the Milkmen and then we'd shoot 'em all down. I took a peek behind me to see the rest of the squadron had turned tail already and were setting up the trap way behind me, so I turned too, dove down to 10,000 feet and poured on the coal. Boy, can that Corsair accelerate in a dive—I was down to angels ten in no time."

Don saw the reporter was lapping it all up. Bud continued his story. "Soon I was goin' like a scalded dog with the Japs in tow and I was sure they'd all be goners real soon now, what with all our guns on 'em, but then the trap kinda didn't happen when the squadron pulled out in front of me, and I went way too fast for the Japs to follow too, so they were small specks again in the distance, and in the end we just landed back home. But I was real proud of myself thinking up the trap in the face of eight Japs, and I was almost given a gong for my brave behavior in combat, but I guess it got lost in the mail."

The reporter was by now beginning to look distraught, and the photographer was smiling to himself behind the rudder.

"Let me elaborate a bit on the squadron nickname, if I

may," Don went on. "We thought of many adjectives to attach to it, such as *Bloodcurdling*, or *Ferocious*, or *Raving Lunatic*, but somehow they seemed too aggressive when seen against the background of our operational record.

"*Bloodcurdling* was almost selected because of the association of curdling with milk, but we dropped that too and went for the clear, concise Milkmen, which, I may add, has been endorsed by all the other squadrons on the base. And so everyone always refers to us by that name and never as VMF-288."

By this time Don's plane captain had had enough. "Sorry, sir, I gotta go check if the cigarette lighters have come in yet." He exited but did not manage to fully conceal his smile, which got the photographer even more suspicious.

"Cigarette lighters?" asked the reporter.

Don took on his schoolmaster look. "That's right, one of our guys read it somewhere that the German general, Galland, has had a cigarette lighter and ashtray installed in his personal plane. That's all very well but we don't really have personal planes here, so to go that extra mile, we decided to install cigarette lighters in every mount, just to be on the safe side. We just can't afford to have the Krauts lead the pack in plane accessories, can we?"

This was the last straw. All of the crew members burst out laughing and in no time at all, the reporter had whisked himself off in the direction of the base commander's tent. The photographer also set off, but only after giving the team a double thumbs-up. Don responded in kind, and watched the photographer walk away, laughing to himself.

"Good work guys, that oughta teach him," Don said, gracefully accepting the adulation of the crews. He stood up, stretching. "Anyone for some coffee?" The men all mumbled some excuse, and finally only Jack was game for java. They started off towards the canteen, pausing at the runway before crossing it to watch an SBD squadron take off into the hot, humid air.

As they reached the far side of the crushed coral runway, Jack ventured to ask: "What is it you got against the reporters, anyway, Don? They're just doing their job like us."

Don stopped in his tracks and turned to face Jack. "You know, so they are. They have a job to do here, and that's fine by me. That's not what I'm against. I'm against the way they report what we do out here. They present us like a blood-thirsty gang intent on shooting down people in flames, like kills are the only thing that matters to us. I'm not here for the kills, and I sure as hell don't want to be portrayed as one who is."

He took a few more steps and then stopped again. "The way I see things, I was handed the keys to the most bestest, fastest, greatest plane there is, have been given as much flight time in it as I can possibly want and then some, and all they want in return is that I shoot down a few Japanese planes. Hell, that's fine by me—I guess the Japs love their 1,300 horsepower sports plane which just happens to carry two cannon and two machine guns for the purpose of dismissing a couple of our folks. I'm not against Yukio or Mitsuo or Mitsubishi or any Japanese pilot up there; I just need to relieve them of the use of their flying machine. I hope they feel the same about me, so that when we meet, it's just two pilots in two great planes, and that they're only interested in disposing of my fighter."

Now he picked up his usual springy gait. After a short dis-tance, he stopped once more and turned to Jack, spreading his arms. "You know, Jack, it's just that I don't like to advertise our line of business. Fact of the matter is, we deal in death. An aircraft carrier, or this base for that matter, that's our wholesaler. And you and I, my friend, we do the retailing of an undesirable product. One customer at a time, we deliver death to them. But to advertise, I think it'd be bad taste. You don't see other players in this business, mortuaries or pathologists, advertise by the numbers. *Forest Lawn Mortuary—more than 150 cadavers processed since July!* or *Our hospital opened more stiffs in January than any other major hospital in California!* Doesn't sound right, does it, but that's exactly what the press is doing with our kills." With that, he turned around and took off in the direction of the canteen.

Jack thought once again he understood Don a bit better. It was just his friend's total disregard of authority, rank, kills, all that mattered to most pilots, that was still a mystery to him. He would push the issue further when the opportunity arose, he thought, and started after Don.

When the base commander met Don that night, he was in no great mood. The reporter had returned, complaining of wanton ridicule and threatening to write such a loud-mouthed piece of journalism that its fury would go all the way to Washington and echo back again with results for everyone in command on the island. It had taken the commander a fair bit of time and effort to get him to cool down, and to top it off he had personally given an interview to the reporter about life on Munda from the perspective of a temporary resident.

The commander buttonholed Don outside the canteen. "You know, Wheeler, one day you'll trip over yourself being so cocky and clever. I had to talk to that guy for an hour before he even put his feet back on the ground. I know it was bad judgment from me to send him to you in the first place, but I thought I'd give you an equal chance of spotlighting for the press. Apparently you don't need the publicity."

"Sir, I'm sorry, but—"

Don was cut short. Even more loudly, the commander went on. "I know you don't like them, but hey, it's a long way Stateside from here, and as I happen to know you don't write too many letters, I thought you'd let your Mom know you're half all right. If you don't like that, it's fine by me. I won't be pointing any more newshounds your way, rest assured. Dismissed."

Before Jack and Don could get away, the commander added, "Just one more thing, Wheeler—I may be the Old Fud to the personnel of this base but to the Press and the rest of the world, it's Commander Wade, if you don't mind."

For the first time ever, Jack saw Don was embarrassed. "Yes, sir," was all he could manage.

To Jack's surprise, more chat came that evening. Due to an incoming weather front, the base commander declared the base closed for the evening and the next day, when it was supposed to rain heavily. In practice, closing base was an automatic invitation to have a party with a movie and beer in the canteen, so everyone finished up ongoing business as soon as possible, secured everything for the night, and retired to the canteen, behind which was a huge tarpaulin painted white.

Across the tarpaulin, cracks had appeared in the grayed-out paint, giving every movie shown a curious craquelure appearance, but the crews couldn't have cared less. All they wanted was for the movie to be shown in its entirety before the weather set in, and then pray the beer coolers didn't conk out. The island base had received a priceless treasure by some quirk of fate—*Sullivan's Travels*, doubly-valued because it starred Veronica Lake in a comedy. The whole base just couldn't wait for the sun to set and the show to begin, and already the best seats were taken for the movie.

Jack and Don took up a great spot on top of the roof of the canteen. Don brought up a roll of rubberized canvas, some boards, a hammer and a pocketful of nails. When Jack saw this, he tried to ask after the plan, but Don hushed him up. He built a collapsible shelter out of the assorted bits he had and said, "Ever watch a movie that didn't end in a torrential downpour? Right."

When the shelter was finished, Jack and Don set up camp in it and watched the opening titles roll on the screen. "Perfect timing," Jack said, opening another can of beer. The movie was among the best comedies Jack had ever seen, and the base enjoyed it thoroughly, but as so many times before, rain set in ten minutes before the credits. The base endured the rain for just as long as it took for Veronica Lake to disappear, and the resulting scramble for the dry canteen and the not-so-dry tents was amusing for Jack and Don to watch from their snug base on the roof.

"Lemmings," Don said, before sipping from the can.

Jack had a sudden impulse to solve a mystery. "Don, you mind if I ask you something?" A grunt in response. "What makes you so fiercely independent?"

Don looked out into the gloom of the tropical rain. "It's a long story. Really." He sounded to Jack almost relieved to have been asked. "I haven't set out to be like I am but there were some things which happened to me which formed my views of life, and of other people as well. Are you sure you want to hear?"

Jack nodded, and Don told him he might as well tell him if it was of such interest to him. "But first, you have to clamber down and get us some more beer."

Jack climbed down, getting very wet in the process, and

returned with six more beers in a bucket of ice.

"Nice touch!" Don said, settled down in a reclining position, and started his tale.

"Up until the age of twelve I was a real bastard. Worse than I am now, believe me. I was the proverbial rich kid on the block, with a daddy whose pockets were deep enough to get me anything I needed, or didn't need but wanted, or to bail me out of any trouble I got myself into; and a mom who only cared about pampering me by any means possible. And man, did I ever make full use of my privileges. I bullied any kid I felt like bullying, I tied firecrackers to the tail of Mr. Rainier's dog, I threw a baseball through Mrs. Dimmond's dining room window on purpose—there was just no end to my mischief. My folks called it *mischief*, but in retrospect I think it should have been called hell-raising."

Don opened another can, spraying white foam into the rain.

"Then I turned twelve. On the eve of my birthday I wasn't feeling so hot, so I went to bed early with all twenty of the gifts I'd received. In the morning I felt even worse, so Mom called Doctor Walters over. He decided I had scarlet fever, and a bad case at it too. He recommended I take it easy as there was not much more to do for me anyway, so I just lay there in my bed for a couple of days. Then I got worse, way worse. The doctor came back and I can still see the worried look on his face when he told my Mom I should've gotten better already. Apparently the scarlet fever was running worse than what he'd ever seen."

Don was speaking softer now. "Two more days passed, and I went unconscious. My folks were of course beside themselves with worry, but there was nothing to do except change the wet towels on my forehead.

"Then a funny thing happened. I had no recollection of the past couple days, but all of a sudden, I could see someone lying in my bed. This of course knocked me sidesaddle so I screamed, but nothing came out of my mouth. In fact, the kid on the bed that was me, he just lay there, the only motion being his chest rising and falling real fast. I rolled out and watched my room from the ceiling. It was real odd, I could move at will without moving anything like a muscle—I didn't have any muscles. I did have a body though, I could see it." The phantom of the memory had appeared on Don's face.

"My parents were there, sobbing, and the good old Doctor was saying it wouldn't be long now. I couldn't make heads or tails of what he was talking about. Then I heard my kid brother, who was eight at that point, asking my mother if he could have my stamp collection after I died. My father flung him out of the room by the ear in a rage. And I understood it wouldn't be long for me to kick the bucket—I felt that if I lost sight of my body, I would die. For real."

Though it was hot on the roof, Jack felt a chill down his spine.

Don almost whispered the next part. "That scared me much worse than the realization that it was me on that bed. I felt like something was pulling me out of the room, through the ceiling, but I wouldn't go. I fought the notion real hard, screaming silently that I wanted my own body back and that I didn't want to go anywhere without my body.

"I made one last lunge toward my body, something snapped, and then I saw the room from my bed. I could feel the cold towel on my forehead and the sheets all wet from my sweat. I tried to speak but my mouth was all dry. The doctor sat beside me and offered me a drink, his eyes full of bewilderment as he had expected me to die on the spot, not regain consciousness. I was very weak. I couldn't do anything but suck in air and drink water by small sips, but soon I fell asleep. In the morning I felt much better, and the next couple of days had me feeling almost well again. I was kept in bed for five more days, but then I got up. I was all well in about two weeks. Since then, Doctor Walters would refer to me as the 'miracle kid'. My parents donated a hefty sum to the local children's hospital in my name to offer thanks for my recovery."

Don looked into the rain as if to see his past through the streams of water. "To say the experience changed me is an understatement. It transformed me. I was given an entirely new look on life. I never thought after that I could take life for granted, and after that I also thought my life was entirely my own. Some people say we're all on loan to each other: kids to parents, parents to kids, siblings, friends, and all that. I agree fully, with the focus on the word *loan*. When the loan is due, you're on your own."

Don's eyes were hard but honest. "I also thought that since I had a transparent body while I was watching myself from the ceiling, it made no sense to collect stamps or anything else you couldn't carry."

He took half a can's worth of beer in one swallow and wiped his mouth of the foam. "I donated my stamps to my kid brother, and I may say that before the event, stamps were my only passion in life. I gave them out at dinner one night, saying that even though I didn't die, he could have the stamps, and boy, did I ever startle the family with that act of generosity! They knew I was out cold when my brother asked for the stamps, but I never told them what I'd heard, or how. In fact, they don't know of this episode, and neither does anybody else, besides you. I'd sure appreciate if you kept it to yourself."

Jack assured Don he had no intention of divulging any of the story to anyone.

Don said he didn't think so in any case, but he had to make sure. "You must see now why I live the way I do. I collect emotions and memories, because I know I still had those when I was on the ceiling. That's why I don't want promotions, or medals, or newspaper articles, because when I die one of these days, they'll be just junk, so much metal and ribbon, no connection to anything anymore."

Don tugged on his collar, his finger on his lieutenant's insignia. "I've seen how guys here have asked for their rank insignia or hat or something to be sent to the family if they bought the farm, but none of that's for me. If I auger in here, I want my family to bury or burn anything I ever touched and just remember me every once in a while. No headstone, no brass plate at the family vault, nothing." He straightened his shirt and tucked it in his shorts.

"On the other hand—I did see your disapproval when we went out with the two girls in Pearl before we came here last time, remember? That's something you're entitled to, but I can still remember how she felt and what her perfume smelled like, and how she liked to be tickled behind the neck. Sure it was a fling, for nothing but a couple hours of necking—I don't think you scored, right?—but even if I die tomorrow, my soul or whatever it was on the ceiling will still know and feel and remember even those stupid little details of a passing encounter on the brink of the combat zone. And to me, that's more valuable than three Navy Crosses."

Jack could not help feeling like he was listening to a fire-spitting preacher. This was testimony, pure and simple.

"Come to think of it, even flying is important to me almost only because of the sensations and emotions I get from it. Surely you can remember your first solo flight, the thrill you had right down in the balls when you realized you could handle it and survive? And the first combat, when you wore out your gun barrels shooting at a Zero from about five miles out with just one long burst? And especially the chewing-out the master armorer gave you after landing?"

"Heck," Jack demurred. "You didn't have to remind me, Don!"

"Well, I just happen to know that you *can* take something with you when you go, and it's your memories. Make as many as you can, good, bad, lukewarm, hot, no matter what, as long as you make a lot of 'em."

Jack stared out at the rain, feeling as if he'd just climbed up to a mountaintop. "All that makes a lot of sense, Don, actually it makes a huge lot of sense. Thanks for sharing with me."

"Anything for my pal, Jack, anything for you," Don said, and handed the last beer to Jack. "I'm not sure I know what you really think of all this, but at least you have a better idea of what makes me tick."

"I sure do—and I believe you. Maybe I'll start collecting my own memories one of these days."

Don slapped Jack on the shoulder. "Get some gals in them memories, pal—nothing warms you up on a cold patrol up at twenty thousand feet like a hug from a pretty girl in your memories."

They climbed down to the soggy ground and retired for the night. Late in the evening, lying in his cot, Jack tried to assemble his memory collection to see what he had in there. He found that he had to sort them by intensity, not by chronology, and that his efforts really didn't bring much order out of the chaos. He smiled in the darkness at some silly little things he could remember much better than his high school graduation day; all he could remember from that day was Amy's smile as she caught his eye across the row of graduates. But that was enough.

Thinking of his childhood days produced an endless parade of sunshine days, with the occasional snowball fight thrown in. He decided to start harvesting memories right now.

10

Jack's schoolmate James Schwinn was the champion model maker of the town. In 1929, at the age of eight, he had arrived from Chicago with his father. The appearance of an uptown doctor in a rural community such as Winton was initially a source of great interest to the well-connected ladies of the town, but Doctor John Schwinn set up his practice and stayed anyway.

Eventually his story of having moved out of the Windy City because of his son's asthma and because he was a small-town boy himself was generally accepted; it even overrode the interest in why he moved in without a Mrs. Schwinn. This question of the doctor's social life enjoyed a brief revival when, eight months later, a young and very attractive housekeeper arrived at the Schwinn residence. But by this time the doctor had become an accepted part of the community and apart from a couple of diehard gossips, no one really took notice of the warm relationship in the household.

The doctor adored his son, and as so often is the case, he took full advantage of his doting dad. There was no end to the lad's requests, and his father dutifully delivered on all. James's favorite hobby was modeling and for that he had a fully equipped woodwork shed. Mr. Schwinn made sure his son never lacked new tools or the latest scale plans. Whether due to the advantage in capital or his raw ability, James was quite the accomplished model maker, and he frequently crowed about his handiwork at school, much to the annoyance of the other hobbyists.

Jack and Tony never took James on about his braggadocio. They saw there was no way for them to compete with him, given the unlimited resources at his disposal. Still, it irked them to watch him win first prize for the school hobby project. When Jack went to see the rubber-band plane which was deemed the best project in the school's history, he could not contain his envy, saying under his breath, "I bet I could make one just like that."

To his bad luck, the boy standing next to him was Danny White, one of James's best friends. "Oh yeah?" Danny scoffed. "Hey, Jamie—this guy says he can build just as good as you!"

James sauntered over, full of the glow of victory after hearing the headmaster's praise. "Well, Jack—maybe then you can tell me why the ribbon is on my plane and not yours?"

Soon there were more friends of James's listening to the discussion, and Jack immediately went on the defensive: "You know why. You have the tools." He knew it was the wrong thing to say even as he said it.

James reared back in mock disbelief. "My tools? It's my tools that build my planes? Wow. I always thought tools were just things that help you make what you want, but maybe I have a shed full of automatic tools!" James's cohorts chuckled at the thought.

Jack felt stupid, but felt his anger building. "No, it's not the tools. It's your stupid push that gets you the ribbons. I don't have the tools you have but I can build a plane that flies better than any plane you have ever made!" The gauntlet was on the floor.

James was only too glad to pick it up. "Jack, there's a way to settle this little problem. It so happens Dad went to Chicago last week and brought me back a set of scale plans. It's a new plane called the *Meridian*. It's a rubber type, all balsa and pine, with paper-coated wings. Eight hours is the estimated building time. I dare you to build it. Just you and just me, with no help from anyone, OK? You can copy the plans at my house, we build, and then we take our planes up one-on-one and see whose plane flies better. If I win, you have to admit I'm the best model maker."

Jack crossed his arms. "And if I win?"

Studying his cuticles, James said, "I don't know if I'll bother to think of anything suitable just now."

His friends burst out laughing, and even though Jack knew he was putting his neck in the noose, he said, "Okay, you're on. When can I come over to copy the plans?"

"Anytime, pal." James was pleasantly surprised at having his bluff called. "I can even give you the paper to copy on. See you later!" And he left with his court in tow.

Jack felt blood rushing in his ears and he knew his face was flaming red. He went to the front door and started homewards from school. Kicking stones and thinking furiously about how he could get out of the sticky situation, his progress was slow. He was only halfway home when he heard someone running up to him. It was Tony, who had run all the way from school upon hearing the news.

"Jack, the word is out you challenged Jamie Schwinn to build planes with you—I told them it was a lie, but then he came up himself and said so. Is it really true?"

Jack nodded and continued delivering aimless kicks to pebbles.

"Oh boy." Tony cast his eyes heavenward. "That's the cleverest thing you can think of? There's no way you can build a plane as smooth as he can! This is something they'll rub your

132

nose in your whole life!"

Jack looked at him like a sick puppy. "Tell me something I don't know yet."

Tony saw there wasn't anything left to say about the idiotic gambit Jack had taken, so it was time for constructive suggestions. "Okay. Let's think. What plane are you building?"

"A Meridian, a new type he just got the plans for. He hasn't even built it yet. He'll let me copy the plans and then we'll build the planes. Building time's eight hours. All balsa-wood with paper-coated wings."

"Do you have the balsa?" Tony asked. "I have some left over sticks you can use, and one sheet of 1/16" with some parts cut out of it."

Jack shrugged. "I have two sheets of 1/8" but I haven't seen the plans yet. I have to see them first to know what I need to build it." He sensed his voice raising, so he toned it back a bit. "Besides, I can't take any help from you on this. Jamie and I agreed on that."

"Well, I can always look over your shoulder and see if you're about to mess it up, right?" Tony winked and chucked his brother on the chest. "Come on, gloomy Gus, cheer up, the game's not over till they blow the whistle!"

For a moment Jack actually felt better, but then the task ahead fell back in his mind like a ton of bricks, and he went gloomy again.

The next morning Jack showed up at Jamie's house early. In fact, Jamie was still in his pajamas when he led Jack into the shed where he built his models. Jack had to admit he hadn't seen such a wide array of tools anywhere, not even at the local carpenter's workshop. On the table was a three-view, folded-out plan of the plane they were to build—the Meridian. It was a simple sleek rubber-band powered plane, nothing too demanding for either of the boys. Jack felt a bit better when he saw the plane really wasn't something Jamie had picked just for its complexity.

"Here's a sheet of sketch paper, and a pencil and a ruler, and here's my eraser. Copy it all and just make sure you don't forget parts. I'll go and eat breakfast meanwhile." He left Jack to the task, and he set out to copy the drawings through the semi-transparent paper. It was a bit hard to get the lines entirely straight as the original had creases on which the copy tended to bend up, but he used a heavy metal ruler to get the copy to stay straight.

Half an hour later Jack was done. He had meticulously copied every line on the drawing, as well as the list of parts and supplies needed. He rolled up his copy and folded the original back into its paper envelope. There was an extra fold in the original, but as he was already a bit late for school, he didn't pay much attention to it. He placed the tools and pencils back in their trays, and left the shed.

At the door he met Jamie, who said, "Did you get it all? You won't get to see the plans again."

"Of course I did," Jack snapped. "See you in school!"

They met in the school hallway later that morning to finalize the rules: How well the planes flew was to be decided by the distance covered and the time aloft. Three mutual friends were nominated as judges, and the day for the final match was set for next Sunday. This gave the builders five evenings to work on the planes. A worried Jack and a self-assured James shook hands on the deal and went to class.

That night Jack went home by way of the general store of Mr. Mitchell. He was a kindly old shopkeeper who had started to stock model-making materials at his store when he heard from Reverend Ackermann that it was a popular hobby among youngsters. He never made any money out of them—he actually made a little loss on the stock—but nevertheless he kept a steady supply of the things the boys needed.

On this visit to the general store Jack had no money, so he had to buy his materials on credit. This was another of Mr. Mitchell's public services—kids had unlimited interest-free credit if the stuff they bought went towards a good cause. Jack made a deal to pay up in three months' time, after his birthday, when he usually received a small sum from his grandfather. Fortunately Mr. Mitchell had on hand everything he needed, from piano wire to engine rubber, and Jack happily went home with his bag of supplies.

Once home, Jack went to his crude workshop to find that all his tools had been serviced by his father. All blades shone newly-sharpened, and on the table there was a tool he had coveted for a long time: a new jigsaw.

He was still turning it in his hands, admiring it when his father came in. "Thanks, Dad!" Jack exclaimed.

"I heard what you have to do, and thought I'd help you out a bit." Jack saw his father smile, which was rare. "This is all I can do under the rules, right?"

"Right, Dad, this is just great. With these tools I can really do my best and have my best shot to win!"

"Okay, son, you'd better get to it. Remember, you can only do your level best, and if that doesn't cut it, it's no longer in your power anyhow." With this last bit of wisdom, Mr. McGuire left Jack to decide where he should start.

That night he spent making wing spars and ribs. There were eight different ribs in the wings, and the differences between them were minuscule. With his crude but very sharp tools he did good, careful work and had all the parts cut he needed by nightfall. The next night he cut the parts for the fuselage and assembled the wings, and he spent the third evening making the tail assembly. The fuselage assembly took the whole of the fourth evening and afterward all that remained for him was to cover the wings and fuselage with paper and to make the propeller.

At this stage he panicked, frantically sorting through his tracings. He had brought home no plans for the propeller. It must have been in that last fold of the plan, he remembered, and raced out the door to Jamie's house. Arriving all out of breath, he knocked at the door and asked for Jamie. When he came down, Jack asked to see the plans again to draw the propeller.

"No dice, pal. You had your look at the plans and that's it!" With that, Jamie steered Jack out the door. Jack was too stunned even to complain, and simply trudged home.

When he reached their yard, Tony came out to find him. "What was that all about? Where'd you go?" Jack told him about the missing propeller plan and how Jamie had declined to show him the plans again.

"I'll aim for his nose next time I pitch for him!" Tony vowed. "But c'mon...let's see whether we can work some magic."

Still dejected, Jack went to the workshop with Tony. They assembled the plane for the first time so they could see how it looked. Even the rubber band was put in its place inside the fuselage. The plane was a very elegant little machine with perfectly proportioned wings and fuselage, but without its propeller it looked quite sad.

"Jack, how many propeller types have you built so far?" Tony asked, and Jack counted them using his fingers.

"Six."

"Okay, six. How different were the props from each other?"

Jack frowned. "Whaddya mean? A prop is a prop—it's the proper dimensions I need for this one. Too small won't go anywhere and too large won't work either."

"What if we measure the relation of the propeller diameter to the wingspan of the plane?" Tony suggested, already scribbling. "Or the length of the plane, or the weight? That way we can at least get you a propeller that's something like your other planes, and hey, some of your planes have flown just fine, right?"

Jack brightened up. "That's a great idea, Tony!" He lined up all his planes on the table and got out the ruler. He asked Tony to make a table of his findings. "Okay, here goes. *Stork*—wing span 40", prop diameter…8". *Altair*, wing span 32", prop diameter 6". *Lone Eagle*, wing span 34", prop diameter, 6 ¾"."

Tony did some quick math. "I think it's safe to say the relation of wing span to prop diameter is roughly one to five. What's the Meridian's wing span?"

Jack looked at the plan. "42 inches."

"That's 8 3/8 inches. Do you have anything around here which might fit the bill? Any of your planes have a wingspan like that?"

Jack went through his collection. "No, the only one I have is the Stork. What if I just make a prop with the same dimensions but a little longer?"

"Since you can't get the real thing, and time's running out, there's nothing else to try. Get to it."

Jack pulled out the only prop-sized block of balsa he had left, cut it to size by removing an inch off its length, and drew the lines on it. He began to whittle the wood away carefully and within the hour he had a passable first cut of the prop. He fitted it onto the nose of the plane and it looked just about right, so he set out to carve the more delicate lines to it. He used his father's old knife which he had sharpened so many times it was down to a third of its original chord and half its old length; made out of a file by the blacksmith, it held its edge for a long time and he had become very adept in using it.

In an hour more he had finished the form of the propeller and sanded it first with coarse sandpaper and then with gradually finer papers, until it felt smooth to the finger. Then he inserted a bit of piano wire into the axle hole and balanced the prop on two razor blades, using very fine sandpaper to take out minuscule traces of wood, until it sat perfectly balanced.

Tony came back to admire his handiwork. "Know what, Jack? That looks like the best prop you ever made. I'm sure it'll run just fine on the plane."

Jack felt pretty proud of it himself. He made the axle on which the propeller rotated and produced a little metal wedge that acted as the holder. A glass bead was inserted to act as a bearing between the prop and the holder. He placed the rubber band in its hooks and ran fifty rounds into the band, and let the propeller loose. The airflow was smooth and the propeller ran frictionless, without any noticeable vibration. He took the plane in his hands and ran it through the air.

"I gotta show this to Mom and Dad!"

Tony grimaced. "Shouldn't you cover the wings before showing off? You're short of time and I'd sooner get it finished than show it off just now."

Jack was already at the door. "I'll be right back." He ran to the door of the house, but just as he was about to open it, someone came out and the door crashed into Jack's outstretched hand that held the plane. The right wing leading edge smashed against the door and the edge along with two ribs were cracked. Emily was in tears but that helped little.

Jack could feel his hopes crack along with the wing. "Oh, crumb!" he cried out as the gravity of the situation hit him. He had no time to rebuild the wing. The only thing he could do was to replace the cracked parts, but even that would be a rush job because he still had to cover the wings and tail.

He ran back to the shed where Tony was waiting, hands in pockets. "So was it worth it?"

Jack was almost in tears. "Quit teasing and help me fix this!" he said, dropping the plane on the table.

Tony had a look. "Oh, well ... you have enough balsa to fix it, but you're out of time. I never got both the wings and the tails covered in less than four hours and it's almost eight in the evening already."

A challenge. Jack rolled up his sleeves and sat down. "Watch me," he said.

First Jack slit open the cracked leading edge with a slanted knife cut. He carefully prised out each of the ribs, discarding the cracked ones. In the process he damaged one more rib, but he had enough balsa to build spares. The wing tip had not been well attached to the leading and trailing edges and it came off easily. Jack was happy at the discovery—it might have foiled his attempt in flight.

The spares were soon cut, and Jack reattached the ribs to the leading edge. Fashioning a new wing tip took more time than he had allocated, and it was already late when he was finished with that stage of the operation.

Tony came in for one last look before heading for bed. "So ... you coming or will you go the last mile today?"

Jack had just to surface the wings. "Give me 30 minutes," he said. Carefully he spread a very thin layer of glue on the top surfaces of the leading and trailing edges and ribs. Then he laid on a sheet of thin blue paper. In just ten minutes the paper was firmly attached to the wings and Jack triumphantly sprayed water on the paper to make it taut.

"Whoa—easy on that water now!" Tony cautioned.

Jack dropped a few final drops on the right wing tip. "There! Now I can go to bed. In the morning my plane will fly the socks off everything," he said, leaving the shed for bed. Sleep was uneasy, and in the morning he was not feeling fresh at all.

Before breakfast the next morning, Jack went to see his plane. With Tony beside him, he opened the door to the shed and almost fainted with shock. His carefully crafted and repaired wing had badly twisted as a result of the drying paper pulling itself too taut. The leading edge of the right wing tip was a full inch higher than the trailing edge. Jack tried rotating the wing straight until it creaked, but as soon as he let go, it jumped back to form.

"All l can say is, that last splash of water was one too many. The unit of measure is a drop, not a bucket," Tony eulogized, leaving Jack to mourn his inevitable defeat.

Jack felt numb all over. There was no way out whatsoever. In two hours he would have to go face the onset of years of ridicule at the flight line. He pondered calling in sick, but Jamie could always demand that Tony fly Jack's plane. He also wished he had never spoken to Jamie, or muttered loudly enough for Danny White to hear. At the last minute, with a defiant huff, he collected the plane from the table and started walking to the field they'd designated the competition site.

Jamie and his pals were already there. True to form, his plane was picture-perfect. There was nothing in it that could have been called a flaw. Jamie idly spun ten rounds into his engine and let it run them out. "So ... here we have the competing planes," he said, unable to suppress his gleeful smile.

Jack meanwhile was again twisting the wing to hide the error he had made with it, but as soon as he let go, it sprang back into its shape like a terrier's tail. It was painful for him to remember he hadn't even had time to put in any trimming flights.

Tom Manston, serving as referee, called out the rules. Jamie handed him his father's chronometer which was to be the official timekeeper of the contest. "Jamie, wind her up with fifty turns and stand ready to fly your plane," Tom said, and Jamie rolled up fifty revolutions. He held the plane high above his head. Jack noticed Jamie's father had joined the crown of onlookers.

"Three, two, one, GO!" said Tom, and Jamie let go of his plane.

Jamie's Meridian gained up to thirty feet in height in a slight turning climb, and then it settled to a gentle sloping glide back to the ground. It was a textbook flight. The plane stayed aloft for sixteen seconds and even though it wasn't part of the contest rules, the boys in the crowd measured the straight distance covered as eighty feet. As the onlookers applauded, Jamie could hardly conceal his pride in the plane when it finally landed.

For Jack, this moment felt even worse than his infamous oral presentation in school. Amid sneers and giggles, thundering in his ears and nearly drowning out the hissing rush of blood, he too rotated the propeller under the watchful eye of Tom the referee. He held his plane high and as Tom reached the word "Go!" he let it fly, closing his eyes in the piercing sunlight. Behind his eyelids he saw only blood-red, which suited his feelings.

He only opened his eyes again when someone said, "Look

at that darn thing climb!"

Jack had to search for the plane, because it was much higher than he could have ever expected. It was drilling a hole in the sky, rising like a bee in a vicious twisting corkscrew of a climb. Hanging on the edge of stalling out, it was twenty feet, then thirty-five, then fifty feet and finally some seventy feet over the gaping group of people.

After it had run its rubber band out of all energy and the makeshift propeller had transmitted it to the air, it went into a graceful, wide descent which curved to the left. It had been so high when it started the descent that it made almost two hundred feet before touching down five feet shy of a bush. Tom Manston almost forgot to stop the timer, but when the plane landed, he clicked the knob and read out the results. "Forty-two and a half seconds!" he announced to the spectators, who broke out in wild cheers.

"And 150 feet!" someone else shouted. In a split second popular opinion swung in Jack's favor, and he found himself being thrown in the air by the loud crowd. His own eyes were still fixed in the sky, and as he was thrown up four, five, six times, he experienced a curious feeling.

Time slowed for him. His flights in the air, really a second each, felt like minutes. He could only see his plane fly up, up, to join the clouds and he merged with it. He saw the ground recede below him, and his senses lied to him: it was as if the Earth weighed his one hundred pounds, and his own body had the massive pull of the planet—as if he were attracting the Earth. For a moment he was one with the air and the sky, and its wide curve and deep blue hue filled all his senses. He didn't realize Jamie was leaving with his plane and pals; he did not care that he had won the competition. All he felt was a carefree union with space, wholly out of time. Even when those tossing him let him back to the ground and he stood upright on it again, he was smiling like an idiot, shaking hands thrust at him. He stood there for a long time after everyone but Tony, Nellie, and Amy had left.

"You lucky fool," said Tony. "Have you any idea just how lucky you got there? That plane of yours could have fallen like a rock instead of taking off like that. It was touch and go with you just now," he admonished his still-smiling brother.

Jack spoke for the first time since the launch. "Yeah. I know," he managed.

Nellie hugged him. "Maybe that'll shut Jamie up—I can't stand that braggart." She took Amy in tow, leaving the two brothers alone in the warm evening sun.

Tony took the plane from Jack and put fifty more rounds into the engine. As he let it fly, it went in a very fast circle around the boys, and struck the ground after three seconds and two laps. The brothers looked at each other and agreed that the wing had been twisted in the first landing. At any rate, it was twisted now. After Jack gathered up the ruined plane, they started homeward, and when Jack finally got home, he went straight to bed, exhausted.

The next morning, Jack was surprised to see a small gift-wrapped box on his breakfast table. He picked it up and went downstairs to the kitchen. "Mom—where's this from?" he asked her.

His mother smiled. "Doctor Schwinn brought it for you last night, after you were already in bed."

Jack sat down at the table and opened the package.

He found a wooden box with a manufacturer's label on it. "Boyne Medical Instruments, Smyrna, New York," he read aloud. On the top of the box was a card.

You taught Jamie a very necessary lesson—thank

Jack opened the box underneath to see it contained a surgical knife with eight interchangeable blades. It was just like the one he had briefly admired at Jamie's workshop. He felt the knife in his hand and imagined just how well it would work cutting balsa and other materials. His father came over to him and placed his large hand on his shoulder. "Well, son, Tony told us how it went yesterday. I'm proud of you, and so Dr. Schwinn seems to be too. You tried your level best and pulled through. Good work."

"Thanks Dad, but it was mostly luck—had you seen the wings of the plane?"

"Those wings carried the plane to victory—be content with that and learn the lesson." Mr. McGuire left for the shed. Jack's mom gave him a big hug and a wink.

In school, Jack found to his surprise that he had more friends than yesterday. Jamie was nowhere to be found, and Danny White was absent as well. They did turn up the next day, and Jamie announced he was building boats now, as they were much more demanding to build than any plane. This raised muted chuckles among the people who knew about the competition and its outcome. Jack didn't take advantage of the situation because of his timidity and his well-founded suspicion that fame was passing anyway and should not be exploited.

One upshot of the plane contest was that Jack finally caught Amy's eye. At that age, notions of the opposite sex are vague at best and translucent at worst; Jack's thoughts of being alone with Amy made him prone to walk about aimlessly, to respond dimwitted to external stimuli, and to act like a jerk in general. While it was a minor nuisance to everyone else, to Tony, with much more determination in his drive, it was a major headache.

So, as Jack once again drifted in the general direction of the river in his daydreams, Tony decided to stalk him a bit. Jack had a spot at a river bend where he liked to hang out in case he had time for himself, and this is where he gravitated again. Tony guessed his destination and made his way to the spot from the opposite direction.

Jack lay down on the sand with his hands behind his back, enjoying the afternoon sun on his face, dreaming of Amy's smile warming his face instead of the Sun. He had nebulous thoughts of having her lie beside him, but he was too shy to allow himself to proceed any further than that, even to conversation. Nevertheless, his daydreams were most enjoyable to him, and most boring for Tony.

At some point Jack wondered what he could actually do with her. He tried to imagine hugging and touching her a bit, but this conjured a forbidding rejection in his mind. Finding something to think about that would allow touching but not imply impropriety was harder than he first guessed.

Tony hid himself in the bush like a cougar, wondering about Jack's amorous contemplations. He was just about to spring to his feet and scare Jack witless, when Jack stood up first. He pranced about a bit, drew a home plate on the ground and lined up imaginary foul lines.

"So, this is what you do!" Jack exclaimed in his illusory solitude, after finally hitting on an idea. "You take up your place at the plate and look at the pitcher. No, not just at the pitcher, you look him in the eye. Make him understand that there's no pitch you can't hit. Then you weigh the bat and swing it back and forth, to get the heft of it." Jack was holding an imaginary bat and doing as he said. "When you're done, rest the bat on your shoulder."

Now he was imagining Amy here, with him, and posing her to the right posture, now lifting her left elbow, now correcting the chin to bring about a murderous stare at the pitcher, the bridge of her nose wrinkling in a way which melted his insides. Thinking of touching her brought forth sweet music inside him, and behind his closed eyelids, she smiled at him.

Tony was watching the show with raised eyebrows. Man, that brother of his was so shy he couldn't even think of a first base outside baseball. He shook his head slowly and decided he had to step in.

"So, Jack, you'd like to teach baseball to Amy? First off, I can see two problems there: one, girls don't play baseball, and two, what makes you think she'd be even remotely interested in either baseball or you? And you really need to think baseball when you should be thinking of girls for their own sake?"

Jack was thunderstruck, hit isolation demolished by a direct hit to his deepest feelings. "Tony! Damn you, I nearly had a heart attack!"

Tony smiled his most irritating Cheshire cat smile. "Heart attack…funny you should say that. You probably have a heart attack for Amy all the time, am I right or am I right?"

Jack sulked. "Why can't you let me think what I want to think and more, let me do what I want to do?"

"Because you need action with Amy, not imaginary baseball practice inside your thick skull."

"Really?" Jack decided to go on the offense. "And just how much action have you had with Nellie? Huh?"

Tony looked at his fingernails, as if evaluating the need for filing them. "Lots."

"Lots? Yeah, right. *Lots* means many times a lot." Jack felt very disapproving. "And as I seem to remember, you haven't spent that much time alone with her. Come to think of it, I've seen you disappear from my sight for maybe two hours last month! Did you spend that time with her?"

Tony looked triumphant. "Yessirree, I did!"

Jack's disbelief was tangible. "Alone?"

"Yessirrreeee!"

"Alone, as in you and her only? With no one around?"

Tony had been too well-trained by his father to speak the truth. "Well, mostly."

This was Jack's wedge to crack. "And just how much time you had with her alone?"

"Ten minutes or so."

Jack delivered the stab. "Not much of a lot then. You've got nothing to brag about, and yet you rub my nose in it." Tony managed to look both defiant and embarrassed. Jack turned to leave. "I'd really prefer it if you let me take care of my own business, and when you come back to brag about something again, put your money where your mouth is. Agreed?"

Tony stayed behind at the river bend, looking at Jack's diminishing back, determined to stay one step ahead of Jack when it came to girls. Even considering this latest rebuke, with Jack so shy, it wouldn't be too hard.

11

Two weeks after Kay had returned to the United States, Jack received a telegram from New York. It was not very informative:

TRUST YOU HAVE VACANCIES ON NOV 9 TO NOV 14.
WILL NEED TWO ADJACENT SINGLE ROOMS. ARRIVING AT
HONIARA NOV 9 1430. SIGNED WILBUR R WALLACE

"Vacancies? I have nothing but," Jack muttered as he strode to his office to mark down the dates. He entered them in his reservation book, promptly forgetting the issue.

On the evening of November 9th, Jack was sitting on the office porch sipping some whiskey when a curious party arrived at the hut. It consisted of an old man with silver-gray hair and steely eyes, dressed in tropical outfit complete with pith helmet, and his apparent manservant, fully clothed in British tweed. They were followed by three young natives carrying two large trunks and a box made of teak wood measuring four feet by two by two. Jack watched the procession with half-amused interest until it struck him that this was Mr. Wallace and party, due today.

"Mr. McGuire? Wilbur Wallace. I cabled you about rooms a few weeks ago."

Jack stood up. "Hello, Mr. Wallace, nice to meet you. Your huts are close by. Please follow me." Jack walked to his left down the path which led to Huts 3 and 4, situated on a grassy knoll overlooking the sea with no palms in front of them. When they got there, Jack opened the door.

"This is your hut, and your … assistant will have the next one," Jack said. He motioned the old man to follow him into the hut and showed him the facilities. The man told his servant to get settled in the next hut and then return to this one. The natives put the trunks on the floor, laying the wooden box on top of them with a loud bang.

"Careful with that!" the old man shouted. "It hasn't come halfway round the world just to be dropped and broken!"

The natives looked apologetic enough, and the old man whisked out a one dollar bill for each for them.

When they'd left, the man sat down on the bed, wheezing. "I haven't walked that much uphill since I was fifty, you know." Wallace fanned himself with his helmet.

"I'll have some refreshments sent to you straight away, sir," Jack said, telling as much to one of the natives in fast, rattling pidgin. The youngster sped off in the direction of the kitchen.

"Thank you kindly, Mr. McGuire. Now, allow me to introduce myself properly. I am Wilbur R. Wallace from Boston. I was referred to your hotel by a mutual acquaintance of ours, namely Kay Wheeler, whose father is an old friend of mine." The old man shut his eyes, but kept on fanning. "Kay had just returned to the States and as she knows my story, she told me she had a perfect hotel for my needs."

His interest piqued, Jack said, "Well, Kay apparently is a very good advertiser. I haven't had any lodgers referred to me before." Jack sat down on the chair by the dresser. He could see the man was about to tell more.

Wallace continued, "You see, I have wanted to come to the area since 1942, but as you must know, it was not an option until the end of the war. I had a son, Richard, about your age, who was in the Navy. He served on the destroyer *Walke*, which was sunk in the naval action of November 12—you may have heard of that one?"

Jack nodded. "I was stationed on Guadalcanal then, so I remember it well. It was a huge battle in the dark of the night." Jack began to understand the reason for the old man's visit.

"My son, along with seventy-nine others, perished when the *Walke* was hit by a torpedo and sank. We got only the official word from the Navy that he was dead. We had nothing to bury. My dear wife was hit so hard by the loss of our only child that she died in March '43. I too have been depressed ever since, but since then I had a chat with Kay—what a wonderful girl!—and decided that if I saw the place, perhaps I could get over this thing once and for all. She told me she had been feeling refreshed after visiting your hotel, so I took the bait and cabled you."

The native boy arrived with gin and tonic and two glasses on a plate. The old man's butler took the drink and gave the boy another dollar, at which his ever-present smile widened even more. The butler poured the drink with the precise hand movements of a seasoned valet, and delivered it to the waiting hands of his master.

He took the glass without acknowledging his butler. "And here I am now, and although I am a well-traveled man, I've never been in these parts. I have a shipping company back east, but I mostly deal in the European and South American trade." The man took a sip from his glass. "I wonder if you could help me out. I need to find the place where the *Walke* went down, or at least get close to it, and then perform a small ceremony. Do you have a boat or do you know of someone who would be able to take me, and Alfred, my butler, over there?"

Jack nodded. "Well, I don't have a boat, but I can get one from the wharf. When would you like to go?"

"I was hoping for Saturday. That's the twelfth, and it's the seventh anniversary of Rick's death."

"Of course. I can arrange that. I'll get to it straight away. But for now, why don't you wash up and get settled. We'll be serving dinner around eight at the luncheon hut down that path, close to those palms there. I'll see you then." At Wallace's nod of assent, Jack left the hut and went to the kitchen to tell Wilma to spruce up the dinner a little.

At eight o'clock sharp, the old man and his butler appeared at the luncheon hut. Jack was already there, overseeing the dinner arrangements. Martin was on hand tending bar. Jack was a bit surprised to see the butler herding a pair of teenage natives who were carrying the teak box. The natives put the box on the floor, and the butler handed them a couple more dollars.

A delicious smell emanated from the kitchen, where Wilma was working hard to produce a meal fit for the guests. Jack greeted the guests and directed them to their seats, and then Martin served them some appetizers. The butler looked as if he wanted to take part in the arrangements, but Mr. Wallace pointed at the seat for him to sit down. Over the drinks, Mr. Wallace said to Jack, "Perhaps you might be persuaded into hearing why we are here?"

Jack nodded. "Yes, I'm keen to hear why a man of your standing would want to visit these parts."

"It will take some time."

"That's no problem," Jack said to his guest. "We have all night."

"Ah. That's good. I need to hear whether you think I'm a

fool to come here. Let me start my story in 1920." And the old man took another sip from his glass, squinted his eyes, and squinted at Jack. "How old were you then?"

"In 1920, I wasn't born yet," Jack smiled.

"Ah, yes. Of course. Anyhow, in April 1920 I met a ravishing young lady, twenty-two years my junior, at a social occasion in Boston. She was the queen of the party, and all the men flocked to her like moths to a flame on an August night in Georgia. I went to her and said, 'Come with me; you know it's the best thing to do'. She gave her hand to me and never let go until we were married three months later. Ten months after that she gave birth to our son, Richard, our only child. We were heartbroken to hear he would have to remain our only child, but we had no choice. My wife's health would not have permitted another one. From the start, he was the brightest little boy you ever saw."

Opening his eyes, the old man continued. "I was overjoyed, and so was my wife. Already I was in my forties, but now I had a baby boy who would eventually take over my business, which I had built up through years of hard work before I met my wife. It's a shipping business, imports and exports, and even though I worked it up from nothing, I can safely say it is now one of the best going companies in the business. With the family I found myself in a new situation; and I made the decision to leave the day to day running of the business to my trusted partner, one Mr. Wellington, and dedicate myself to my family.

"We traveled, enjoying summers at Martha's Vineyard and winters in southern Europe, Australia, and South America. By the time Rick was ten, he had seen thirty countries and could speak fluent French and German. I'd hired a tutor for him, and this gentleman, Signor Bottazzi was his name..."

"Bottezzi, sir," the butler pitched in.

"Bottazzi, yes, he was a very diligent person indeed. Rick proved to be a good pupil too. He met every academic standard with ease, did his homework well and then returned to his sailboats. You see, sailing, and boating of all sorts, was his life. I was happy about that, because to succeed in shipping you really need to love the sea. Rick sailed all types of boats, and he was good at it too. He also piloted my speedboats—my heart was more into engines and speed than sails. All of this is required for you to understand the contents of the box we have brought here from Boston."

"I see." Jack signaled Martin that he could start serving. With a gorgeous millionaire's salad, they started their dinner.

The old man pointed to the box at the door. "In that box, Mr. McGuire, is a perfect copy of an Italian Riva Serafino speedboat of 1935. It is built to scale, and the only difference between it and the real thing, besides the size, is the engine. I commissioned the woodwork of the boat from a craftsman in Italy, across the street from the Riva factory, and a clocksmith in New York manufactured the precision spring-loaded engine. He also made the steering device in which you can set eight different paths for the boat to travel." He got up and went to the box. "Have a peek in here. I doubt you'll ever have seen anything like this." He punched buttons on the box's heavy combination lock, and pushed back the lid.

Jack looked down into the box to see a magnificent replica of the classic boat. He had seen a Riva at the wharf of San Francisco in 1947, and it had made an impression on him. This model was truly a gem; every detail of the original had been painstakingly included, from the mahogany woodwork to the brass propellers to tiny rope railings. Beside the boat there were eight strange-shaped pieces of metal fastened to square metal pegs some three inches long.

The butler opened the engine cover to reveal a clockwork engine. It was about the size and shape of the original engine drawn to scale, but it was spring-loaded. The engine crank for the spring was fastened to the engine cover. The butler removed it, cranked the spring a few rounds and then fastened one of the metal pieces into a hole in the top of the engine. Jack realized that it was the steering device as the butler set a peg to follow the turning piece of metal.

"See that, Mr. McGuire? It can run circles, ovals, figure eights, squares and more. With the spring fully wound up, it'll run for ten minutes—the spring is so powerful. Rick would run this boat in the pool or out in the sea for days on end, until he turned sixteen and was given a real speedboat." The old man was obviously pleased to see Jack marveling at the device. At his signal the butler released the catch, and the propeller of the boat started whirling. Jack could feel a definite stream of air being pushed by it. The rudder of the boat slowly moved, and Jack could see that in water, it would steer the boat in a lazy figure-eight.

"That sure is a great boat, Mr. Wallace, and I can see why your son would like to play with it," Jack said as he stepped back from the box. The old man too went to his chair and sat down to continue dinner. The butler wiped the boat's deck clean of any fingerprints and placed the boat in the box.

"So Rick was enthralled by the sea, and anything even remotely connected with it. He sailed all the time he could spare, changed boats all the time to get bigger and faster ones … he was just a nut for sailing. But, seeing as he did well in school, we didn't mind. In fact we encouraged him." The old man tried his salad, and an expression of surprise came over his face at how good it tasted.

154

Jack smiled in his mind—Wilma had done it again.

"As he came of age," Mr. Wallace said, "it was clear to everybody he would want to join the Navy. I wasn't worried about that at all—I knew he would do well there, too. He went to Annapolis and was admitted as one of the top applicants. Now, if he was happy somewhere, it was at Annapolis. He loved every minute of being a cadet, every drill, lecture, trip, all the things they do there. I was hoping he'd get his fill of the Navy life there, maybe have a short commission to a real ship and then he'd come to work for me, but it soon became apparent that the destroyer he was posted to was his new home." His forehead now wet with tiny drops of sweat, Mr. Wallace accepted a handkerchief offered by the butler with which he dabbed.

"So, when the war began, he got posted to the destroyer *Walke*. He was so happy about that posting, he just couldn't keep still when he heard the news but came home to us to celebrate. We were less than happy, given the fact that those tin cans go pretty far into harm's way, but after all parents have no say in a grown man's life. He was promptly made gunnery officer and he, along with the rest of the crew, put the *Walke* through its paces really hard. They were good and they knew it, full of fighting spirit. But you must know all this, having been a pilot yourself, you still remember how kids are at that age.

"In late summer '42, Richard was on leave, but getting ready to return—it was a matter of time before his ship would sail into combat. It was of course not known to us, but we could tell he was about to leave. He was more sentimental than usual, made a point of meeting old friends, such as were still around, and spent a lot of time with us. It was his last night home before he went to his ship when he sat around the pool with me and my wife, when all of a sudden he bolted off and hauled out this speedboat. He carefully wound it up and put it into the pool, and watched it run its course."

"He said to me, 'Dad, I want you to send this boat out to Merle. He'd want to have it after I don't need it anymore.' Merle was his ten-year-old cousin in Los Angeles. I said, 'Rick, we'll keep it here so you can pass it on to your own son when you return from the war,' but he would have none of that. He insisted I promise to send the boat off to Merle right away so he could play with it. Though I saw it was futile to try to talk him out of it, after he left for his ship I tried to do just that, but couldn't. So strong was my conviction that Richard would walk back to me after the war, get married and have kids of his own who would like to play with the boat, I couldn't even contemplate the alternative."

Mr. Wallace took a sip of his drink and reclined in his chair. "Once he left, I couldn't start any work. I wasn't able to concentrate on anything until we got the final post card from Rick, in which he urged us to carry on with life even though he wasn't there with us. The postcard was from Panama— they passed through the Canal on their way to San Francisco and on to the war zone. For some reason that postcard reinvigorated me and I returned to the office."

Jack could see that relating this story to him, a stranger, was both a strain and a relief to the old man.

Mr. Wallace took a moment's breather and then carried on. "We had no idea where Rick was. We thought he was too busy to send us mail. This later turned out to be true; as soon as the *Walke* went for the combat action, they never took a moment off from the battle. We felt he was doing his best, and doing something he really loved. Still it was a terrible moment when we got the War Department telegram. I just sat there staring at the text on the paper, not really seeing it, not understanding any of it. Our son was never coming back to us, there'd never be a Richard Junior—hell, it felt like there was no life at all after that damn telegram."

The story was taking a physical toll on the old man; his shoulders dropped as if bearing a great weight. "My wife had a nervous breakdown of some sort, not saying a word for weeks after that. She was never at peace again. In January 1943 she told me she had cancer of the stomach, and she died soon after that. I was a broken man for a long time, but I still could not send that boat off to Merle."

Alfred poured some more wine in the glass of the old man. His story seemed to be building to a climax. "Then, one night, way past midnight, I was again in Rick's room. I usually go there when I can't fall asleep, just to look at things. I'd been talking with Kay over dinner at her parents' house, and she told me of your hotel, right here on the spot where Rick died. As I looked at the boat it occurred to me that if I sent the boat to Rick—would it help me get on with my life? I immediately woke Alfred up and told him to start arranging this trip. And finally, we're here."

Jack looked the old man in the eye. "That's quite a story, sir. I'll arrange the rest so you can send the boat to its owner. Don't you worry about a thing."

The old man smiled. "Thanks, Jack—may I call you Jack? That means a lot to me. But now I feel I should go to bed, as it's been a long day, and a long journey, and a long story." Aided by Alfred, Mr. Wallace stood and, bidding Jack a good night, left for his hut.

Jack sat for a long while on the porch, alone, listening to the noises from the village and the incessant concert of nocturnal animals. He felt it his duty to see to it that Mr. Wallace should get to do what he had to do.

In the morning Jack dispatched Martin to the pier. He was to get the biggest of boats in the harbor to take Mr. Wallace and Alfred out to Savo Island on the twelfth. They didn't know exactly where the *Walke* had sunk, but Peter, the owner of the boat, claimed he had a good idea where they ought to look.

Mr. Wallace, happy to hear that the boat was already in order, spent a leisurely day on the beach and on the porch of his cabin, resting from the journey. They ate dinner that evening with another pair of Jack's guests, who were traveling up the Solomons chain and had been happy to find a hotel in the area. It was a much more light-hearted evening than the previous one, and everyone felt refreshed by the time they retired to their cabins.

In the morning the sky was overcast, and a light drizzle filled the air. A worried-looking Mr. Wallace came up to Jack's cabin. "Jack, can we still do this even with the weather looking so poor?"

Jack reassured him that even if he wouldn't go flying in this weather, the boatmen of Tulagi were still fully capable of going safely out to sea.

"I have another request, Jack—if you don't have anything you need to do right now, would you join us on the trip? It would mean a lot to me." Jack was happy to oblige. Relieved, the old man with his ever-present companion went to enlist a few native boys for the task of carrying the boat box to the harbor piers.

Peter met the party at the pier. He had cleaned out his boat of nets and other fishing equipment, but the sea stench of the boat was almost overpowering. Mr. Wallace told Jack, who looked a bit apprehensive, that the smell was not half as bad as on some of the ships he had on his company's books, and that he was used to such things. Alfred the butler looked less certain of his ability to filter out the stench of marine life, and discreetly held his nose.

Peter pushed the boat away from the pier and headed out west for some time, and then turned north-northwest. After about half an hour of travel he shut off the engine and a dead silence came over the boat. There was no wind at all, and only a seagull could be heard mewing high over their heads.

"Well, Jack, this is it, then," Mr. Wallace spoke up. "Are we on the right spot, Peter?"

"As far as I can tell, sir, this is where the ships fought and this is where they sank too," Peter replied.

The old man nodded. "Alfred, the boat, with full winding of the engine, please." Alfred took the crank, opened the engine compartment, and wound up the clockwork. Then Mr. Wallace said, "Figure eight—no, make it a circle. A full circle, the large one."

Alfred inserted a round piece of metal on a stick into the engine's steering device. Then he handed the boat to Mr. Wallace, who was about to put it into the sea, when Alfred said, "Sir—the plug."

"Oh yes, the plug," said Mr. Wallace, and removed a plug from the bottom of the little boat. Now the boat would take in water as it went. Mr. Wallace flicked a lever on the engine and the little propeller started revolving. With some trouble, leaning over the side of the boat, he set the boat in the water where it began to do majestic circles with a diameter of eighteen yards, skimming over the oily-smooth surface of the sea. For four minutes the party watched as the boat sped on its route. When the engine began to slow down, more water began to seep into the hull. The boat started to sink slowly, pulled down by the engine and the ballast. Soon it was down to crawling speed with its deck approaching the sea surface, but the plucky engine kept on turning and the boat was still moving on its predestined path when it finally went in below the surface.

Only a diminishing row of bubbles marked the spot where the boat had begun its descent to the bottom of the Slot, where it would join bigger ships and its rightful owner. When the bubbles vanished, there was nothing but the sea, the clouds, and the solitary seagull up in the sky.

No one said a word for a while, but then Mr. Wallace said with an unwavering voice, "There's your boat, Rick—goodbye, son."

Jack had to swallow tears. When at the end of a few moments of silence Mr. Wallace looked at Jack, the younger man could see that the little ceremony had been beneficial; his eyes were bright and he smiled. "Well, Jack, what if we went back for some lunch? I seem to be a bit hungry already!" he said, and with that Peter guided the boat back towards Tulagi.

Peter had asked a sum of three dollars for the trip, but Mr. Wallace paid him twenty, thanking him for the good service and wishing him good fishing. He also left the boat's box with Peter, who was astonished at the present. During lunch Jack was surprised to see a new glint of vitality in Mr. Wallace's eyes. It seemed that now he was eager to get back to the United States.

When they had had coffee, Mr. Wallace nailed his assistant with a steely look. "Alfred, pack us up. We are going home, since there's work to be done. Jack—I will remain in your debt for helping to make this little ceremony possible. I hope everything goes well with your hotel and that you become a prosperous man. I'll return one day for a real holiday."

"It was an honor having you here, sir, and please come back any time," Jack said, emotion choking his voice.

Alfred packed their gear, Mr. Wallace settled their bill, and after a noisy procession of natives had carried their luggage to the pier, they embarked for Guadalcanal. Jack waved to them out on the pier with Martin, until the boat disappeared from sight into the fog. He didn't think they'd get a flight out of Guadalcanal that evening but he didn't want to ask them to stay, so obvious was the old man's will to leave. There would be a cargo plane of some sort passing through Guadalcanal almost every day.

After Mr. Wallace had left, Jack again sat alone on the porch of his cabin, sipping the whiskey which the old man had left behind, peering out to the darkening ocean. He thought about the old man's life and his work, how all his hopes had been crushed in a span of six months during the war. Again he couldn't help wondering what war was all about—was it just an unavoidable natural feature of mankind, or was it a divine tool for forcing people to take charge of their lives instead of just living them out? The question went unanswered in the changing light of the sky.

Night fell like a butcher's cleaver, nocturnal birds began playing their flutes, and crickets and frogs crowded the soundscape. All of a sudden Jack felt immensely tired, as if he had just walked the eight thousand miles between Nebraska and the Solomon Islands. He once again tried to figure out how his life might have fallen together if the war hadn't interfered.

He wanted so badly to picture himself leading a normal life in the United States, with a wife, a couple of children, a steady job and a home, even the farm. But as always, the people in this imaginary family had no faces—he had never been able to create the complete image in his mind. His fatigue gave way to self-pity, isolation, and deep melancholy. When his mind hit the image of Kay, and the fact that he was probably never going to see her again, it was like a physical punch to the gut. He reached for the bottle of whiskey he had on the floor at his side, but it wasn't there.

He looked around the porch, but all he found was Martin holding the bottle in his hand. "Jack, it's better to call me first, before you open the bottle. I thought we agreed to that." Martin sat down in the chair beside Jack.

"Aw, I was just having a couple of nightcaps before going to bed," Jack lied.

Martin didn't buy it. "It's fine by me if you want to drink whiskey in the night, but the sun will rise no matter how much you try to push it back, and we have work to do tomorrow."

Jack was at once irritated by Martin's patronizing tone and relieved to have someone to listen to him.

"You know, Martin, you're right. There's really no point in drinking, especially alone. But you have to tell me this: What would you be doing if the war hadn't come? Where would you be now?"

It was Martin's turn to look pensively into the darkness. "I can't say. I don't know, honestly I don't. The nuns always said they'd send me to Sydney to go school, but hey, if I went to school in Sydney, what good would that do me? Nobody would give me a job in Australia. Back home, what good would a diploma do me? The only thing I ever thought I could do with a degree would be go get a job with the British administration here, but I couldn't live behind a desk. Besides, there's enough people in England available for the Resident Commissioner's office, they wouldn't want to hire me. So, in essence, what I'm saying is that while I'm truly grateful for the nuns of the mission for the support and schooling they gave me, I'm even more grateful to the war."

"Grateful?" Jack sat up in complete surprise.

"Sure. Take you, for instance. The war brought you here. The war set you up with a love for this place, and the will to return. If it wasn't for the war, this place would be just remote backwoods nobody knew about, and I would be a really bad fisherman. Now that you're here, I have a stake in a hotel which'll eventually become successful, and I believe it's the best thing that's ever happened to me. Sure, the war did a lot of damage to the islands and the people and the waste and death was terrible, but there's something good in everything." He poured Jack another drink, and one for himself too.

"Let us toast the departed, and the past, and celebrate the future—may we live long and prosper with Tulagi Hotel," he said with ceremony, and Jack nodded, convinced by Martin's steadfast testimony. They stayed up a long time, idly chatting with long, pregnant periods of silence between brief snatches of conversation.

Finally Jack stood up, slapped Martin on the shoulders and said, "Let's go to bed. As you said, the sun will rise, and the work will not leave us."

Martin nodded and started down the trail towards his hut by the beach. Jack relieved himself at the palm sapling he selected as having the greatest need of fertilization, and meandered up to his hut and bed, much like a bee that has dipped in one too many roses. He fell asleep instantly.

Next Monday Jack had to go over to Guadalcanal to buy the usual eight barrels of fuel for the plane. This time he wasn't looking forward to it, because his cash box was showing its bare bottom, and his quarterly money transfer from his investments in the States hadn't arrived yet. He'd have to ask for credit, which he hated to do, but this time there was no way around it.

At the airfield Jack talked to Bill Peet, the airport caretaker. He dug a hole in the ground with his big toe and felt like he was again at Mr. Mitchell's general store, asking for balsawood and rubber. "Listen Bill, I have to ask you something. Is it possible for me to get the avgas but pay up like next week or the week after that? I have none over on Florida but I'd need to have some, because I have guests arriving in a couple of days and I hope they'll want to fly with me. If it's a problem with you, don't worry about it. I'll go and get a little loan from someone, or something like that."

Bill didn't look up from his papers. "Sure you can. Pay me next week, the week after that, whenever you want. Or don't pay me at all, if you don't want to. See if I care," he added, scribbling his name on some papers.

Jack was baffled. "Like how? It's a lot of money for eight full barrels, but I need it."

Bill looked up from his papers. "Did you have a guest on the island just now? An old guy, traveling with a real butler and all, a pommy bastard at that?"

Jack acknowledged this.

"Well, it so happened he was waiting for his plane over at the lounge and asked me who sends you your gas. I said I get it from Trans-Oceanic and they get it delivered here by Southwest Pacific Shipping, and as I said this, he said, 'Let Jack have all the gas he wants and send the bill to me.' He gave me his card and said he'd settle it directly with Southwest—he had some business deals with them or something. So the net result is, you can fly all you want on his expense."

Jack was flabbergasted. Bill went on: "He mentioned you had helped him in some kind of ceremony and that he was homeward bound. Now, if you don't mind, your gas is in the hangar as usual, and I have some work to do, so see you later, mate."

Jack borrowed Mr. Wallace's business card from Bill, went to the post office and sent him a post card, thanking him profusely for relieving him of his biggest expense. He knew well that it was no hardship for Mr. Wallace, but it was a major relief for Jack. He bought the rest of the items on his shopping list and returned to Halavo by boat, this time savoring the smell of the sea.

12

During Advanced Fighter Training, Jack and Don saw men washed out of the program for a variety of reasons. Some failed to grasp aerial gunnery; others didn't manage to land on a carrier deck painted on the tarmac and had to be let go before attempting a real carrier landing; yet others failed to grasp tactics and would have posed a threat to their squadron mates in combat.

The progress of cadets was assessed every day. Any infraction of rules and regulations, or bad flight performance, was marked with a down grade—and three downs were enough to see a pilot out of Advanced Training. Consequently, all cadets paid close attention to whatever they were doing to avoid the downs. Having made it up to fighters was everyone's dream come true; washout, with the inevitable transfer to bombers or other flying duties, was a common nightmare.

The only man in the class who didn't worry about downs was Don Wheeler. Given his long experience of flying, his skills were of course well above average, and he also possessed a rare skill in aerial gunnery. He was consistently at the top of his class in anything having to do with flying or shooting, and just as consistently at the bottom when it came to studying.

Jack, on the other hand, was of the standard type of cadet who had only flown the regulatory hours and had to keep up with every subject given to the class. Despite all his efforts, Jack was given one down early in the class, when he got completely lost on a navigational test flight and had to seek refuge at a bomber field to refuel and to re-situate himself on the map again. The same test flight saw eight others also fail because of a low overcast which appeared after take-off; those who hadn't been extremely vigilant had been bound to lose their way.

Jack's second down came when he attempted to land wheels-up in a night exercise. He remembered the gear at the last possible moment, hit full throttle and despite having already lowered the flaps, managed to pull up and go around for a more conventional landing. The bad news was that Lieutenant Commander McMahon, a fiery Irish instructor pilot, was watching the class perform the exercise, and he gave Jack a down for the near disaster. It was a matter of some controversy whether the down was justified—Jack had not damaged government property, but he had very nearly done so.

Jack tried to decompress with Don afterwards. "I just don't get it. I mean, I was doing fine today, you saw me fly like an angel, and then he gives me a second down. Just for almost ruining the plane and possibly myself too. All I need now is a third one and I'm off to the trenches...can't imagine how I can avoid that third one."

"Listen, pal, you have two options," Don said philosophically. "Look at it your way and be absolutely certain of getting that final down, or look at it this way." He tilted his head sideways at the neck and looked up out of the corner of his eye.

"You bastard!" Jack had to laugh. "I'm serious about this!"

"So am I," said Don. "You can put up a fight if you don't just walk into that third down like it was ordained by God himself. What you have to do is to figure out a way to do so well McMahon simply can't fail you that one more time. I've gotta say that this time I think he was right downing you for that gear-up landing approach. Just think of the repaint operation it would have caused. Excuse me, I have to go to the little boys' room for a sec, but when I get back we'll make a battle plan for your upcoming grand finale with McMahon."

On his way to the men's room, Don paused to glance at the corridor wall. Originally painted a weird whitish hue with no relation to the overall color scheme at the Altitude Bar, such as it was, it had long since been scrawled full of messages from members of graduated classes to peons still in the pipeline. It was common courtesy for cadets to refrain from writing as only graduates had the privilege to immortalize themselves for posterity. Among all the meaningless inside jokes, obvious hoaxes and bad wordplays, a familiar name in one scribbled message caught Don's eye:

```
McMahon always washes out exactly 20% of any
class plus one.
```

This interested Don very much. He started going through the wall systematically and soon found another message alluding to McMahon:

```
If McMahon calls you 'Flyboy', don't worry about
not becoming a fighter jock; you'll learn to
enjoy flying bombers and other fine multiengine
types.
```

He searched even more carefully and finally found what he was looking for. A third reference to McMahon said:

```
To McMahon, life is just one never-ending poker
game.
```

168

He made his way to the rest room. Sitting on the can everything became clear to Don. First, he had seen Jack on all the flights but the one when he got the downgrades. Then, he had not been able to see anything wrong whatsoever with Jack's performance. Second, he had been on the tarmac when McMahon received Jack from his successful cross-country navigation flight. He had stated: "Nice work, flyboy, but the landings still stink." Don felt a chill down his spine. McMahon had targeted Jack as his patsy for Class 42-C, and Don had to do something quickly if he wanted to get to fly with him in combat. He also quickly resolved not to say anything to Jack just now. He had to get to McMahon alone to force him to keep Jack on the program.

To confirm the basics of his plan, he went on three separate nights to Chez Paris, the bar of choice for training staff, and true to form, McMahon was on the poker game in the early evening and playing craps by 2 AM. While Don couldn't see how he would be awake enough to take off at eight the next morning, he was now sure he had something he could use in saving Jack.

The next Monday, Jack and Don were part of an eight-plane flight doing field carrier landing practice. In the FCLP exercise, the cadets had to fly a simulated approach to the airfield as if it were a carrier deck, hitting the tarmac at the same relative spot as would have been appropriate for a real carrier. McMahon was on the tarmac acting as the landing signals officer, complete with paddles, and he had two lookouts, one of whom played the role of the radioman and clerk. The other's task was to check with a pair of binoculars that the approaching cadet had gear, flaps, and hook down, and convey the information to McMahon. If one of the three was not down, the cadet would receive a wave-off and a down grade.

Jack performed his first approach with trembling hands; he was very careful to work the plane into the groove in a coordinated turn, and he also remembered to lower the flaps, gear, and hook. The lookout yelled, "Gear, flaps and hook down, sir!" and McMahon guided Jack in. His contact with the tarmac was picture perfect. As he throttled open and started to accelerate again for a new round, he could see McMahon give him a thumbs-up. That took all worries off his mind, and he did six more almost as good go-around landings.

On the eighth and last approach, the lookout again yelled, "Gear, flaps, and hook down, sir!" But McMahon said, "What hook? I see no hook!"

The lookout was completely baffled. "He has the hook down, sir, I can see it clear as day with the binoculars!"

"Damn it, Seaman, are you saying my eyesight is bad? I see he has no hook down, and *you* note it down *now!*" He pointed at the other lookout with the log. The radioman cowered under the thundering voice of McMahon, who was known for his rough treatment of lookouts. He noted "Hook up" in his log, even as Jack flew by and landed with a perfect touchdown, and the plane correctly configured.

After all the cadets had landed, McMahon assembled them at the flight hangar. "Gentlemen—today's exercise almost went well. Most of you found a way to hit the right spot with the right configuration, but McGuire and Landis didn't. Both had hooks up, McGuire once and Landis twice."

"Sir, that's not true!" Jack shouted. "I had it down every time!"

"Let me be clear about this, McGuire—you just got yourself the third down. I am sure you'll thank me one day for not letting you go get killed crashing a barrier on a carrier with that tail hook up. Dismissed." McMahon started on his way to the instructors' office.

Landis was cursing his first down, but Jack was almost in tears at the injustice. He knew the lookouts would never dare take his side if he dragged them to the commander of the school. Don slipped away from Jack and went to meet McMahon in his office.

McMahon was surprised to see Don. "Well, what is it?"

"Sir, can I get off the record with you and talk to you in private?"

McMahon waved the clerk out of the room with an impatient wide circle of his left hand. Once they were alone, he said again, "Well? What do you have to say? I got a lot of paperwork today, so let's be snappy with it."

Don took a deep breath. "Sir, you are one of the biggest bastards I have ever had the displeasure to come across in my entire life."

McMahon dropped his pen on the table in shock.

"What's that?" he exclaimed.

"Come to think of it, you are *the* very biggest bastard. I think it's a result of three separate causes. One, you are only five-foot-six. Many men that size try to compensate by acting the way you do: controlling, authoritarian, even dictatorial."

"Big words from a cadet, Wheeler," said McMahon, puffing himself up to size.

"Second, I believe you have stepped on someone's toes on your way to your current position as an instructor pilot, and so you're stuck here while your own classmates are fighting in the skies all around the world every day. And if you make ace while here, well, you'll be fighting for the wrong side."

McMahon came out and nearly stood chest to chest with Don. "Have you any idea how far out of line you are right now, cadet?" he said, peering at Don through squinted eyes.

"Sir, for all I care, the line could be in Kansas. I don't give a shit what you think, but let me tell you the third reason why you're a bastard. Somewhere down the line when you figured you'd be pinned down here till the war ends, you decided to take a gamble on cadets. You decided to wash out men by quota, not by skills, and that's what you were doing today too. Your gamble is that no one will ever have the guts to stand up against you. Jack McGuire had nothing wrong in his FCLP and you know it."

"Wheeler, were you there on the ground?"

"No, sir," Don had to admit.

"Well then, would you really say that flying your own plane, a thousand yards away from him in mid-air, you had the time and the eagle eyes to check on McGuire's approaches to the last detail?"

"No, sir, I would not. But after his last landing, the hook was down, and you claimed to have seen it up."

"It was probably jarred loose by the impact of the landing for all I care. It was up when he flew in. And that's final. Dismissed." McMahon returned to his desk.

Don said, "Sir, I have one more thing to say. Let me challenge you to a dogfight. If I win, you take out Jack's downs from the records."

McMahon squinted again. "And in the much more likely event *I* win, what do I get?"

Don leaned forward. "You can wash Jack out with his downs, *and* you can give me an LMF."

McMahon whistled through his front teeth which had a convenient gap for that purpose. "Lack of Moral Fiber, eh?" LMF was the most feared of all labels in the naval aviation, its bearer seen as unfit for any duty beyond the kitchen. "Let me get this straight. You're willing to risk an LMF for yourself to save your pal, who I'm about to wash out anyway?"

"That's right, you little twerp, it's time to show you that you can't play games with cadets."

McMahon stacked all his papers on one pile and called in the clerk. "Sort out this mess. I'm taking a flight with this here cocky cadet, right now." Then he picked up the phone and called the hangar. He ordered the crew to prepare two Wildcats with tanks half-full and no ammunition, but gun camera film loaded. "Wheeler, you're on. See you at the flight line in thirty. We take off, head out to sea, climb to fifteen thousand, fly opposite directions for a minute and then it's a free-for-all, okay?"

"Yes, sir," Don said, and went to collect his flight gear.

In thirty-five minutes' time, two Wildcats sped down the runway, took off, and turned out to sea. They disappeared in the pale-blue sky dotted with high but small cumulus clouds. The ground crew was cursing the lack of flight plan information, but thought it better not to record the flight anywhere and risk McMahon's wrath later on.

On the ground, Jack had gone looking for Don, but was unable to find him anywhere. He went to the flight line to see whether Don was chatting with the ground crew as was his habit, given his interest in all things mechanical, but the crew had gone out to the canteen to wait for the planes to come back. While he was at the hangar, a flight of four TBM torpedo planes landed and taxied in. The lead pilot hopped out of the plane and said, "What's the fight about out there?"

"What fight?"

The pilot grinned at Jack. "We were doing this triangle flight, and on the overwater leg we passed these two Wildcats that were both going for the jugular...never seen such a ferocious fight with two Wildcats engaged in it. I mean, we did a three-sixty turn around the pair just to watch them trying to get at the tail. I don't know who they were, but they both were pretty damn good!"

It all became clear to Jack in a flash. He smiled to the other pilot. "I think I know who we have up there…let's see what happens!"

Half an hour later, Jack greeted the crew on their return. Soon he heard the sound of two planes returning to the field, and after a few moments, they landed in formation.

When they had taxied to the hangar, the pilot from the first plane exited in a rush and stormed out to the crew chief. "Get both gun camera films out now, and get them to me. Don't give them to anyone else. Don't develop them. And patch up that wingtip. And McGuire—you get your flight log to the records clerk right now. MOVE IT!" He wiped sweat off his forehead and half-walked, half-ran towards his quarters.

Don sat down on the wing of his plane. "That sure was fun," he said, blasé, and lit up a smoke despite the pained look on the crew chief's face.

"What was all that about?" Jack asked. "Why does he want my log book?"

"It's because he's a good gambler and he always puts up. He lost, fair and square. I waxed his fanny four times, he got me once, and I forced him so low he actually hit a palm on the beach! Man, that was fun!"

The ground crew chief went to the right wingtip of McMahon's plane and pointed at a definite green dent in the leading edge. "This plane sure went in pretty low," he said. "We'll need to change the wingtip."

Don nodded to Jack. "Better go and collect your winnings—get that log to McMahon before he forgets he lost."

Jack sped away to his quarters. There he picked up his log

and hightailed it to McMahon, who apparently had already told the clerk what to do. The clerk took the log and went to his room.

McMahon's face was still the color of raw liver. "McGuire, are we clear on the fact that this flight I took with Wheeler never happened?"

"What flight, sir?"

McMahon looked to the wall behind Jack. "Dismissed."

Jack took to his feet and ran back to the hangar, but Don had already left. The crew chief told him Don had gone in for a shower and that he expected to meet Jack later at the Altitude Bar.

Jack went to eat, then returned to his quarters to change clothes. When he was about to leave the room, the clerk was at the door, delivering his new log book. Instead of his own book, written in his handwriting in a variety of pens, this book consisted of the same information but written in someone else's hand—*and* missing the downs. Every flight was there, every minute of flight time, all the notes, but the only thing missing were the downs. Fascinated, Jack went to the base gate and hitched a ride from a couple of other pilots who were going downtown past the Altitude.

By the time he got to the bar, Don had already found a date for the evening. He greeted Jack with his trademark grin and held out a beer. "Here's to your new, improved, industrial-strength logbook!"

Jack took the beer. "Look, Don, you just got to level with me. What the hell happened there? I have to know."

Don turned to his date. "Colleen, meet Jack. Jack, this is Colleen. Jack just got a better chance of passing the course because his logbook no longer contains any bad marks, only great ones." Colleen giggled and toasted Jack with Don.

Smiling, Jack sat down. Hard as he tried, he could not get Don to talk about the deal.

"Look, pal," Don frowned, "all you really need to get out of this outfit is a logbook that has all the necessary information, with no downs. You got one now, so why worry? I bet Colleen knows that gorgeous brunette over in the corner table because she waved to her just now, so what say we ask her over and get us a great foursome for the evening?" Don started waving to the girl, who feigned reluctance at first, but eventually hopped over and joined the little party.

Jack was still too geared up with the logbook issue, but Don buttonholed him. "Jaysis, Jack! When will you learn to have fun when it's possible and worry when you have nothing else to do? Look at Colleen and this other gal, and then tell me you want to discuss logbooks. This is going to be a seven of a night, so let's not waste any more time, OK?"

Jack put up his hands in mock surrender, and looked at Colleen's friend, who at least in the dim light of neon signs and beer ads looked very pretty. He smiled to her, learned that her name was Jo Anne, with a space and a capital A, and steeled himself for a fun night out.

It did turn out a great night after all, and it was just barely before curfew when Jack finally assisted a very drunk Don back to the base. They had kissed the girls goodbye outside the last bar which had admitted them, and as usual Jack was prepared to make sure Don did not go AWOL. He decided to try once more to find out what had been in Don's mind when he pulled his stunt on McMahon, and he propped him up against the wall. "Don, level with me now. Why did you fly today?" he asked.

Don smiled the low-beam smile of a properly-marinated man. "I have a hunch you may turn out useful someday, Jack my lad. If you do, fine. If not, I had some fun at McMahon's expense today. To me, that's reason enough. Hey, why did you bring me back to base? I want more beer!"

Jack decided he had his answer, or some answer at least, and as Don had just passed out while leaning on him, no more was forthcoming tonight. He carried his friend past the sentries, shushed them with his index finger, and laid his human cargo to rest on his bed as gently as he could.

It remained to be seen whether Don's hunch or McMahon's third down would carry the day.

13

Roused from a little afternoon snooze on the porch of the operations hut, Commander Wade, head of the recently established island base on Munda, was less than happy. It was a Sunday afternoon, and he had just been given a note by Beep Coleman, the radio operator, on which was a hastily written message from headquarters at Efate in the New Hebrides.

It took Wade only a few seconds to read it through and see what was in store for him and the base. He rose from the wicker chair and strode over to the end of the porch. Across the swath of land cleared from the jungle, he could see the planes of the air base milling around, taking off, landing, and taxiing about, like bees in their colony. "Damn, we need these like another hole in the head," he said, and turned to face the messenger.

"What is it, sir?" Coleman, like all radio operators, had taken down the message without thinking about the content at all. It was more like automatic writing than anything else.

"We're getting yet another distinguished visitor from Stateside. Another big shot congressman intent on hanging a Samurai sword on his office wall. And it's only a month since they declared Guadalcanal safe for visits like this." Wade rolled the paper into a ball and threw it out into a large bucket full of rain water. "But this isn't Guadalcanal. This is Munda and we're still full of Japs in the bushes. And Rabaul likes us so much they still pay us a visit every day. Goddamn it, can't they see back in the States how we fight over here without sending us these freeloaders every two weeks?"

"Which one is it this time, sir?" Coleman asked, without actually thinking the bit of information would be of any use.

"Grundy, another member of the Naval Affairs Committee. Apparently he wants to see for himself how we turn fighters into floatplanes and work this rainy hellhole like it was a Naval Air Station in Florida."

"When's he coming in, sir?"

"Tuesday. Off again on Wednesday. On a PBY, Wildcat escort from there, since Guadalcanal is safe, remember?" Wade was striding up and down the porch. "And if he's shot down, I'll get my ass chewed for sure. Oh well, go get me McGuire and Wheeler, and what, two others ... Jones and Becker. Now."

"Yes, sir," and Coleman was already well on his way to the pilots' area.

When he reached the tents, Coleman found Don halfway through shaving, using a well-polished piece of sheet metal as mirror. "The old man wants you. Where's Jack McGuire? And Jonesy and Becker?"

"Whoa, Beepie, I got half my face to do still! Hold your horses, I'm not leaving till I'm soft as a baby's butt on both cheeks."

"I think you'd better drop it and finish up later, like next week. He's mighty geared up already."

"Is it that bad?"

"It is that bad," Coleman confirmed.

Don washed the lather off his face. "OK, sonny, I'll take your word for it. Becker and Jonesy are up on CAP, but Jack is having a nap in his tent. Tell him I already went."

Coleman found Jack in his tent, napping, just as Don had said. He shook him gently at first, but soon resorted to combined shaking and talking. Jack was woozy for a bit, but at Coleman's persistent pushing stood up and started towards the command post.

Commander Wade took a somewhat suspicious look at Don's appearance but decided not to ask about the shave. "Don, Jack, good to see you—where're Becker and Jones?" the commander asked Don.

"Up on CAP, I think."

"That's right," said Jack, "they had the afternoon hop today."

"Never mind. Boys, we're about to be greeted again by a Congressman. They've been popping in and out of islands in the region lately, but I have a bad feeling about this one."

"How come?" asked Don.

"Beats me—but then, I've never been wrong yet. I had this same feeling at Guadalcanal before the battle of Savo Island, and remember how *that* went? Right. Now, as this concerns you, I want to make sure you're up there with Jonesy and Becker for this fella's arrival and departure. Guadalcanal will supply escort with a bunch of Wildcats—just as a precaution, as they say—but you'll go out and meet him as far as is needed, and make sure he gets out safe too. Go cancel all your hops for Tuesday and Wednesday; you'll only fly these escort hops. And make sure your planes are well-trimmed and loaded for action. If I'm proven wrong, you'll just show him the sights, but I feel it in my bones he's in for more than he signed on for. And Wheeler, you just gotta learn how to shave properly." The pilots mumbled acknowledgement, Don rubbing his jaw absently, and went their way to the tents.

"What do you think, Jack? Is the Old Fud finally losing

it?" Don asked as they wended their way among the puddles.

"No, I think some folks really can smell trouble," Jack said, "and Wade is about as keen as anyone. Let's just buy his hunch and see if we can keep the distinguished visitor out of harm's way."

"OK, but I bet you three to one it'll be a milk run."

"Well, milk runs are fine in between the real stuff, eh? I like just flying around sometimes—I don't want to have to dodge tracers every time I go up. I want to fly in peace every now and again!"

"Ya ya ya ... pacifist!" Don winked, and ran away from Jack's irritated swing.

In about fifty minutes, Jones and Becker landed from CAP. They were sometimes referred to as Munda's very own Laurel and Hardy, since Jones was tall and lanky, with little hair on the top of his conical head, and Becker used to look like he never missed a meal. In fact, he'd had some trouble getting through flight school and keeping regulation fit, but after a few months at Guadalcanal and Munda, it was only his round face which showed his former glory. No matter how much they were joked about, no one contested their abilities in combat aviation; Jones had 4.5 and Becker 3.5 kills and they were popular pilots when special missions were sent out.

Jack and Don went to the pierced-steel runway to greet them. As Becker hopped down from his Corsair, Don shouted to him, "Guess what, Becker? You're on special duty! You'll be babysitting a Congressman!"

"Shut up, Wheeler, and let me go get something to eat. I'm real hungry now and I don't want to be bothered before I grab a bite!" Obviously Becker didn't believe every word he heard from Don.

"I kid you not, Becker, Jack and I are on it too with you

and Jonesy. Did you have any planned missions for Tuesday and Wednesday? Too bad, because they're off now. You'll be up with us to greet this great representative of our glorious country and make sure he gets here with a full set of tail feathers. And out of here too!"

Becker wiped sweat off his brow. "Oh, not again ... babysitting. Nothing to do except do needlework around some PBY flying at a hundred knots and try to avoid stalling. I hate babysitting."

"Well, who doesn't, but go tell the Old Fud you don't want to do this, and you'll find yourself up with fifteen CAPs per week," Don said, patting Becker's shoulders.

Becker aimed his walk towards Jones's Corsair whose engine sputtered and coughed into silence.

"Jonesy, Jonesy...we're doomed again!" Becker called to Jones, who extricated himself from the shoulder harness and stood up in his cockpit.

"Can't be any worse than this already is." Jones took off his flying helmet and adjusted his retreating hair into a passable formation. "What are you talking about?"

"We'll get to babysit some grandstanding Congressman from stateside again. McGuire and Wheeler are in it too."

"So what? It takes us off CAPs, right? I don't mind a few rings round a flying boat if I don't have to face forty Zekes in the process." Jones hopped onto the wing and then onto the ground. "So let's just guard his honorable butt and see how easy we get to have it in between the escorts."

This was not the response Becker had expected; he remained standing there open-mouthed as Jones walked to his tent. His ground crew already had his plane under maintenance and they very politely moved Becker off from under the wing to access the hatches.

Don had an idea. "Hey guys, if we're off the roster for to-day and tomorrow, why don't we liberate a jeep and go see the sights? I've heard that the road to the village near the beach is actually possible to run with a jeep, and the few Japs on the wayside don't pose much of a problem!"

"I don't think that's a good idea, Don," Jack said. "There's way too many Japs for my liking in the jungle and if we get hit by them there'll be not much left for the next of kin to bury."

Don pouted. "You're such a spoilsport. And a wimp. And chicken. Jonesy? Becker? Come on guys, I want to see some-one wear something else besides government-issue flight gear or greasy coveralls! Like a sarong round the waist, and nothing else? Come on, I've seen 'em in National Geographic! They're all over these islands!"

Jones and Becker looked at each other, negotiating the is-sue without words. Jack had no choice but to assent to the majority vote.

Without further talk, they went each to pick up a bag with some necessary supplies, and then proceeded to the jeep depot of the base. Don dug up a sturdy staff sergeant who was in his debt from a poker game that had run deep into the night and left him with nothing in his wallet, and precious few other valuables either.

"Jorgenson! How are you, pal?"

The sergeant eyed the four flyboys. "Uh oh, Wheeler … what do you want with me now?"

"Nothing much … just a jeep with a tank of gas."

"A jeep? To drive where? To the other end of the runway? Why don't you walk?"

"Quit stalling, Jorgenson, you know full well where we want to go. Which one'll we pick? This one? No, the paint needs work. Here's a good one, and … yes, it has a tank full of gas. Hop on in, fellas!" Don climbed in with all the litheness of a weasel. Jack, Becker and Jones took up the rest of the seats.

Jorgenson wrung his hands in anguish. "Wheeler, do you really have to do this to me? If the captain runs in and wants his jeep, I'll be shot at dawn!"

Don nonchalantly waved his hand. "Tell him it was requisitioned for a special mission involving penetration behind enemy lines and reconnoitring uncharted territory." He started the engine and gave it a few good pumps of the pedal. "And quit worrying! We'll get her back to you in just a few hours. Say, five hours, give or take another five." And with that, he sped off towards the base perimeter fence and its gates.

At the gate, Don produced a paper of illegible scrawls on a piece of official letterhead. After some shouting, the bewildered guard was eventually persuaded that Don had permission to go past the perimeter to the road that led to the shore and the village.

"Man, you really got a way with words," said Becker to Don as they sped along the bumpy road that descended towards the sea.

"It's all in the brain of the listener, pal. Just sound confident, and the listener's head will do the rest for you." Don avoided a large hole in the road by turning the wheel very abruptly, almost throwing Jack off the front seat. Jack was feeling awfully stupid sitting there, being definitely and irreducibly AWOL. Jones and Becker, the two less-than-formal Marine aviators, were enjoying the scenery and their stolen freedom to the hilt. Jack told himself that since he was in for punishment in any case, he might as well enjoy earning it, and gave in to a feeling of lightness.

Don steered the jeep into the village, and asked passers-by for directions to the beach. None of the first people they met could understand a word of English, but then they ran into a Catholic priest. "Hey, Padre! Which way to the best beach in these parts?" Don asked the churchman, who seemed astonished at the question.

"Son, I've never been asked that before, but I think the best way would be down the road and then right at the river." Don tipped his cap to the elderly priest and sped off.

"You can always trust a priest to know the road to the beach," he said. Jonesy and Becker nodded approvingly. Not sure what Don's pronouncement could mean, Jack shook his head as the last twinges of guilt were flushed from his thoughts. It was not long until the palm trees gave way and the road widened to meet the beach. Don stopped the jeep while they were still within the shadow of the woods, and then he rose up to look at the view. He pushed his cap to the back of his head. "Gentlemen, I present to you the beach as God himself meant beaches to be!"

Jones, Becker and Jack admired the stretch of sand. Even though the beach on the base was by no means ugly, this was much finer. It was wider, and the sun glittered on the water, through which it was visible that the shallow water extended much further into the sea than at the base. Not a soul was to be seen here.

Jack had to agree. The beach was the finest he had seen in his life. Don parked the jeep in the bushes, took his bag and proceeded to the shoreline. Jack, Jones and Becker followed suit, and they all stripped and went to swim in the glorious water. After a long swim they each dragged themselves up to the beach and dug in their packs for cans of beer. Don opened his and took a long drink.

"I think that if you have to go to war, this is about the best way to go," he said, squinting into the horizon.

"Hear hear," said Becker, "though I do think we've paid for this pretty heavily already. Just think of all the folks we've lost from the squadron already. Here's one for them." He solemnly lifted his can of beer and had a gulp.

"Guess what, Becker? Their tickets just didn't carry them this far. They had to get off the boat at Guadalcanal, or off Santa Cruz. We're along for the ride, and there's no way to tell where your stop is. Hell, this whole war is just a giant rollercoaster—might as well enjoy the ride!"

"I don't think this is just a picnic, Don," Jack heard himself say. "It's a war against another nation, an all-out effort. It's no laughing matter."

"What, America against Japan? Just tell me what America is in the first place! Look at the squadron; we have Canucks, Polacks, Norwegians, Limeys in the pilots, and some Mexicans in the ground crews, and Lahte's even a Finn, if I remember correctly! There's no such thing as America fighting this war. It's the United Bastard Pilots of the World against Japan, lemme tell you that much! And I'm happy to have the fellows along when I fly, but if they're shot down, well, they went away. That's it. No more than that, they just left and that's it. I think we're all on the journey alone, and it's good to have someone along for the duration, but no one gets to leave here with someone else, so why bother?"

Jonesy, not generally known as a deep conversationalist, pitched in: "So you don't think there's anything beyond the world we see here, Don? Just this ocean, and the planes, and the bullets and the dogfight, and after that, goodbye? Well, though that's pretty gloomy, I must say I'll drink to that." He did so.

Becker begged to dissent. "I'm luckier than you boys. I know there's a Heaven, and with my three and a half kills of the ungodly Japs, I'm guaranteed prime real estate up there."

Jack was uncomfortable with the whole discussion. He had been raised to believe in Christ and salvation and the works, but what he had seen of the war waged in the Pacific had made him suspicious. He had seen such destruction as he could not believe possible, assuming there was a God controlling the world and its goings-on.

He realized that Don's outright atheism and Becker's straight—forward Christianity were bound to turn into a heated discussion later on if this line of discourse went forward. "Guys, what about our mission?" he asked, but got only three quizzical stares in response.

"Come on Jack, I was just getting interested!" exclaimed Don, who liked to argue his unorthodox views, especially with Christians present.

"Besides, a babysitting mission is a babysitting mission. What's there to discuss?" Becker wanted to know. Jack felt stupid. An awkward silence fell on the party.

It was broken only when Jonesy called out, "Hey, look at the strike coming home! That SBD won't get to land!" They all looked to the sky and saw eight SBD bombers approach Munda from the west, one of them far below the others, trailing smoke and seemingly hanging in the air by the sheer will of its pilot. Even as they watched, the SBD's engine quit, and the plane went into a stall, spinning into the ocean some four hundred yards from the beach. As it hit the water, it exploded, hurling debris in all directions. But after a moment, the only sounds they heard were the other SBDs landing, and the hiss of the waves on the shore.

Don pointed to the place where the plane went down.

"That goes to prove my point, boys…his ticket was punched. Nothing we could do would have helped him Or his radioman, for that matter. In fact, not anyone in this world could have helped him. May they now go from here to wherever pilots and radiomen go when they die. I hope they share a heaven, since they probably shared an awful lot of miles in that *Slow But Deadly* of theirs."

Don put his can of beer on the sand and went for another swim. Jones munched on his C-rations, deep in thought. Minutes later Don returned, still dripping.

"Maybe, boys, I'll take this opportunity and thank you for having flown with me, even saving my neck on occasion. Still, one day I'll see the bullet that bites me, and all your efforts will've been in vain. I'll just cease to exist as Don Wheeler. Further than that, I don't know, and I actually don't even care. So from now on, you can't ever say I never gave you credit for anything." Don toasted the boys.

Becker snorted. "Brother Wheeler is waxing mighty deep here."

"Yeah, Brother Becker, he is deep indeed," Jonesy said. "In fact I think he's so deep the fish would benefit from his sermon today. Don't you agree, Brother McGuire?"

"Yes, Brothers, he's deep enough. Let's deliver him to the God of the Ocean!" Jack yelled. To a man they grabbed Don, and despite his vigorous counterclaims, pitched him into the sea, into one of the big swells, under which he remained for some time before his head popped up for air.

"You bastards! Three against one! And I was just getting dry!" Don raged in mock fury, scrambling to his feet to catch Becker's waist and throw him into the swell as well. In no time the free-for-all had all four of them gasping from the exercise. After some more conventional swimming, they

188

retreated up the beach and their banter turned to more mundane matters, such as the film to be screened later in the evening at base, and as always, the leading lady in the movie.

It wasn't until the sun was casting the deepest red veil across the Western horizon that they loaded up the jeep and set course for base. Getting back onto the base was much easier than getting off it—a mere salute did the trick. Jorgenson was about as happy to see them as a puppy whose master had returned from the first day of school. He immediately set about to scrub the jeep clean so its owner would never know it had been the getaway vehicle for four AWOLs. The guilty foursome split up, but even with no words said, everyone felt good about the trip, they felt refreshed, and they knew it was moments like these that fenced away the madness.

Jack found it hard to fall asleep, though, because once again he'd tried and failed to find his place in the world. *Is it all here and now, with nothing beyond the final bullet? Or is there something waiting as you draw your parting breath?* It was already the wee hours when he ceased tossing and turning and enjoyed a restful sleep for the remainder of the night.

Jack awoke to the distant roar of the huge Pratt & Whitney R-2800 engines of their Corsair fighters being started and run warm. He remembered the day's mission and kicked Don in the butt. Don awoke, cursing the kick and the rudely-interrupted encounter with Dorothy Lamour. After breakfast of sorts they went to their planes, engines running, already serviced. Becker and Jonesy came out too, and the four of them set a simple battle plan for the mission. They were to relieve the Wildcats a half-hour away from Munda, at 1500 feet, so they decided to go in at 2500 feet and look for the party of one PBY flying boat with four Wildcats.

They took off in formation, a neat trick which required

experience. Crew chiefs and members exulted in their pilots' skill, bragging as if it were their own doing. It wasn't long before Don, leading the flight, levelled off at 2500 feet at a bearing of 165 degrees. They all throttled back and began to pay attention to the sky all around them. Below, the sea was glimmering as if a mirror were broken on its surface and the sky was reflected from each of the tiny pieces, and again for a few moments they all felt curiously detached from a brutal war.

"Let's keep them eyelids peeled, boys. If the PBY is on time, it's at twelve o'clock any minute now," Don's voice crackled in the earphones. All of them began to scan the front quarter more carefully, until Jonesy called the flight.

"PBY and Wildcats all right, one o'clock, slightly down," he said, and all four pilots saw the Wildcat escort rush up to make a positive identification of them. They liked what they saw and waggled their wings as the Corsairs took up station around the PBY, weaving above it to make sure there was no section of the sky left unscanned for the enemy to zoom in from.

"Hello PBY two eight niner, this is the Munda Marines, and you're in good hands," Don contacted the PBY pilot who acknowledged and expressed his relief at being escorted by Corsairs, whose firepower was much better than the Wildcats'.

"OK boys, let's keep Dumbo here out of harm's way. Becker, Jonesy, right side. Jack, take my left." Don had the situation under control, and after an uneventful thirty minutes of flight time, the PBY settled onto the strip at Munda like a pregnant whale. The fighters took another three rounds in the landing circuit to stay aloft until the floatplane had been relieved of its prize cargo of congressman and party.

"That wasn't so bad," said Becker to Jack when they were

walking away from their planes they'd parked in the shade of the palms. "I kinda like these trips—not that much chance of scoring but not that much chance of becoming a star on the side of a Zeke either."

Jack saw that the whole base, minus sentries and perimeter duty troops of course, was arrayed for review. Congressman Grundy was walking in front of the lines, admiring the greasy look of the crewmen and the informal pilot apparel of the flying personnel, when all of a sudden the air was pierced with the sound of an incoming Japanese projectile from outside the perimeter. The Congressman and party hit the plentiful Munda dirt faster than anyone thought possible, and indeed, no other man standing did the same, since it was evident from the sound that the projectile had little chance of hitting a target even the size of an airfield.

Slowly the esteemed visitor extracted himself from the dirt, to the chuckling of the troops, but soon another sound caused a great commotion. This time the troops recognized a true incoming shell and took cover, while the perplexed Congressman, standing, watched them. The shell exploded between two revetments nearby.

"You'll soon learn the difference between the two," Commander Wade consoled Grundy.

The rest of the day was spent with the Congressman poking his nose into every possible corner of the American-controlled part of the island. He was a general pain with his boyish enthusiasm and pointed inquisitiveness. His powerful and numerous public relations department didn't help either, as they intended to photograph the Congressman toiling away on his part of the war effort. They only failed to record the moment when the Congressman, posing as a participant in the overhaul of a Corsair's engine, turned the wrench one time too many on an oil-drain plug before the crew chief could restrain him. During the next hour the base commander was at his leisure as the Congressman was re-outfitted from his underwear up.

Meanwhile, Jack and the rest of the escort crew had a day off, which they spent lazing it up in their cots and playing cribbage. In the evening the base assembled in front of the movie screen set up between two palms at the far end of the landing strip, and the Congressman gave a too-long speech. He praised all he had seen, professed his faith in the success of the US Armed Forces in the Pacific, and tried to collect laughs recollecting his own experiences of Verdun, but the only time he got more than isolated chuckles was when he produced his true gift to the war effort, a brand new movie by M-G-M. The crowd burst into cheers as he passed the reels to the machinist, and not a moment too soon the movie was under way.

Later in the evening Congressman Grundy cornered Commander Wade at dinner. "You know, Commander, I met the Wildcat pilots and I sure want to meet the Pirate pilots."

"Corsair," was Wade's only reply, the correction whispered. He sent for Jack, who might be trusted to handle the situation with no sarcastic or otherwise embarrassing comments to the Congressman.

When Jack arrived, Grundy set out on yet another lavish monologue of praise. Jack listened with a small, shy smile, nodding every now and again as Grundy extolled the virtues of the US Military and especially its Navy and Marine pilots in the war against the Japanese. Though Jack mumbled comments every now and again, as usual, the Congressman's attention was much more on his own ideas and his performance for the benefit of the newspapermen in his entourage. Jack soon concluded there was not much point in hanging around, and he excused himself from the Congressman's company, claiming he needed the sleep before tomorrow's escort duty.

In the morning Jack, Don, Jonesy and Becker were awakened by Beep long before first light would break. In the pitch dark of the tropical night they made their way to the canteen for a cup of java they could have done without, and continued on to the flight line. Crew chiefs were already out, making sure the Corsairs were completely up to their task. One by one the engines bellowed to life, producing the gut-wrenching roar which only pilots and crewmen are permitted to like.

The four Corsairs were joined by the twin engines of the Catalina, which the Congressman had clambered aboard after profusely thanking Commander Wade for the opportunity to visit this outpost of American military might. After two final pictures of Grundy in the gangway, the door shut, and four Corsairs led the way into the air for the lumbering Catalina.

Once again Don was in command, and his team began their customary weave above the Catalina. First light had broken and the reds and oranges of the eastern horizon were magnificent. The stunning morning did not keep the escorts from scanning the skies for hostile aircraft and maintaining a light banter with the Catalina pilots. After half an hour there was still no sign of impending danger, and Don began to relax a bit.

Then he happened to glance to his seven, and for a brief few moments he saw white wakes in the sea, which came to a sudden end. There was only one possible cause: seaplanes taking off, probably Rufes, the float versions of the Japanese A6M Zero fighter.

"Bogeys, seven o'clock. Rufes. Jonesy, Becker, check 'em out. Jack, we'll cover the Catalina. Dumbo, stay tuned for more." Don's instructions were clear, calm, and concise, and Jones led Becker down to investigate.

It wasn't long before they came on the air. "Definite Rufes, eight of them, now at a thousand feet, split into two groups of four. Taking on the first four," Jack heard Jonesy say before his machine guns burst into life, flaming their first target.

Don didn't worry about the first four being engaged by Jonesy and Becker, but he was straining to see where the other four went. "Dumbo, open up and head for the deck."

"Roger," the Catalina's pilot acknowledged, and Jack saw his exhaust stacks flame up blue as throttles hit the firewall. Picking up speed, the big floatplane nosed down and began descending swiftly towards the sea.

"Splash two," said Becker on the radio. Don picked up the four remaining planes, which by now had split further into two pairs. One was straining for altitude to attack Jack and Don, but the other pair was not in sight.

"Don, let's get the two below and behind," said Jack.

"No way, we need to kill the missing pair first. Otherwise the Dumbo is dead meat," Don said, and even as he spoke he took his plane through a lazy barrel roll. "I see them!" he yelled, "right behind the Dumbo!"

The two fighters had not left the wavetops, correctly figuring the Catalina would descend to pick up speed and to avoid attack from below. Jack took a look as well and there they were, gaining on the cumbersome Catalina, trying its best to pass off as a racing plane. Even though Jack and Don simultaneously slammed their throttles they could see the Rufes had a crucial lead over them; they'd arrive at firing range before the Corsairs could hit them.

Don called Jack to tell him they only had one option. The Catalina would have to do some great evasive action and they themselves would have to hit the attackers from afar. It called for a joint action.

"Dumbo, on my three, pull up and left as hard as you can!" Don hailed the Catalina. "Jack, take the one on the left." Jack made sure his six guns were all hot. "One, two … three!" The Catalina pilot, assisted by his co-pilot, pulled in the control columns with all his might. The Rufe pilots were delighted to see the big plane help them out in reaching firing range, but the sudden movement of the Catalina threw off their aim for a second.

During that second, the two Corsairs put all their eggs in one basket and fired all their guns from almost six hundred yards. The Catalina looked like it was in pain as it went into a great turn. The Rufes tried to follow the turn, but as they finally managed to reverse their heading, they lost all interest in the Catalina, and instead decided to try to dodge the steady flow of lead from the Corsairs' wings.

They didn't make it. Even as the Catalina again reversed course to continue in the general direction of Guadalcanal, one Rufe was sheathed in flames from engine to rudder, and the second was dropping aimlessly into the sea, its pilot having been fatally hit by Jack.

Don had time to see a fifth Rufe explode in midair and the remaining three mount a retreat. "Five out! Anyone see that? Nitpick won't allow that as a kill with no confirmation!" called Becker, and the escorts again took their positions on the Dumbo.

Don went in close to see how the floatplane pilots were doing, and he got near enough to see the sweat pouring down on their faces. "How you guys doing?" he asked, getting a shaking thumbs-up as an answer.

Five minutes later, the party of five planes saw eight Wildcats approaching. As Jack listened to Don handing over escort to the Wildcats, the pilot of the Dumbo also came on and said Congressman Grundy had told him he owed every Corsair pilot one.

"Don't worry about it, it's all in a day's work," Don told the pilot. One last wag of the wings to the Guadalcanal fighters, and Don's flight turned towards Munda.

No banter came over the air during the return flight, because the pilots were all too aware of the float plane threat; eight had been here, and more could be hidden below the trees overhanging the island edges. But nothing happened, and after safely landing, the pilots proceeded straight to their debriefing by the air intelligence officer. Lieutenant Mitnick, whose last name stood no chance against the rhyming skills of the pilots, was happy to hear of the fate of the five Rufes; he also could relay that Guadalcanal had radioed to him news of Congressman Grundy. Apparently he had been taking a sip from a canteen when the pilots did their sudden pull-up.

"So, what will you do with the favor you have up your sleeve from the good Congressman?" Becker asked Don over another cup of java that might as well have not been drunk.

"You know, Becker, the three least valuable possessions I have are the altitude above me, the fuel I left back at base, and a Congressman's thanks without an attached pay hike. You're welcome to my favor as well if you can find some use for it." Don took another sip and frowned.

"Hello boys—glad to see you again, " Commander Wade said as he sat down. "You must now think I am a sorcerer with my ability to tell when trouble looms up ahead." The four pilots all agreed it had been a good move to send out the four-plane patrol to guard the Catalina. "But here's another piece of free advice: don't ever look down your nose at a Congressman. They may yet help you out. You're back on the strike roster now, boys, there's one up your street tomorrow. Good work!"

With that, Commander Wade went his way. The pilots shot the breeze for a few more moments before retiring to their bunks. Jack experienced the unfamiliar feeling of being a professional, like a painter or carpenter, who had put in a full day's worth of his trade.

14

The month of November 1943 was a bad one for VMF-288. In the span of three weeks, the squadron lost five pilots in exchange for only three enemy planes. In addition to ferocious air battles, anti-aircraft fire was proving deadly accurate above the Japanese bases under attack. Strafing the barges the enemy was using for transport was also dangerous and many pilots were lost in these attacks.

When these factors were combined with nightly nuisance raids by Japanese twin-engine bombers, which rarely caused casualties but deprived the base of sleep, squadron morale began to falter. Don was the first to approach Bunny Radner on the issue.

He joined Bunny on his way from morning chow. "You know, Bunny, we got a problem. The new kids on the team aren't doing too well. They don't see us winning the day, let alone the war, and they think the Japs are too good for us to beat. One of them even wanted out of 288 and into some other gang with less responsibility and easier targets. I told him I'd sign his transfer request any day, but if he backed out now, he'd miss out on a feast later when our luck turns again. He stays for now, but that's the kind of sentiment in the air." Don scowled.

Bunny nodded. "Yeah, it's a real problem. Losing five for three is unsustainable, and none of the new guys have hit any enemy planes. I've been thinking what to do to make it better for them, but the only idea I've come up with so far is to increase gunnery training."

Don shook his head. "Naah. They've practiced enough. It's between the ears—I've talked with them and I know."

"I take it you got a solution I don't see yet. Let's have it."

"One word: luau."

"*Luau?* You finally gone crazy?"

Don smiled. "Listen for a sec. What we need is a wake. We got to send off the dead guys and start looking forward. It won't hurt a bit to get the new guys bashed out of their skulls in the process, either. Think about it: we'll stack up on beer, go pigsticking for a few porkies, and roast 'em up. All we need is for the weather to close in for a couple days so we can safely numb the brains of our kids."

Bunny thought for a second. "Right. Have you seen how the locals send out a squad of their warriors and a couple hours later they carry in three pigs and four of the hunters? The hogs they got out here aren't your local farm piglets. They got to weigh in at four hundred pounds."

Though the words were cautious, Don knew he had Bunny now. "We'll speak softly and carry enough firepower."

"Okay, but what about beer? We don't have a stock. We'll have to ration it for a while and build a party stash."

"Listen, Bunny, let me worry about the drinks. Let's just say I have some friends in the business."

Bunny raised an eyebrow. "I'm sure I don't want to hear it all, but we can give it a try. We can always train more kids later if your plan goes down the tubes. Let's keep this under wraps though ... it's not really by the book to boost morale by getting drunk."

Don saluted and went his way. "OK, Skipper, you're in for the party of your life!" He bounced off, leaving Bunny to wonder whether he'd called it right.

The first person Don needed to find was Jack, who conveniently happened to be having a haircut at the canteen. "Drop everything, Ace, I got work for you."

As Jack was already done, he paid up and left, with misgivings, with Don. They made their way to one of the empty revetments where they could talk undisturbed.

"So what's the action?" Jack asked.

Don looked around slyly. "Bunny wants us to throw a party to get the morale up."

"Does he now?"

"Yeah, so I planted the idea in his head. That's not important right now. What *is* important is that as you remember, the torpedo squadron left the island a few days ago."

"And?"

Don explained with a schoolmaster's patience: "And, the torpeckers are out there somewhere in the Pacific Ocean. We know they're no longer here, they know they're no longer here, but the transport ship captain in the harbor doesn't know they left. He unloaded fuel for 250 torpedoes this morning because that's how it was written in his orders. That's two-hundred-and-fifty jerry cans, some sort of backup fuel dump, I guess. The harbormaster almost bent the captain's teeth when he heard it. The captain wouldn't believe there's no torpedo planes on the base any more, and didn't want to load the cans back on his ship to be taken to some needy torpecker squadron on some other base." He pointed towards the sea. "See that ship out there? That's him, bound for Fiji— he didn't want to tool around till someone found him a new destination to deliver the goods to."

Jack shrugged, but said the story sounded good so far.

"Here's the punchline: when the harbormaster was left

with the 250 orphaned jerry cans of fuel, he made a beeline for the Old Fud and spilled the beans. Wade told Beep Coleman to radio Fiji to report the cans. He did so, and they'll pack the juice on a transport plane that's passing our way today. Beep didn't tell the commander about the reply just yet. We have to act real fast if we want to liberate some!"

Jack held up his hands. "Whoa, Don, you just lost me there. Why the hell would you want torpedo fuel?"

Don smiled. "This is proof positive you slept in class. Don't you remember what torpedoes use for fuel? Thirty-three pints of 200-proof alcohol."

"Aha." Jack whistled through his teeth. "The missing link."

"Right. With the torpeckers and their storekeeping people off the island, the harbormaster was left in charge of the goods, and he hates it. He wants to get rid of the cans in expedited protocol. All we need is one jerry can, on loan just for the time it takes to unload the contents to some medical containers being arranged by Doc Mendel."

Jack was baffled. "So have you mobilized half the base for this op? What does Bunny think of siphoning five gallons of 200-proof?"

"Aw, he's just fine about it. But now we got to act fast."

Jack thought for a moment. "So you'll refill the can with some other liquid, like water? The torpedo that gets fueled up with water won't run worth a damn."

Don shrugged. "Well, if you listen to the torpecker brothers, none of their fish work anyway. And I bet you they take a swig now and then of the stuff they fill 'em up with, so they'll find out soon enough."

"Fair enough. Just one more thing: how did you get the word on this?"

Don smiled. "Beep Coleman listened in a bit when the

harbormaster stormed the premises. He told me, and here we go. Are you in or what?"

Jack shrugged. "Sounds like fun so count me in."

"Thought so. Beep is sitting on the message that seals the fate of the cans. He has to tell Wade and the harbormaster about the transport plane in an hour at the latest."

"So how do we pull this off, then?"

Don started drawing in the sand. "Beep told me the harbormaster stashed the goods in the central warehouse in the harbor. He then drafted two young Marines who happened to walk by and set them to the task of not letting anyone in the warehouse. One's guarding the door and the other's walking around the building. The harbormaster also said that should anything happen to the cans, he'd personally execute both of 'em."

"And how do we get to do the lifting if there's a guard and probably a lock on the door?"

Don drew a square in the sand. "I did a quick recon mission after Beep alerted me. It so happens the door is indeed locked, and there are two meek-looking junior Marines on guard. However, the back wall has a couple of loose boards, so after checking the door lock from a distance, I followed the walking sentry and scanned the back side. I pried open a crack in the wall and had a peek. The cans are laid out in ten rows of twenty-five on the floor of the warehouse. They don't stack that well, and I think they're laid out like that just so you can see at a glance that they're all home. I mean, the harbormaster's no fool: the island *is* full of would-be party people. It's almost completely dark in the warehouse but it's still easy enough to count the cans. Or to see one is missing at a glance."

"So what you're saying is that we have to swipe one, get

the contents, and replace the can before they do a nose count on them?"

"Egg-sactly, Jack my boy!" Don stood up, touched his forehead with his index finger, and gave Jack a whack on the shoulder. "And just in case the harbormaster gets itchy, we just so happen to have a spare can of the right size, but wrong color, unfortunately, to suggest the missing lamb while we get the juice. We can't just leave it there with the others because of the color. I found that my crew chief had pinched one can off the torpeckers for some obscure reason—may have been just the thrill of doing it, for they have to account for every can. Though it was empty, it served as a pretty good trophy just as well—hell, he lost a Corsair propeller blade in return to the torpecker team one night." He grinned. "Anyway, it wouldn't pass in daylight, but in a dark warehouse it'll fool them long enough for us to return the real McCoy."

"I guess you have a plan for getting the guards off guard," Jack said, already knew what Don would say.

"Sure I do. All I need is this nice stack of less-than-decent gals and the kids will be in the palm of my hand while you go in the warehouse, pinch the can, leave the decoy there, run off to Doc Mendel, and return with the empty can. Or wait— let's make it so that you fill it up to some capacity so that it weighs about the same. Doc'll know what to do. Any questions?" He didn't wait for an answer. "Okay, let's roll."

They made their way to the harbor. As expected, the central warehouse was indeed locked, with a guard at the door and another walking around it slowly.

"That's the target," Don whispered. "The decoy can is in that bush over there. I'll go to the kids now and get them interested in this deck of cards. Then you can go and do your switch with the can."

"Okay, go for it!"

Don sauntered over to the young Marine sitting on the door, a Thompson submachine gun with drum magazine lying across his lap. With eyes closed he was probably dreaming of the Untouchables with the classic weapon at his disposal, but scrambled to his feet and made an attempt at saluting when Don approached him.

"Man, it's sure hot today, ain't it?" Don took off his cap and with an Oscar-winning performance wiped his exhausted brow.

"Lieutenant, please clear out from the vicinity of the warehouse. You aren't allowed here by order of the harbormaster." The Marine held his Tommy out.

"Whoa, pal, what's that all about?" Don made as if he was trying to look around the kid. "Whaddya got in there, state secrets?"

"I'm not allowed to tell you. Please leave, so there's no hassle."

The other Marine completed his round and joined them at the door. "What's the trouble here?"

"Come on, fellas, I'm harmless. Hey, have a smoke." Don pushed out an open pack of Camels. "It can't be so bad that you can't take a break for a refreshing smoke." The guards hesitated, but accepted the cigarettes and lit up.

Meanwhile, Jack slipped into the bushes and found the can.

"When are you guys due for leave?" Don asked them, all innocence.

"We have R&R coming up in just eight weeks. We're going to Sydney."

"Is that so? Wow—you two are sure lucky devils. Sydney's nice. The girls're especially nice. Either of you ever been there before?" The guards shook their heads.

Behind the diversion, Jack made his way to the back of the warehouse, behind which there was nothing but a few empty crates before the bushes. He inspected the boards until he found two loose ones, just as Don had said. He pried them until he was able to push the can inside, but trying to get through the small slot was a lot harder. When he pulled the board, a nail shot out of the wood making a sharp cracking noise.

"What was that?" One of the guards started to look around.

"Come on, someone probably was just cleaning his rifle out there and shot one off by accident. Nothing to it. As I was just telling you, Sydney gals're great. In fact, I just happen to have some pictures of 'em right here—"

Don pulled out the stack, but frowned. "Or *are* you interested to see what you're going to find there? You guys look awful young to me. You ever been on leave anywhere but around the soda pop machine at the corner store back in Yodelville, Kansas?" The Marines, oblivious to the fact that they'd abandoned their task altogether, again shook their heads, though reddening this time.

Don added steam to the engine. "Man, oh man ... you kiddos ever even *seen* a naked lady? I just ask so I don't shock you with these, they're pretty hard stuff—leave nothing to the imagination. Second thoughts, maybe I'll just let you alone to guard the warehouse. See ya fellas later." Don began to walk away.

The Marines almost begged him to return and to show the stack to them. Checking around like a true black-market shark, Don came back. He gave them half a stack each, and after casting furtive glances around them, the young Marines learned an awful lot about female anatomy as they flipped through the cards.

By now Jack was inside the warehouse, and he placed his can in the spot of one can in the last row. Then he reconsidered and placed the decoy can as the second can from the second row. This left only the top of the can visible, making its detection even more difficult. Getting out from the hole in the wall was easier than getting in, and after rearranging the boards, he left the warehouse and walked speedily to the road leading up from the harbor. He signaled Don to let him know he had the goods.

When Don saw him waving, he bid a hasty retreat from the guards, pulling the stacks from their greedy hands. He also reminded them they should do some guarding too, lest the harbormaster have their asses for breakfast. Chastened, they resumed their duties, blissfully ignorant of the visit paid to the cans.

"Piece of cake, right?" Don asked Jack when they met back up.

"Easy enough—now, let's get the rest of the plan going too. I'm not too comfy running around with this baby."

"Don't fret, chum. We'll go and see Doc Mendel right now." At the sick bay, Doc Mendel left the final stitches he was applying to a flesh wound for a medic to complete.

"So, you have the goods?" he asked Don and Jack.

"Yes sirree, right here. Let's … um … fill up the medical stores, shall we?"

Taking the jerry can, Doc Mendel left for his store, coming back a few moments later with the can weighing about the same as it had before.

"Thank you kindly, gentlemen, I was running a bit low already. I trust you can dispose of this properly?"

Don took the can. "Yes, sir, we will make this right."

Once out of the sick bay, Don peered at the can Doc had given them. "Look, he even made the seal look like it's still unbroken—the crafty bastard!"

They half-ran back to the harbor, where Don returned to the Marines for part two of the diversion. On sighting Don they stopped their rounds right away, and as Jack returned the can to its proper place and removed the decoy, Don made five dollars from selling the stack of pictures to the young Marines. "Nice going, eh? We have five gallons of 200-proof and five bucks on the side!"

"Yeah, not bad at all. So what do we do now?"

"We sit tight and wait for the right moment. We have to hear from the weather boys that the flying weather will close in for at least forty-eight hours—then we go and kill some pigs, roast 'em, and make punch out of the load we have here. I've also secured a supply of beer for those unfortunate bastards who can't drink hard liquor."

Jack smiled. "I'm sure this breaks every rule in the book, but I'm still on board with the idea."

"Of course you are. It was my idea and I never have bad ones." In the distance Don saw Beep Coleman, looking very distressed. He signaled with his hands and Coleman shot off towards the base commander's hut. Now that the jig was in, he could go and tell the commander and the harbormaster there was a plane coming in for the torpedo juice.

The weather stayed agonizingly good for the next four days, and the flights went just about as bad as before. On the fifth day, though, the weather service reported a massive weather front coming in which would cancel all flight operations for at least forty-eight hours. Silently rejoicing, the conspirators finally publicized the luau, which was greeted with enthusiasm. Arrangements were made for an entertaining program. The country boys of the squadron were tasked with finding a few wild pigs for the kitchen to prepare for roasting, and departed into the nearby bush armed to the teeth. They returned five hours later carrying three massive and very dead pigs in triumph to the base, with no human casualties.

The squadron chorus had rehearsed five new songs. A few theatrically-oriented individuals, from both ground crew and pilots, came up with a new interpretation of a classical tragedy in two acts, and if their three previous presentations were any indication, it promised to be hilarious.

The party started at six in the evening in a slow drifting rain. A huge drum of fruit punch greeted the participants at the side of a grill system of four oil barrels sawed in two longitudinally. Generous chunks of marinated pork sizzled on top of the grills, wafting mouth-watering scents to the passers-by. More barrels had been converted to function as coolers filled with crushed ice and cans of brew, placed in strategic locations around the grounds. The entire party area had been made effectively rain-free by ingenious use of tarps and ropes, and all those present were able to enjoy the food and drink as well as the program in relative comfort.

Don made his rounds among the party crowd. He was sure that as people got enough alcohol in their systems, tempers would start to flare, and the men would start yelling at one another. He prodded the party, listening in on the conversations until he found a knot of several new pilots on the brink of a fistfight. He sat down on a palm trunk and studied the pilots to see if these men would work as his target audience.

After ten minutes he felt ready to barge in. The young pilots had worked themselves down into a defeatist mood and were thinking of ways of getting the million-dollar-wound, a non-fatal injury which guaranteed exit from combat but would heal completely in time.

Jumping up, Don stretched and entered the circle.

"Look, guys, you're forgetting something important here. Million Dollar Wounds sure are nice, assuming you can get the Japs to do it properly, but you got to remember this one thing: Not one of you was forced to take flight training. No one was dragged kicking and screaming through Pre-flight, Primary, Basic, and you didn't bribe anyone to let you skip Advanced. In fact, *all* of you competed to take part in this and get here—now live with it!"

He took a slight pause for effect, letting his words sink into the soaked brains of the pilots. "You just can't be a little bit pregnant, and you just can't be a part-time fighter jock."

The juniors sized him up with their eyes but let him continue, since he was widely acknowledged as one of the true stars of the squadron.

More people joined the discussion, but mostly they let Don speak. Some offered their support, others challenged him, but gradually it became his monologue. Only expressions on faces, visible in the flickering yellow light of torches and lanterns, betrayed the feelings of the participants.

"I guarantee it," Don said, "out of us fifty-odd pilots, maybe five more will die in two weeks. In the next month or so, maybe eight more will die. A couple will crash but live. Some will be hit, some will burn. One may get the silver-lined Million Dollar Wound in the ass. That's not important. What *is* important is that out there beyond the horizon there's a carrier with replacement pilots, ready to take on whatever Japs are left after you go through them. But if we don't do the job, it'll be *their* carrier, not ours, sailing under the Golden Gate. Your call."

By this time, the general murmur of the rest of the party had all but petered out. People were gathering around the little circle of pilots Don was addressing.

Jack, watching from a bit further away, suddenly thought that the concentration of people around the small but vocal discussion looked like a tornado brewing. As if on cue, the rain began to intensify, and the sound of the heavy drops on the leaves of the bushes became louder. Don raised his voice to match the noise level.

"So we lost five for three. Too bad. That's just the way it happened, and the guys we no longer have among us are gone for good. They met the bullets which had their names on 'em, and that's it—doesn't make any difference at all to them what we do or say here. Besides, all of us, I mean one-hundred-goddam-prrrrrcent of us, will wind up dead one day. So what difference can it possibly make how it happened? There's but one guy in all of history who didn't buy the farm. No, wait—he did buy one, but he got refunded a couple days later."

Though a few like-minded pilots chuckled at the joke, this did it. One of the newer pilots threw his metal cup down on the ground in anger. It hit a stone and clunk-bounced loud as he shook his fist at Don. "It's fruitcakes like you who'll get us all killed flying out here! I've had enough!" He stormed out towards the tents, followed by a second, then a third. Don watched them leave, then watched the remaining men. He could see in their eyes the balancing act they were doing in their heads.

Then, Don shouted to the backs of the men leaving. "Guys! Hey, guys, before you go, think on this: that Death, he's a persistent bugger. You can try and run away from him, you can even try to fool him. That's what you'd be doing, running and fooling, if you went off and got posted to fly

CAP over Chicago. I'll sign your transfers with no problem whatsoever. But over here, you can really do the only thing with Death which matters: looking him in the eye. Scythe and cape and skull and empty eye sockets and all. You look him in the eye, or the socket at least, like in a staring contest back at school, remember? And that, my friends, is what we do here. You can look him in the eye later too if you wish, but one day, he'll be there to stare you down. Prepare yourself."

The men who'd challenged him left, one by one, but the majority stuck around to see what would happen. As his last trick, to breach the awful, dead silence, Don began to whistle the chorus of the squadron song *Check your six!*

Everyone in the squadron knew the song. Easy enough to be sung by absolutely anyone, no matter how tone deaf, its verses were numerous and ever-increasing in number. Eleven verses had become more or less canonical and thus known to all, and some twenty more apocryphal ones could be heard at times. Each verse dealt with the benefits of looking behind once more before committing oneself to any act. In the original song these ranged from stealing apples to kissing the quarterback's girlfriend, with many lewd or just plain stupid variations found in the evolving collection of verses, but the chorus was always the same:

Check your six, check your six, there ain't no better way,
If you wanna lead a healthy life and fight another day
'Cos there's always one more enemy comin' down from out of the sun
So check your six, do your tricks,
And be prepared to run!

211

Don was sweating as he whistled. Though he had the party just where he'd wanted it, the morale situation was far worse than he'd thought. Everyone just looked around, trying to see how the others were taking all this before committing themselves. The only sound was the lonely whistle of some nocturnal bird in the jungle.

Don went into the chorus a second time, and then a third, very slowly. Jack, Bunny, Jonesy, Becker and all the old-timer pilots held their breath, hoping for the juniors to take the cue. Finally one of the juniors began to hum the song and then, apparently deciding that Don was right in his pep talk, started singing. Now that the ice had been broken, one by one the squadron pilots picked up the song, and by the time the eleventh verse rolled around, the sound could be heard all over the base. Don walked around with a bucket of punch, replenishing cups left and right. More food was made available and consumed, and the party atmosphere brightened back up.

By the time even the most earnest party people had either left for their cots or lay passed out in the party tents, Jack sought out Don. "Don, I think what you did was top-notch stuff, and the kids really needed to hear it, but I really think you could have left Jesus out of it. The point was already made."

Don agreed. "Yeah, I know. I shouldn't pick on him. He's done a lot of good to a big bunch of people. It's just that I've been there, done that, and I never saw the guy."

Jack thought a second. "Maybe you didn't die well enough back then." He left Don fumbling for a snappy answer and retired to his cot. Later, he would come to remember it as the only time he ever got the last word over Don.

Early in the next morning, Don was roused by an insistent messenger, Beep Coleman. "Lieutenant Wheeler, sir, please wake up. You've got a briefing in fifteen minutes." Beep flashed his light into Don's eyes, which drove the pilot's aching head under the pillow.

Don mumbled, "Beep, you're a nagging bastard, and you're wrong about the day. There's no flying before the day after tomorrow, the weather boys said so."

"Sorry to say, but there is. The weather's clearing up." Beep looked around the hut, seeing half-dressed, still-drunken pilots everywhere.

Don attempted to get accustomed to the light but was not able to open his eyes. "No way. It was raining last night, remember? Now get out of here and let me sleep. Go find Noah, that's how much it rained. He'll help you out."

"Sir, it's like this: They have a submarine outside Rabaul, and they said they can see loads of stars in the sky and loads of Japanese ships on the surface, all pouring into Rabaul. MacArthur is sending everyone but the Marx Brothers up there. I have to find seven other semi-sober pilots, or pilots who can fly okay drunk, because Commander Wade already promised eight Corsairs from 288 to go and strafe the Rabaul fields in front of the B-25 bombers which are now in the air from Port Moresby. There's sixteen other Corsairs from other squadrons and the Navy'll put up sixteen Hellcats. You have to be in the air in an hour, if you're gonna meet the heavies before they turn back home already. So please get up and help me find the rest."

"Okay." Don clambered to his feet. "Go get Jack. He can fly drunk just as well as I can. Jonesy and Becker. That's four. Can Bunny fly on this one? It's his squadron."

"I think he's already at the command post. That leaves three."

Don considered. "Find Stoney Stokes. He's the only teetotaller on the island."

Beep sorted through the snoring bodies of pilots in the tent, which added up to five pilots. "High as a kite … skunk drunk … this one can't remember he has legs." Don dressed and went to the door, where he was met by two junior pilots of the squadron.

"Lieutenant, sir, we'd like to join the strike, if we can."

Don recognized one of them, a skinny college kid from New York who had been doubtful of his talent as a fighter pilot all along.

He looked each of them in the eyes. "Fellas, I have to tell you this: there probably ain't a worse place to be right now than Rabaul. Are you sure you're up to this?"

The taller of the two nodded. "Yes, sir. We talked at the party last night and thought this is what we're here to do. We have to fight 'em and fight we will, if you'll let us."

"That's the spirit." Don hid a smile. "One of you will fly with Bunny Radner and one with Stoney Stokes. That way all you have to do is to stick with your section leader and do as you're told. See you at the briefing." The pilots took off to get their gear.

"How'd you like that, Beep? The party's working already," Don said. Beep smiled and went to find Stokes.

At the briefing at 0400, while the rain was still pouring, Lieutenant Mitnick was already posting notes on a large map of the area when the VMF-288 pilots joined him. There were also sixteen other pilots from two other Marine squadrons. Mitnick greeted all of them grimly, waiting for the chitchat to fade before he started. He went to the map and pointed at Rabaul, the main base of the Japanese Empire in these parts.

"Gentlemen, we have to go here once more. We got a submarine monitoring the St George Channel, and he says there's ships aplenty going into Rabaul, many separate convoys, lots of ships, both cargo and warships. The B-25 groups in Port Moresby are already airborne with everything that has wings and can lug a bomb. They have trouble getting enough protection from their own P-38s, which is why we've been tasked with helping them out. The rain we have here will end soon, since the sub can see no clouds and the wind is from the northwest. In any case, we'll fly out due west until out of the rain and then north to meet the bombers. Here's the battle plan."

He pointed back to the map. "All B-25s will go for the main anchorage in Simpson Harbor. Our task is to strafe Lakunai, Tobera, and Vunakanau airfields to get as many defending aircraft down as possible before the heavies roll in to bomb at low level. The Navy Hellcats will be top cover, and we'll fly at 9,000 feet before descending to strafe."

Don put up his hand. "Hey, Nitpick, can't you make it angels ten?"

"Why's that?" Mitnick asked.

"We want to go on oxygen so we can stay awake."

Mitnick smiled. "See if I care if you suck up all your oxygen. Fly at 9,000 and go on oxygen anyway. That's where the bombers are too. You won't need the oxygen for height on this one."

Jack found it hard to concentrate. The alcohol in his system was still numbing his thinking. He tried to focus and scanned the faces of the pilots. Some were calm and professional, like builders reviewing the plans of the house they'd build. Others tried to conceal their fear by smoking, but the jerky movements of their hands when they struck a match betrayed them. Yet others discussed the upcoming mission in subdued voices, shaking their heads and letting the clenched jaw display their apprehension.

It occurred to Jack what a lottery it all was. With the millions of bullets and cannon shells they'd be facing, planes would be hit. Some pilots would be killed; others would be incapacitated and destined to crash into the Pacific in their stricken steeds. One or two might escape the bullets themselves, but the planes would be damaged badly enough to force a crash-landing in the sea or on the Japanese-held islands.

And there was simply nothing he could do about it except hope for the best for himself, Don and Bunny, and for all his squadronmates. He would be having that void feeling again upon landing, seeing crew chiefs sitting around and waiting in the empty revetments of planes which would never return. Jack had come to hate that period between a strike returning to base and the ultimate deadline of fuel depletion passing— when they finally counted the noses.

Then he realized his own plane's revetment might be vacant after this mission, and he shivered. The only way to dismiss the thought of a random death roulette was to focus on what the Intelligence Officer was saying. Jack just shook himself awake a bit too late—all the important information had already been passed on to the pilots.

"...any questions? Okay. See you at the strip in thirty minutes."

The pilots picked up their gear and formed small huddles to discuss their own plans. Jack and Don went to Bunny, where the new guys were already talking with him.

Bunny was telling the young pilots how he appreciated their effort and guts in joining the operation, but didn't pull any punches. "This will be your worst strike yet, fellas. There's a lot we have to do, first navigate out of this pea soup into the clear on instruments, then meet with the heavies, get in front of them, strafe a busy airfield, and then fight any Zekes who show up at the assembly area. You'll do just fine, long as you remember what we taught you here. Stay close. Avoid any unnecessary moves. Save fuel until in combat, make sure you stick with your section leader. You, Tanner, will fly with me. Smith is with Stokes. Questions? Let's go then."

In the predawn darkness the sound of the engines starting up was even more impressive than it was in daylight. Birds fled from bushes as twenty-four Corsairs started up, to be followed by sixteen Navy Hellcats. Pilots turned on their navigation lights to assist in the difficult task of flying out of the weather front, and then, at the appointed moment, Bunny Radner and 2nd Lieutenant Tanner led the way down the runway and took off into the darkness.

Jack was flying on Don's wing, and to make his headache go away, he sucked greedily on the sweet-tasting pure oxygen. It made him feel nearly normal, dissipated his headache, and even though he still had alcohol in his blood, it didn't seem to hinder his thought or movement. As Don opened up and blazed down the runway, Jack followed him neatly to the right and slightly behind him. The troublesome weather made them fly a bit further apart than they usually did, but Jack was able to follow Don's navigation lights. After only ten minutes of flight, at about ten thousand feet, they popped out of the cloud and joined up into a flight. Bunny set course for the base at Bougainville.

The landing and topping-up at Bougainville took only fifteen minutes. They took off again and this time charged their guns and test-fired each of them. Exactly one hour later Jack could hear Tanner's excited call on his radio: "Bombers at 11 o'clock!"

Bunny congratulated him on his eyesight and told the group, "Okay, folks, this is it. Let's pass by the bombers to show them we're here for them, and then I'll lead you on to Tobera. All of you—let's not risk anything this time. One pass. If you can see planes, fine, if not, strafe the buildings or anything else worth your shots. Don't waste ammo. We'll need it at the assembly area."

Jack's mouth felt flannel-lined once again. He settled to his seat a bit lower and checked all his equipment once more. The lumbering bombers waggled their wings in acknowledgement as the Corsairs zoomed over them, turning slightly north as they went. Bunny signaled for more speed, and also started a slow descent. Soon they were above the New Ireland coastline, coursing at a speed of 300 knots, guns armed. As soon as the Tobera airfield was in sight, Bunny turned slightly south to align them with the runway. There was much activity on the field: planes were started, tankers were getting away from the planes, and field personnel busily prepared planes for flight. Don, Jack, Jonesy, and Becker slowed slightly to form a second wave behind and to the right of Bunny's division.

Lowering his plane's nose, Bunny yelled, "At 'em!"

All eight planes spouted lead from their six machine guns. Bunny's division, going on the left side of the strip, spotted more targets than they had time to hit, but the four of them did manage to cause damage. Planes burst into flame. Armorers jumped off wings and tried to run for cover, only to be caught in a fireball from an exploding tanker. Tanner, the other young pilot, managed to concentrate on flaming a Betty bomber, while Smith let out short bursts at three separate Zekes parked on the side of the runway.

Jack saw that there were four Zekes about to take off at the far end of the runway. "Get those Zekes down there!" he yelled, and all three of his division mates responded. They ceased strafing the ground, pulled up, and focused on the Zekes. If they didn't split right now, the experienced Americans would pick them off. They failed to split, and each of the chasers poured bullets into the Zeke in front of them. Two exploded; one shed a wing and spiraled to the ground, and only the one in front of Becker evaded bullets. The Marines were still going very fast, and they were away from the field in an instant, using their speed to collect altitude and climb away from any eventual followers. At seven thousand feet, they relieved the tension by wild whoops into the radio, comparing what they saw happening.

"Good work, boys!" Bunny commented as he led them away and around Rabaul to the assembly area.

The new pilots were exuberant with their achievements. Bunny had to cool them down. "Boys, don't let go now. The deep end of the pool is round that mountain—that's where the Zekes will get real mad with us." He led his flight round Cape Tavui. They could see that despite the strafing attacks, the Japanese had managed to get many fighters airborne, and they were busy engaging the bombers.

"Pour on the coal!" Bunny yelled over the radio and they all started to accelerate to top speed, picking targets at the same time. There was a B-25 nearby whose starboard engine was smoking, its propeller having been feathered. Its pilot was working hard trying to reach the relative safety of other bombers, but it had been targeted by three Zekes which were taking turns shooting at it. The gunner who'd had a chance of shooting back was dead already, and the bomber was defenseless.

Bunny came on the radio. "Don, get up and get that bomber safe with your division. My division, follow me to the left to those two bombers. Now *split!*"

Don pulled up with his three planes to allow Bunny to pass under him. Even the greenhorns flew like old hands when they covered their section leaders into the engagement with five Zekes. They seemed surprised by the attack, aborted their pursuit and turned towards the incoming Corsairs.

In a display of marksmanship, both Bunny Radner and Stoney Stokes fired at and hit Zekes rushing at them with a combined speed of more than 500 knots. Their wingmen observed both Japanese planes plunging into the sea, burning. Tanner received a cannon shell through his wingtip, but it did only superficial damage. Bunny and Stoney were already pulling up to gain altitude for a new attack. As ordered, the junior pilots made sure they stayed put on their leaders' wings as if glued there.

Don directed Jonesy and Becker to attack the nearest of three Zekes while he and Jack floated apart to get at the pair of Zekes making a pass at the stricken bomber. It was not the first time they'd let their section come loose; they knew they could trust each other to follow the situation and come to help in need. The Japanese pilots had become too fixed on their target. Neither of them saw the Americans before they were in range to fire, and they wouldn't miss a shot at a target which didn't even attempt to evade. Jack hit the tail of one Zeke, which tore loose. The pilot stood up in the cockpit and managed to get out of it before the plane spun down out of control. Jack registered the pilot's parachute opening when he zoomed past the enemy plane.

Don hit his quarry directly in the wing tank and the plane became a fireball through which he had to fly. Oil and debris rained on his plane, nicking his propeller. He had to decrease throttle to keep vibration to acceptable levels. He approached Jack, patted the top of his head to pass the lead off to him, and settled on his wing.

After five more minutes, the bombers were all assembled into defensive formation. Two of them were smoking, but were apparently managing to stay with the group. The Marines and Navy Hellcats stayed with them for some time, making sure all Japanese planes were off their tails and returning to Rabaul. Then the fighters departed for Munda.

The trip back was uneventful and all fighters landed in short order. The new pilots were bursting with pride and joy over the successful strike, and they rushed to Bunny's plane as it rolled to a stop.

Bunny hopped out of his plane and grabbed the two lieutenants by the shoulders. "Atta boys! Well done!" he said, and the youngsters gloated as he pounded their backs. "Now go ye forth and spread the good word. The Japanese are not invincible, and now you know it. Make sure you tell everyone what happened, and frankly, I don't give a damn if you spruce it up a bit—you did well out there just now!"

Buoyed, the pilots bounced off in the direction of the mess. Their crew chiefs went to work patching up the Corsairs, which were in surprisingly good shape considering the amount of ordnance they had encountered in the air. The only major rework needed was Don's propeller, which was badly out of shape and had to be replaced.

Bunny wiped sweat off his brow. "I got to hand it to you, Wheeler. You were spot on with that party idea. They had excess steam and now that it's out, they can handle the grind again. Just one thing: next time you get ideas like that, tell me beforehand, so I can stock up on aspirin."

Don grinned and slapped Bunny on the shoulder. "Sure thing—can we get some sleep now? Nitpick can debrief us later, right?" Bunny sent them on their way with his blessing.

Jack and Don stopped in the canteen for some java and then walked slowly to their tent.

"Man, I'm beat," Jack said, "but I don't think I can sleep. I'll go and write some letters. Great work out there, pal."

Don smiled. "All in a day's work, McGuire. See you later."

Later that day, Jack was mildly amused to see the following young Tanner and Smith had assembled. They were once again re-telling how it all happened, swinging their hands in the air in wide arcs, their thankful and rapt audience never tiring of the story. Jack just hoped the attitude would last.

15

As if in a waking dream, Jack stood at last outside Kay's apartment house on Joy Street in Boston. Five months had passed since she'd left Tulagi to go home, and Jack had never written so many letters in such a short span of time. He wasn't alone in the loop; more or less every time, the mail boat had something from Kay for him. He'd snatch the letter from the mail-boat driver, drop whatever he was working on, and rush to his solitary spot on the top of a hill with a view to the sea.

Jack read each letter many times over, imagining Kay sitting at the porch of his lodge talking to him about the things in the letters. For the first weeks he could easily conjure up her sweet, tingling voice, and even catch a whiff of her flowery perfume, but as time went by, it became increasingly and painfully harder to do so. He did have the stack of pictures she sent right after her visit, but he didn't look at them for fear of seeing shadows.

The change in him was gradual, but unmistakably powerful. At sunrise or sunset he'd stop to admire the view on the beach and turn to share it with her, and then would remember with a shiver that he was alone. In the night he'd lie awake and walk the paths of Halavo with her in his mind, and once more feel desolate and stranded.

Jack fought having to confess to himself just how much he missed her, until he had no choice but to take the long trip Stateside. He wondered long and hard how to put the case to

Martin. He couldn't just say straight out, "I miss Kay so much, I got to go and see her again, or the rest of my life will be hell." Could he, now? One day, as they were working on the engine of the Kingfisher, he thought he'd hit on a good excuse.

"It's a good thing to get the gearbox in shape. By the way, I think we need new gauges for the instrument panel, too. I didn't think the altimeter would start acting up, but only last week, I was at 10,000 feet, and all of a sudden it read 3,000. Then it jumped to 12,000 and when I landed it was still at 3,000. And the compass was stuck the other day. Too bad I didn't buy spare gauges then at the Navy Yard, 'cause now it's kind of hard to get them. I don't think they have a mail-order service. Maybe I should pop over to San Francisco and get some, eh?"

At the conclusion of this hasty monologue, Martin stared at him a full count, then laughed so hard that he almost fell off the wing of the Kingfisher.

Jack started to backtrack on his travel plan right away, worrying about the expenses: "Naaah, never mind. It'd cost me an arm and a leg. We have some spares in Sydney, and with luck there're gauges in that crate I never opened."

Martin controlled his face just long enough before cracking the widest grin ever. "Look, Jack, this thing with Kay—so far, it's cost you a heart and a brain, so why start cutting corners now?"

Jack started packing that evening.

It was a long trip, Tulagi to Sydney to Fiji to Hawaii, and on to San Francisco. Then a cross-country train trip took him to Boston, and he eventually settled in at the Back Bay Hotel. He hadn't written to Kay he was coming, and only when he signed in at the hotel did it occur to him that warning her might have been a good idea.

Nevertheless, now he finally stood at the door of the apartment house on a Saturday at noon, double-checked the address from Kay's latest letter, and went in. Kay's apartment was on the fourth floor. In the stairwell Jack found himself slowing down as he got higher, not for lack of strength, but lack of willpower. The last eighteen steps were the hardest to take, but at the end of the trek he stood at her door.

He checked his bouquet and wondered whether he should unwrap it, but then thought the wraps would be problematical to hide. He straightened his tie and pushed his hat jauntily to the side, then re-thinking, pulled it back to the businesslike look.

And during his deliberation, Kay opened the door, looking radiant in her made to measure skirt suit. To Jack, the sight of her was tantamount to a blow on the head. Her eyes flew open and the eyebrows which Jack loved so much arched above them, black and trim and expressive.

"Jack! What are you doing here?" She rushed into his arms. He hugged her without a word, then pushed her to arm's length, and enjoyed a second helping. She giggled and kissed him on the cheek, then pulled him inside the apartment for more hugs. Jack managed to keep the bouquet unharmed and presented it to her when her wave of amazement gave way.

"So I managed to surprise you?"

"And how! What lovely flowers too! How *did* you know I was going to wear red today?" she cooed as she ransacked the cupboard for a suitable vase.

Jack took a look around the apartment. It was furnished to a high standard, even he could tell that. The hum and honk of traffic carried through open windows and Jack realized how different the sounds of the city were from his jungle. The door to the bedroom was slightly open and he caught a glimpse of a vast bed with all kinds of accessories thrown over the spread. Maybe it hadn't been so easy to pick today's colors, he thought.

"Where are you staying?" Kay yodeled from the kitchen, over the noise of the running tap.

"The Back Bay," Jack answered.

"Oh, that's very convenient!" She entered the living room with the flowers and set the vase on a round glass table, then propped the flowers this way and that way, until she was satisfied with the arrangement.

"I do hope you have a week or two on your hands? I won't let you leave in a rush!" she declared. "Unfortunately, you just caught me at a moment when I need to go downtown and meet some friends. Will you join me? Oh, please say you will!"

"I wouldn't feel too comfortable barging in on your appointment," Jack admitted. "But if you're free in the evening, maybe we could go and have dinner somewhere? I have no idea where, but you probably know a nice, cozy restaurant in the neighborhood, eh?"

Kay thought just for a second. "I'll think of something. Why don't we meet in the lobby at Back Bay at around ... eight?"

Jack smiled. "I'll be there. Let's go now, or you'll be late for your appointment." They went down the stairs as fast as Kay's heels allowed her, and Jack hailed her a taxi. She leaned towards his cheek and left a very red stain with her kiss, then rubbed it off with her handkerchief. "Eight it is! Oh, I'm so happy you're here!" she told him from the open window, and then the taxi merged into the traffic and bore her away.

Jack stood still for a moment with his eyes closed, inhaling the city's scentscape and letting its vibrations permeate his body. Car horns honking, the clatter of heels on the sidewalk, a police whistle—all merged in his head and welcomed him back to civilization. Then, opening his eyes and tipping his hat to a passing old lady, he started towards his hotel with a wide grin on his face.

He was ready for Kay by six thirty, and thought he'd go down to the lounge bar for a drink while he waited. "A martini, please," he said to the tuxedoed barman, whose moves he could only envy as he remembered how haphazardly drinks were mixed at Tulagi. He selected an armchair at the back of the lobby and sat down to enjoy his drink.

Time crawled. He glanced at his Navy-issue watch every three minutes, and yet the wait in itself was wonderful. Here he was, thousands of miles from home, awaiting the company of a wonderful woman. When Kay sailed in through the doors, dressed in a blue off-the-shoulder dress with a cover-up jacket, Jack felt his heart take a few triplet beats before settling to an even, yet accelerated, pace. Kay was stunning, as always, and for once in his life he enjoyed being the guy in the lobby she singled out from the crowd.

"Hello again!" She kissed him on the cheek. "I thought we'd go to Parker's Restaurant for dinner."

"Anywhere with you suits me just fine," Jack told her, coaxing the smile he'd wanted.

"It's a twenty-minute walk, but we can take a taxi," Kay said, leading him out of the lobby. Jack wanted to walk, to prolong the time with her, but it was cool outside, so he suggested they take a cab. He'd have her attention for the whole evening.

Once they had selected their meals from the extensive menu at Parker's, and had tasted the wine, Kay rested her arms on the tablecloth. "It's so wonderful to see you here.

227

When I left Tulagi, I was hoping to get back as soon as possible, but you know how it is, with work and all."

"You know," Jack mused, "I have to admit that I never asked you a thing about your life. I don't even know where you work!"

Kay smiled demurely. "We've had other things to discuss. Anyway, I'm a financial administrator at the Boston Public Schools. Much as I like what I do, Don and I were going to open a flight school after the war, with him teaching and me managing the place."

Jack reached into his pocket. "Speaking of Don, once more, I have something for you." He took a small book from his pocket, leather-bound and read a thousand times, and handed it to Kay. "I took this from Don's belongings after he was lost. I don't really know why. I've read some of it. Must be the first book of poems I've read since high school." He handed the book to Kay.

"Well, well, well," said Kay, sinking back into her chair. "I never expected to meet Mr. Khayyam again."

Jack smiled. "Then you know this book was sort of an owner's manual for Don. There was an endless supply of wisecracks and pieces of immortal wisdom in it, and he dispensed them whenever the opportunity arose." From the shadows moving through Kay's face, Jack was starting to wonder whether bringing the book had been such a good idea.

Kay looked at the book for a long while. "*Operator's*, not owner's," she said finally. "Don had no owner, and he made that very clear to me. But yes, this book is full of little stories which appealed to him. This one is the Fitzgerald edition, the 'field companion' so to speak, as you can tell by the stains and worn edges. He had the Whinfield edition too, a very beautiful hardcover book, but that was only read on Sundays. He

228

used to compare the two and pored over them for hours on end."

Kay browsed for a second and read to Jack:

Ah, with the Grape my fading life provide,
And wash the Body whence the Life has died,
And lay me, shrouded in the living Leaf,
By some not unfrequented Garden-side.

"That's quatrain 91, one of his favorites." Jack nodded as he recognized the words. "He usually recited 91 whenever he'd been out drinking and only felt the escapades of the night the morning after."

Kay tilted her head. "Did he never say anything about 'having a 74'?"

Jack racked his brain to remember.

"As in, 'I think it's better to have a 74 tonight and not try to decide on the house'?" Kay clarified.

Jack heard Don's voice echoing the words as Kay said them. "That sure rings a bell. He sometimes threw in numbers which seemed kind of random, but with us not having the code book, we just ignored them … I guess now it makes perfect sense, though."

"Have a look." Kay tossed the book to him. "See if you can crack the code now."

Jack leafed through the stained brown pages until he found the page:

YESTERDAY This Day's Madness did prepare;
TO-MORROW's Silence, Triumph, or Despair:
Drink! for you not know whence you came, nor why:
Drink! for you know not why you go, nor where.

Jack smiled. "That's pure Don speaking, with or without numbers. That last line is something I can especially remember hearing at Altitude."

"While in the air? Really?"

Jack smirked. "No, Kay, Altitude Bar was our favorite haunt in training…we hung out there an awful lot."

"I see." Kay smiled mirthlessly. "Unfortunately, I also found out that Mr. Khayyam can be pretty nasty sometimes. When I wanted to plan for the future, or create a schedule of sorts for our life, or talk about starting a family, I was told that I was a nagging 55."

Jack again turned the pages, this time with much less enthusiasm. He read it to himself instead of reciting it out loud:

You know, my Friends, with what a brave Carouse
I made a Second Marriage in my house;
Divorced old barren Reason from my Bed,
And took the Daughter of the Vine to Spouse.

Jack shook his head. "I'm so sorry. I know he was a bastard sometimes, but to treat you like that … I never would have thought it possible." He managed to cut his statement short before saying something foolish like, "*I* would never do that."

Kay sipped her white wine. "He wanted me to be as carefree as *he* was, to harvest memories and create as many of them as possible, but someone had to keep us firmly rooted on the planet. It had to be me, since he couldn't even balance a checkbook. I tried to take his behavior as a token of love, but I sometimes think that he wanted to hurt me for being so orderly and sensible and boring."

Jack had to protest. "I won't buy that, Kay. You're anything but boring. You're the most stimulating company I've ever had!"

Kay smiled and thanked him, but reminded him: "With Don on the scene, anyone was boring, wouldn't you agree?"

Jack shrugged his assent. They fell silent for a moment. Jack told himself that there was very much more to his late friend than he'd ever thought, and he also had to admit to himself that being with Kay was a delicate mixture of pleasure and pain. He had to work hard not to fall all the way for her. It was torment.

Once more they managed to turn the conversation away from Don, to safer waters. Kay asked all about Jack's recent projects at Tulagi, how the hotel was doing, and how Martin was, and a million other things. Jack had intended to find out when Kay would return to the island, would she marry him, and would they stay together there happy ever after, but true to form, he never managed even to introduce the most innocent of these issues. He felt the same, intense frustration as always in these situations, only this time it was more bittersweet than ever before.

The dinner was wonderful, and they stayed until late. Then Jack walked her home, which was only a few minutes away. At the doorstep, Kay took up the poem book once more. "Don gave me a single number when he left the last time. '45', he told me, and then he said that it might take until 1945 for him to get back for real. We both knew he was referring to Mr. Khayyam, and I knew what he wanted me to do with it. His mother never forgave me, but I did put it in the newspapers. Goodbye, Jack—I'll call you tomorrow!"

Jack walked back to his hotel, just to revel in the enjoyment.

In the morning he went out to find a taxi. He asked the driver for an antiquarian bookstore, and was driven to Brattle Book Shop on West Street. Jack went inside, and headed straight to the poetry section. He found a few copies of Khayyam; Quatrain 45 in the illustrated and leather-bound Whinfield edition did not strike him as especially meaningful, but when he read the Fitzgerald edition, he had to sit on a stool for a while, so much of Don entered his mind at one flash:

'Tis but a Tent where takes his one day's rest
A Sultan to the realm of Death addrest;
The Sultan rises, and the dark Ferrash
Strikes, and prepares it for another Guest.

He bought the book. It was a long, slow, thoughtful walk back to the hotel. The little book weighed heavily in his pocket.

For his daytime entertainment he went on an aimless stroll. The busy streets and multitudes of people rushing by him were a source of enjoyment for a while, but he also found it tiresome; while at Tulagi, he had not stayed alert for long periods of time, except when flying, and even then only if the weather demanded it. Dodging taxis was fun for a while, but when he had lunch at a basement cafe, he found himself longing for the sound of the palm trees in a gentle wind, and the lapping of water on the float of the Kingfisher.

But then, when Kay phoned him around three, he was full of energy and anticipation, and the prospect of meeting her again filled him with joy. This time she said she'd meet him at the lobby in fifteen minutes, if that was fine. Jack was downstairs in ten. Kay barged in through the revolving doors, raising her eyebrows once more. "Jack, I just thought of something. I'll tell you in the taxi." She tugged at Jack's arm and he complied.

They sat in the cab outside the hotel, Jack watching her with expectation. Finally she cleared her throat. "At first I thought we'd just go for coffee or something, but then I thought I should ask you this: would you like to visit Don's grave? We don't have to if that's not what you'd like to do," she added, solemn for once.

Jack had never considered the possibility that Don would have a grave. After a second's thought he felt sure he wanted to see it, mainly because Kay seemed to want him to. "Yes, I would like to do that," he smiled.

"It's just that it occurred to me I haven't been there since I came back from Tulagi. Driver—Mount Auburn Cemetery, please." As the taxi joined the flow of traffic, Kay fumbled in her purse for a lipstick and applied it to her flawless make-up. Jack could see the gesture was a smokescreen and left her in peace until she was ready to speak to him. The remainder of the trip they talked about the places they passed and of life in Boston.

They bought a small blue and white bouquet at the flower shop in Mount Auburn, then walked slowly down a wide road and up a succession of smaller ones, until they came to a little hill. There, on the top of it, was a slab of white marble, almost featureless except for an arched top and gilt letters which read, *"Don Wheeler USMC"* and the dates of his life. Kay placed the flowers on the ground in front of it.

Jack stared at the little headstone for a good while. "It's just as I think he would have liked it, no frills," he said and looked at Kay. She gave a short, sad little smile to him and pulled out a handkerchief from her purse.

"He abhorred the self-absorbed monuments some people have here. We never talked about this, but I just knew what to do. My mother wanted one of those car-sized ones, but I put my foot down."

Jack was struck by a thought, and he worked it through

out loud. "You know, that's the first headstone I ever saw for a wartime friend of mine. It's not for want of people who needed them—I think we lost maybe thirty, no, forty pilots during the war ... but they all just failed to return. One of them died on the ground in a landing accident when a plane landed on his, and we got to bury him, but all the others just faded from my life. Seeing that grave... I don't know what to say."

Kay took his hand. "I hope I haven't brought you down too far."

He looked up into the green trees and realized it was the first time he'd heard leaves in Boston, and it made him feel better. "No, I'm glad we came."

"Maybe you now understand why I looked you up in Tulagi? I came here for years to see this grave, and to find some solace. For a few years it worked, but the day came when I decided I simply must find out what happened. Burying a picture of him and me, and the leather-bound Whinfield edition of Omar Khayyam wasn't enough, but when I met you and heard what had happened, it really set me free."

They stood there for a moment longer, two people at the headstone of a third, united by war and divided by it. Then Kay offered him her arm. "Shall we?"

Jack took hold of her and they left, not looking back.

*

All too soon it was time for Jack to head home. They spent their last evening together at the Hi-Hat restaurant, enjoying a fabulous meal and entertainment by Erroll Garner. When Jack walked Kay home, they stood at the doorway for a long while, staring into each other's eyes. "Would you like to come up for some coffee?" Kay smiled that smile Jack had come to love.

Jack was certain coming up could not make his life any harder. He'd fallen for her so bad that the thought of the trip back home was already killing him. "Sure," he agreed, and they went upstairs. They kissed when they closed the door behind them, and kissed their way into the bedroom. When they lay together in the bed, her skin soft and warm on his, Jack felt a singular contentment.

He woke up when she sat on the bedside in her morning gown. "Here's the coffee I promised you," she smiled, setting the tray in his lap. Jack had a sip of the steaming coffee and grinned. He applied some butter and jam on his toast and munched it while studying her face intently.

"Why are you doing that, Jack? Watching me, I mean. I'm not exactly at my freshest," she said with mock coyness.

"I need to take in the prettiest sight in the world," he told her. "I have to bring something of you back to Tulagi."

"I was going to ask you about that," she said. "Will you stay there all your life, or would you consider moving back here to the States?"

Jack held his breath for a while. "No, Kay, I don't think I'll be coming back. Somehow I feel my home's now there. When my father died, he asked me to live my life my way, and right now, that's how my way feels."

Kay's disappointment showed on her face for a fraction of a second. "But you just have to come and visit me again! Or I can come down there, if there'd be a cabin free for me?"

Jack was happy she let him off so easily. "You know cabin number nine is always free for you." He could almost feel the pieces of his heart rattling around in his otherwise-empty chest.

After they took turns showering, he bade her farewell. The

last kiss, and the last hug, and the letting-go emotionally and physically were a strain, but one he'd gone through in his mind many times already.

When the door closed behind Jack, Kay was at a loss as for what to do next. She sat down for a while and tried to read, but soon enough went to the phone and called her mother. She was happy to hear Kay wanted to have lunch with her; she needed to hear what Kay had been up to.

They met at Parker's Hotel. Kay didn't talk at all about Jack, but kept on chitchatting of everything else. Finally, Mrs. Willis couldn't take it anymore. "Well? What *about* this Jack? Is he still here? Will you bring him for us to see, for dinner maybe?

Kay shook her head. "No, he left this morning. He wanted to go by the Navy yard to see if they had some parts for his plane, and then he'll leave for the Solomons."

Frowning at this, Mrs. Willis wanted more. "I hope you're not harboring any fantasies about joining him down there, dear?"

Kay struck back immediately. "And why would that be such a bad thing?"

"Oh, come on, you know what I mean. You're not cut out to live in a jungle, for heaven's sake. You're a city person, you couldn't possibly be happy living in a treehouse."

"It's not a treehouse. You saw my pictures and know perfectly well how nice the hotel is. Besides, he'll work on the main lodge of the plantation and renovate it when he has the time."

"Oh, Kay. I do wish you'd find a nice man right here in Boston and settle down once and for all. A man who'd make you feel safe and content so you could finally start a family. I mean, first Don Wheeler, and then that Max Jeffries, and now this Jack...what *is* it with these pilots?"

Kay snapped with some venom: "They can make you fly high."

Her mother rolled her eyes up to the restaurant's ceiling. "Sometimes you're just impossible, Kay. I feel I have to warn you—don't start squandering your future building romantic castles in the air, or in the South Pacific for that matter. Let this man return to Fiji, and concentrate on your life, which is here with us."

Kay backtracked a little. "I'm not moving to Tulagi right now, no need to worry. But I *will* say this: when I find a man as good as Don was, I will act on a hunch if need be."

Her mother poured some more wine. "That's fine with me, but please—find a man who stays on the ground for a change." Kay gave her the briefest of smiles, and then buttoned her lip for the rest of the lunch.

When they parted, she wanted to walk home to clear her head. She was quite sure she wanted to remain in Boston, as certain as Jack seemed that Tulagi was for him. But his presence still seemed to walk beside her, as if they were back on the island paths, and she kept looking over her shoulder to see him. Already she missed him, but hoped the feeling would fade away as time passed.

16

In the two weeks after Don's death, Jack flew every available mission. He flew Combat Air Patrol, the aerial counterpart of walking the perimeter; he flew fighter cover for dive bombers; he went on fighter sweeps deep into enemy territory. For fifteen consecutive days he didn't have a single day out of the cockpit. On the fifteenth day, just after he taxied his plane to its revetment after spending four hours over the beachhead at Bougainville, Jack was greeted by the squadron doctor. Doc Mendel was accompanied by a pair of burly Marine military police and one of the new pilots, a 2nd Lieutenant. A funny party, Jack thought to himself as he shut the engine down.

"Hello, Jack—been busy lately?" Doc asked, as Jack released his harness and deplaned.

"Well, you know how it is, covering the landings is critical, like at Bougainville," Jack answered.

"Do you really need to fly two or three missions a day?"

"Well, not necessarily, but then, the new boys are just being broken in…"

"Jack, did you really hit this young man and pull him out of his plane yesterday?"

Jack studied the kid for a moment, and yes, it was the pilot he'd grabbed and thrown out of the cockpit of a Corsair. "Sure, I think it's him. Sorry about that black eye, pal—no offense, but I needed that plane, and I thought it best you not go on that particular mission, as it was an incoming fighter sweep, they're pretty rough sometimes."

Again, Doc interrupted Jack. "You know if you're not on the roster, you don't fly."

"I do know, but I was kind of hoping to keep the kid out of harm's way, and that's why I took the plane."

"He's received extensive training in flying into harm's way and surviving it, just like you. Jack, these two gentlemen are here to make sure you follow me to the sick bay. Get down here and walk with me, and we'll have a talk. Otherwise, they'll arrest you, and *then* we'll have a walk and a talk."

"Come on, Doc... you're kidding, right?"

"I'm afraid not. Now get down here and come with me."

Jack saw that the MPs were briefed to do Doc's bidding, and he obediently walked with them to the sick bay.

Once there, Jack was directed to sit on the bench outside the doctor's tent. Doc came out of the tent, stretched himself and sat down on a rock he used as his chair when addressing patients. In the tent, an opera played on the gramophone, and every two seconds, a loud click accompanied the orchestra.

Doc looked at Jack with a resolute gaze. "Jack, I'm thinking of having you sent Stateside. You have too many problems right now, and you're no longer safe for yourself or for your squadron mates."

"What? Look, Doc, I may have flown a bit too much and I may be a bit tired but that's all there is."

"No, Jack. You know just as well as I do. You're stressed far beyond safe limits. Since Don died, you've popped down to the ground only to eat and crap, and then you've gone back to fight the Japs. That doesn't go, as far as I am concerned. You're grounded."

"Doc, there's nothing for me to do but to fly and *you* know it," Jack tried once more. Doc stood up and dug a cigarette from his shirt pocket.

"Jack," he began, lighting the cigarette, peering out into the jungle but not looking at anything, "there's a limit to everything. You can only eat so much, or drink so much. There's also a limit to how much a pilot can fly, and you've gone way past that. The other day you punched a junior pilot in the eye and dropped him off the wing of a Corsair, in the process of which he sprained his ankle, and the day before that you flew balls-out into a nine-plane formation of Vals with no tallyho and without letting anyone in your squadron hear what you were doing. That's not exactly the way it's spelled out in the regulations, is it now?"

Doc took a long drag from his cigarette, kept it in for a long time, and let the smoke out his nostrils very slow. Jack was sweating in rivulets at the thought of being grounded, and he didn't want to hear Doc out.

"Worse yet—I talked with Bunny Radner. It'd come to his attention that you hardly sleep at all. Why is that?" Doc sat back on the rock.

Jack shrugged. "I guess I don't need the sleep."

"All human beings, including and especially hotshot pilots, need sleep. If you don't sleep, there's a problem. Let me have a go at the reason why: you miss Don. You don't sleep and you fly like a reckless maniac, no—strike that—like an *idiot*, because you don't care any more. Am I right or am I right?"

Jack was uneasy. "Sure I miss him, but I don't think it affects me that much…"

"Did you have problems before December sixth?"

Head down, Jack had to admit that he hadn't.

Doc flicked the cigarette butt accurately into a small puddle of brown water by the tent, a target already littered with bullseyes.

"I see two possibilities here. One: I send you back to the States on the next boat out. I hear the fishing at Pensacola is great this time of year. That's the easy option for you. Two: You sleep for four solid days and nights in the sick bay. And then you promise me that you fly only the missions Bunny gives you, and even then, you only do what the squadron does in the air. No hot-shotting, no single-handed attacks at the Japanese Emperor and his loyal pilots, no devil-may-care reckless leaving-behind of wingmen. In short, you're back to flying the way we do it. If I get one more report from anyone that you deviated from this plan, consider yourself packed in a cage on top of the slowest available freighter headed for San Francisco. Are we clear on this?"

Jack nodded slowly.

"Good. Now go get your stuff. You're confined to the sick bay for four days, and then we take another look at you." Doc strode off in his usual brisk manner. "Oh, one more thing, Jack," he added over his shoulder. "I hear there's a trainer assignment coming your way anyway, so you'd better get used to the idea sooner or later. Preferably sooner, if you ask me." And Doc was off to tend to some other problem, leaving Jack in the care of the two MPs who assisted him to the sick bay.

"I take it you're not leaving until I'm sitting nice and tight on my bunk here in the sick bay." Jack squinted at the corporal.

"Got it, sir, those're my orders," the man replied.

Jack went with them to his tent, collected all he thought he would need, and returned to the sick bay with his bag, wondering what the hell he'd do for the next four days.

By eight o'clock, Jack had had a nap, eaten, and been for a walk. He had also collected every scrap of reading material available in the sick tent, but it was a pitifully small canon. It consisted of three technical leaflets describing various aspects of radial engine maintenance, *Life* magazine's June 1941 issue, and the ever-present Bible donated by one religious organization or another. He decided to leave the Bible to the more religiously-oriented, the maintenance manuals to the ground crews, and settled down to enjoying the sumptuous, if a bit worn, magazine.

In fifteen minutes he had read it cover to cover and was again out of anything to do. He tried to get into the frame of mind to write letters, but found that there was nothing he wanted to share with anyone. Then he remembered his mother's birthday was coming up, and so he wrote her a short letter, all roundabout, obscure sentences from which she would be unable to figure out his state of mind. By nine-thirty he had already had an evening snack and was lying in his bunk, staring at the roof, bored stiff.

He drifted off into an uneasy sleep. At first he dreamed he was back in school, being bullied by the biggest kid in the class, and Tony nowhere in sight to fend him off. After he received a complete working-over from the bully, his dream switched into his first experiences in combat flying, and that terrified state of mind came vividly back to him. He felt helpless and vulnerable, as if he were flying into combat with a plane whose guns were inoperative. Rolling in sweat in his bunk, he kept many of the soldiers at the sick bay awake most of the night with his shattered sentences and babbling. When he woke up, he felt not a bit refreshed.

In the morning, the private in the next bunk asked him, "What did you dream about, sir? Sounded mighty bad."

Jack did not answer but went to wash his face and clean up. His bunk was still all wet from his night sweating. He ate breakfast and then remembered he still had three more days of inactivity to look forward to, and his morale sank even lower. Luckily, a fellow pilot was admitted to the sick bay with such a bad case of dysentery that he'd been taken off the flying roster. Now, at least Jack could relate to another fellow inmate. Joe Wunderlich was prepared a bunk next to Jack's, and he settled down for a couple of ground days.

Wunderlich was very handy with a knife. He was constantly whittling away, even when the pilots were on scramble alert. He said it took his mind off the upcoming action to carve native figurines, and that one of the upsides of being in the South Pacific was having no shortage of tropical wood to use. His figurines were eagerly bought and sent home as souvenirs. From the shelves in a supply room, Jack had located a chessboard with half the pieces missing. Wunderlich said he would carve new pieces, but that it would take him a couple of days to finish them. In the meanwhile he quickly made a set of wooden pegs out of light and dark wood, so at least they could play checkers. He bet Jack he'd beat him eight times out of ten at it, and Jack just had to take on the challenge.

After ten games it was six to four to Jack, so they played another ten, after which the score stood at eleven to nine to Wunderlich. After lunch and a nap, they went on to battle yet another ten games. Now Wunderlich took seven of these, and now it was Jack's turn to demand rematches. By seven o'clock that evening they'd finished forty games, and the score stood at 21 to 19, Jack.

"As a kid, did you ever figure you'd like to play forty games of checkers in a sick bay in the South Pacific while recovering from the runs?" Jack asked Wunderlich, who was putting the finishing touches to a mighty fine-looking chess knight by the dim light of a lantern.

"No, not really ... but then, I doubt any of us really had

this in mind when we enlisted. I mean, Marines are supposed to just fight battles and win 'em all, you know, go in, take care of the trouble, and come out, not sit around and get bogged down on islands like this." Wunderlich blew some wood chips off the horse's head and examined the piece against the light, then drilled an eye with the knife tip. "Still, I'd rather be here than on the carriers. This one won't sink from under me."

Jack finished his cigarette and lay back on his bunk, placing his hands under his head. "I never thought I'd see the South Pacific in the first place. I thought I'd finish school, go to college and get back to the farm." He closed his eyes. "Now … having been here, I don't have a clue what I'll do after the war. For some reason, the farm doesn't seem like a good idea."

Wunderlich pointed at Jack with the knife. "Listen, bud, thinking about the post-war times is a bad idea in general. It makes you lose your edge in the air, which makes you a good target to the Japs. It's better to go up and fly like there's no tomorrow at all. That way, you can concentrate all your energy on flying that plane just on that particular mission, and if you get back, then you can look back and see you made it once again. That's what I do anyway: live mission to mission. Now go and get me some ashes or coal."

"Coal?" Jack was surprised.

"In chess, you got white pieces and black pieces, right? Get some soot and make these pieces black with it, then polish 'em up with a rag."

"Got it," Jack said, and got up. Outside the sick bay they'd burned a fire earlier in the day, and he picked up some coal and ground it into soot, mixed in some water and soon had his hands full of black goo. Wunderlich gave him half the pieces; Jack rubbed them black and finished the surfaces with an oily rag.

244

When he was done, he assembled the pieces onto the chess board. "Now that's a good thing … in the morning I'll have your butt with black."

Wunderlich grinned. "You're on."

"In the meantime, let's go for a snack. I'm hungry." Jack stood up and washed his hands in a bucket, whose water, and insides too, turned so black he had to pitch the water and wash out the bucket from a barrel full of rain water.

"You go on. I think I'll skip it and hit the hay." Wunderlich flexed his fingers after having whittled so long. "Damn it … I gotta go, but then I'll just get some sleep." He got up and disappeared into the darkness in the direction of the latrines.

Jack stretched and went out to the medics to get a piece of bread and some canned meat. After that he went back to his bunk and tried to sleep, but once again found it difficult, and even when he did finally drift off, he was plagued by visions. Jack had been on the flying roster when the Japanese had tried to run down The Slot with four transports filled to the brims with men and ammunition, and when the SBDs had stopped the transports, the fighters were sent in to strafe them.

While the ships burned, fighters swooped as low over them as they dared, letting fly with all six .50-caliber machine guns. Jack would never forget the stench of gunpowder and burning ships, although in the daytime he was usually able to shake the feeling of awe and disgust he'd felt during the attack. But at night, there was no escape from the nightmares which would see him jump to his feet from his bed as if he were pitched out by springs.

There seemed to be no escape from the dreams. One frightful mission after another they came, forcing his body to twitch and his mind to grow more and more tired as the hours of the night trudged on. Frequently he woke up, imagining his feet on the pedals and his hand on the stick, and the finger keeping the trigger down. Trying to settle back to sleep was useless, or that's how it seemed to him, at least.

His third night in sick bay went just as poorly as the first. Doc visited him around midday and saw that the ace was in a bad way. He resolved in his mind to start the paperwork which would release Jack from the torment of combat and ship him back to a training command. The risks of flying would still be there, but at least he would escape the bullets. While Doc Mendel knew the way Jack took to combat, he could not bear to see him fade away like this. When Jack had his blood pressure measured four times a day as per Doc's order, it was found to be consistently in the region of 180 over 110, which further confirmed Doc's decision to have Jack removed from front-line combat. Doc tried to discuss the issue with Jack, but the pilot would hear none of it.

On the fourth night, as Jack had again settled down with no real hope of a peaceful night, he surprised himself by falling asleep almost immediately. This time his dreams were not as chaotic as before; there was more of a foggy, undefined atmosphere in which Jack was merely drifting. He did not find this dream unpleasant in any way, but he was startled to be roused from the sleep by someone sitting in the rickety chair he had at his bedside. His initial wonder turned into sheer terror when he saw that the chair was occupied by Don Wheeler, looking as dapper as ever. Jack looked at him in complete awe, unable even to say a word, but then he heard Don speak.

"Hello, Eightball." Only Don had ever used that nickname. "Once more we meet."

Jack looked again and in the dim lantern light he saw Don was not sitting in the chair but actually slightly off it, and yet the chair moved as Don straightened himself out.

"What's this?" Jack gasped. "Who are you?"

"You got to let me go, Jack," was Don's reply.

"What do you mean?"

"Jack, we all go someday. I'm gone, but still you keep me around when you think of me all the time. I gotta go, and you gotta let me go my way."

Jack could not believe what he was seeing or doing, but slowly he came to his wits. Maybe Don was dead, but not all of him. Jack could not think of much to say. "I see. Yeah, I see what you mean," Jack said, and Don got on his feet from the chair.

"So long, Eightball. And hey—you know what? The bullets really are numbered, and you fire them, but they're not your bullets. You didn't do the numbers. Get it? And another thing is this: the ripples are yours to keep. Nothing else is yours. Just the ripples."

With this Don faded from sight, leaving Jack repeating over and over again, "I see. I see it all."

A very tired voice from the other end of the sick bay said, "Oh great. Now the basket case lootenant can see in the dark."

When Jack woke up in the morning, it was way past reveille. He felt refreshed for the first time in a very long while. He went out for a walk and found who he was looking for—Doc Mendel was out by the hut he had as his office. As usual, he had *The Flying Dutchman* playing on his gramophone, and he frequently closed his eyes to savor a particularly felicitous cadence in the music.

He looked up from his papers when Jack greeted him.

"Okay, what happened? Be snappy—I am not in a good mood. Not after they send me a case of crickets and a box of bones and expect me to fix heroes out of them," he growled.

"You won't believe me if I tell you, so I won't. Let's just say I feel better after a relaxing night of sleep."

"Try me." That was all Doc would say. At the resolute gaze of Doc's eyes, Jack pondered what to do now. "Shh! Listen to this! It's my favorite aria!" Doc closed his eyes, conducted a palm tree orchestra for a few moments, and then remembered his patient was standing there with a story to tell.

"Really, Doc, it's just that I feel better after a good night, that's all," he tried.

"No, that's not all." His voice was rife with irritation.. "Let's have it."

Jack hedged once more. "Doc, you won't—"

Doc's gaze ended all resistance. "Jack, I know every pilot here. I know how they are. There's nothing they can tell me I won't at least think over, so spill it." Doc took up his habitual pack of cigarettes and guided Jack out to the rock he liked to sit on. *The Flying Dutchman* blared into the jungle as Jack saw that he had no choice, and reminded himself the worst that could happen was that he'd be sent home.

He took a deep breath. "I saw Don Wheeler last night." He looked at Doc to see his reaction, but none was apparent.

"Did you, now?" was all he said.

"That's all?"

"What did you expect? A straitjacket?" Doc said, puffing at his cigarette as if to extract all its nicotine in five seconds.

Jack didn't know what to say. "Something like that, I guess." Again he tried to decide whether he was being taken for a ride.

Doc finished the cigarette and dispatched the butt with the accurate finger-flip into the puddle on the ground, already littered with butts. "Well, let me tell you something. Before the war, you'd already be on your way to the funny farm. No question about that. You see dead people, you're sent to reinforce the basket-weaving squadron. But now, with this war... I don't know what's true and what isn't."

Doc looked at Jack with his piercing eyes. "You think you're the only one with that story, right?"

"I don't know of any others, at least."

"You're not. Remember Duggan, the RAF Brit we had? He saw his mother here, on this island, the day after she died. And Taylor talked with his sister, only the sister died four years before. Potter was a raving madman, that's why I had him sent away—not because he frequently chatted with his squadron mates, none of whom were on the roster any longer."

"Well, I'm happy you're not assigning me to the funny farm now," Jack said, "but what made you change your mind?"

"Long story. To tell you the short version, I had a teacher in medical school who was a down-to-earth researcher, no possibility of spirits outside the 86-proof ones whatsoever. For him, nothing beyond the body ever existed. He had a funny— no, that's not the right word, weird is more like it— experience, when he himself had to have an operation. Under anesthesia he could see the doctor fighting to smother a big hemorrhage in his stomach. He could see the entire team almost in panic, and he was just watching serenely by. He said it was as clear and understandable a situation as any he had ever seen in the operating theater, and he even tried to give the doctor advice at some point. Anyway, at some length he felt a need to go back into his body, which he did, and afterwards he woke up very weak. The operating doctor was terrified when he related the worst part of the operation to him blow by blow."

Doc seemed unwilling to talk about this at length, but Jack's nod pushed him just a bit more. "So he concluded that there's the physical part, and then there's a spiritual part. I talked with him at length on this and he convinced me to think again. And then the war came. You know, I've heard so many stories of dead people and living people in the same happy bunch that I've had to begin to think differently. That's why you can keep your job out here."

Doc Mendel looked Jack in the eye to level with him. "I won't send you away solely on the basis of that meeting with Don, mostly because I think you aren't lying, and secondly, I think it takes a lot to admit it ever happened. I'll place an additional stipulation on that, though; you stay one more day, see if you can sleep okay, and your condition gets better. Is that clear?"

Jack smiled. "Sure is, Doc, and thanks. You'll keep this to yourself I hope, though?"

"Hey, while I hear weird stuff, I don't pass it on." Doc returned the smile. "Now get to lunch and have some rest. If I do release you tomorrow, you know you'll be on the roster straight away anyhow. I'm off to do some fishing, so get going."

Jack saluted and left. Doc watched his gait, which had taken on a new bounce. He grinned to himself and went to collect his fishing kit.

In the evening Jack felt both drained and revitalized. He went to sleep instantly and slept all through the night. In the morning his blood pressure was found to have normalized, and the only remaining problem in his condition was loss of weight. Doc Mendel signed his release to flight status, and Jack went to the squadron commander to report.

Bunny Radner was watching a flight of torpedo bombers

arriving when Jack found him. The roar of engines drowned communications for a while, but after the planes were taxiing to the revetments, he greeted Jack warmly. "Good to have you back on the flight line, Jack."

"I miss my flying too, sir," Jack replied.

"Are you *okay* now, or A-okay, Jack?" his commander asked with a wry smile.

"I believe I'm A-okay now, and glad to get back to operations."

Bunny Radner looked at his watch. "Good. The first one is a handful—an escort to Buka and Bonis. We want their runways looking like the full moon. I was hoping to have you back today. I need all the experience we can muster."

"All I need is my flight gear. When's the takeoff?"

"At 1300 hours. Briefing at 1230. You take your flight and Jonesy has his, and you have twelve Avengers to nurse there and back. I sure hope you've got it all with you, this is no milk run."

Jack smiled. "See you at 1230 then!"

The flight went well, and while accurate anti-aircraft fire claimed one bomber, no fighters were lost. To the strike's surprise, no Japanese fighters were to be found in the air over the bases. All planes formed up and flew back to Munda, where Jack and Becker let the bombers land first while the fighters circled vigilantly for Japanese surprise attacks on the landing circuit.

After the landing, Jack emerged from his plane and went to meet his crew chief. "Good work, Jack," the chief told him.

"Really? Even if all I do is take your plane out to be shot to pieces?" Jack teased.

He left his plane to the crew to check and rearm and went to the pilots' mess. Joe Wunderlich was there, too, having

251

recovered well enough to return to flight status. He waved Jack over and handed him a paper bag.

"Here's your chess set," he said.

Jack opened the bag and found thirty-two beautiful, accurately shaped chess pieces in it. "Hey, thanks! These are great!"

"At some point I'll make you a board, if I have the time. I got one under way, but it seems to take a lot of time to finish." But Wunderlich knew that Jack appreciated his eye for detail and would not worry about that.

"No rush, pal. Boards are easy to come by but these chess pieces are hard to get out here." Jack closed the bag and went to his tent, where he placed the pieces in his trunk. It felt good to be back. He felt more alive than in a long while.

On the way back from the strike, Jack came in over Florida Island as the last plane of the escort flight. Some foul-up on the field caused a delay in going down to land, so Jack did a couple of circles above Halavo Bay along with three other fighters. Just as Jack completed his third circle, he spotted a flash in the jungle. He looked that way with a quick turn of the head, and saw that in the jungle, almost completely hidden under the lush canopy was a small plantation. In a moment he had sped past the plantation, but its image etched into his mind. The plantation lodge was a white two-storey, colonial-style building, not very big, but not just a hut either. A couple of sheds and a damaged pier jutting out into the water completed the set, along with tall, straight palm trees planted at regular intervals. The place seemed to exude peace and tranquility in a world of jagged edges and cold steel. Jack wanted to have another look, so he started another circle, but before he got any further, radio traffic called for him to leave the pattern and head for Henderson.

In the evening, when the oil drums used for lighting the

runway for late arrivals were extinguished and the stars above took over, Jack sat down in his plane revetment and watched the pinpricks of light on the pitch dark sky. The vision of the plantation didn't leave him; he could see it again and again when he closed his eyes. He wondered whether it ever would, but the persistent warm feeling it gave him didn't frighten him. Quite the contrary.

17

One fine day in March 1944, Jack's afternoon nap was cut short by the roar of eight Corsairs approaching Munda from the south. He stood up and rubbed his eyes to see what was happening. Ground crew members lined the runway to watch pilots land the new replacement planes, and then to direct the new arrivals to the plane revetments below the palms. The two divisions landed in short order, one after another. Or at least the first seven planes did.

The eighth plane seemed a bit uncertain in its approach, its pilot jockeying the throttle like a motorcyclist intent on waking up the neighborhood at two in the morning. The large plane wavered and wobbled around as it got closer to the runway, and every man on the base watched it coming in with much interest. Fifty feet off the ground, the pilot attempted to flare the plane, then had to compensate and push the nose down to make it dive towards the ground with much too much speed. Ground crews, always on the lookout for something to place bets on, wondered whether the plane would survive touchdown.

"Here's five bucks saying he'll ruin the gear and belly that plane," said a technical sergeant to a group of mechanics.

"You're on. That Hog is as tough as any bird they ever made, and that's a new one. It'll get in all right on a runway, but I wouldn't bet on it on a carrier deck. Here's my five for survival," said one of the mechanics.

After a final set of swerves and jinks, the plane slammed onto the runway, bounced high a couple of times and went into a relatively straight taxiing run. Only the good workmanship put into its construction enabled it to survive touchdown.

"Awww hell!" the sergeant bellowed. "I was certain he'd pop it down from forty feet, but somehow he slipped it in!"

"Well, Vought didn't take any Chances when they built the Hog," the mechanic said and snapped the fiver from the sergeant.

"What a punster we have here—a regular Shakespeare, eh? Chance-Vought Airplane Company... Sheesh! Now get back to them planes and quit bugging me or I'll have your asses for supper," the sergeant growled, dispersing the mechanics to their charges.

"Now that's an artist of a pilot," Jack muttered as the plane followed its guide to its revetment. He watched the pilot unstrap himself and hop down off the wing. Jack was sure the pilot was the shortest he had ever seen when he saw him report to the base commander under the wing of his plane. The new pilots were shown their tents, and they all went on to settle down.

Half an hour later Jack chanced to pass the new pilots' tents, and in front of one there was a sign, so freshly-painted the paint still glistened in the afternoon sun. It read, "*Ye Olde Nose Art Shoppe*" and below that, "*No Idea Too Bad—No Image Too Hard*". At the bottom of the sign was written, "*Inquire Within—The Artist is IN*" with the word IN on a separate patch.

The planes at the base had only recently been taken out of a plane pool and assigned to individual pilots. Consequently, nose art had begun to appear on the engine cowlings. Jack had at first thought such an art form as an unnecessary extravagance, but after he found he was regularly flying the F4U Corsair whose Bureau of Aviation number was 17576, and that he was in principle assigned the plane for good, he thought he might as well have something painted on the nose to customize it.

Until the arrival of James Rogers, the artistic pilot, and the grand opening of his Nose Art Shoppe, the names and images had been painted on the planes with stencils and only rudimentary artistic vision. Consequently the designs and results were usually less than spectacular. A couple of weeks into the venture of the Nose Art Shoppe's entrepreneur pilot, though, planes were quickly turning out from the works adorned with quality designs. Jack chuckled at some of the combinations of names and images, but he didn't want to have something painted on his old 576 until he had a really good concept in mind. He toyed with a few ideas, saw a couple of them appear on other planes by coincidence, but then one morning as he watched his armorers loading up the six .50 caliber machine guns for a CAP Mission, he came upon the name for his steed: he was going to call it *Haulin' Ass* and have Rogers paint a warlike donkey on the engine cowling.

After the CAP Jack went to see Rogers in his shop. He found him reclining on a hammock slung between the landing gear of his Corsair, fast asleep though it was a busy day and planes were roaring low above him at infrequent intervals. Jack kneeled down by the head of the hammock and wondered whether to wake him up or to let him sleep.

Rogers solved the dilemma by opening one eye and checking Jack out with it. "What can I do for you, Lieutenant?" he asked.

"Well, I was just wondering about this nose art ... you do that, don't you?"

"Yes. I do nose art. I'm a nose artist. My nose art is the best in the Pacific, if I may say so. Say, lieutenant, your personal nose is beyond my help. I'm a nose artist but I don't do nose jobs. My brother-in-law does 'em, though. He could fix that nose in fifteen minutes flat. He works in Hollywood; most of the real good nose jobs in West Hollywood are done by Eddie Thorne. If you want to look him up, just go to Max Shultz's and ask for Eddie. Tell him Jimmy sent you and he'll give you a ten percent discount."

Jack instinctively touched his broken nose, which he'd earned at Guadalcanal. "No, I think I'd be satisfied with just nose art for the plane."

"Do you have a design for it? Name? Theme? Picture of your sweetheart? Veronica Lake? Mae West? Rita Hayworth? Douglas MacArthur? Any gal with big tits will do, although I am slightly bored with gals on planes. I'd rather do something of real cultural value. No one has commissioned anything like, say, Michelangelo's *Creation*. You know, with the newly-created Man on the engine cowling and God on the fuselage. Now that'd be a real challenge, and a nice conversation piece besides. Besides, no Jap would dare to shoot at something like that and risk ruining the painting. Order now and get yours done before Christmas!"

Despite the persistent ringing in his ears, Jack began to like the talkative little fellow. "Well, I was kinda thinking that the name *Haulin' Ass* and a corresponding image of a pissed-off donkey would be good," Jack suggested.

"*Haulin' Ass? Haulin' Ass*! Wonderful! That's extra clever! Simply great! Fannn-tastic!" Rogers bolted up from his hammock to the tent and came out with a scratch pad and pencil, and within five minutes he had portrayed Jack's idea to the hilt. Jack could not help laughing at the belligerent donkey he'd drawn, standing on its hind legs with machine guns in its front hooves and two ammo belts hung over the shoulders. The cigar it chewed took it up a further notch.

"Something along those lines?" Rogers asked.

"Yeah, just like that. Say, you should be working for Disney!" Jack was no artist but he could see that Rogers surely would have a fine career in cartoons.

"Funny you should mention that," Rogers said, and went into the tent again and came out with a letter in a picture frame.

"Have a look at this," Rogers said, with more than just a hint of pride in his voice. It was a letter of acceptance, typed on Disney Studios letterhead, and signed by the chief of animation. "They hired me two days after I'd finished flight training. I got the letter a day before I shipped out—had a little trouble getting it framed so fast. I called 'em from Los Angeles and they said they'd wait for me till the war's done. I do nose art to keep fit, so to speak." Having finished his monologue, Rogers polished fingerprints off the glass with a puff of breath and his elbow.

"OK, that'll be good enough for me," Jack agreed. "Size it so that the text can be read from far out."

"Will do. When's your next hop?"

"I'm on the roster for Combat Air Patrol tomorrow afternoon."

"That's fine, I got fast drying paint. What's your plane?"

"It's old 576 over there, the one that has no propeller. They've found a new one for me which is why I won't be going up today. Oh, how much will it cost me?"

"I usually charge fifteen bucks and three packs of smokes, but this one is so good and business is booming, so I'll do it for free. You'll see a finished design if you drop by tonight around eight."

"Let me just pay your regular charge, like everybody else," Jack said, and they shook on it. "Well, see you then." Jack started out towards the operations hut.

After supper Jack returned to The Shoppe. He found Rogers toiling over a large piece of engine cowling. He had marked out the outline of the donkey, complete with machine guns, and had traced the name "Haulin' Ass" on it too. The artist, clothed in just his pants, was deeply immersed in painting the hind legs of the donkey.

"Boy, that looks like a regular piece of art!" Jack said.

"Well, this time the name was so good I thought I'd go all out," Rogers said, wiping sweat off his brow. Jack admired the level of detail and the sheer whimsical 'what-the-hell' nature of the image. The name had been outlined in gold, and Rogers said he'd fill it up with white. Together with the deep blue paintwork, it all made very good nose art, the best Jack had yet seen.

"I added a revolver on a belt to him, hope you don't mind?" Rogers asked as he touched up a foreleg.

"No, don't mind at all, it fits fine in there. Say, when will this be done? It looks pretty far down the road to me."

"I'll keep this plate here overnight, and your crew chief said he'd fit you a spare one in case this isn't finished and dried by the time you need to fly."

"OK then, all is well. I'll bring you the money and the smokes tomorrow morning. That work for you?" Jack asked.

"No rush ... I trust you won't run away from me or escape this island for that matter!" Rogers commented, and returned to his work in earnest.

Jack watched him work for some time, but then decided it was better to leave the artist to it. He went on to the mess for a cup of disgusting coffee.

In the morning Jack found himself on the roster with Rogers on his wing. Apparently the base executive officer had decided to shuffle the wingmen around. The mission was just another CAP, and while they were up, Jack was surprised by Rogers's skillful flying. He seemed to be just in the right place for a wingman, and when Jack turned, Rogers lost no time in getting to the spot again.

After fifty minutes of uneventfully running rings in the sky at 12,000 feet, Munda Base came on the air. "Cricket 3, Cricket 4, this is Moses. Large plot of bogeys, fifty miles, angels 8, vector 290. Buster."

"Cricket 3, roger that, Moses. Balls to the walls, boys!" Jack called out, and his flight of four turned fast to heading 290. The Corsairs accelerated as the pilots pushed the throttles forward to full, though short of War Emergency Power, reserving water injection for battle. Jack fired his guns in a short burst to test them, and the rest of the flight followed suit. Fifty miles is not a big distance for two groups of combat airplanes rushing headlong into each other, and in a few minutes, Rogers tallyhoed the group of enemies.

"Tallyho—nine bombers, eight fighters, below us, 11 o'clock!" he said into the radio with a very businesslike voice, void of any emotion or excitement, very unlike his usual friendly banter. No one could see a thing in the direction he'd mentioned, and all three members of the flight said so over the radio.

"Tallyho—nine bombers, eight fighters, below us, 11 o'clock!" Rogers reiterated without changing inflection. The others strained their eyes to see the planes against the sea glimmering blue below them. One by one they found the combatants, not more than tiny specks of silver to the naked eye but definitely arranged in vee formations. Jack marveled at Rogers' eyesight. Apparently he belonged to that elite group of pilots whose eyesight could save their necks in the heated battles they met.

"High side, left, spread out!" Jack called out to his flight of four. They spread out and prepared to attack the Japanese, who could not see them as the Corsairs were approaching from the direction of the sun. Soon Jack was looking directly into the bomber formation, an escort of Zeke fighters coursing overhead. Jack throttled back a bit to keep from flying too fast into the formation.

Just then the fighters noticed them and began to pull up and try to get a shot at the descending American fighters. Jack opened up and hit the lead Zeke squarely in the engine. The plane exploded instantaneously, and Jack pulled up to avoid the debris. This placed him again on a rising path of flight, so he traded some of his speed into altitude and turned back to fly after the bombers. The Zekes lost all sense of formation and were easy prey to the Corsairs. The other flight of Corsairs arrived to the scene and went after the bombers, who dropped their payloads and headed for the relative safety of the deck.

Jack was surprised to hear Rogers transmitting in short sentences. He was apparently reading the air battle as if he were a sports commentator relating a football game to his radio audience: "There's one to your left, crossing to your right, too close to hit him now...watch the one that's below you to the right and climbing...Zeke at your 3 o'clock, just turn and shoot...."

Jack did so and found a Zeke, a sitting duck in his sights. A brief volley of machine gun fire took the left wing off the Zeke which went into a corkscrew dive into the sea. Jack looked to mark Rogers' location. He was on Jack's right wing, a bit behind and a bit above him, watching Jack's every move, and in the process keeping tabs on nearly every enemy plane in the sky.

The battle came to an end as Boots Singer, another rookie in Jack's squadron, scored a direct hit on a Zeke coming headlong at him. However, as Singer had no time to evade, his canopy was shattered when he hit the Zeke's wing wildly fluttering in the air. He managed to duck his head, which saved his life, but his rudder suffered serious damage. He fought to regain control of his plane, and managed to do so only a couple hundred feet off the ocean.

"Can you fly it, Singer?" Jack asked, and the pilot gave him a thumbs-up. "Let's head home, folks!" Jack transmitted, waggling his wings again to collect his division. No Corsairs were harmed save the crippled Singer, so they turned towards Munda with Singer closely guarded by the other three.

The other CAP division had downed three Vals and got 2 more as probables, and they were already on their way to Munda to continue patrolling until their relief flights got there. Jack's flight helped Singer nurse his fighter towards the base maintaining a close watch on the sky all around them. Jack notified the base of Singer's plight, and the damaged plane got to land first. Singer made it without incident, after which the rest landed in quick succession. Rogers was the last man in. Again, as always, he made his landing look like the plane was extremely reluctant in getting back on the ground. For some reason his flying abilities surfaced at about a thousand feet and above, Jack thought to himself.

After the debriefing with Intelligence, Jack took Rogers to a cup of coffee at the mess. "Say, you got mighty fine eyesight. I couldn't see the first speck yet when you first called out the bandits."

"Well, truth be told, I must admit I'm pretty good at picking up things from afar." Rogers had a sip of his coffee.

"And that play-by-play reporting of the battle. I'm impressed," Jack said. "Made it much easier for me to fly and just check on targets, when you covered me so well. Where'd you pick up that ability?"

"I've thought that it's probably my abilities as an artist which give me the three-dimensional edge there. I just gauge the speed and the height difference of every plane I see, and somehow I get the knack of where they're headed, which of them are potential threats and which are just targets."

"Well, I'd like to have you as my wingman. I could use the quick thinking and sharp vision you just showed me."

"Sure thing, lieutenant. I'd rather get accustomed to someone's flying style than get yanked here and there to fly wing on all the pilots on Munda."

"Good, I'll settle it with the exec. We have the evening hop tonight, so fill up with coffee." Jack stood to go to the operations shack to secure Rogers' assignment.

From there on, it was McGuire and Rogers, Jonesy and Becker in the same flight. Flying wing never did offer much opportunity for making ace, but Rogers didn't seem to mind. He was content to make sure Jack wasn't hurt, as Jack clearly had more abilities as a marksman. Jack rarely missed a plane he shot at, while in the following six weeks Rogers managed to collect only half a share in a probable; he just did not seem to have the vision of seeing where he should aim to hit a plane that was in the air with him. Consequently, Jack's score stood at eleven by the first week of May, and Rogers still had his half share of a Zeke someone had seen limping back towards Rabaul after both Jack and Rogers had taken a shot at him.

Rogers was still unable to land his plane without having all free personnel flock to the runway to see the spectacle. "Here comes the cavalry!" was the call to get to watch Rogers touch down. It was a constant source for wild bets to see if this would be his last landing, but luck was always on his wing and he never did anything worse than bounce a few times. Rogers thus gained the moniker "Jockey" for his bouncy landing style.

Eight weeks into his tour, Rogers was up with Jack over Buka. At some point the battle, which had begun as a fighter sweep, developed into a real furball of planes going every which way and quickly expending ammunition. By this time, Jack had come to rely on Rogers' running commentary, sometimes too much, as he constantly reminded himself. He could see Rogers maintaining his position as if he were glued to his wing, and he delivered his observations in terse comments over the radio, as if it were Cornhuskers-Sooners instead of Corsairs-Zekes.

Just as Jack was preparing to shoot at a Zeke which was crossing his field of vision at a 90-degree angle, he thought he heard a popping sound in Rogers' commentary. The flow of messages ceased and Jack lost sight of Rogers for a few moments. The battle waned and planes grouped together for the return flight, and it was then that Jack found Rogers again. He seemed to be in some trouble, and there was a row of bullet holes across the fuselage at the cockpit.

Jack used hand signals to establish communication with Rogers, who indicated his radio was out and showed that he was bleeding from his left hand. Jack urged him to pour on the coal and pulled ahead of the rest of the flight to escort Rogers home.

As usual, all available personnel were lining the runway since Rogers was out on the hop. Bets were being made, and speculation on the landing was rife. To the disappointment of the crowd, Rogers pulled in as the first plane, executing a flawless landing. All onlookers were amazed at the smooth operation, and some who had bet on a full-blown cavalry-style landing were crying foul play, even accusing Rogers of switching planes with another pilot.

When Rogers finally rolled to a stop at his revetment, his crew chief climbed on the wing and pulled the canopy back. He took one look inside and yelled "MEDIC!" with wide, panic-stricken eyes before he started to unharness the unconscious pilot. Apparently Rogers' willpower alone had kept him flying, because there was blood spattered all over the cockpit, and he needed to be lifted from the plane.

Rogers had been badly wounded in the left wrist. A bullet had pierced his forearm laterally, blowing the bones into bits and piercing the artery. In-flight he had wrapped his scarf round the wrist to suppress the blood flow, but so much of his blood had already been spilled all over the cockpit.

Rogers was put on a stretcher and rushed to the sick bay, where Doc Mendel had to make a fast decision: what to do with the wrist and hand, after the bleeding had been suppressed and a transfusion arranged. He tried to see if the wrist could be formed into at least a static array of bone to save the hand, but to his dismay he could not find a single piece of bone large enough to start building on. With a sick feeling in the pit of his stomach, he performed an emergency amputation.

Jack and the crew chief were waiting for news on Rogers' condition outside the sick bay. Doc Mendel emerged from inside, and the look on his face told Jack that there had been no choice. As had most of the base, Doc knew of Rogers' artistic capabilities and the job he had waiting for him back at Disney. "Sorry, Jack, you'll just have to find another wingman. One-handed pilots don't do that well," he said, shrugging his shoulders, and went back inside.

Jack heard the crew chief curse under his breath. He was trying to think what would become of his wingman's future job. Maybe he would still be able to draw for a living, and retain the job. For that matter, Jack had no idea of how animators work. It might just as well be impossible for Rogers to work as one. He resolved to take the issue to the other pilots and his crew.

Over evening chow, Jack addressed the assembled pilots. "As you all know, my wingman became one-handed today, courtesy of a Jap 20mm. You also know the work he has been putting in as our unofficial nose-art master. He has a job waiting for him at home as an animator at Disney—does anyone know if his wound will make it impossible for him to do his job, or whether they can still use him?"

There was a mumble of discussion, until Lieutenant Mitnick, the air combat intelligence officer, spoke up. "I used to work at this ad agency, and I've seen some animators at work, and these guys at least had several sheets of paper on which they drew their pictures, and they arranged 'em between the fingers of the left hand. Then they flipped 'em back and forth to see the animation they were doing, adding a line at a time in the papers. So I don't think he can do the flipping without a left hand. But I'm no pro here, this is just a guess, so if someone has other info, spill it."

Many pilots now agreed with Mitnick's assessment, and it seemed to Jack there were no opposing ideas on the matter. This would then mean that his wingman was not only invalided by the war, but also forced out of his dream career by it. He felt terrible for Rogers, as did the entire squadron. Still, there was nothing they could do to help him.

In the morning Jack went to visit Rogers, who was lying on his bunk in the sick bay. He was pale as ice and very weak, but worse, Jack could also see the fire in his eyes was smothered. "Hey there, ace, how's it going?" Jack started.

Rogers smiled, but the smile waned fast. "As you can see, Jack … not much left of my hand," and he raised the bandaged stump for him to see.

Jack patted him on the shoulder. "Come on, champ, you'll be up and around in no time. Besides, that'll get you out of this goddamn war and back to civilian life, and you have that job to go back to. You'll be turning out new 'Dumbos' in no time!"

Rogers closed his eyes and turned his head away from Jack. "I don't think I'm any good for Disney now, Jack. Not much work for a one-handed animator."

Jack put on a cheer he didn't come close to feeling. "Aw, come on, they'll love ya! You've done such a great job with our planes and all, and besides, you got that letter of acceptance from them. You'll do just fine there."

"Y'know, it's nice of you to try to cheer me up, but one, the planes stay put when you paint 'em, and two, when they hired me, I had two hands." Again he turned his head away to face the wall. "Now there's one too few."

Rogers turned back to Jack surprisingly fast. "In fact, Jack, do me a favor? I need to dictate a letter."

Desperate, Jack grasped this straw earnestly. "Sure, pal, lemme grab that pad and then you can start."

"To: Personnel department, Disney Studios, Burbank, California, United States," Rogers started.

Jack lifted the pen from the pad. "Awww! I don't want to write *that* letter!"

Rogers looked him in the eye. "That's the only letter I

want written just now. I want to let them know I won't be coming. And if you don't help me, I'll ask one of the medics to write it."

Resigned, Jack put the pen back to the pad and started writing. He had a plan evolving in his head. Rogers wanted him to write about his wounding and based on his incapacitation as animator, he asked Disney to release him from employment. Jack held the pad up to the wounded pilot and he signed the letter in a feeble hand.

After the resignation letter was completed, Jack ripped the paper off the pad. "Listen, Rogers, I got some envelopes in my tent, and I have a couple letters I gotta mail myself. I'll go by your tent and get the address from the approval you got in your tent—where is it, exactly? Then I'll mail your letter."

Rogers instructed him where the letter was in his things. "Jack, thank you. You're a true friend indeed. Please send that letter as soon as possible."

"Sure thing, pal, just rest and get well, and I'll take care of this letter. See ya later!" And Jack left the sick bay for Rogers' tent.

On the way there he met Jonesy and Becker. He showed them the resignation letter and they shook their heads.

"That's just too bad to see," Becker said. "He really wants them to kick him out, but there's gotta be *something* he can do there, even if he doesn't animate."

"Yeah, that's exactly my point. Let's not send this letter."

"But you promised the man, Jack."

Jack touched his temple. "I know, but I have a plan. All we need is sufficient press, and they'll be glad they had him coming over in the first place. Let's find a reporter, there's always a couple hanging around."

Jack entrusted the letter to Jonesy and went out towards

the canteen, where most of the reporters loitered when they were not working. It wasn't long before Jack found a reporter, surrounded by the off-duty men whom he was interviewing. Jack was about to enter the circle of interviewees when he recognized the reporter: it was the same man Don had kidded six months earlier. Since then, he'd been made a captain in the Army. Captain Welch, as Jack saw on the reporter's nametag, recognized Jack immediately. Too late to retreat and find another writer.

"Captain Welch?" Jack grinned. "Remember me? You were here in November and you interviewed my squadron mate for your paper?"

The reporter looked at Jack with the expression of a sly fox.

"Why, sure, I remember you. The Milkmen, wasn't it? The squadron with the impeccable no-kill record and cigarette lighters in your planes?"

Jack blushed. "Sir, I'm truly sorry about that bit. That was Don Wheeler, my wingman—all the time he was alive, he just couldn't keep it straight for a minute and you happened to get in the prop wash."

The reporter looked around the ring of people, most of whom remembered the incident and were smiling either openly or in hiding. "You can say that again about the prop wash. May he rest in peace. He nevertheless took me on a ride, around the Pacific to be exact. What makes you think I would be as gullible now? I think I learned my lesson then."

Jack forged ahead. "Sir, this time I've got something for you that'll make a great story. You can help a wounded pilot rebuild his life in civvies, and it's going to be just great. All I need is some of your valuable time, but I'm convinced your readers will be really interested." Jack could see he still wasn't amused, but the old newshound was beginning to smell something worth checking out.

"Okay, flyboy, give me the quick version and I'll tell you whether you have my ear for the whole shebang. Thanks, fellas, I'll get back to you later." The reporter dismissed the ring of people around him.

"Thank you, sir," Jack nodded to Captain Welch. "Let me frame the story for you now, and then I'll show you some of the nose art I'll tell you about. You'll see that the pics and the story will work perfectly together."

The old reporter pulled out a notepad that looked like it had been in every battle since the Somme, and made a quick indexing entry on the top of the page. Jack then went on to give him the short version of Rogers' story. Captain Welch made a few cursory notes every now and again and asked a couple of clarifying questions, but Jack could see he was hooked. Then he asked to see some of the nose art Rogers had created.

They had been walking slowly along the runway as they chatted, so already they were close to Jack's mount. Jack took him around the nose to show him *Haulin' Ass*, and Captain Welch deemed it one of the best nose art jobs he had ever seen. Chuckling at the donkey, he wanted to see some more, and Jack told him every fighter nose art on the base had been made by Rogers, except for the one on the squadron's communications plane, which had been produced by an over-confident crew chief early in the conflict. Captain Welch asked a private walking past to find his photographer and send him towards Jack's plane.

When the photographer arrived, he too remembered Jack straight away. He gave him the thumbs-up, and Jack smiled vaguely back, not knowing exactly how to respond.

He need not have worried, because there was a journalist on the trail of a great story. "Morton, you still got that roll of color film in your bag?" Captain Welch asked the photographer.

"Yes, but—"

"Ya ya ya, I know you want to make the cover of *National Geographic* with some tastefully-artistic color snaps of native naked ladies, but at the risk of denying teenaged American boys their first erotic experience, I am commandeering the film for a real story. Grab a pic of every nose art you see on the base, and make sure you get them all. This is going to be the best story yet on *Stars and Stripes*!" The photographer went to get the film, his head sagging, but when he returned and started shooting the nose art, even Jack could see he got caught up in it.

Captain Welch asked Jack a few more supplementary questions and prepared to go on his way, when he asked one more thing. "Where is this guy now?"

Jack said, cautiously, "He's still in sick bay."

"I'll go over right now and get the story straight from the horse's mouth!" Captain Welch exclaimed, folding up his pad.

"Sir, I'd really ask you not to do that. He doesn't know what we're doing. Matter of fact, he asked me to send out a letter to Disney telling them he was resigning."

"Hell no!" said the Captain, "there's loads of things he can do over there! Let's get this story out and they'll both be happy, Disney and this guy, that he didn't send that letter—or did it go?"

"No," Jack answered.

Captain Welch smirked knowingly. "Confiscated?"

"Yes, sir."

"Nice work, Lieutenant!" the captain said, patting Jack on

the shoulder before leaving with the photographer.

The next day Rogers was evacuated on a R4D transport plane to Efate in the Fiji islands. He was carried onto the plane, and the last his squadron saw of him was a feeble smile on a pale face, his remaining thumb raised to the sky. The next day, Captain Welch left the base, taking with him the story and the rare color shots of the nose art. The squadron was left wondering whether the story could carry Rogers to fame, or at the very least contentment, at Disney Studios.

Two months later, mail call carried two very different items to Jack. One was a letter from Rogers, and the other was a signed copy of the latest edition of *Stars and Stripes*. In it, Captain Welch had done a superb job in describing Rogers's artistic flair and the contribution to squadron morale on the remote Pacific island base. He also mentioned Rogers's future career plans with Disney enough times that they couldn't even consider *not* taking him along. Jack cut out the article from the magazine and posted it by the squadron's victory table for all to see.

The letter to Jack was more personal. In it, Rogers explained how he had been approached by Disney while he recovered at a convalescent hospital in San Diego and how they adamantly worked him into accepting an even better position at the animation studio—how they re-recruited him. After Disney saw the photographer's prints of nose art he'd designed, he'd been placed in the character-design group of a forthcoming full-length animation movie—a significant upgrade from the position of junior animator for which they'd originally accepted him. Rogers thanked Jack many times in the letter for trying to keep his spirits up, and he was optimistic about his prospects after his release from the hospital and from active duty.

The only thing he was unable to explain was why Disney had forthrightly rejected his resignation; in fact, Disney never mentioned the letter at all. He also wondered whether Jack really did send it, but after the way things turned out, he was much happier this way. He closed the letter with warm greetings to the entire squadron and wished them well in continuing the fight.

Smiling quietly to himself, Jack went to the squadron's victory table to pin the letter right next to the *Stars and Stripes* article. There was hope after all.

18

Well before reveille, Jack was already dressed up and sitting on his bunk, watching out of the window. It was his first day as an instructor at the Naval Aviation Station, Pensacola, Florida, and he was far from looking forward to it. He could feel himself sweating just thinking of facing the eager new cadets, looking up to him to teach everything they needed to survive combat. He could not shake the memory of his past experiences at public speaking, none of which had been great successes or pleasant experiences.

He had tried to mention this uneasiness to many people, such as Doc Mendel, Bunny Radner, and every officer he thought was able to rescue him from this training assignment, but to no avail. It was standard policy to rotate experienced pilots to instructors, and that was the end of it. He was going to have to take six months to a year at Pensacola, like it or lump it.

After reveille was sounded, he had breakfast, such as it was: the great food they were offered, of which back at Munda they could only dream, Jack cut short to two cups of coffee and some orange juice. He could not force himself to eat anything solid. He thought he might go to the classroom where he was supposed to be giving his lecture on the general nature of the air war in the Pacific Theater of operations. Then he remembered that the class was supposed to get there first so Jack could be formally introduced to them. So instead he went back to his room and again sat down on the bed. He began to think of his speaker's block and how it all started.

He went back in time to a September long past, to a classroom in Nebraska. He was in second grade, and his assignment was the classic prompt, "What I did on my summer vacation." Sure, every other kid had had the same assignment, and the assignment had been known to him all summer long, but he had just ignored it until the very last opportunity. The evening before the presentation he had tried to piece together a coherent history of his summer vacation, but he got so distracted thinking of the swimming trips and harvest and visiting Aunt Clara in Omaha and all the other events that by bedtime, he had a great story, but nothing written down on paper. He could think of a million things he did over the summer, but the concept of standing up to tell others of them got him all stifled.

Tony had it all neatly laid out during the summer, and all he had to do was to piece it together; he was sleeping peacefully by the time it dawned on Jack he'd have to talk without a paper to rely on, since there was no way of getting one done by morning. He had little sleep overnight, fretting over his impending failure.

The presentation was just as big a catastrophe as it could possibly be. Every kid in the class had his shot at fame and they all took home some sort of praise from the teacher, all except Jack, whom the teacher dismissed from the podium after an embarrassing four minutes of false starts and toe-digging. He had turned a shade of red from his knees up, or so he felt, and the kids in the class wasted no time in rubbing it in. He only wanted to melt between the floorboards and escape, and for him it seemed like the longest school day ever.

When the bell finally rang, he ran from the school and

didn't go home until after dark, much to the worry of his parents. They tried to console him after he had confessed to the failure in between sniffs, but the damage had already been done. After that, he could not enjoy public speaking, but rather turned to writing. His essays were always best in class, and he pleaded with the teacher to be able to write reports on themes instead of presenting them before his fellow pupils. For the most part, his counterproposals worked.

Now, however, there was no writing his way out of this situation. Stiffly he stood up at 0743 to cross the sandy yard between Bachelor Officers' Quarters and the lecture hall. This took him two minutes, so at precisely 0745 he opened the door to Hall 102 and entered. The cadet master called the class to attention and announced the class: "Class 44-B assembled for your lecture on Air War in the Pacific, sir!"

"At ease, gentlemen, be seated," Jack said, walking to the podium. He could feel all forty pairs of eyes glued to him. *Here is a genuine flying ace, the man himself, the guy who has done in twelve Japs and lived to tell the tale*, they all thought in his mind.

The ace they were admiring wasn't with them for a second. This was the same classroom in which Jack had met Don Wheeler, and seeing it again sent him on a quick tour to the distant past of his own flight school. Don sat behind him on their first lecture. After a few minutes of listening to the lieutenant, he had leaned over to Jack, and in a theatrical whisper said, "Stick with me, kid, and we'll make ace in no time!"

The lecturer had picked up what Don had said, but could not believe his ears. "Cadet, what did you just say to the one in front of you?"

"Sir, I said, 'Stick with me, kid, and we'll make ace in no

time,'" Don answered nonchalantly.

The lecturer faked surprise. "Ace? Gentlemen, we have a real prodigy among us. At this stage of the training, he already knows he's destined to make ace. Such divine intuition deserves a round of applause," he said, and started clapping his hands. Don was not at all ashamed as the class joined the lecturer, but smiled and acknowledged the applause left and right with benevolent bows.

The lecturer smiled as he continued. "Gentlemen, the action is at such levels these days around the globe, that it's indeed possible for some of you to make it big. Some will get official recognition for their efforts, such as medals; others may yet make ace, and—" he let the smile drop off his face like a knife—"yet others will die trying." The ensuing silence lasted a good while. Jack could still remember how embarrassed he had felt.

Shaking himself out of the stupor of memory, he went over to the podium and grabbed the stick to focus his hands on something solid, decided it wasn't needed and put it back, only to pick it up again in a move of desperate indecision. The cadets waited anxiously, ready to suck up every word the man from the combat zone would say to them.

"I'm not too good at this," Jack heard himself say.

This baffled the cadets. All the other instructors they'd ever seen had been quick to assert their authority over the fledgling pilots, to tell them they had nothing to their name and that without the gems of knowledge presented at this training session, they would continue to have nothing, and then here comes this double ace, starting off like *this*. Pens were taken off papers, eyebrows went a bit higher, and everyone waited for Jack to start anew.

"I mean, I'm not good at public speaking. I've flown in

combat in the Pacific and survived, so I guess I must be somewhat good at that, but this training assignment isn't at all what I'd asked for. While I understand it's not your fault that I stand here now, trying to teach you what I know, I must ask you to be patient with me. It may take some time for me to learn how to do this. It also may be better if we train not with lectures, but with more like question-and-answer sessions. But at any rate, let's just see what comes out of all this." Jack was mildly pleased with himself now. He had confessed to the class that he was not going to try to be the hotshot everyone expected him to be, and that he wanted interaction instead of dictation.

"The Pacific is a big expanse of water with isolated pockets of Japanese planes and pilots in it. We have to find them and get them out of the air so the Navy and Army can come over and take the islands." Having served this indispensable piece of advice so early in the lecture, Jack wondered what the hell to say now.

"If you want to make notes, well, that's the whole gist of things, really." This got a shy laugh from the group and Jack felt even better.

"I guess I was handed this particular topic because other instructors know about things in Europe and you guys don't know yet where they'll ship you. The Pacific Theater is weird, because practically all fighting is done over water, and the airfield shifts around at thirty knots, whereas fields in Europe stay put. But let me start a bit further along first, and if anyone has a question at any point, just let me know and I'll call on you." Jack was feeling surprisingly good now. He decided to keep the lecture very personal and talk only from experience.

"The thing that gets me the most is navigation. Think

278

about it; you start here, fly that way for two hundred miles, fight around for half an hour and then try to figure out where you should go to get back. And while you were fighting, the airfield moved fifty miles northwest. So my first rule—and write this down—is: *Learn navigation and get real good at it.* No amount of great flying will save you if you don't know where you're going. And believe me, the sight of the ocean below you without a clue of where to turn to isn't a pleasant one." Pens went to paper as cadets thought that this man really knew his stuff. All eyes again focused on Jack after the note was made.

"Second, don't ever buy into the idea that the Japs are second-rate pilots with bad planes. I know this has been a standard call over here, but it was a goddamn rude awakening for us to see how well they flew their planes, which also could fly circles around our Brewsters and Wildcats. So my second point is, *Take every engagement as if you were facing the best.* I know full well that their training is lagging behind, and that they no longer have the best pilots in play, after Midway and the Guadalcanal campaign, but among the tyros they still have some absolutely first-rate fliers, the old hands. Meeting one of them by chance and thinking he's not that good will be your death, make no mistake about it."

Jack leaned against the blackboard. "Third, I guess I should say that first you need to learn real great flying, and then, in combat, you need to learn some unconventional flying too. I want you guys to get real snappy at every possible maneuver, like take-offs and landings of course, carriers and airfields, but also turns, aerobatics, crossovers, and the Thatch Weave. Basic was nice flying, wasn't it?"—here he looked around for approval and got ample amounts of it—"but this is where the going gets rough. You'll be surprised to discover how little time you have to aim and shoot at that Jap on your one o'clock, and if you screw around with basic maneuvers taking up all your time, soon either you'll be dead, or your wingman will be. *Snappy* is the right word for how you need to fly out there; that way, you'll have time to fight."

Jack strolled the aisle. "Unconventional—with that, I mean that you will have learned how to make a nice coordinated turn with your needle and ball indicator and airspeed and whatnot. That's all fine. You need to have that under your belt so well you can fly your bed in coordinated turns." Jack paused to allow the chuckles to die down.

"But in combat, the guy who makes a coordinated turn is the easiest target. That's how you can tell a newcomer Jap from an experienced one. If you set your sights on one of them making a turn, and he stays in your sights, he's a tyro. If the guy starts going sideways to throw off your aim, flips around in a jiffy or pulls another stunt, he's an ace and now you know. You need to be the same way when facing the Japs. Turns are just one feature of the battle, but get wise on them. It all comes back to the snappy flying; if you can fly snappy, and wrong, and support your pal who's flying wing on you just like you, you'll all get out of there okay. Those of you who fly by the book will get in trouble, and when I say this, I'm in no way meaning people teach you the wrong things in here. Let's just say no one else teaches you the way I'm going to; let's just leave it at that. Look at it this way: I came back from there and am able to tell you these things."

Jack paused again. To his complete and utter surprise, he had the undivided attention of the entire class. Everyone was listening intently and making notes, and it seemed to Jack it was fine to go into Q & A for the rest of the lecture. He asked for questions, and got thirty hands up almost instantly. Going through those took up the rest of their hour, so he had to ask the cadets to write the rest of their questions down so they could return to them next class.

After Jack dismissed the class and the last cadet had passed out the door, he hightailed it to his quarters, and promptly vomited in the toilet. Half an hour later, he was feeling nearly all right again, and was mildly proud of his achievement, having put in a decent presentation for once in his life.

The class took to Jack like puppies. They listened to his every word, and in the air, they tried their damnedest to emulate his wild flying. It seemed to Jack that after three weeks, the group he was teaching was picking up everything better than the others. They were more advanced in their formation flying, take-offs and landings, and it was clear they all wanted to fly 'snappy'. Jack settled down to a routine of lectures, training flights, some grab-ass flights with other instructors, and mock dogfights.

Days of curriculum became weeks of schedules. He became more active in staff, too, having been at first somewhat of a loner, and he even showed up at the parties on Saturday nights. Happy as he was, making progress in all these matters, he still felt he was not doing his best to promote the war effort. He wanted to be out there, doing it instead of telling others how.

After three months Jack felt he could not take the routine any more. He went to the commander to submit a transfer request, but was stared out of the office. Word got around that he wanted back to the combat zone, and many folks thought he was out of his mind to ask for another tour in the Pacific. The base commander's recommendation was essential for transfers to go through, but after trying in vain to submit another, he realized such a note would not be forthcoming.

His popularity with the classes slowly waned as he became more introspective and moody, and after one training flight where he was chased by seven cadets and managed to stay out of every gunsight in the air, he felt that he'd had his fill. Surely there had to be a way out.

The staff had an ongoing tradition of going for drinks every Friday. Jack had made friends with one Lieutenant Tom Allen, a decent chap who appreciated Jack's timid ways. Jack had confided in Allen so far as to say he was not entirely happy with the training assignment, but one Friday at the bar he felt he could not keep his wish to leave to himself. After buying two beers, Jack cornered Allen at a table. Jack had already had a couple, so he was beyond exercising his right to free speech. "Tom, I want to get back to combat," Jack said without warning.

"Don't we all? THE HELL WE DO!" roared Tom, who'd also already had a few beers.

Jack put his arm around Tom's shoulders and elaborated:

"Tom, I am not an instructor. Really, I am *not*. I'm a combat pilot and that's it. I really want to get back to where the action is."

Tom looked at Jack, his head swaying slightly from one side to the other, focusing his eyes between Jack's.

"Really? You wanna get back to b-being shot at fer *real*?"

"Yes." Jack took another sip.

Tom couldn't believe his ears. "Lemme get this straight. You went there. You had your hide pierced a couple o' times. You got your plane shot out from under you. People were aiming the business end of every conceivable weapon at you, and you want to go BACK?"

Jack reiterated that that was the general idea.

Tom tried again. "Listen, pal, over here, you got it better

than great. Fly all you want, eat all you want, womanize all you want, and if someone shoots at you, all it means is that you volunteered to fly the target tow by mistake. And you want to trade all this in for another chance of getting *killed*?"

Jack began to feel that seeking Tom's confidence been a bad mistake.

This was confirmed when Tom stood up and silenced the barroom with a few loud bellows, then bawling, "Ladies and gentlemen, I've got an announcement to make. My pal Jack McGuire over here, the best goddamn instructor I ever saw, a double ace an' all, wants to leave us and go back over to Guadalcanal or wherever and get shot down again, this time being relieved of the use of his life. I call for a moment of silence. SILENCE!"

Tom's drunken portrayal of a solemn moment was so funny to watch that instead of granting the asked-for silence, the entire barroom burst out laughing with whistles and applause.

Jack could do nothing but smile, but he did also leave the joint at the first opportune moment. In the morning, Tom Allen was suitably embarrassed, but they didn't broach the subject again until much later.

One Friday at lunch Jack was going through the *Herald Tribune*. Page 2 featured a large picture of Congressman Grundy presiding over the Naval Affairs Committee. Jack was already about to turn the page and look for the comics, when he happened to remember Grundy from the babysitting mission he did way back when. Grundy had promised each pilot a favor, and Jack would now need to find out whether he was a man of his word.

That afternoon, between two flights, Jack locked himself in his office and went to the telephone.

He asked the operator to connect him to Congressman

Grundy in Washington. Of course he was sure to be put through to a secretary instead of Mr. Grundy himself, but even so, the harsh tone of the secretary came as a shock.

"Congressman Grundy's office."

"Can I talk to Congressman Grundy, please? This is Lieutenant Jack McGuire of the US Marines from NAS Pensacola."

"The Congressman is in a meeting."

"When will he be available?"

"He's in meetings all day."

"What about tomorrow?"

"More meetings. Send him a letter."

Jack decided to go for the kill. He had little to lose anyhow.

"Lady, please tell me this: Are you the Congressman's private secretary?"

There was a startled silence for a brief moment. "Yes. Why?"

"Have you been his secretary for long?"

Another pause. "Twenty-two years."

Jack knew he had her now. "Would you be working for anyone else in Congress if Mr. Grundy wasn't there?"

"Not very likely, no," the lady said.

Jack shot his bolt. "Thought not. Lady, if it wasn't for me and three other pilots, your boss would've been dead since last November, and you'd be assembling torpedoes for the war effort. Now, get me Congressman Grundy!"

At that Jack could hear the clacking of heels on the floor and a door being opened, a switchboard clicking, and then the voice in the phone changed.

"Lieutenant! What can I do for you?" Congressman Grundy sounded very pleased to hear Jack calling him.

Jack took a deep breath, and started to tell his story.

"Sir, I realize I'm way out of line calling you like this, and please tell your secretary I'm sorry for having attacked her like that, but you're my only chance of getting back into combat. I was one of the four pilots who covered your flights to and from Munda, and we brought down a few Rufes that were bothering your plane, and you said then that..."

"Yes, I remember," interrupted the Congressman with a hint of a smile in his voice, "and you'd like to collect on my promise *now*, I presume? What would your request be exactly?"

"Sir, I know there are men out there in the combat zone who would give anything to be where I am now, training cadets stateside, but this job just isn't for me. I can't think I'm doing all I can over here. I really would like to get back to the combat zone, but my superiors won't even take my transfer requests any more. So I thought I'd cash in my chips on the odd chance that I'd get in touch with you. Maybe you could put in a word for me and make my commanding officer take in my request and get me back to the Pacific, where my squadron's still fighting. I mean, training is okay as part of the war effort and all that, but I'm no instructor at heart. I am a combat pilot, and that's it."

Jack paused to draw some breath. Now he was sure he could hear the Congressman smile as he responded.

"Lieutenant, let me see what I can do. I do know a couple of folks over at the Pentagon. You'll know soon enough if I succeed. In the meantime I'd rather you didn't tell anyone of this conversation, by the way." The Congressman was apparently quite terse when he meant business.

Knowing he'd pressed his luck as far as he dared, Jack thanked him and put down the receiver. Only then did it hit him head-on what an audacious move it had been to call the Congressman cold.

Eight days later Jack was summoned to the base commander's office. Colonel Turner shoved a paper in Jack's face. "McGuire, what is this?"

Jack studied the paper, which was indeed a transfer order for him. "It's my transfer orders, sir. I'm to rejoin VMF-288 without delay."

"That much I know already. And just how in the hell did you get this paper to be drafted? You know full well no one leaves this place unless I say so, or someone from upstairs decides that way, and somehow you found a way of getting upstairs without my help. Just to make sure it doesn't happen again, I want to know how you managed *this* bit of trickery!" Colonel Turner was almost purple in his face.

"Sorry sir, that's classified information." Somehow Jack managed to suppress the smile he felt forming.

"*Classified*, my ass...I hate being told to release someone, especially if it's someone as good as you. Still, I have no option but to sign the receipt of this since it's already signed by a major general at the Pentagon. You need to be out in San Diego by the eighteenth of this month. Here's your paperwork. Sign it and get out of my sight!"

Jack signed the dotted line, collected the manila folder, and saluted snappily. As he turned to leave, he heard the colonel call him.

"McGuire?"

Jack turned around.

"Yes, sir?"

Turner seemed to be chewing his tongue. "Aww ... just get the hell out of my office!" The old colonel turned to look out of the window at some cadet coming in for a bouncy landing and cursed.

Jack smiled and left.

Once in his room at the Bachelor Officers' Quarters, he started packing. It was now the sixth of the month, so he had almost two weeks of leave before he had to report to San Diego Naval Station for transport to the combat zone. He had no clue as to what he ought to do. He briefly toyed with the idea of going to New York, as he'd never been there, but ruled it out due to the sheer expense. A holiday in Miami was a distinct possibility, since while at Pensacola he'd visited there many times and knew where to board for a very reasonable price. The absence of friends there eventually made him abandon that idea too.

At the back of his mind he knew he just about had to go home, but the notion of up to nine days there did not appeal to him. Counting his money and weighing personal comfort against familial duty, he decided to pay Mom and Pop a visit. He cabled them and finished packing. While thinking of what to do in the meantime, he idly browsed a two-day-old copy of the local newspaper. In the sports pages was a story of Tom Allen winning a springboard diving contest. In the picture of the medallists, taken outside under a cloudy sky, Tom was the only one with a very definite shadow.

Jack felt the familiar twist in his stomach. He only wondered how long it'd take, and whether he'd hear when it happened.

On his way out, when he reached the front gate, he heard someone calling his name. It was Tom, who ran up to Jack and, on reaching him, first had to catch his breath for a second.

"I just heard...how did you do this, you bastard?"

Jack smiled. "It's just knowing who to call, pal, that's all," and he patted Tom's shoulder.

Tom grew serious. "Listen, Jack, the other night, the reason I staged that scene was that I want to get out of here just as hard as you do, but I can't. I tried the old man three times and the last time I put in a transfer request, I only got my hearing back the next week. I want to find a way out, too!"

Jack had to tell his friend he could not help, and that he couldn't even reveal the method which got him back on the road to combat.

Tom shrugged. "Oh well, when you get there, take care, and take out a bunch of 'em while you're at it, won't you? We'll meet after the war and laugh about the training command, I'm sure. Keep in touch, OK?" They shook hands and parted company, Jack keeping the sense of doom to himself.

Two days after leaving the base Jack had to call the base from Cincinnati to ask them to send him some papers he had left at the office. During the call he was told that Tom Allen had bought the farm, running into his cadet wingman who'd failed to note that Tom was turning right. There was just one molten mass of metal on the ground—the planes had fused together when they collided and burned.

Jack put the receiver down on the hook and stared out the rainy window.

The train ride back home to Nebraska was just about as boring as it ever could be. The Midwestern scenery failed to grab his attention, no one he knew was on any of the trains, and he had to change trains eight times. Only as he neared his home town did he start to feel a bit better. The sight of familiar places appealed to him. To his great surprise, he found himself missing his boyhood pals, most of whom he had not seen in years, or did not even know whether they were alive.

Next to the station he saw the warehouse window Tony

had broken with a well-aimed pebble—apparently nobody had bothered to fix it even after all these years—and the apple orchard of Nielsen's widow, still looking like the pilferers' paradise it was when he was a kid. Every detail in the scenery spoke to him in murmurs of memory, filling his head with an undefined but definitely warm feeling. It lasted until he remembered Amy.

From the train station, Jack got a lift home on the mail truck. It was nice to chat about local things with Hank Weddell, the mailman. Though much had changed, it fundamentally felt the same. The ride home took half an hour but it seemed like less than a minute to Jack when he got off the truck by the roadside in the noontime sun, as Hank went on his way.

Jack did not hurry along the poplar-lined road to the house, choosing to soak in the familiar sights and scents. Everything was just as he remembered, down to the last spade forgotten by Tony at the side of the ditch. This gave him enormous comfort after surviving such a chaotic world as the Pacific Theater of war, of some things in this world at least remaining constant. He thought of sitting down by the shade of a huge poplar tree and closing his eyes, but he was spotted by his sister Emily who let out a wild whoop and rushed to him, dropping her laundry basket.

"Jack! We didn't expect you until tomorrow!" she greeted him as she gave him a hug. "Mom will be so happy to see you, and Dad too. Anna is in town, but she'll be home soon."

"Sure is great to see you, Emily. And hey, thanks for all your letters. They were more important to me overseas than you could ever imagine."

Taking his hand, Emily led him up the road to the house. "It's hard to imagine where you were when you read them. Is it really all just like a jungle?"

Jack was hard pressed to find an answer.

"Yes, and not really—it's more like just blue sea everywhere and then a few islands that are all green and here and there the odd reef with not much on it. It's really just so different from all this. I can't explain it but I hope you get to see them one day, they're really quite beautiful." They walked up to the house talking, hardly giving a turn to one other.

Jack's mother stepped down from the porch to greet her son. "It's so good to see you all right, Jack! You don't know how many War Department telegrams they've had even in this town after you left. It was just awful, waiting, but I'm so glad to see you!" She kissed and hugged Jack until he felt smothered.

"Well, Mom, I'm home for the week, so we have a little time to catch up on everything," he said, picking her up and carrying her up the stairs to the porch.

"Oh, put me down, why don't you? Lunch will be ready in an hour, so why don't you go and get freshened up? It must have been a long train ride. Dad's out with Joe Mellis and they will be back for lunch." Jack agreed, and picking up his duffel bag he went upstairs to his room.

Here, nothing had changed. His baseball bat was still leaning against the bedpost, the balsa planes still hung from the ceiling, swaying gently with currents of air, with a layer of dust cloaking the brightly-painted wings. On his desk his mail, whatever had not been forwarded to the combat zone, was neatly stacked in three piles: mail deemed by his family to be of little importance, mail from the university, and personal mail. He opened the letters in the personal stack and found little he wanted to know, so he placed all of those in the wastebasket. The same fate awaited the other two stacks.

290

He picked up a plane from the wall, gave its rubber-band engine a few twists, and let it run in his hand. The current of air felt cool on his hand, and he wandered in his memory back to the carefree days of model building with Tony. He felt a sharp pain for his brother's death once again, even though most of the time he'd been able to suppress it altogether. He put the plane away, took another one up and did the same rounds for it, but its rubber band had become brittle and it broke as he turned the propeller. Somehow he felt this plane was a lot like his life.

"Jack! Good to see you, son!" Mr. McGuire burst into the room. "Safe and sound, eh? You're the talk of the town—everyone knows your score and they all slap me on the back for having an ace in the family!" He shook Jack's hand.

Jack surprised his father by hugging him warmly, but he responded gladly when he did so.

"Good to see you too, Dad, but the kills—they're all teamwork. I didn't do them on my own, no way."

"Come on, son, there's no one in that plane but you. It's *your* skills that make the difference. Have you been fed already, or are we still waiting on lunch? I saw you ride in with Hank and told Joe to finish up outside by himself. I wanted to get to see you soon as I could." Mr. McGuire put his arm around Jack and began to steer him downstairs.

"Lunch is all but ready," said Jack's mother. "Come and sit down, it'll be just a minute more."

Jack took his old seat, at the side of the table facing the sink. It felt odd but still comforting to be able to sit there once more, taking in the scents of the lunch Mom was preparing, seeing Emily and Dad in their seats.

Just as they began to eat, Anna came in from town. It took some time for to calm down from the thrill of seeing Jack after so long, but finally they had their lunch. Over the meal Jack felt at ease for the first time in a long while.

After lunch, Mr. McGuire said: "Son, if you'd care to, I'd like to take you for a walk. I have something to tell you." Jack's mother and his sisters lowered their faces.

Not good, thought Jack, but agreed to go with his father.

Mr. McGuire got up from the table, picked up his hat, and extended his arm to Jack. They thanked Jack's mom for lunch, and as they went out of the door and onto the farmyard, the women came to the window to watch them walk away.

Jack already knew where they were headed. The few moments of rest his father allowed himself were invariably spent on a little hill, on top of which grew a lone tree. It had become known as the Leaning Tree, as Mr. McGuire liked to rest his back against it, the perfect height for someone his size. As a special treat for himself, on summer Sundays with great weather, he'd take along a book and read for a couple of hours up on the hill. Such days were very rare though, and Jack had come to associate them with a particular jovial mood of his father's.

Ordinary walks up the hill were usually signs of a good mood, but Jack had a curious feeling about this one.

First, Jack's father was not walking with his usual brisk gait, and in fact he appeared to be fatigued. Second, he breathed very heavily, also unusual for him. Jack stayed a couple of steps behind his father, watching. After twenty minutes they reached the tree up the hill, and for one silent moment they admired the landscape which opened around them. Then Mr. McGuire set himself against the tree and looked down at the farm below.

"Jack—I have to be blunt. I am going to die soon."

Jack had anticipated everything short of this statement. He

drew in a long breath of air. "Die? What from?"

"Cancer in the stomach somewhere. Or everywhere. Can't you see the jaundice? My gall bladder is overflowing and it's making me yellow in the eyes."

Jack was unsure how to react, so he remained silent.

"I see you're at a loss for words, son—I would be too. No need to say anything. It's in me, and it won't go till it takes me with it. So, there's a couple of things I wanted to talk about, which is why we're here. I didn't want to ruin your leave, but maybe it's better to get on with this and then you can rest and relax."

Mr McGuire closed his eyes.

"All I ask is that you take care of your mother when you get back from the war." Jack started to say something, but a wave of his father's hand silenced him. "Yes, I know you will. But with Tony gone, and your sisters marrying at some point and likely moving away from here, and me dead, I want to know you'll see to her so she can go on living as well as possible. At least arrange for her well-being, if you can't do it in person."

Jack felt hoarse. "Sure thing, Dad, you know I'll do that, as far as it's ever possible for me. I got to get out of the war first, but when I do, I'll take good care of her."

Old McGuire smiled feebly. "I know you will, Jack, I trust you with all my heart. And as for the war, I just have this feeling it won't do you any more harm. Don't ask why, but I just feel that way. I'm happy this part is over now."

Mr. McGuire spread his arms. "Look at this, Jack, look at *all* this, and suck it in. Take it back with you. Put this peaceful view of home in your heart for the times to come, and it'll ease your mind every time as it does mine, whenever I'm troubled. But now, the second thing I wanted to talk about."

Jack wondered what would be coming up now. It was hard thinking it would be anything but a pledge to keep the farm.

"Jack, I want you to do something for yourself." Old McGuire looked Jack in the eye. "I want you to live for yourself. I've been taking stock of my life lately, and I came to an unpleasant conclusion: I failed to live my life."

Jack again prepared to protest, but was silenced.

"No, it's true. I lived for the farm. I didn't even live for my family, but for the land itself. That's a mistake I don't want you to make. I started out my life as a poor son of a poor man, and when I saw my opportunity for getting out of poverty, I jumped at it. I worked my land, sailed right through the good times and the bad times, even the Depression, not looking left or right for anything besides the land." He lowered himself down to squat against the tree, and Jack sat down on a stone.

"Remember how I came up here with a book sometimes? Just to spend some time up here?" Jack nodded. "Well, let me let you in on a secret. I never read a single page up here. All the time I was just thinking about the farm, how to make it better and bigger and finer than anyone else's. I may have looked like I was reading, but my mind was always on the land. Some of my best ideas for the farm were hatched up here," and again he made a sweep of his hand to indicate the farm's expanse. "But...now I see it's all come to nothing in the end. I have a nice farm, we make a good living, and that's it. I haven't got anywhere myself."

Jack had to protest. "Dad, that's not true. You're too hard on yourself. Your work on the farm made it our home. Us kids, we had a great childhood here. We were always warm, well-fed and cared for, and it was all your hard work that got us all that."

"Now, son, don't forget your mother. When I was out in

the fields, she was working just as hard in the house. That's another disappointing thing I realized—I never appreciated her enough for what she did. I was always too busy talking about the farm to hear what she had to say."

Jack went on pleading. "Yes, Mom was there too, sure—but she was working *with* you *for* us children. I don't know anyone who had it better than we did, and that's the truth!"

Mr. McGuire looked Jack in the eye. "But you know, Jack, the funny thing is that when someone tells you you're going to go—in my case it was Dr. Schwinn, who told me there's maybe a few months more—you look back and it all gets a new perspective. I want you to know that now, since you can still do something about how you see your life. So what I want you to do is to make your own choices."

"But I've done that all along," Jack said.

Looking down at the farm buildings, Mr. McGuire said softly, "No, you haven't. I never asked you if you wanted to study agriculture. I didn't ask if you wanted to study something else, or to study at all. I didn't ask Tony either, and look where it got him. I've blamed myself for his death all along, because it was because of me alone he went the way he did."

"Dad, it's a war out there. You can get killed doing anything in it. And hey, you can die for many other reasons too, outside the war!"

"Yes, son, you can, but it was so wrong of me to do that to Tony. That's also why I want you to promise me you'll do it differently. I want you to think every decision through from this point of view: is it good for *you*?"

Jack suddenly felt very close to the old man. "What do you want me to do?"

His father looked at him and smiled.

"First off, the farm. If you don't want to live here and farm it, sell it. Although no one ever tells me anything, I seem to understand there's a lieutenant here that Emily goes for—a nice boy, one-armed though. He says the last thing he remembers of Europe was looking for his left arm on the beach where they landed. Anyway, they might want the farm if you don't. It may be my life's work but it doesn't have to be yours. When I'm gone, I won't have need for more soil than the six feet they put on top of me. Oh, don't look so surprised. I am old, I am sick, and I have thought of this long enough now to say this."

Mr. McGuire closed his eyes and rested a while. Then he spoke: "Follow your own mind after the war. Even if it takes you somewhere else, make your life your own. All I ask is that you make sure your mother has it all right, but outside that, don't let anyone tell you what you need to do. You'll know inside where you need to be, and what's there for you to do— it'll all come to you. Just stay aware of the decisions you take, and make sure you alone make the calls."

Jack smiled. "I promise." They shook on it and started down the winding path. Jack looked at the back of his father as he walked slowly down the hill, and imprinted the whole scene in his mind, clear and crisp.

It was the fastest leave Jack ever had; it seemed to be over in a day. He managed to see some old friends, help out on the farm, talk more with his father, entertain the girls with his Pacific stories, and sleep a lot. For three days he put off visiting Amy, but then he decided to bite the bullet and go see his only, if very distant, love. In the barn he found his old bike and decided the tires had enough air in them to ride a few miles.

Here, thousands of miles from the combat which was tearing the Earth itself apart, riding his bike along his old paths seemed like time travel. Nothing much had changed, apart from trees and bushes growing and some new fields being carved out of the wilds. All the old houses were still there, now maintained by the old generation, and from every porch he got at least a wave, if not offers of lemonade.

Amy's house stood alone amid the fields, and the road leading to it was lined with poplar on both sides. As he reached the house, Amy's mother came out to greet him. "Jack! Is that really you?"

"Yes, ma'am, it's really me. I'm on my way back to the Pacific, but I have a few days of leave. I was wondering if Amy was here?" Jack anticipated a 'no'. Had Amy been home, he was sure she'd have rushed to the porch to meet him, but Mrs. Miles had bad news.

"Sorry, Jack, but Amy's been in Omaha for almost a year now. She went there to become a nurse, but with the war, she's working at a munitions plant for now. She'd have loved to see you." Mrs. Miles rolled her hands in her apron as she spoke, confounding Jack a bit.

It seemed to him there was more here than was being told.

"Too bad … I'll just write her a letter, I guess," he said.

Mrs. Miles jumped at the thought.

"Yes, dear, please do! She loves letters." More fumbling with the apron.

"Maybe you can give me her address?" Jack said.

"Oh, why don't you just write us here and I'll forward your letter along with the other ones, I mean, with her ordinary mail. Oh, she'll be so pleased to hear from you!" Mrs. Miles smiled and Jack was now certain he had no need to write. He promised to do so anyway and bid his farewell, mounting his bike and pedaling downhill.

After a few more days, Jack's departure was at hand much

too soon. The whole family came out to the whistle-stop to see him off. The girls cried and hung themselves on him, while his mother offered reasonable advice on how to dress in the tropics. His father mostly smiled in the background, and when his turn came to send his son off, the engine was already puffing. Mr. McGuire shook Jack's hand and said, "Son, keep the pledge. Goodbye."

Jack had to hug him, tears in his eyes. "Goodbye, Dad. Thanks for everything."

His father gripped him tightly, then let him go. "The train's moving, son."

Jack hopped onto the last car. As the train pulled out, he knew it was the last he would see of his father. By the time the train went around the first bend, hiding his family from view, he was feeling miserable. Rather than cry in public, he left his bag behind and climbed to the roof of the passenger car. There he sat down, leaned his back on the air vent, and let his tears flow. The slipstream of the train dried them off as soon as they emerged from his aching eyes, but it took him a long while to calm down. Just as soon as he felt he'd sent off his father, he remembered Tony, and after that his friends who'd fallen from the skies over the Pacific. He was glad it took time for the train to reach the next station.

The trip back to the combat zone was uneventful, as far as such a thing was possible in times of war, but in the first batch of mail he got a letter in his mother's tiny handwriting. He knew the contents before he read it. She explained how his father had passed away eight days after he left, and the family had decided not to do anything about the estate until Jack had made it back to Nebraska. Jack put the letter in the envelope and stashed it away.

19

The morning of February 18, 1946, found a very tired Jack McGuire twiddling a spoon in his hands. He was sitting on a stool in Lou's Diner just off campus, an empty coffee cup in front of him, trying to figure out what to do with his life. While he was sure every other student at the university was faced with the same dilemma, he was in a defeatist mood and was certain that the others all had an escape plan of some sort, and that he was the only loser on the entire campus.

After his release from the Marines, he'd actually looked forward to getting back to civilian life. His combat record had earned him enough points to be released among the first (the officer who released him had quipped, 'Hell, with these points you can buy half your squadron off the books!'), so in late September 1945 he'd turned in his military gear and walked away from that part of his life. He had hurried back home to spend a few days with his family, but he had also felt a need to get started with his studies as soon as possible. Making it back to civilian life after years of sustained danger felt like a dream come true.

He had managed to join his class in early October, and for a time felt welcome and full of energy about it. He enjoyed getting back to studies, and found agronomy very interesting. He enrolled in all the required courses he could fit into a schedule. Extracurricular activities, too, caught his fancy, and he started bowling and joined the theatre ensemble. The latter, he admitted to himself, was not for a particular love of theater, but rather for the prospective leading lady.

By the end of November, however, things started going awry. He was having trouble sleeping, and being constantly tired made him perform poorly in his studies. His schedule was proving too busy to be enjoyable any more, and to add insult to injury, the lady he had followed through the portals of the theater proved to be more into football than flying. This last straw notably affected Jack, considering his scarce success in the feminine world. He had been cultivating far-ranging pipe dreams and life plans with this girl, and when he was ditched in favor of the fullback, he found it very hard to take.

On this morning at Lou's, he was considering his options once again. Sure, he had a GI Bill education in the making, and a farm back at home where he could put it into good practice. He still felt damn sore about the ditching, but hoped he'd find that special someone for himself. Then, two more years of school and he could go back home to run his first-class farm the way it was meant to be run.

The big fly in the ointment was that he was far from sure he wanted to go home in the first place. With his parents and Tony gone, Anna in Berkeley studying psychology and only Emily home to welcome him, he wasn't sure he'd want to make a living out of farming. It was no fault of Emily's—she loved him as much as ever and was eagerly awaiting his return.

Suddenly the radio started playing the Gershwin tune *"But Not For Me"*. It could have been Ella, or Billie—Jack could not identify the melancholy, deep and feminine voice. But the words struck home. He listened even though he knew the words well enough by heart. Jack marveled how well Ira had captured his situation right down to his ill-fated romance with

Jessica in the halls of the theater:

"... *I guess she's not—she's not for me...* "

Jack asked Edith, the morning waitress, for another helping of less-than-fresh apple pie and some more coffee. She reminded him of his mother and sometimes she also acted the part. But now, as she was busy flirting with a truck driver, she merely plopped the goods on the counter in front of Jack. He thanked her, though she could not possibly hear at the far end of the counter, and certainly did not care.

Thoughts ran rampant in Jack's head: studies, love, the farm, work, sleepless nights, nightmares. They took on the shapes of thoroughbred racehorses galloping round the track, all vying for first place. None of the problems managed to get a sufficient lead over the others and thus get resolved; when Jack decided to clear up love, for example, in the back of his head the farm demanded a working plan for dividing it among Emily, Anna and himself, or his future as a farmer wanted to be more clearly defined.

To take a respite from the race, Jack grabbed a newspaper from behind the counter. Surprisingly, it was only two days old, and the top right corner held an interesting teaser: "Air Force of One". Jack turned to page fourteen, where under a stain of chicken broth or some other yellowish substance, the byline read: "Local pilot purchases fighter plane".

Jack read on. "Frank Aioli, a wartime pilot from the legendary 357th Fighter Squadron, bought his favorite plane at a government auction last week. Fending off scrap metal dealers, Aioli paid $1,220 for a P-51D Mustang, fully-functional though without guns. 'This is a dream come true,' the proud owner commented. 'The Mustang carried me through the war and I came to love the plane. So it was an easy choice when I had to decide whether to invest in a company or buy this plane. The surplus auctions offer unbelievable value for money, and with the reduced Army Air Force of today, there's plenty of real gems out there.'"

The story went on for a generous share of space on the page, but Jack didn't read it all. He looked at the picture of the pilot holding his plane by a propeller blade and noted how his shadow fell in a different direction from the plane's. "Hope you enjoyed the plane before you crashed in it," Jack muttered to himself as he folded the paper away.

The race had not reached any decisive stage in Jack's absence. The thoughts were just as busily running the course, jockeying for position. It occurred to Jack that a scorecard might help him sort them out, so he asked Edith for some paper and a pen. Since the trucker was showing interest, she was very annoyed by such a nonprofit request and slammed her order slip stack in front of Jack. "Need more, the stationery shop's down two blocks that way." She returned to her ongoing project and Jack smiled at her back.

He overturned the stack and tore off one slip. He drew three columns in the back of the paper. One was labeled *Issue*, the second *Status*, and the third, *Outlook*. Quickly he filled in the first column with *Studies*, *Family*, *Farm*, *Career*, *Romance*, *Money*, and after a little thinking, *Health*. After some additional pondering he added *Interests*.

To get on with his table, he filled in the *Status* field of *Studies* with "OK". It was true enough for the classes he had cared to take seriously, but less so for some others. *Family* got a status of "Needs attention soon", since the farm ownership issue would have to be resolved. The same note was carefully written for the *Farm* and its *Outlook* was awarded a cheerful "Good".

Jack felt this was finally getting him somewhere. Tools

were all-important. *Career* was another easy fill—a successful life as a farmer—and he duly noted "Good" in both entries. *Money* was covered by the GI Bill as far as the studies were concerned, and the farm was in good shape and therefore valuable. Monetary status and outlook were therefore "Good".

With the scorecard half finished, he saw the tricky parts were all left. *Romance*—should he strike the entry altogether? He had had quite enough of it lately. Maybe he should just give it up cold turkey. "*Status*—Dismal" followed by "*Outlook*—Nonexistent" appeared on the sheet. He let out a silent sigh. All his friends were on their way to the harbor of matrimony, it seemed. Seeing those words stare at him was like a slap in the face, and yet he felt that admitting a problem existed was the first step in getting it sorted out.

Health was assessed as "Adequate" in its status, but *Outlook* got an energetic "Work on this". As an afterthought he added, "take a trip to the sun". He had many times wanted to feel a really hot sun on his face after his return from the Pacific, but he had consciously pushed it away as something from the past.

Interests. This proved to be the toughest nut yet. In the vein of honesty he had shown in the *Romance* field, he decided to finally look at what he really wanted to do. He took a separate slip and started listing his interests. "Flying, working with people, travel, flying" were written down in short order. He drew a big black plus sign to the left of these. Below, he drew an equally menacing minus. "Studies, graduating, agronomy" appeared on the sheet much to his horror. He was studying agronomy, for God's sake. He also noted he had listed "flying" twice, but that probably only reinforced the yearning he had to get back in the air.

He'd liked working with other people for the first time ever in the Marines, and for the second time, in the theater ensemble. The director of the play had noticed his social awkwardness the very first time they'd had a larger congregation of actors at the stage, but he had urged Jack to work on his disability and eventually to turn it into a positive force. He felt he had succeeded in it, even to the extent that he was actively thinking of ways to allow himself to interact with others. To him, it was a major victory.

As for travel, ever since he'd seen the South Pacific, he'd been injected with a desire to see what was beyond the horizon. In a sense it went back to his boyhood plane rides with Old Joe Selig, but now he had found he could daydream of palm trees even in the middle of exams. He had no idea where he wanted to go, but wherever it was had better be far from Nebraska.

Suddenly he thought he detected a pattern forming on the paper. He had to get the farm ownership sorted out, that much was certain. He also needed to find a vocation which would not be a lonesome vigil by a field of ripening harvest, and to find a way to see palm trees. Above all, he had a yearning to fly that was like a dull ache in his backbone, alleviated only by changing the G force through aerobatics. Quickly he noted all these down on a third page, and drew a large circle encompassing them all.

He picked up the paper again, and looked at the price the pilot had paid for his surplus Mustang—$1,220. What if *he* went and bought himself a Hellcat? Surely the Navy was auctioning out stuff as well? But he promptly ruled it out. Barnstorming was a thing of the distant past, and outside the Reno Air Races there was not much flying to be done in a Hellcat. A gas guzzler like that would eat up too much money even to get airborne.

Then he thought about buying a PBY Catalina, but quick-

ly overruled himself on the grounds of not having a multiengine pilot rating. Besides, maintaining that plane would be
a big burden and probably required forming a company to run
it. He did, however, allow himself the luxury of remembering
what it was like flying in a transport plane over the azure
waters of Fiji. Daydreaming this took so long that his coffee
went cold. Gulping it down nevertheless, he remembered his
talk with his wartime crew chief, in which he had first thought
of relocation to Hawaii.

Already on the way back from combat in late August 1945,
he had seen that the islands were on their way to becoming an
integral part of mainstream America with people and crowds
and vigorous development, and he did not relish that prospect
at all—Hawaii was not for him.

Suddenly he hit the jackpot. His thoughts zeroed in on the
scout and observation plane used in the Navy. He knew in an
instant that the Vought-Sikorsky OS2U Kingfisher was his
plane. He could buy one off the Navy, move somewhere
south, and start a company for sightseeing flights. San Diego,
perhaps, or Florida—Cuba? Or Mexico, maybe. Travel would
only grow down there. Sure, why would he have to keep to
the domestic sites? The further south, the better!

Come to think of it, Sydney had been a very nice place for
R & R, he thought, and saw in his mind's eye a company sign
in Sydney Harbor proudly advertising "McGuire's Pleasure
Flights". He'd have a hangar built right by the side of the
harbor where all the tourists flocked, and he'd make a fortune!

His subconscious mind, timid as ever, forced a reality
check. A one-plane flight company wouldn't cut it. It would
have to be just one part of a larger venture. Still, by now he
was getting really interested. He sent a spaniel glance in the
direction of Edith, who, having had to release the trucker

from her voluptuous lure as he left for Albuquerque, got the idea and filled his cup with hot coffee. He blew her a kiss and resumed his search for the solution, a parent operation for sightseeing flights.

Two words appeared out of nowhere and filled his head like a Times Square neon sign: *Tulagi Hotel*. That was the name and the place—and the operation. The Solomon Islands were where he'd jousted with Death and emerged victorious; there he'd seen how the natives lived peacefully, close to nature, with incredibly beautiful places around every corner. He also would escape the crowds, which he had never really liked, but on the other hand, when travel picked up in the region, he would already be the established proprietor of Tulagi Hotel and its sightseeing flight services.

He tore one more slip from the pad and triumphantly labeled it *The Master Plan*. It comprised several items:

```
1) Sell farm to Emily and Anna (if she wants a
share)
2) Drop out of college
3) Find Navy surplus sale and buy a Kingfisher,
Duck or other floatplane
4) Get all of the stuff over to the Solomons
5) Start Tulagi Hotel and settle down. Live life.
```

He stared at the paper in disbelief. Here was his ticket, his plan, his direction for all eternity. The race ended and he dismissed the horses from his head. He flippantly stuffed three dollar bills down Edith's breast pocket and threw her a kiss. Out on the street, he half-walked, half-ran up the street to the post office where he had found a warm telephone booth. There were two calls to make, one to Emily and the other to Anna.

The first went through in five minutes, and he asked Emily to get a quote on the farm's value from a realtor, and to consider whether she could manage it. The second call took longer to go through, but was over quicker. Anna, though cross over being abruptly awakened, agreed to come home for the weekend to settle the open issue. That done, he went to a class on agricultural chemistry, never a favorite with him, with a broad smile.

On Friday, Jack went to class as usual. At 2:30 that afternoon he boarded a bus for Winton, where he arrived around five. He was home by six for the dinner which Emily had prepared for him. Leftovers were dutifully saved for Anna, who would arrive later from California.

Emily handed Jack an envelope. "Here's the envelope from the realtor. I haven't opened it, because I thought you would want to see it first," she said. Jack took it and smiled.

"Thanks! I'll go through the farm papers and this stack later."

Over dinner, Jack had the pleasure of finally meeting Emily's one-armed suitor, Victor Vaughan, who turned out to be a very nice fellow, exactly the sort of person he'd expect Emily to find. Jack vaguely remembered Vic from school and thoroughly enjoyed talking with him, and found him entirely suitable for the plan he'd hatched. Vic did not stay the night but agreed to return in the morning.

After Anna had arrived and had eaten, the three McGuires sat around the fireplace. Both Anna and Emily had been bugging Jack all night to tell them why he'd assembled this reunion, but he'd only smiled. "All in due time" was his only reply. Emily had made a pot of hot chocolate, thick and creamy, just as their mother had made it on winter evenings, and they sat sipping it silently. There was no need for words in their small circle; every one of them felt the soothing warmth of the large fireplace, like a mother's loving hand, and savored the presence of their siblings, along with the bittersweet yearning for childhood and days so long past. It was late when they finally went to bed, after the red embers succumbed to the night.

In the morning, Vic was the early bird. He prepared breakfast for the others with surprising agility for a one-armed man. Jack said as much, but Vic thought nothing of it. "Got to make do with what you got," he said cheerfully while pouring black coffee out of a battered pot.

Jack filled his lungs with the nearly tangible, wonderful smell. "You sure know how to brew some wicked coffee."

Smiling, Vic handed him his eggs and bacon. "Save your praise till you taste our local specialty, Bacon Vaughan." Jack devoured a hefty and very tasty portion.

By noon, it was time. Jack, having assembled the meeting in the living room, got the ball rolling. "First of all, thanks for coming. I believe it's time to settle all the issues in the air surrounding this farm and its future, and all our futures as well. Mom and Dad worked real hard on this place, and left us a great inheritance. I think we all need direction and purpose at this point in our lives, and together we can make sure we all make the best of it."

Emily and Anna nodded and Victor sat quiet by the fireplace. Jack gave him a smile to tell him there was a part for him to play in this plan.

"I've come to the conclusion that I'm not going to come back to the farm after I graduate. Matter of fact, I'm not sure I will graduate at all. I've decided to take my life in a different direction, and I hope you all see the reasoning behind the plan I'll now explain." This unexpected announcement received startled looks from the girls, since everyone had always assumed Jack would take the farm and pay off the sisters. Now, everything was up in the air.

"Emily, I'm very happy to see that you've found a man like Vic here. He's the perfect partner for you as you take on the farm."

Emily blushed at the mention of Victor, and invited him to sit with her.

She put her hand on his shoulder. "We can manage, Jack. I'm sure of it. We can, because we'll work hard like Mom and Dad did."

Anna looked happy for her sister too, but she also seemed anxious about her own share of the farm.

"Anna," Jack continued, "I believe you and I are in more immediate need of money than acreage. You need to finish your degree, and then I think you want to go on and get a PhD in Psychology, isn't that right?" Anna nodded.

"Okay, then. I have a proposal to make. What if we calculate the value of the farm, the land, buildings, livestock, the works, and put it in the same stack as Uncle Nathan's securities and stocks. Then we deal out the goods and the greenbacks, and we all will have enough to get ahead in our lives. How does that sound?" Everyone smiled at Jack. He put out a paper on the table and started to write figures on it.

"I asked Emily to make some enquiries as to the value of the farm at current land prices. From the realtor's letter and the farm papers, it seems that Dad left things in such great shape that it's actually very valuable. It paid off handsomely to install that irrigation system even if he took a great gamble with it. I got the figures here, but let me give you the big picture."

"The net worth of the farm is $33,200. This, of course, is

all fixed assets and not really there, except for the bank account. Then, we have Uncle Nathan's stuff. I asked the solicitor who was managing the portfolio for Dad, and he said there's liquid assets to the tune of $14,500. This is real money. This can be set free any moment." Jack again looked all around. "The question, then, is how much does each of us get? I calculated that yesterday, and then we can see how we finance the entire shebang. Bear with me for a moment more."

Jack took a deep breath. "I'm going to relocate to the Solomon Islands in the Pacific. Therefore, I want to sign over my part of the farm to Emily in exchange for liquid assets. I would guess that you, Anna, also would rather have money in hand to finance the rest of your degree. I'm therefore suggesting that Emily and Vic increase the mortgage a bit so they can pay us off, and then they'll have sole ownership of the farm for themselves. How's that sound to you all?"

Jack looked round. Emily showed enthusiastic support; Anna was thinking hard; Vic was beaming.

Anna was the first to speak up. "Actually, Jack, right now I don't need that much. I have my job with the Department, so money, while it would be useful, is not too big an issue right now. I also would like to retain a share of the farm, because later on I'd want to build myself a little cottage for writing. So, what if we set aside a little land out by the stream, you know, on the knoll by the river bend? Other than that, I can postpone payment on my share of the farm, or you can pay me in instalments. Looks to me like Jack is the one who needs money now."

Jack gave her a warm smile. "You hit the nail on the head, sis. I've come to the conclusion I really need to do this for myself, and I do need money."

"Jack, have you figured out how much each of our shares

is worth?" Emily asked. "And how should we pay you up?"

Jack took out another sheet of paper and resumed figuring. "Each share of the farm is worth $11,070. Of the stocks and bonds, we all should get around $4,800. But, as I said, I would prefer to get stocks and bonds so I can liquidate what I need and still have something to fall back on."

Vic picked up the thread. "So, if we give you our share of the stocks and bonds, we still owe you some $6,200?"

Jack jotted it down on the paper. "That's right, roughly that much. Is that a problem?"

Vic shook his head. "No, I'm sure we can get the mortgage up that much. That is, if Anna really doesn't want anything for herself now?"

Now Anna shook her head. "No, I'm fine with the stocks and bonds. I can sell off some now and renovate my apartment a bit. I won't be asking for the farm share up front, so you can pay me maybe five hundred bucks a year?"

Emily hugged Vic. They both found it hard to conceal their excitement. "Yes, we can surely do that, and you can have as large a plot by the river as you like!" Emily declared.

Jack was happy to see it all working out. "It's a deal, then. Let's write this up on paper and get the notary to sign it, and then I can call the attorney who manages Uncle Nathan's portfolio. One thing I wonder a bit about, though. Vic, with just one hand...do you think you can manage the farm work? I don't want to be rude, but might some of the heavy lifting and such be difficult for you?"

Vic took it calmly. "You're fully entitled to ask that question, Jack. Well, it so happens that Dim Jim is my cousin. I'll ask him to move in as our farmhand, and we'll be just fine."

Jack remembered Jim Smythe, of whom it was said that he had the brain of half a man and the strength of two. It sounded like a perfect solution to have Jim on the farm, as it had the extra benefit of saving Jim's aging parents from having to care for him. Jim was docile and hard-working, but his limited understanding made him useful only to the people who knew him well.

The foursome celebrated the deal over lunch, after which Jack drove off to the town with Vic to have the notary draw up the final papers. Jack found it hard to concentrate now that he had everything ready for the next step. He wanted to pack straight away and go kick-start his new life. He did make a mental note of having to call the University Department of Student Affairs, telling them he was dropping out. After that, nothing bar gravity could hold him to the ground.

Before leaving home for good, Jack decided to try and talk to Amy just one more time. He thought she'd returned from Omaha and was living at home for now. He decided to walk over to the house so he could figure out a clear and concise way of expressing his plans and his wish of her joining him. He was still figuring when he arrived at her family's place, so he dragged his feet walking to the house.

This time, Amy was home and came out to meet him at the porch. Leaning her back against the pole, she put her hands in her apron pockets. "Hello, Jack."

Jack found his brain wiped clear of any premeditated speeches, and even complex phrases. "Hello, Amy," was all he could come up with.

A long pause ensued.

"I was hoping to see you, so it's lucky you were here," he finally began.

"Yes, well, I've been here for a year now," she said.

Jack decided to cut off the small talk. "I'm going away, Amy, and I was kind of wondering about you, whether you'd like to come with me? I thought of moving to the South Pacific to start up a hotel."

"Really, Jack?" Amy stood up straight from the pole. "You're moving that far, and happened to think of me? How nice." The sarcasm was stinging. "After all these years, you finally come up with a plan."

Jack already sensed it was a mistake to have come over. "Well, sure, I know it's been some time since we, um, talked, but I just wanted to let you know what I was up to. It's going to be real nice down there once we get it started, and I'm sure business is going to be brisk after the first couple of years."

Amy shook her head and looked up to the sky. "Jack... you are such a sweet, sweet idiot."

By now Jack was *sure* it was a mistake to be there.

"You know, there was a time, somewhere between first grade and high school, actually, up to the end of the war, you could have come over with a crazy plan like that. And I would have jumped at it, dropping everything for you and your crazy plan. But that time's passed, and it passed with the one-letter-a-year policy you had. You could've told me you were hatching a plan in your mind, Jack, just a little sentence somewhere in a letter, and I would've waited for you. But your letters never said anything, anything at all that would have applied only to *me*. All I could read was something which could have been from a letter to your mom, Jack."

She looked pained as she continued. "I understand that you're shy down to the core of your heart. And I know you felt for me, just as I felt for you. But feeling for someone has to turn into action for someone sooner than later, if you don't want to let it go to waste. And action, Jack, that's the one thing you never had much of. As for me, not even having to search very hard, I found someone who has a balance of feeling and action, and I've made up my life plan up here, around me and that person together."

"Amy?" The male voice came from inside the house. "What is it, hon?" An unshaven man in coveralls appeared in the front doorframe, wiping his hands on a rag. "When's dinner? I got to go over to the north side tonight and fix the fence." He saw Jack standing in the yard. "Hello, I don't believe we've met."

Amy exchanged glances with the man. "Rick, my husband—Jack McGuire, my longtime friend. Oh, by the way, my name is Hoover these days. Rick and I've been married a year and a half now."

Jack put on a benign face. "Must be wonderful," he said, more to himself than to anyone else.

Rick was in a hurry. "Look, darling, can you fix me some sandwiches or something? I really can't hang around waiting for dinner now."

Amy turned to him and patted him on the chest with both hands, then kissed him. "Sure, in a moment. Just give me a sec, will you?" she said, and Rick got the hint.

"Nice to meet you, Jack," he said, adding, "You must come over for dinner someday. Eh?"

Jack thanked him with a fleeting smile. "Sure, someday." Then Rick went back inside the house and the old school friends were alone again.

"I know I didn't manage this too well, Amy—I just had to see you one more time before leaving."

Jack's downcast face sent a wave of compassion swimming across Amy's heart, but it had to run against the shore.

"Thanks for that, Jack. In another time, and a different set of circumstances, it might have worked out, but... this isn't our time. I hope everything turns out well for you down there, wherever it is you're going." Amy's voice was tender and wavered a bit.

Jack started up the stairs to shake her hand, but after intercepting him Amy hugged him tightly and gave him a kiss on the cheek. "I'll always remember you," she said.

Jack nodded and retreated down the stairs. The walk home was a blur.

Next day it was time for him to leave the farm for good. His luggage consisted of three battered suitcases and one briefcase, which Emily had found in his father's old things and had presented to Jack for his documents. When he stood out in the yard, taking in the last view of his home, Jack's heart was devoid of feeling. He knew it was the end of an era for him and the start of another, an era of which he knew nothing, only a vague plan for it hastily concocted in a diner and spelled out on the back of an order slip.

Anna had left for California, Emily and Vic were out working the farm, and Jack was here, alone. He scanned the yard, turning around in a full circle, hoping to transfer every blade of grass and tree twig to his memory so deeply that he could always recall them on demand.

As he picked up his belongings to start his walk to the station, he remembered something.

Dropping his suitcases, he returned to the house. There, on the fireplace mantel, as he remembered it, was the brass matchbox cover, with the enameled word "Sverige" imprinted on it. Jack picked up the little object and turned it around in his hands. He had no idea why he'd returned for it, and had no name for the need to possess it, but just the same he put it in his jacket pocket.

Then he returned to the yard, picked up his stuff, and walked out of his old life.

20

As the misty March morning reluctantly turned into a gray day, Jack stood outside the gate to Hunters Point Naval Shipyard. A marginally-sized naval base in southeastern San Francisco, Hunters Point had become well-known in two circles for its surplus sales. Scrap dealers and aviation enthusiasts alike made careful note of the days which the Navy dispensed of materiel it deemed no longer useful.

This Monday it was announced that the lots on sale included PT boats, World War I vintage tugboats, disused naval artillery, and various aircraft and aircraft parts. These were not elaborated upon in the cursory brochure which had been mimeographed for the benefit of the buying customers, who had arrived by the dozen to see what was up for grabs. Jack felt distinctly out of place standing at the gate among all the scrap dealers in coveralls, as they all waited for the gate to open, and then the convoy of buyers would be escorted to the largest hangar on the base, where the sale was to take place.

Jack could see that there was little of interest for him in the brochure until Lot 42, noted as *Floatplane*; after all, he was not in the market for quad-AA guns, five-inch destroyer guns, expended shell casings, or anchors. All these were eagerly bought by the scrappers, because the cost per pound was minimal and the metal in the scrap lots was of very good quality. He was mildly interested in Lot 33, *Fighter Aircraft, used, without guns, non-flying condition*, until it turned out to

316

be two Wildcats: one with a broken back, the other without engine and in a generally sorry state.

He fervently hoped that the floatplane coming up in the auction did not share the condition of the F4F, and that it was not a PBY Catalina two-engine flying boat, as it would be beyond his reach anyway. He needed either a Vought OS2U Kingfisher or a Grumman J2F Duck, but he'd have to wait and see.

The scrappers eagerly barked out their offers and then, when one of them pushed the price out of the others' range, mumbled to those close by about the buyer's lack of business sense. Jack stayed mute but alert. Chief Petty Officer Morgan, who was running the auction, came to Lot 42. "Gentlemen, this is the pearl of the show. We have for you, finally, something far from scrap. This is a flyable OS2U Kingfisher, Dash 3—latest model!—straight off the destroyer DD-78; one owner only, the ship chaplain, and he only flew it on Sundays." This brought mild chuckles from the scrappers and a smile to Jack's lips that would have blown his poker game.

"It's out for sale strictly due to budget cuts. Nothing at all wrong with it. Turn the prop and off you fly. They don't make planes like this any more. What do I hear for this great plane?"

"Forty bucks!" shouted one of the scrap dealers, a burly man with enough eyebrows for four.

Morgan took this as an insult. "Listen, Klinghoffer, I just told you. This is not scrap; this is an airplane. Almost a work of art, if you ask me. There's a difference between this and junk metal. What do I hear?"

"Forty-five!" shouted the same man, to howling laughter from the crowd.

"Two hundred," shouted Jack, taut as a bowstring.

The laughter died. Suddenly Jack was the center of attention, something he'd always hated.

"Say, you don't look like a scrap metal dealer to me. Am I right to assume you'd like this plane for flying?" Morgan asked.

"Yes, sir," Jack answered. The old sea dog smiled.

Klinghoffer was not amused at all. "Three hundred!" he put in.

"Four," said Jack, sweating though the air in the hangar was very cool. He'd thought he could go as high as a thousand, but that was it. Klinghoffer clearly was one of the regulars and could outbid him just to have a bit of fun, and sure enough, he put in a bid for five-fifty straight in. Jack turned and started to walk away. His master plan had a major flaw: the plane he needed would simply cost him too much.

"HEY! Hold on, it's not over yet. If you get the plane for three hundred, will you fly it?" Morgan asked Jack, looking directly into his eyes.

"Well, yes. I need a float plane. Actually I need two, but this is a good start."

"SOLD to the gentleman with adequate funds AND the right spirit," Morgan shouted, "for two hundred dollars!"

"Come on!" Klinghoffer began to protest. "You can't just ignore the highest bidder like that! I know my rights! Besides, you've been selling them for a lot higher than that if they fly."

Chief Petty Officer Morgan cast a sideways glance to the man that made even bystanders feel drafty. "*Mister* Klinghoffer, perhaps you'd like to watch the rest of the auction from outside the perimeter? I mean, it's my auction and I run it as I damn well please. The plane is sold, and you can turn your attention to lot number 43, *Anchors, ship, used*. And you, sir, you who just now bought yourself an *airplane*, should come here first to sign the paperwork, and then wait for Lot 66, which contains another plane of this same type, albeit boxed up for easy delivery. I think we can come to an agreement on its price as well."

Morgan was pleased by the applause which arose from the crowd as Jack went to the orderly who was taking payments. Jack signed a paper which transferred the plane to his ownership, collected some instructions as to how to get it registered with the Civil Aviation Authority, and sat down to wait for Lot 66, all the while keeping an eye on his own Kingfisher. To him, it looked beautiful as it stood parked by the hangar.

Jack got Lot 66 for three hundred dollars, and after paying up went to see it in the hangar. It consisted of four large crates. One, more than thirty feet in length, contained the fuselage and wings. The second crate housed the engine, installation accessories and cabling, and the third one held the tail assembly and assorted odd pieces. The floats and other landing gear were stacked in the fourth crate along with the propeller blades. To Jack it looked like a king-size puzzle, but he was assured that the documentation contained within the boxes would enable him to assemble the plane.

Later, after the auction, Chief Petty Officer Morgan came over to see Jack. "So, son, you're building a naval air force for yourself," he commented, patting Jack on the back. Smiling, Jack explained his long-range plans, which seemed to please the man very much.

"Let me tell you, son, I was there. I was right there in the South Pacific with the construction battalions, and you probably flew off the runways we constructed. Those were the days … now I make my living selling these anchors and whatnot to the people who stayed here and made fortunes on the war, and couldn't care less what happened. I'd do exactly what you're planning to do if I were younger, to get out of the Navy and go back, but…it's too late for me."

His gaze lost its focus somewhere on the horizon. "Speaking of late, it's getting late now, too. You've spent some of the twenty-four hours already. Have you arranged for the transport?"

Jack was caught off guard. "Transport?"

The old man smiled. "So you didn't read the papers you signed. Nobody does on the first time."

He explained that all purchased material had to leave the base within twenty-four hours. Jack would therefore need to go out and find a trucking company that would take his crated plane to the harbor, where he'd find trans-Pacific shipping. As for the flyable plane, he could fly it out to the harbor and have it hoisted onto the transport ship. But Jack had made none of these arrangements beforehand, and the subsequent stress in his face at this realization made the other man just laugh.

"Listen, son, let's don't worry that much. I'll hide the crate in my hangar, and ask some of the crew chiefs if they can make believe the plane is still theirs, and look after it. Why don't you come back when you get it all set up? Try to make it in a week or so. It can get a bit tricky for me if the others get wind of the arrangements, if you get my drift."

Jack thanked the man profusely, but the Navy man just waved him off.

"I just like to see some of the stuff I sell wind up with responsible people, that's all. See you in a week, or even earlier, if you can manage it."

Jack walked out of the base, took a taxi and went to the harbor.

He had all the details worked out in two days. A truck went to the base and collected the crates, and took them to

Oakland harbor. There they were loaded on a rusty Liberty ship, itself surplus, of the Anglo-Pacific Shipping Company, which was running an Oakland-Sydney route. Jack went with the truck to the base, tried to find the auctioneer but failing in that, left a bottle of Jack Daniel's in the care of a subordinate of his. Then he went to the hangar in which his Kingfisher was parked, and had it pulled out.

In training he had never looked at a seaplane twice, but now, after the war, he was keenly aware of the services these durable planes brought to the effort. Practically unarmed, these planes had been flown into battle where everything was touch and go, and hundreds of pilots had been rescued by them. Jack felt proud of his plane and was even more sure of his plan.

He confirmed with the crew chiefs that there was enough fuel in the tanks for him to taxi over to the Pier, where it'd be hoisted on the ship. He didn't want to fly it off the base because of his limited knowledge of floatplanes, but he felt confident enough to taxi with it. He'd have plenty of time for reading documentation on the ocean crossing. While he was taxiing across the busy harbor, he was unable to hide the proud smile on his lips. He had his plane and one in reserve as well, so all that remained was to get the hotel too.

The ship wore on its hull every nautical mile it ever crossed. Murky, rusty, in bad need of paint but with a good engine in its heart, it chugged from Oakland to Hawaii to Fiji and onward to Sydney. Jack enjoyed his first peacetime Pacific cruise to the hilt, poking into every last nook and cranny of the plane, and reading the papers which he'd found in the engine crate. He was sure that flying the Kingfisher would not pose much of a problem at all: floatplanes are docile and easy types to fly.

All in all, Jack was in a great mood all through the long voyage. He slept under the plane, as the accommodations inside the ship left a lot to be desired, and since it allowed him to relive many of the feelings of years before.

On disembarking in Sydney, Jack found a wharf-side storehouse by the pier which was affordable and located close to the gate. He set out to prepare the next leg of the journey right away, contacting the Burns Philp Company for transportation to the Solomons.

A representative of the company came over to see how much material Jack had to ferry over to Guadalcanal, and as he saw the crates, he let out a long whistle. "Know what, mate? That thirty-foot crate will be a handful in the Solomons."

"You don't have a big enough ship, is that it?" Jack asked.

"No, we have ships as big as you'd need, but getting it off the boat may be tricky. At least on the Tulagi side, if that's where you want to put it. What's in it anyway?"

Jack explained.

The man said, "Over there, putting it together can be a problem, unless you know how to do it and have done it before."

After consideration, Jack had to admit he probably would have trouble assembling the plane. Still, he'd need it in case the flyable plane needed spares.

The man had a plan. "In that case, I'd suggest you send the plane over to the airport and strike up a deal with one of the airlines. They have people who can strip the plane and pack up all the parts you need."

Jack thanked the man, they shook hands, and Jack went straight out to the airport.

None of the bigger companies wanted his business, but he

found one which ran an air taxi service. After an hour's nego-
tiation, Jack had struck a deal, sending his crates over to
Haggard Aviation for safekeeping and eventual parts delivery.
They had a large maintenance department and assured Jack
they could handle anything. Even a description of a malfunction would enable them to find the right part, and if it was
one that wasn't in the crate, they'd find one through their own
channels.

As it stood now, Jack's main concern was not the crated
plane any more but the flyable one. It had been offloaded
from the ship and now it was tethered to the end of a wharf in
Sydney harbor. He had an itch to go and fly it, but first he
had to work out the arrangements for the trip up.

When he was getting ready to go to bed at a hostel, it
struck him he had been just too busy to feel anything over the
move to a remote location so far from home. This made him
feel lonelier than ever before in his life. In fact, he felt awful,
the depth of his solitude hitting him all at once. He sat on the
edge of his bed, thinking how no one would even know if
something happened to him out there, and in a way that
thought terrified him.

Still, at base, he felt confident that his plan would eventually work. To make himself feel better, he started a list in his
head of issues he needed to resolve, but before he got anywhere with it, he fell asleep. In the morning the only thing he
remembered was that he really needed to make that list, but
not now.

The next morning he went downtown and bought all the
available maps on the South Pacific, such as they were. The
eastern seaboard of Australia was well-covered but he could
find few maps of the islands. One map did show Southern
Papua, and another was a superficial one of the Solomons, but

as he had no choice, he bought all he could find. Then, maps in hand, he planned his route.

His flight plan would take him up the coastline first to Brisbane and then on to Townsville, from where he planned to cross the Coral Sea into Port Moresby on Papua. From here it would be a simple flight due east to reach Guadalcanal and Tulagi. With a range of 805 miles, and a cruising speed of 119 miles per hour, he was looking at a leisurely five hours or less in flight time for each leg, except for the Coral Sea crossing. He was so excited to finally get to fly that he was hard-pressed to sleep.

It was a Sunday morning when Jack started his push for the Solomons. He had checked and re-checked every part of the plane, filled the tanks to capacity and stashed six jerry cans of fuel into the plane's cavernous hold for emergencies. At 8:05 AM he started his engine, checked his taxiway across Sydney harbor, and at the sight of a half-mile of unobstructed, calm water, he pushed the throttle forward. At first the plane seemed hesitant in collecting speed, but when the main float began to aquaplane, acceleration increased and soon Jack was able to pull the stick back. He was airborne.

He relived the first solo flight he made, the barnstorming flights of youth, every one of his most memorable experiences in the air flooding his mind. Whooping alone in the plane, with a grin across his face, he did a farewell circle around Sydney and spotted the hangar owner at the waterfront waving with his hat. Jack could not wipe the grin until his jaw ached and he was halfway to Brisbane, flying at 5,000 feet above the Australian coastline. It demanded no navigation at all to find his way up to Brisbane, and he had ample time for sightseeing.

He put his plane down after some four hours of flight time

and moored in Brisbane harbor. It was easy to find high-grade fuel right there in the harbor, so he topped up his tanks, had lunch, and set out again for the five-hour hop to Townsville. Here he found his first customers, a couple of missionaries on their way to the Solomons; they promised to come and stay with Jack as soon as he had his hotel up and running.

In the morning it was a bit cloudy, but Jack decided to take off anyway. He found himself wishing for the weather service of the wartime US Navy. It had been so much easier just to go to briefing and get all the latest weather data, but now he was limited to listening to the radio with the other civilians. He managed to get a weather report by phone from the Townsville airfield, according to which there should be no real danger from the weather on his next leg, but in the evening he did a couple of navigation exercises in his head, just to brush up.

Tuesday morning broke in a patchy, overcast sky. Wind was slight, from the northeast, so it would push Jack southward and off-course. It was nothing like what he'd had to fly through during the war, so he hopped in his plane, started up, and took off. Only five hours later he congratulated himself on keen navigation, as he made landfall directly over Port Moresby.

He decided to stay a day and have a look at the town of which he had heard so much in the war, but which he had never before seen. The rapidity with which the scars of war were being eradicated surprised him. He had a good meal at a local restaurant and a good night's sleep at a hotel and in the morning pushed out once more.

The longest leg of the trip took him due east, over the tail of New Guinea and the d'Entrecasteaux Islands, and then a long strip of empty water until he sighted the Solomons. His heart pounded as he studied the familiar shapes of the islands, and admired once again the lush green forests and deep blue sea, fading into sandy beaches. He felt at home, and at the same time, very, very far from home; last time he had been part of a huge machine, but this time he was on his own.

He decided to fly around Guadalcanal and zoomed down on Savo Island, before setting down on the waters off Honiara harbor. The flight didn't weigh on him at all; he felt refreshed and good as he jumped from the wing of his plane onto the pier. Now he was finally where he'd wanted to be so long, and now he could start to build his dream.

The first thing was to get connected. Leaving his plane in the harbor, he hitched a ride to the airfield which had once been called Henderson Field. Seeing it again was a profound experience. Here he had escaped death by the skin of his teeth and lost so many good friends, and the field had been buzzing with activity, dawn till dusk. Now, in peacetime, there were only a couple of transport planes parked in the sweltering sun, and a few hangars which served as airport.

He made the acquaintance of the ground-handling foreman, an Australian named Bill Peet. Bill had been in the Australian Navy during the war, and he and Jack hit it off right away. He arranged for his fuel supply with Bill so that on request he'd send the required number of barrels down to the harbor for Jack.

By the time Jack made it back to his plane, he was surprised to see a young local man peering into the plane as he stood on the wing. Like most natives, he was not very tall, but his muscular frame told of countless hours spent canoeing, and he had a crew cut, unusual for a native. He was dressed in military fatigues cut off at the knee with loose strands flowing down, and a sleeveless shirt.

When Jack got close, the man paid him no attention, so Jack cleared his throat. "Excuse me, can I help you?"

The man didn't look down. "What took you so long?"

Jack recognized the man in a flash. "Well, Martin, I had to take care of some loose ends first, but here I am. Want to do business with me?"

Martin turned to Jack, his face alight with a grin, and he hopped down to the pier. "Yes, sir, I sure do want to do some business. What shall we do?"

Jack took him to a bar, and over beers explained his idea of the hotel to Martin. "Not in bad shape at all," Martin nodded. "In fact, I think we can get off to a flying start. I've been dealing in scrap and sundries while you were away, and I have eighteen Nissen huts crated in the stockhouse you see there. I just collected them when the Americans left, seeing as they didn't seem at all interested in hauling them back to America. I've been waiting for some use for them."

Jack brought two more beers for Martin and himself, and Martin went on. "And I know just the place for the hotel. It's over there on Halavo Bay, by a stream from the hills. An old plantation, a few palms here and there, no leftover ammo from the war, sunset view, and if you cut down some trees, you can see the sun come up too. Besides, it's close to the seaplane base, which may come in handy. I'll call on the owner today."

Jack smiled. "How much do you want?"

"What do you mean?"

"For the huts, of course."

"They're not for sale," Martin said, "but if you want to have them you can," and he smiled his irritating smile.

Jack shook his head in disbelief. "Okay, buddy, here's what we do. We go to the commissioner or whoever runs the show here, and we set up a company in which you have half and I have half. You own the huts, and I own the plane, and the hotel comprises them both. How's that? And I want to see the place as soon as possible."

Martin took his hand and shook it. "Yes, boss. Sounds fantastic, boss."

"That's the first thing you have to work on right there. I am *not* your 'boss'."

"Fine, boss," Martin said again before he bounced off somewhere to get transportation for the crated huts over to Halavo. The hotel wouldn't be on Tulagi proper, but close enough, as Tulagi was still recovering from the war. Jack was very excited about the prospect.

It took Jack four hours to reach Halavo by boat and canoe. Martin met him at the beach and they walked north. When they approached the plantation that Martin had told Jack about, he began to have feelings of déjà vu. The location was somehow familiar, even though he had never been to the island of Halavo before.

When the winding path straightened out of the jungle to open up to a small but beautiful plantation, Jack finally realized what he was seeing. It was the same site he had seen from the air during the war, coming back to land on Henderson. It struck him, just as much now as it had then, how the place exuded peace and tranquility, and even in its dilapidated state, it looked like the spot for his dream to take hold.

"Martin, this is perfect," Jack practically whispered to Martin. "The question remains: will he sell it to us?"

"Oh, he will. He's been fending off all the big players—Lever, Burns Philp and the rest—and has vowed he won't sell to any of them. Still, he's pushing eighty, and as the place hasn't turned a profit since the Japanese came over, he has to sell. I've heard he wants to go back to England for his remaining days and only wants enough to cover the mortgage and a ticket back home."

Martin walked up the creaky stairs to the porch, pointing out some badly rotted planks. "It's a load of work ... but just think of the end result."

Jack followed him up and knocked on the door. An old man with snowy hair and a flax suit hobbled down the hall to the door to meet them. "Hello! Welcome to my humble abode," the man said, extending his hand. "Ingram, Thomas Ingram. What can I do for you?"

Jack shook his hand, noting the steely grip. "Jack McGuire. I've just arrived here and I'm looking for a property to purchase. We're hoping to set up a hotel here, and Martin told me about your plantation, which I understand is for sale?"

Mr. Ingram put his hands, thumbs extended forward, into his vest pockets. "It is, *if* you're not acting for someone else."

Jack was taken off-guard. "No, I'm acting for myself and my friend Martin. This is a long-time dream of mine, and Martin here knew of your property. So, if you'd like to sell it to me, I'd be very happy to pay you whatever I can. My assets aren't great by any means, but I'm hoping we could come to an agreement over the price. I'm going to set up a partnership with Martin to run the hotel. Maybe you'd like to consider investing in it? That might be one way to settle the price."

Mr. Ingram relaxed and asked the men to join him for some drinks in the library. Jack followed him down the hall, admiring the rows upon rows of books on the shelves. On closer inspection, however, he found most of them musty and stained with mildew.

"I see you have an eye for books," Mr. Ingram commented.

"I brought them all with me when I arrived here in 1907, with the thought of finally getting to read them all. Running this plantation allowed for little spare time, I am afraid…they're unread still, for the most part. Maybe you'll have better luck." He pushed glasses of whiskey into the hands of Jack and Martin.

"So, you'd like to invest in a bit of land, eh? Marvelous idea. I am toying with the idea myself." Mr. Ingram smiled, his eyes twinkling.

"Really?" Jack was surprised. "Here in the Solomons?"

The glint still shone from Mr. Ingram's eyes as he continued. "No, not here, but back in Weston-super-Mare. Nothing big… maybe eight-by-three."

Jack and Martin exchanged a muddled glance. "Eight-by-three?" Martin asked.

"Feet, my dear boy. That should suffice. And six feet deep. I am seventy-eight, so there's not much point in trying to turn a profit from properties. The same applies to this place. Before I expire, I owe a certain amount of money to a bank in Australia, and while it is by no means large, it is not within my means to pay it off just like that, not until I settle my late brother's estate in England. Therefore, if you put up enough to cover my immediate costs, I am willing to sell. With the clause that you will never sell the property to any of the big copra companies. That is my only demand, outside purely financial issues. They were after me from day one, and I do not want to see them happy."

Mr. Ingram seemed to decide he liked Jack well enough to proceed to the next stage. "Why don't we bypass the chitchat and go to the larger issue. How much money do you think you could offer me for this property?"

Jack did some quick math, and gave Mr. Ingram a figure

that was some three-fourths of his assets.

"Tsk, tsk, tsk. Sorry, my lad. Burns Philp sent their third-in-command over last week when they learned of my imminent departure. They offered me five times that much."

Jack's heart relocated into his knees. "I'm sorry to hear that. Well, we'll be off then."

"That's their problem. I told him to go back to Australia."

Jack wasn't sure he was hearing right. "So... this place is still available? If I go and find more money, you could sell it to me still?"

Mr. Ingram's smile widened. "When you get to be as old as I am, you'll understand what I will now tell you. You see, the pockets on the funeral shroud are so small that not even your funds would fit. I'm not looking for money, Mr. McGuire, I'm looking for a way home, and a way to maintain one small piece of my personal history on this island. To do that, the new owner needs to have a heart, and none of the companies has one, that's for sure." Mr. Ingram gestured for the men to move out of the library and on to the porch, and then down the rickety stairs.

A narrow pathway started from the corner of the house, winding its way slightly uphill to a hillock, on which stood a solitary palm. On the side of the hillock facing the sea, Jack could see three slabs of stone. The grass on the hillock had been kept scrupulously short. Fresh flowers were placed on the ground before the stones. As they walked around the hillock, they came to see that they were headstones, the middle one slightly bigger than the other two. On it, Jack could make out the words:

Beloved wife
Mother of James and Thomas
CORA NATALIE INGRAM
b. 1/11/1887
d. 4/12/1914
Requiescad in pace

Mr. Ingram said as an aside, "It was the first time the local stonemason had to inscribe anything in Latin. I didn't have the heart to make him do it all over again."

On each of the other two stones was simply a name, with the same date for death.

"It was a fire one night. Started from a crack in the stove-pipe. The house burned down in fifteen minutes. I got out through a window with only minor burns, but they were not so lucky." Mr. Ingram faced the sea for a while. "After that, I rebuilt the house to look exactly like the old one."

"Sorry to hear of your plight," Jack said.

"Well, you know how the world goes. One plans and builds and toils, and then one morning it's all in cinders. Anyhow, this is why I wanted to sell to you and not to BP. It's now, what ... thirty-two years since I lost them. Not a day goes by without me visiting this place. But if it's thirty-two years since I lost them, I thought, maybe I could relax the watch and think of my own burial too. I want to see my old home before I die, and there I have a small cottage. When I sell that one, it will cover my mortgage and other debts. Your money will fly me home. With a proviso in the deed, that is."

"Sir, I think I get the point. Believe me, I'll maintain this plantation as well as you have."

"I would just want to know that until my dying day, there are fresh flowers on the grave. After I die, there's no one left in the world who would remember the three people buried here."

Jack felt a lump in his throat. "I understand. You won't need to worry."

The old man led them down another path, away from the grave. With Martin a bit behind them and out of whispering range, he motioned for Jack to cock his ear his way. "I used to see them, you know," he said with an impish look on his time-engraved face.

Jack heard him perfectly, but just to regroup, he said, "Sorry—I didn't catch that?"

"I saw my wife and my sons after the accident. For years, actually. They'd be pottering about the lodge, or playing in the palms, or running up and down the stairs of the house. But then, they gradually came less often, until I saw them no more. Mind you, for years even after that, I felt their presence. And there's the hammock, of course."

Jack was amazed that the old man was telling him of ghosts and wanted to hear more. "The hammock?"

Mr. Ingram pointed to two palms some twelve feet apart. They both had a ring in the bark around the trunk, now much too high for any comfortable hammock, but probably perfect for one years ago. "She used to take her evening tea here, after the boys had been put to bed, in the hammock. I put up a tarpaulin above it, and sometimes she sat here in the rain, just enjoying the sound of the water rushing down. You'd hear the sound of the hammock ropes creaking against the trees, and that sound was the last reminder of them, even after the hammock had rotted away." He started down the trail again, with his hands behind his back, the epitome of a plantation owner.

"Are you a religious man, Mr. McGuire?"

Jack took a couple of quicker steps to catch up with him. "I'm probably what they call a token Christian."

Mr. Ingram now knew the path so well he could afford to close his eyes and walk blind. "I used to be more of a religious man. But somehow, it has worn off me. And when I lost my family, the remnants of religion blew away from me like so much dust. But I have always respected graves, mind you. That's what kept me here—the grave. And yet…"

Jack tried to walk silently to hear the man better. "And yet?"

Mr. Ingram stopped and looked Jack in the eye. "Why did they stop coming?"

"Your family?"

"Yes. Why can't I see them anymore?"

Jack felt very much out of his depth, but decided to try anyhow. "Maybe they've moved on."

"Exactly! I like to think they've gone on. How wonderful of you to share my opinion." He started down the track, but stopped and turned again. "And that's why I feel I can move back to England and still not forsake them. If they're not here anymore, they won't mind me going back to see my old home. Does that sound logical?"

"Sir," Jack said with a smile, "I assure you, I can see the logic in that."

"Good. Then we can head back to the lodge." Back there, he entered the library and started fumbling around. "Where's the damn thing … I'm sure I left it here … ahh! Here it is," he said as he pulled an old photograph from between two huge leather-bound books. He proudly presented it to Jack. In it, a young version of Mr. Ingram could be seen shaking hands with the Resident Commissioner at Tulagi. In his other hand, he held a deed. "There's the original deed. I have just purchased this land, and you can see the joy in my eyes. Ah … the days. Anyway, I would like to have a picture like this taken with you and me in it, just for posterity's sake, if that's all right?"

Jack saw the joy in his eyes, but he also saw the definite shadow behind the man in the picture. "We'll get one just like this," he swore. They agreed to meet at the commissioner's office for the deeds in two days. Jack and Martin took their leave from the old man, who could be seen waving his hand while they walked all the way to the edge of the jungle from the house.

Martin followed him out to the path. "Well, is it perfect or what?"

"It sure is, pal. The main lodge is a bit of a problem. It'll take lots of work to get the way we want it. Do you have any larger Nissens there in your stack? If we had one big enough to make for a kitchen and dining room, it could double as a main lodge as well. That is, until we get this lodge fixed. We need carpenters, a bunch of them, and people to assemble the huts as well."

Martin nodded. "Finding labor will not be a problem, not at all. I have three big ones and lots of medium sized huts. Let's go check them out and start planning the landscape, eh, mister Hotel Proprietor?"

Jack couldn't hide the smile. "I like that, thank you very much, but just remember, you're one too!" They sauntered up the path towards the marketplace, talking all the while, planning as they went. Jack felt expectations rising within him, and the thought of all the work ahead made him a bit light-headed.

21

After taking his leave from Kay, Jack had gone to the Boston Navy base. There was no surplus auction coming up in the near future, but he was taken to the engine shop anyhow, because they were discarding bits and pieces they had no more use for. He was allowed to dig into the piles of parts and supplies and see whether he could find any useful material. After a good two hours of looking around, he went to the chief of the shop with two cartloads of miscellaneous parts he reckoned he could use. These included some miscellaneous engine parts, an air speed indicator and a tachometer (both of which had given him trouble in the past), and a new stick. The shop chief had a cursory glance over the material and signed a shipping list valued at $6.75, claiming Jack's findings to be *Misc. aircraft parts*. He directed Jack to the base commander's office.

Jack paid up at the office, then called a local trucking company and asked them to come to the base with two crates and packing material for shipping the parts back to Tulagi. Inside the crate he placed four large and well-padded bottles of Jack Daniel's, which was hard to come by in the Solomon Islands. He labeled the crates, signed the bills of lading and watched the truck take off with his crates. Then it hit him that he was now done with the official part of the visit, and having said his goodbyes to Kay, he was now on his return trip. Suddenly he felt very far away from home.

He had told no one that he had built an extra day into his itinerary. He had correctly guessed it'd be rough seeing Kay and leaving again, so he'd left one spare day for going to New York. He had some money left, his return ticket to Sydney was open, and—he had to face it—no one anywhere was missing him. He made his way to the South Station, bought a ticket to Penn Station and a snack along with a *Saturday Evening Post*, and spent the time people-watching in the grand hall before the train left.

He spent the entire trip looking out of the window and watching the scenery roll by. Arriving in New York, he was happy to see the Pennsylvania Hotel right across the street from the station. He signed in and spent some time resting in his room, and then he went out to dinner at an Italian place on Madison and 48th.

That was one thing he missed a great deal in the Solomons: he had grown to like Italian food very much during the training assignment in Pensacola, and now that he could, he intended to have some for every lunch and dinner until he left. Following dinner, he found he was very tired, so instead of going to Radio City Music Hall or another show he just bought a fifth of whiskey, went to his room, had a couple of drinks and slept like a log.

The next morning, while sitting at the window table in an unassuming coffee shop, watching people on the sidewalk go by like bees in their hive, Jack thought of Bunny Radner. Kay had said he owned a shop in Manhattan. After some deliberation he decided to look him up and pay him a visit.

Jack had enjoyed working with Bunny all through his assignments in the Pacific, and as a squadron commander, Bunny had been highly esteemed even outside VMF-288. Jack now felt sorry for the way he'd let his contact lapse with all his wartime friends, but he also faced the truth that with the loss of the shared framework of life in the squadron, they once again had little in common. Jack asked to borrow the coffee shop's phone book from the waitress.

From there he found what he wanted: there was only one Manhattan company with Radner in its name, and it was located on 22nd, half an hour's walk away. It began to rain when Jack left the coffee shop, so he hailed a cab.

After a short ride, he reached his destination. In front of him now was a small shop with a sign above its door which read *Radner's **Office** Office*. Gingerly he opened the door and entered the shop, which was laid out around two long rows of freestanding shelves. Against the walls there were eight shelves on each side, and all of the shelves were meticulously laid out with every possible type of office equipment represented among the selection. Along the back wall of the shop was a mirror with a door set into it, the mirror covering all the wall space. It made the rectangular shop appear even longer and narrower than it actually was. At the cash register was a tall blonde woman labeling miscellaneous supplies with price tags.

Jack went up to her.

"Hello, I was looking for Mr. Radner. Is he in?"

The lady put away her labels and flashed Jack a smile. "Sorry, he's out on business. May I help you with something?"

Jack smiled too. "I was in his squadron during the war and thought I'd say hello, as I happened to be in the neighborhood."

"I'll be sure to let him know you dropped in, Mr...?" The lady held out her hand.

"McGuire. Jack McGuire," Jack said, and shook her hand.

"Dorothy Elkin. Friends of Mr. Radner are always welcome here. I'll let him know you stopped by." As she spoke, the door on the far wall silently opened inwards. "Oh, he must have come in through the back door already," she lied smoothly. "Please go on in." The lady motioned towards the door.

Jack mumbled his thanks, walked through the aisles to the back of the store, and entered the dimly-lit room. It was now clear the mirror was in fact two-way, and the store was in full view from the room. By the wall facing the store there was a large desk, and in the large chair behind the desk sat a man in profile.

"Hello Jack, long time no see," he said.

Jack was baffled. The man sounded nothing like Bunny Radner. As he turned to face Jack, he didn't even look like Bunny. All he had on his head were a couple of isolated tufts of hair, hideously-burned remnants of facial features, and the tiny ears of a mouse.

"Bunny?" Jack held back a gasp. "What the hell happened to you?" He went to shake Bunny's hand, which was rough with scar tissue.

"Oh, nothing much. I was testing an FD-1 jet fighter in January '46 and landed with my wheels up. I said it was a malfunction, but they weren't so sure. Anyway, when it finally came to a standstill off the runway, I was burned up pretty bad."

"But you were lucky you made it through, right?"

Bunny looked out into the store. "They said straight away that had I crashed anywhere but NAS Patuxent, I would have died. Bethesda managed to keep me alive. Such life as it was. I was with the hopeless cases for about four weeks, but then they had to move me out to the burns ward when I didn't kick the bucket."

Jack felt sick. He'd seen his share of badly-burned soldiers while in the Pacific, but none of them had ever come back to meet him. They had either died or faded out of his life.

Bunny went on. "They moved me out to England for almost two years. They had this doctor, Archie McIndoe, who had worked out new techniques for us roasties. He got me started on the road to recovery, and because of his encouragement I didn't kill myself. He also got me looking like this. They couldn't have made such a Dapper Dan out of me over here." His lipless slash of a mouth might have been smiling.

Jack sat down on a chair. "I see ... all I heard was that you were out on a medical discharge after an accident, but I didn't think—"

"That I'd look like a baked potato? Nah, that's just the way it went. So after the war I'd got out of the Marines and gone into the Navy, because I figured the Marines were going to get chucked altogether, and with the Navy I was able to get into the test-flight unit. For a while life was good. I flew all I wanted, tested some really great planes, and they even paid me well enough. I married my old high school sweetheart and we got a great house just outside the base. But, after the accident, my wife took one look at me when I was still attached to all the hoses, and left. Luckily we had no kids."

Bunny obviously wanted to tell the whole story, so Jack stayed silent.

"I first thought of continuing to fly, but my hands don't work well enough, and my eyes are out of whack too, especially in the dark. So, for some time I just brooded, but I wasn't allowed to go really under, because the limeys showed me how to cope with the burns. They had these two fellas out there who looked like breakfast bacon at a bad motel, and had just two good hands between them. Doc McIndoe had got this factory to build a workshop for his patients, and these two guys worked every day, day in, day out, one holding the bit and the other drilling holes in it. I couldn't do less than that, I thought."

Bunny walked slowly around the office. "Then when I got back to the States, my uncle was set to retire and wanted me to buy this business. He was only supplying small businesses around here, but I've managed to sell to bigger companies too. Funny what you can do on the telephone. But I couldn't let the smaller ones down even though I almost lose money on the retail side—I just had to find someone to run it for me. Take a guess how many people I interviewed before Dorothy came along?"

Jack made a non-committal move with his hand.

"Thirty-seven. Most of 'em fled like so many bats out of hell when they saw me, but Dottie here has a brother who was left even more well-done after a car accident. She has lots of experience with burn victims, so she stuck around. She runs the retail and keeps the books and I sell directly to the bigger clients."

Jack could think of nothing to say, so he simply nodded.

Bunny cracked his best possible smile. "I know, Jack, that's my story and most people go kind of silent when they hear it. But enough about me—what do *you* think of me?"

Jack felt that his old commander was back; whatever else had happened, his humor hadn't gone anywhere. "Ha ha," Jack said, "now let *me* update *you*."

"Yeah, the last I heard was from the *New York Times* that you went off to the Solomons of all places. I still have that story on the wall, see?" he said and pointed to a clipping on a notice board. Jack went over to read it, and looking at the picture of his beach made him more homesick than ever.

"Well, I guess I could be doing better. The hotel isn't making too much money, that's for sure, but I like it there, and I hired Martin to help me run the place. I bought a couple of Kingfishers off the Navy surplus sales, and I run my little air force down there."

"Ah, the Pacific. I wouldn't ever have thought I wanted to go back there, but these days I would. The thing is, over there I had it all: a good job, friends, all the booze I could handle and a lot beyond that. Here, I don't have any of it. Well, the business is good enough, but I've run out of friends. But I'm happy Martin is okay—he was a fun little critter in the war times." Again he stared through the mirror into the store. Dorothy waved to him with a smile.

"Stoney Stokes was here last year, Jack. He chanced to pass the store and thought a Radner had to be me, and he had a brand new wife to show off. He stormed right in, just like he did on strafing attacks, and before I had a chance to go backstage, he was all over my case. One look was it, the lady fainted and Stoney carried her out into a taxi and left. After that, I haven't even heard from anybody, let alone seen anybody." He poured Jack a cup of coffee from a pot without asking, and dropped three lumps of sugar in the mug. "Three, right?"

"Right." Jack settled down again and they continued to talk.

Suddenly there was a little metallic noise from the back alley. Bunny raised his finger to his ghost lips and winked towards a window in the back of the room. Jack watched it out of the corner of his eye. Three kids were slowly pushing their heads up to peek into the room. Bunny waited until the kids were in full view, as they apparently thought the two men in the room could not see them. Then he turned his head very slowly and stared at the kids, who with yelps scrambled off the trash cans as fast as they could.

342

Bunny smirked at Jack. "I found the Karloff stare works best. I tried saying *boo* and chasing them and all that, but a long, slow stare really does the trick. Now they won't sleep for the next few nights. As I was saying the other day to Padre Menozzi—a great guy who runs the nearby church, lost a leg at Anzio charging in with the troops, we play poker on Wednesdays—if I get really pissed off with the kids, I could do the rounds on Halloween and make the bottom fall out of their market. They can't possibly get a better freak to go trick-or-treating with."

Jack couldn't help but laugh at the image.

"So, Mr. Waldorf. Is the hotel going to pick up soon, or are you just wasting your money out there?" Bunny asked. Somehow his nickname seemed even more inappropriate now than when he still had the wrinkly nose the name alluded to.

Jack chuckled into his coffee. "It's going fine, but it's no gold mine. I think the travel will have to grow slowly, but more than that, I'm there just because I like the area. I mainly break even most of the time, and in the dry season I actually come out a bit ahead."

Bunny stared Jack down. "Know what, Jack? Out there, when we chased rats out of our cots and shook snakes from our boots, we swore we'd never return or even look back over our shoulders. But now, I'd do fifty tours for my old face, or any normal face. And just a handful of friends. Fifty, hell... I'd fly the rest of my life against the Devil himself if I could have my old self back."

"Out there, Bunny," Jack answered softly, "you got at least two friends. One is me and one is Martin. There's no one to fight anymore, but when you want to see the place again, look me up. I guarantee you there are no snakes or rats in my hotel, and the rates are reasonable. Besides, you didn't look so hot back then either, so quit your whining and pining."

Bunny put on a ghost of a smile, and Jack could see he meant it even if it looked like a nightmare. "It's good to see you, Jack. Good to see you here." He shook Jack's arm.

Jack got up. "I think I gotta be going. I still have some shopping to do. See you around, Bunny."

Bunny wanted to see him to the door, but with several customers in the store, he stood where he was in the dark room. "Thanks, pal, for popping in. It was a pleasure."

Jack smiled. "Sure was, so look after your store and yourself. See you in Tulagi next?"

"Someday, pal, someday." As the customers paid up with Dorothy and left, Bunny put his arm around Jack's shoulder and saw him out through the store and into the street. Dorothy smiled warmly to Jack as they passed her.

On the sidewalk, Jack turned around. "Say, Bunny, I never thanked you for pointing Kay Wheeler my way. She said she found me through your advice; she was out at the hotel a while ago."

"Kay Wheeler?" Bunny stopped to stare his wax dummy stare at Jack, oblivious to some passers-by who looked at him like he wasn't a member of their species. "Some lady, eh? Don sure had taste. Did you hit it off with her?"

Jack had to smile. "Well, I did visit her now before I came to New York, but not quite in the way I think you mean. We're just friends."

Bunny managed a surprised look, even without eyebrows. "She didn't tell you about me?"

Jack shook his head. "No, she only said you were out on medical discharge."

Bunny whistled through his teeth. "Oh, now I get it. That's why you looked like such a jerk when you saw me." It was Bunny's turn to smile. "Ya ya ya. But better work on that one—she'd be well worth the effort."

Jack smirked. "Sure, she's just dying to fall for a flat-broke hotel owner from the south Pacific. Got to run, Bunny. Take care."

Jack took the long way back to the hotel. Bunny, direct as ever, had managed to hit his sore spot. It was only a day since he had left Kay and he was already miserable. He began listing reasons for going back and reasons for forgetting her, and in moments the list became hopelessly off-balance towards the minus side. To shake off the gloom, he didn't stay at the hotel as he had planned, but went out to buy some new records, including an Erroll Garner, and then to dinner and a Broadway show. Nothing could pick him up though, and he resigned himself to the hope that getting back home to the Solomons would help.

His return trip to the other side of the world took about eighteen days with his economy tickets and less-than-direct routes. By the time he reached Guadalcanal, his spirits were considerably lifted by running into Martin there, who told him the hotel was almost fully booked. A gaggle of enterprising Dutch tourists, who had decided to see islands from the Solomons to the Philippines the hard way, had descended on Florida and upon finding the Tulagi Hotel, with its sightseeing plane, had decided to stay for a week instead of one night. Jack was only too happy to dive right in and become a full-time proprietor once more, with no time for matters of the heart.

Around midnight of his first day back, when he was already dead on his feet, he slumped on his bed, but then he had a funny thought. Now that he had discussed Omar Khayyam's quatrains with Kay, he happened to think about the only occasion he'd heard Don discuss nose art for his plane, with his plane captain on Guadalcanal. He'd wanted a moving finger, or the number 71 for his plane. Maybe it was another reference to the strange little poems.

Jack dug into his still-packed luggage, spilling dirty laundry and travel documents and surprisingly even some clean clothes around his room until he found the book. He went to the porch, sat in a wicker chair, and leafed through the pages until he found quatrain LXXI:

The Moving Finger writes; and, having writ,
Moves on: nor all your Piety nor Wit
Shall lure it back to cancel half a Line,
Nor all your Tears wash out a Word of it.

The moon had traversed half the night sky before he let go of his memories.

22

Jack was completing a smooth landing on a glassy calm sea, having taken three hotel guests over to Guadalcanal. It was a special source of enjoyment to allow the Kingfisher to descend onto the water without the slightest bump and then to see the unbroken curve of water shoot out from the main float.

When his speed went below planing, and the floats began to plow water, he spotted a stocky man standing on the pier. He didn't look familiar, so Jack thought he was just another guest, probably a hitchhiker who'd arrived on one of the fishing boats. The Hawaiian shirt was loud enough to identify the man as American, but it wasn't until Jack was close enough to spot the American Optical, Navy standard issue sunglasses shading the man's eyes, that his identity hit him.

McMahon.

Jack's first instinct was to grab the throttle and push it open, even though he was facing the island, but when he felt the knob in his hand, he decided otherwise. McMahon would have to be just another guest, even if he had tried to wash Jack out of flight training. Gathering his calm from deep reserves, Jack docked as always and supervised the mooring of the plane before acknowledging the man.

"Hello," McMahon said. "Jack, isn't it? Can I call you Jack?" He held out his hand. Jack took it, and experienced a handshake so unlike the appearance: the man still had a limp hand, like cold custard in a rubber glove.

"Lieutenant Commander McMahon," Jack said, in want of anything better to say.

"Mike, if you don't mind. Good to see you after all these years. I left the Navy back in '45." When McMahon grinned it brought back memories for Jack, who had seen McMahon issue a glacial smile only once: when he declared Jack's fighter pilot career terminated.

After a weighty pause, McMahon decided he had to carry the conversational ball for now. "Nice plane you got there. A real change from fighters, eh?" He patted the wingtip of the Kingfisher. "Of course, Hellcats aren't really designed for pleasure flights. Mind if I take a look inside?" With surprising agility, he catapulted himself up to the wing and with a couple of long steps on the wing, he reached the cockpit before Jack even managed to say yes.

"Wow, I like this. You've changed the entire plane! This looks like a flying taxi. How many can this take on now? Four, no, three?" McMahon seemed genuinely enthusiastic, but Jack held his reserve.

"Yeah, I have three extra seats and an intercom for each seat. Took some cobbling to get it to work right, but it's good to be able to talk with the guests when we fly." He wondered why on earth he'd be meeting McMahon again, after all this time, here of all places.

McMahon peered in again and checked the pilot's seat. "How does this fly? Like a pregnant sow?"

Jack could tell the old sense of humor was still with McMahon, the humor he had grown to hate. Besides, he was very proud of his little air force, and any knock on his operation, particularly with that attitude, was bound to be dead on arrival.

"Actually, *Mike*, I guess nearly all fighter pilots would say that, but if you ask any of those guys one of these saved from the sea, they'll tell you it flies like an angel."

Getting the point, McMahon retraced his steps. "Yeah, I bet. It's just that I've never had a chance to check myself out on one of these. Maybe we can take a flight later at some point?" McMahon walked back to the wing and dropped himself on the pier. "That is, assuming you have any vacancies, and if you'll have me as guest. I'd like to stay a week or so, if that's okay with you?"

With the prospect looming of seven days and nights with McMahon on the island, Jack was balancing between a flat-out lie and a grudging assent. But dutifully he pushed himself to say, "Sure, I have a vacant hut for a week, for ten days actually. It's not the best hut I have, but it's okay if you don't mind the limited view." He failed to mention the six other huts which were also free.

McMahon smiled again, this time a hint of genuine feeling inside the smile. "I'm not here for the views alone. I can manage." He grabbed his gear from the pier and started towards the shore. "Which one is mine? There's quite a few huts here, I guess."

Following him, Jack pointed to a hut which lay snugly tucked in amongst a group of huge palms. "That one, number twelve," Jack said as he jumped the gap between the pier and the shoreline. A brief stroll uphill took them to the hut, which was oriented towards the sea.

Seeming satisfied, McMahon dropped his kit bag onto the porch and sat down on the canvas chair with his feet up on the railing. He reached out to his bag and pulled out a pair of shorts to change into.

"This is great. Just what I had in mind for a relaxing holiday far from the hustle and bustle of the modern world."

Jack took a sideways glance at McMahon's kit and deduced the long thin canvas pouch must contain fishing equipment.

"So you're here for some fishing," he said, and McMahon assented.

"Yes, I thought that since I never got out here during the war, I'd like to see the place anyway and maybe do some fishing on the side."

Jack indicated the book which was visible at the top of the bag, *Teach Yourself Fly Fishing*. "You'll be the first guest so far to try fly fishing around here. Most people seem to go for light tackle," Jack commented, wondering whether fishing was really the reason for the trip.

"Well, yeah, I can't say I'm an old hand when it comes to fishing…it just felt like a good thing to try out when I decided to come here." McMahon shifted in his chair. "Look, I got to level with you. I only bought the kit in Sydney. Thought I ought to have some excuse for coming to this place, any reason at all."

Jack raised an eyebrow. "So…let's see now: you went on a cruise halfway around the globe to find my hotel, to fish without any idea how to, and with kit you don't know how to use? Something just doesn't add up here."

McMahon stared out to the sea, where the sunlight broke into a wide swath of gold across the small white swells in the turquoise water. "Okay. I wanted to come and talk to you. So sue me. My life's been put on hold—twice—and I needed some way to get things straight."

Jack was half-amused, half-piqued at McMahon's reply. "Well, you found me. Now that we're both here, maybe you want to fill me in? Or actually, it's getting to be lunchtime, so what if you settle in and we can continue over lunch? It's served at the main hut—see the one there, up that path?" Jack made an undulating gesture with his hand, trying to follow the winding path on the ground.

"Great... now that you mention food, I *am* famished!" McMahon nodded. "I'll just toss my stuff in and we can walk up together."

Jack waited a minute, and when McMahon re-emerged, they set out together along the path. On the way Jack explained his reasons for setting up his hotel, touching briefly on some of his adventures along the way, and McMahon genuinely seemed to admire all the work he'd put into the project. It was looking nice, too, with fourteen Nissen huts up now, and the main lodge customized and spruced up, scattered among palms on the old plantation's rolling grounds, and paths lined with round stones winding their ways between the huts. It was nearer the ideal Jack had built in his mind's eye.

Lunch was once again one of Wilma's seafood specials, and both men availed themselves thoroughly of the delights, not speaking terribly much between bites. Before post-lunch coffee was served, Jack remembered he'd promised to visit Bill Peet on the big island around noon, so he excused himself while McMahon assured him he could manage on his own.

By the time Jack returned, it was already almost six in the evening, but when he went to McMahon's hut, he found him in the hammock adjacent to the hut, with *Teach Yourself Fly Fishing* open over his face at about fifteen pages, the reader fast asleep beneath it. With the palms giving the hammock a gentle sway, it was not at all hard to be lulled into oblivion.

Jack moved quietly away to the main path, retreating to his own cabin. It was Thursday, and this Thursday he was to host the weekly poker game with the mission teachers and Reverend Miller, the proceeds going to local charities, usually the mission. He found in his bookshelf the old green tablecloth which doubled as a casino poker felt, buried under a cribbage board and a checkerboard, beside a well-worn collection of books. Then he reached behind the bookshelf at his knee level, and pulled out a fifth of Jack Daniel's, held back for special occasions. In no time at all, his window table had been converted into a *bona fide* casino table complete with whiskey glasses, a box of cigars, and a worn-out military issue Zippo lighter.

"Perfect!" Jack said to himself just as the mission delegation arrived. Reverend Miller and the two teachers, Dwight Norton and James Tubbs, greeted Jack and went to the table. Reverend Miller produced his prize possession, a small aluminum case of casino chips, and opened it on the table. They all sat down getting their five-card draw game going, grunting comments and cigar smoke gradually filling the room. Jack administered doses of whiskey as necessary, and they were completely engrossed in the game when the door opened and McMahon sauntered in.

"Oh, sorry, didn't mean to disturb you guys—I was just looking for something to eat since I guess I slept past dinnertime," he said.

Jack grabbed a chair by the wall and the teachers hustled sideways to create space for McMahon at the table.

"Sure, dinner's out already, but Wilma will bring sandwich makings and cold cuts pretty soon. You want to join the game?" Jack offered, but McMahon had already seated himself at the table. The mission party gave their names in turn, and McMahon introduced himself as Jack's old flight school buddy. Jack felt a shiver at the bald-faced euphemism, but managed to let it pass without being noticed.

McMahon fitted surprisingly well into the circle of conversation and companionship, and since he was an atrocious player, he was soon out of chips and had to buy more. *All the better for the mission*, Jack thought with an internal smile. Reverend Miller passed a stack of chips across the table and play resumed, only to halt again in half an hour with McMahon again out of money.

By now it was nearly midnight, and the mission people took their chips and money and bid their farewell. Jack and McMahon took one more whiskey and a pair of fresh cigars, and went to the porch.

It was a pitch-black night with absolutely no moon, but the scattered points of starlight dotted the sky, making it almost three-dimensional.

Head tilted, McMahon seemed to be listening to the sounds of the night. After a while he spoke:

"Sounds like Pensacola, only more animals and fewer cars," he said. "I used to like sitting out in the night, like when they threw me out of Altitude and I was too drunk to drive back to base and had to walk. It took me three hours because I couldn't walk a line, and I used to sit down by the roadside and just listen to the frogs and whatnot. Cars would pass me by and not pick me up. I mean, who in their right mind would pick up a drunken Marine, except the MPs? By the time I got back to base it was already light, and I had maybe two hours of time to sleep before the first flights. Oh, those halcyon days…"

Jack sat down on the chair by the window and motioned for McMahon to sit on the other one. He sat down and placed his feet on the porch railing. After a sip of whiskey and a long dedicated inhale of cigar smoke, he emitted four rings of smoke and said, "What if I leveled with you? You caught me out with the fishing already so my bluff has been called."

Bad bluffing—that's been the theme of the night, Jack

thought. "Please do," he said out loud. "Actually, I'd wondered about you on occasion, so it'll satisfy my curiosity to hear what you're doing down here."

"It's a long story, but I'll spare you the details. As you know, I tried my utmost to wash you out from my school, but you got saved by your buddy. Don Wheeler, wasn't it? I never saw such a pilot as Wheeler. I mean, you were actually good enough, but that Wheeler character, he was *one* with his plane, instead of merely being a pilot. Anyway, you probably wondered why I was so hell-bent on getting you out. Before you say anything, I also know about the graffiti on the wall at Altitude, with my alleged quotas for washing out cadets."

McMahon took a sip of whiskey and had a pause to enjoy a puff from the cigar. He continued with his eyes closed. "You know the truth? I had no quota. I washed out everyone I didn't think I'd want to have around me in combat or on board a carrier. Okay, to be completely honest, some of the graffiti was true. I did pick out one cadet from each class and have him expelled just for the heck of it, and in your class, well, you had the distinct honor of being that cadet." He looked at Jack.

"Why me?"

"Because you had a friend who could fly better than me."

Jack let out a whistle between the teeth. "Don Wheeler," he said. "But how does that get *me* washed out and not *him*?"

McMahon looked hard at Jack. "Too many people took note of his flying. The first day he flew Wildcats with us, the station commander told me to watch this Wheeler guy, he'd be going places. So he was, and as such, he was untouchable. I couldn't have any reason for washing him out, assuming he didn't crash, so you got the evil eye meant for him."

It was Jack's turn to have a sip. "But why were you so hell-bent on washing people out?"

"I only washed out people who couldn't survive in combat, and then the one cadet who had some other reason to catch my eye in that regard, like you. Ninety-nine percent of my washouts would have killed themselves at some point, accompanied by massive destruction of government property. You, I just disliked."

Like a back-row schoolboy, Jack leaned back to balance his chair against the wall. After attaining a stable position, he observed, "At least you're honest about it. I did wonder a lot why you wanted me out, but I couldn't find a reason. In a way, I like knowing there was none, really."

McMahon still looked like he had things to tell. "Washing you out was one thing. Why I did that for every class is another, but if you want to hear that too, fetch the bottle."

Jack went into the hut, returned holding the Jack Daniel's by the neck, and poured a stiff one for McMahon.

"Whoa, that's plenty," McMahon held up his free hand. "I've been trying to go easy on the liquor lately. That's another one of my problems, and I like to hide from the others behind it."

Jack sat down. "And what would *they* be?" He wasn't fully sure he wanted to hear it all as he settled back in his chair and balanced it carefully against the wall.

After a long pause, McMahon decided to pull out the chocks. "I've spent so much time hating the Navy, Jack, you have no idea. I was ripped off by 'em for a petty personal grudge, and I lost out on World War Two. I had no chance to prove my mettle, even though I'd prepared for it for years, and I know I could have kicked ass with any goddamn pilot any enemy nation could field against me. And I wanted so hard to make my way in the Navy." He puffed on his cigar much too hard to enjoy any finesse its smoke might have had.

Jack sipped on his whiskey. "Well, I know you could fly, obviously, but I had no idea you didn't get into the fray...what happened? Stepped on some big toes?"

McMahon assented. "I was already a non-factor by 1939. It was a commodore, actually the son of one. This son could fly with a half-decent touch if someone got him airborne and up to fifteen thousand feet, but coming down was a nightmare to everyone. I mean, this kid had no depth perception whatso-ever. So I washed him out. He actually came to thank me the morning he left. When the next class got in, surprise! He was there again. Doesn't that just beat all? I took him off to the side and asked him what the hell happened. His dad had pulled some strings—given the boy's prowess at flight, I'd say they'd have to have been hawsers—and got him back on the fighter course. Same thing happened the second time: I flunked him and he thanked me as he went away. Next week, I was under orders to another station, courtesy of ol' Commo-dore Papa himself. The kid came back once more, of course, but this time he wasn't my problem."

Jack stared into the ice cubes trapped in the amber of his glass. "Let me guess. Something happened and suddenly you were to blame?"

"What, you a mind reader or something? Yup, the guy was sent to carrier training and hit the fantail on the first try. Boom, blaze, nothing left bigger than a cigarette lighter, instant burial at sea. And me, I got Pensacola, but I also got lots of black marks on my record. Enough to keep me from ever getting a transfer to a fighting squadron." He fingered the rim of his whiskey glass as if to try to make it sing, but when that failed, he had a sip. The last puff of his cigar colored its tip a furious red, and then McMahon flipped the butt out to the dewy bushes.

"1939," Jack said. "And you were still in Pensacola in 1942, but you weren't there in 1943 when I had my tour as trainer. So at least you got somewhere else, eh?"

"Sure I got somewhere." McMahon crinkled his nose. "I got everywhere, Jack. They stuck me on a plane flying all around the States in January '43, as Inspector of Quality, Naval Aircraft Production. After all, I did have a degree in aeronautical engineering, earned before Annapolis. Big deal. I was a glorified rubber stamp with my very own plane to zoom around in. Too bad I was never allowed to stray outside the United States. You've probably guessed I got nasty and had very little in the way of a fuse…also, I found that my skills at flying after a drunken brawl were intact, even if the plane wasn't a fighter any more. Many were the bridges I stormed under and even more numerous were the cows who probably didn't give milk for a week after I flew low over their pastures. Like, at thirty feet or so."

McMahon's hand went looking for his cigarettes, first in the shirt pocket, then in the shorts, but after it found just a wrapper, Jack pulled out his Chesterfields and offered him one.

"And then?" Jack asked.

Within seconds McMahon had located his Zippo and lit the bent cigarette.

"And then … I flew around the country, meeting with factory foremen in the day and drinking with them in the night, all through the war. By the summer of '45 I was so pissed off at the system, what with the war already won in Europe and Japan in ruins and teetering on the brink. Still, all my applications for transfer bounced. Until in July '45 I decided to try and see if I could get discharged. Oddly enough, right after

August fifteenth, I was discharged. Honorably, mind you, but man, was I lucky to be out and ahead of all the other folks that were discharged right after me."

Jack nodded. "I know the feeling. I toyed with the idea of trying my luck with the airlines too, but by the time I got out, they'd hired all they needed, and besides, multiengine guys got there first."

McMahon smiled more to himself than to Jack. "One good thing came out of my times as the fastest and most reckless rubber stamp in the world. I got to talk to all these engineering people and know them by name, so when I called one of them for work, I got hired in ten seconds flat. So now I work for Boeing, in the design shop, but I'm afraid I can't tell you more than that. But now, Jack McGuire, we finally get to the reason why I'm here."

Jack rubbed his eyes and stretched. "Will that take as much time to explain as the overture did?"

McMahon got serious. "No, I hope not. You see, I've worked with the Air Force on their designs mostly. But three months ago, I was posted to a Navy project. And like you'd think, I ran into problems almost straight off the bat. You see, working with guys in uniforms brought back memories, not all of them good. Within a few days I was grabbing one of them by the collar. Within a month, I had made the Navy very suspicious of my teamwork skills. At the same time, my wife was taking the brunt of my problems at the office."

Jack lit a cigarette, inhaled a couple of lungsful and blew three smoke rings in succession. They managed to survive suspended in the still night air for some few seconds, just long enough for him to ask McMahon: "I think I'm getting the picture here. You said you'd been put on hold, twice? Bureau and bride?"

"You *are* a psychic." McMahon's eyes gleamed red in the intensifying light of the cigarette tip as he inhaled deep. "Wife, actually—it wasn't too easy on her already when I was stamping around the country, but I thought things would get better when we settled down in Seattle. Fat chance. The Navy thing got its wrenches back in my works, and one evening when I went home, she'd left me a note. She'd be back from Mom's when I was back to my loving and caring self, to the man she'd married way back, and she said nothing less would suffice. So, next morning, I went to the office and had a field day when the Navy guys tried to get something changed. It was like the type of a bolt or something as radical as that, but I blew a main fuse and stormed out to the boss to hand in my resignation. He got me to calm down, but when he found that I'd amassed three months' worth of overtime work in a year, he blew his. He dragged me to payroll, had them pay out two of the three months in cash, and took my ID Badge. 'Come back in a month's time, McMahon, and if you get your shit sorted out, I might give this badge back to you,' he said. Well, that's what I'm here to try and do—sort out my shit."

Jack flipped the cigarette butt into the darkness, and watched it somersault down to the ground, shedding red cinders as it went. A faint *psssht* confirmed its extinction. He looked levelly at McMahon. "Okay. You want to get your life back on track on two fronts. I still don't get what all this has to do with me."

"Beats me, Jack, beats me. It was just a crazy idea coming here. I never had many crazy ones, so I wasn't sure how to handle them. But somehow I thought that if I got here and told you about this, then maybe you'd help me out. I have no clue how, or why, taking into account how shabby I treated you, but, er, I thought that if I, well…"

359

Jack smiled to himself. "Apologized?

"Apologized, yeah. That's another skill I really haven't practiced too much, though my wife gave me plenty of opportunities for exercise."

"Well, if that's your apology right there, then I accept. Not that it makes much difference, I guess, because I don't think you could have hurt me or my life that much, but for what it's worth, I absolve you." Jack grinned.

McMahon didn't seem to know just what to do next. "Thanks, Jack ... one down, some thirty to go. No, make that fifty."

"Come on, you just can't go around searching for all your victims on your vacation. Besides, if there's such a thing as marriage by proxy, why don't you take this as apology by proxy?"

This too was a novel concept for McMahon. "Yeah ... well, yes. Why not, actually? I'd be playing the same record anyway."

"Besides, Mike, I've come to the conclusion that there's no way of telling why things go the way they go. Like, in washing out hotshot cadets, you probably saved quite a few of them from dying in battle. Probably even yourself. Would you say you were a gung-ho pilot?"

McMahon shrugged. "You saw me in the air."

"Most of the pilots who flew like you didn't come back from the war. Even Don Wheeler bought the farm, and you know how good he was. So, if you had been in the fray yourself, chances are you'd be long dead by now, and in my opinion, with the choice of being either dead with a Navy Cross or alive without a Navy Cross, I'd pass on the decoration."

McMahon went silent for a long while. "I sort of get your point. And I sort of know I probably would have gotten myself killed in the war, what with my temper and all. It's just that I waited so long for it and it never happened for me."

Jack savored the whiskey before observing, "You're better off this way, Mike, let me tell you. And so are those who got into your bathing water. Why not just let go and see what's coming up instead of trying to figure what went on without you? I mean, I was there, and it wasn't so great. For every rush I got for scoring, there was a massive down when someone didn't come back from a flight. And now, flying that old Kingfisher around, I can see it would've been better to look to the future even back then. You have it all going for you—a wife and a good job—and you're risking it all for old grudges, against the Navy of all things? Doesn't sound very smart to me, sorry about that."

Even in the dark, McMahon looked like he realized what an ass he'd been. "I know…it's just that, well, you know."

"Actually I don't know, but what does it matter? You've apologized, it's been accepted by me on behalf of all the others, and all is well with the world. Just turn around and face the future instead of the past. Besides, I can let you in on a secret. Sometimes waiting for something to happen is better than it actually happening. This probably is one of those times for you."

McMahon sought out Jack's hand to shake it. "Know what? That's what I'll do. As soon as I get back from this godforsaken island, I'll get a grip on things. No more griping with the Navy. And I'll try to change my ways with the wife too. I don't want to start all over again with someone else, if she stuck with me through the dark times. Cheers, pal!" He clinked his whiskey glass against Jack's so hard as to splash some on his own hand, and he licked it off before gulping off the rest the glass in one go.

"Damn, it must be late. I think I'll hit the sack. Tomorrow's my day to learn fishing, and I got twelve more days till the Trans-Oceanic flies south again." He turned to leave. "Thanks, Jack. I had no idea whether this trip would do anything for me, but it has. Stupid little things like this can make a big difference."

"Think nothing of it, Mike, it's all part of the package. Good night."

Jack watched as Mike McMahon's black form dissolved into the darkness, hearing a loud curse as his guest hit his toe on a stone. Mumbled denunciations were the last indication of him, and soon they too faded away into the night.

Not thinking of the future at all, Jack sat on the porch and intently watched the stars.

23

Jack was on the roof of a hut, fixing a leak which had been reported by the somewhat irate tenants of the previous night. A free weekend added to their stay had placated them, but they did demand a new hut, one with a better view. Luckily such a hut was available, situated on top of a grassy knoll with a breathtaking view to the west. With the sunshine it was a pleasant enough job to patch the roof.

From down below, Martin called up to Jack. He was walking uphill in the brisk version of his stride, waving a telegram in his hand. When Martin reached the hut, he said, "It's not the first odd telegram we've got, but this time I can't make any sense in this. You should have a look."

Jack reached down from the roof, took the telegram, sat down and looked at the piece of paper. It was terse, all right:

JOEL 2:16 2 WEEKS IN 3 BR BR

Jack smiled. "Martin, can you pop over to the mission and ask for a Bible? This is from Bunny Radner, most probably, with best regards, but I need some info on this Bible bit. At least I *think* it's a Bible quote."

Martin flashed a knowing smile and bounded off in the direction of the mission at the bay.

When he returned he said, "They were delighted you finally asked for one, and fully expect to see you in church at ten on Sunday. They also sent these leaflets along with the Bible, which, by the way, you can keep for further study."

Jack knew the missionaries were deeply concerned about his moral fiber or lack thereof, but Martin really didn't need to lay it on so thick.

"Thanks, Martin, and next time, please remind me before I ask you to do something, I'd be better off doing it myself. Now, open the Bible at Joel 2:16, and read it to me."

Martin looked at the index, leafed through the pages, and with an intrepid "Here goes" read with a solemn voice: *"Gather the people, sanctify the congregation, assemble the elders, gather the children, and those that suck the breasts: let the bridegroom go forth of his chamber, and the bride out of her closet."*

Jack whistled through his teeth. "This means work, Martin. We need to get the bridal suite out of our dreams and into reality in two … no, three weeks. So Bunny got lucky. Where did we store that big hut? Is it with the smaller ones?"

"No, it's down by the wharf. Let's go and finish the groundwork first and then I'll get it transported."

Martin had been planning to get the largest hut erected for some months now, and had even started work on the foundation, but lack of demand for such a hut had caused it to drop in priority. It had been thought out as a proper bridal suite all right, with the best views, best amenities, best location, the works.

Jack surveyed the spot they had planned for it and admired the unobstructed view to the west: it was certainly the best available on the island.

Martin arrived with the crew of workmen who had helped Jack lay out all of the huts. Even with just hand tools, it didn't take very long to finish the earthen foundation. Then the crew left to organize the transport of the corrugated iron hut, which was packed up for transport—as it had been since 1942.

Jack fixed Martin a knowing glance. "Well, it looks like

Bunny Radner is coming back to the Solomons. We have to make his stay an enjoyable one, which shouldn't be too hard, seeing he's found a new wife for himself. Remember I told you about his burns?"

Martin nodded. "Burns or no burns, Bunny Radner is a survivor. It'll be good to see him again."

Jack said, "If it's okay with you, I'll leave you to check the setting up of the hut, I need to finally go get the stuff we need for the interiors."

"Sure thing, Jack," Martin answered, and started uphill.

Jack decided to hop over to Guadalcanal, waste of fuel as it was, to enjoy the fine flying weather. At his office he was met by two hotel visitors who had come to request a flight, so it was easy to work out a deal which worked both ways.

Jack flew the Kingfisher higher and with wider turns than usual, just to make the most of the glorious weather. He also flew all around Guadalcanal, made small tight rings around Savo Island, and buzzed a fishing boat whose owner was his friend and would not get mad. The guests whooped with joy at every flamboyant turn of the plane, and when they landed at Guadalcanal, they wanted to book a flight for every flyable day left of their stay. Jack arranged to meet them at the harbor in three hours' time for the flight back.

Jack needed paint, curtains, furniture and advice on all of these. Luckily these were all available at Honiara, and within an hour and a half, Jack had a definite plan on how to make the bridal suite look and feel like one. Deliveries were arranged for the next week, except for the double king-sized bed, which would take more time to construct. Even that was promised to be delivered on time before Bunny and company would arrive. Whistling some tune which even he himself could not name, Jack returned to the harbor.

In two weeks' time, bit by bit, the bridal suite became reality. A very large Nissen hut had a hardwood floor, a hardwood porch, and as a final touch, four hardwood pilasters at the door installed. Inside, the local seamstress had prepared very fine curtains and dividers, and the furniture supplied by the carpenter workshops was a perfect match, with their close attention to detail.

The missing bed was a source of some dismay, but the carpenters promised to deliver it by the time it would be needed. They had decided to make this bed much more solid than the others they'd delivered to the hotel. With this in mind, Jack cited the day before Bunny's arrival date as the last possible moment for installation, just to be on the safe side.

The day Jack had calculated for Bunny to arrive dawned just as magnificently as a day possibly can. The bridal suite still had the slight but discernible smell of paint, as the interior walls of the Nissen hut had been given a fresh coat of paint in three colors. Windows had been placed in the roof and walls of the hut, allowing the soft-hued light which penetrated the palms to enter. Overall, the bridal suite looked very enticing indeed.

The fact that no bed had materialized so far had given Jack some leverage in the negotiations with the carpenters, but it was becoming a headache. A bridal suite by definition must include a bed, Jack tried to argue with the master carpenter, but he was just as adamant that it had to be perfect to be worthy of the bridal suite, not to mention sturdy. Though Jack was irate, he couldn't do anything about it except try to hurry them up.

No visitors arrived with the day boat, and no other boats came in before nightfall. Jack was partly relieved and partly worried. He brushed off any worries with the simple explanation that the telegram was very imprecise in its dates, and that Bunny could descend on them any day now. The next morning and day brought no Bunny, and neither did the next one, but three other guests popped in without notice. By dinnertime, the carpenters were carrying huge wooden constructs in a jubilant procession up the hill and went on to assemble them into the biggest bed Jack had ever seen.

Jack was so happy to see his bed finally delivered that he paid a hefty bonus to the crew, who promptly took their leave to go and celebrate at the harbor. Wilma showed up and made the bed, rolling her eyes at the size of the thing, and before she left, she arranged a set of dividers so that they afforded the bed area some privacy from the spacious living quarters of the cabin.

As Jack was admiring the final look of the suite, he became aware of a commotion coming from the harbor. Apparently a boat had landed, a local event in itself, but this time there were children screaming and adults trying to calm them down. Jack started downhill to see what it was all about, but he ventured a guess it was Bunny Radner and party finally arriving. And as soon as he saw the harbor under its solitary, dim light, he could make out Bunny in tropical gear complete with pith helmet, Dorothy from the store, a third person, and a bunch of natives collecting a large amount of trunks and bags from the boat that brought the people from Honiara. Bunny organized the assemblage into a line of luggage-bearers and set himself up in the front of the whole noisy train.

"Hey, Jack! I made it!" Bunny yodeled from halfway up the hill. "Good to be back! And hey, here is the brand-new, industrial-strength, as-seen-in-hospitals Mrs. Dorothy Radner."

Jack smiled and went down to shake his hand. Bunny ushered Dorothy up to give Jack a hug, and Jack heartily congratulated her.

The three stepped off the path to allow the baggage train to pass, but Bunny said, "Oh by the way, Jack, remind me never again to hire non-natives as bearers. At the far end, you see the one … she's been nothing but trouble so far. She enlisted back in New York but she's been so gloomy and moody and just couldn't wait to make landfall over here. She won't carry anything but her own bag no matter how hard I try to push her. Maybe the two of you should have a talk." Bunny resumed his upward walk with Dorothy in his arm.

Jack didn't want to believe his heart, which was racing out of control, but he soon saw it was indeed Kay who was the person bringing up the rear in the long line of people. He experienced three separate jarring heartbeats which felt like a pile driver each time, but then he felt calm.

"Hello, Jack," Kay said, as the caravan advanced and left them alone.

Jack stared at her, not trusting his eyes. His desperation for her, which had tormented him from the day he left the States, suddenly abated and left only an overwhelming sense of love for Kay. He took her in his arms.

"I'm back," Kay said. "I have something here that I just had to come and give back to you." She reached into her bag, rummaged about, and finally found the small matchbook cover she had pinched almost a year earlier.

"Well, well, well," Jack smirked. "I didn't think I'd see *this* again. I thought it'd been pinched by the eclectus birds and was now a prized possession in a nest. Some of the birds are really obnoxious, and they've stolen loads of stuff off me."

Kay grimaced. "I only took this one thing. Will I be punished for it?"

Jack looked thoughtful. "Truthfully? I think I have two options. I could turn your case over to the British authorities who will deal with you in due course. It'd be a long court battle, and you might wind up doing hard labor in Australia. On the other hand, I could let the locals take you through their justice system. You would probably land in a chicken coop for six months as punishment—they're harsh with people who steal down here."

Kay put on a sorry face. "Can't you try to speak in my favor?"

"Oh, I guess I could try and see if the authorities might release you into my custody. At least until the case is tried, that is, and it may take a while before it winds up in court."

"I'll just have to take my chances then," Kay smiled.

"I know." Jack put his arm on her shoulder. "That's just the way things are. Come up, we'll get you sorted out for the night, and we'll worry about your legal representation in the morning."

Snuggling close, Kay walked up the trail beside him.

After dinner, at which a good-natured Bunny had drunk a lot and had made a lot of noise before retiring to the bridal suite under Dorothy's guidance, Jack took Kay for a walk down the hill to the harbor. It was a very still night, with no wind at all it seemed, and at the moorings of the plane by the pier, only the slightest sound could be heard from the lapping of the water against the main float. Jack held Kay's hand as they reached the end of the pier.

"I'm so happy to see you, Kay ... and I can't believe you're here. When I left Boston, I was sure I'd seen the last of you."

Kay took a small piece of wood from the pier planks and flipped it into the sea. "You know, I thought so too. I actually thought, good riddance to you. I was glad you went, and it took all of thirty seconds for that overwhelming emotion to pass. After that, I've been like a sick puppy: lost, miserable, unable to work, no sleep, no nothing."

Kay sat and pulled Jack down beside her. "My mother thought I'd gone crazy, and so did my boss when I put in my resignation. The only person in the world who understood me was Bunny Radner, when I went to see him in New York to ask for his opinion. Bunny said that he'd known only two really exceptional men in his whole life, and I had already been married to one of them. That was all he'd say, but he did put his itinerary on the table where I could see it. I scribbled down the dates and went home to pack. Then I went home to try to explain to my parents, and after getting yet another diagnosis of acute madness from my friends, I set out for San Francisco. Nice flight, nice cruise from Hawaii onwards … but I just couldn't enjoy any of it. I was so worried how you would take me showing up."

Jack put his finger across her lips. "Shhh … let's just say I think I can manage it." He took her by the hand and led her to her cabin, and from there, to his.

Within three days, Kay had invaded every possible sector of Tulagi Hotel's operations. She would accompany Wilma to the market, marveling at the variety and freshness of the fruits of land and sea, then help out at the kitchen trying to soak in all that the Solomon Islands' cuisine had to offer. Martin had to put up with her very expert-sounding but entirely American visions on color schemes for a new cabin and he was also told the cabin should be rotated forty-five degrees to face more westerly, even considering it was already firmly attached to the ground.

As for Jack, Kay placed a permanent reservation on any flight or any other operation he had in mind which included the plane, and she didn't even mind the cuts and bruises she suffered one morning when Jack asked her to retrieve a wrench he'd dropped inside the fuselage. Kay was small enough to ferret herself down to the floor of the plane but had long enough arms to reach the noisy nuisance of a fallen tool. Triumphantly she presented the wrench to Jack and demanded an hour's flight in return. They made it back shortly before nightfall.

On a bright July morning, Jack was trying to do his bookkeeping when Kay bounced up from the harbor. She was all out of breath by the time she reached Jack, and her mad dash had him rather worried. "Jack!" she shouted. "I know what's wrong with your plane!"

Jack was almost certain his plane was in flames or had sunk at its moorings, but she restrained him from darting back downhill.

"It doesn't have a name!" she exclaimed in triumph.

Jack nevertheless peered down at the pier to see if anything was salvageable there, but then looked at Kay.

"A name? It's a Kingfisher, you know that. It's been a Kingfisher all along, since 1940."

Jack apparently didn't see the point, so Kay pounded her fists on his chest.

"You nincompoop! It needs to have a *real* name! And nose art! Just like you had on the fighters you flew. Surely this one, your very own beautiful plane, can't be left without a name?" And she accompanied the last statement with the pout she knew was capable of melting Jack's steely resolve in seconds.

"A name ... okay, I can live with that. What name do you want? *Kay* springs immediately to mind, of course," he said, grabbing her hand and starting downhill again Wizard of Oz fashion, swinging her whole arm in stride.

She frowned. "That's obvious, way too easy. No, Jack, now you put some thought into this." Kay wrenched her hand out of his and ran to the next palm, then leaned against it with closed eyes and lips fit to kiss.

Calmly passing her by, Jack talked out loud to himself.

"My mother wouldn't probably appreciate flying around the Pacific on the nose of a scout/observation plane. Hmm ... I have two sisters, but they would both want to be on the nose, I guess, so I can't leave one out, or she'd be mad at me. What about Wilma? Yes, Wilma would be good ... let's go and ask her."

Jack received a whipping on his posterior from a cane wielded by a woman scorned.

"Get real, Jack, you can think of a good name. What were the names like back then?" Kay pushed him against a palm and made sure he looked at her by kissing him hard.

"Well," he began, breathless from the kiss, "most of them started with *Miss*. There were lots of planes like *Miss Mabeline* and *Miss Veronica* and *Miss This'n'that*. I had one called *Haulin' Ass*, and Don fought with his plane captain when he wouldn't paint '*71*' on his plane. So you see, even back then I wasn't that hot on naming planes for ladies." Jack switched places with her against the palm and kissed her.

"You ancient brute. It's the height of fashion! *Haute couture*! You don't want to miss the trend and leave your poor old plane nameless, do you? You'd be last in the neighborhood." She played tag on him and bolted off, only to miss her step and fall flat on the undergrowth beside the path.

Jack followed her, pulled her up, dusted her, and kissed her elbow all better again.

"Let me make sure you get down to the pier in one piece," he said, and lifted her across his shoulders. No amount of yelling and screaming, no amount of foul language, got her free. She only regained her self-determination on the pier, when Jack, with the agility of a banana-boat loader, whipped her off his back and dropped her on the pier. He was within inches of his life, her gaze told him, but only for a second. Jack presented her with the plane, with Martin looking on, wondering what was up this time.

"So, Martin, Kay wants to have a name painted on the plane. Any suggestions?"

Martin shook his head. "You caught me off-guard, I haven't thought of any." He tried to pass the buck. "What about you? Do you have any candidates?"

Kay took up the challenge, suggesting quite a few names in rapid succession, only to have each one shot down in flames. Then she walked out to the end of the pier and stood for a long while, arms folded on her chest.

"Martin, what's the word *tomorrow* in your language?" she asked.

"In Pijin it'd be *tumora*," Martin told her.

"That's it then! We'll call her *Miss Tumora!*" She beamed with the internal light of genius, and the men fell on their knees on the pier to worship her DeMille-style. She accepted this token of appreciation as her natural due, much to the amusement of the fishermen on the other side of the pier.

Jack got up and pointed at the lazy plane basking in the sunlight. "I can't paint it on the cowling, that's for sure, but Martin, don't you think it's a piece of cake for one of the guys who paint our huts?" he asked.

Martin agreed and offered to go look for the man straight away, which was very much to Kay's liking.

"Great! Tomorrow we can have a grand ship-christening ceremony with champagne and a party afterwards! Yay!" Kay seemed to regress to five years old in a second, bouncing on the pier like a cheerleader, but her unabashed joy caught on with everyone else. The men exchanged a glance and told her the party would be on soon.

Champagne might or might not be available on Guadalcanal, but Jack jumped on the wing to go have a look. Kay's spaniel look bought her a ride too, so Martin untied the moorings when they were already on the wing of the plane. He watched them take off and went to look for the painter.

It took Jack a few hours to come up with four bottles of champagne, and apparently it was Guadalcanal's entire supply. After the quick hop back to Halavo, they went to ask Wilma for a menu appropriate for a ship-christening, and invited all the guests of the hotel to the grand party on the pier in the evening. By six-thirty, the pier was full of people, and the Kingfisher had been tied close enough to be hit with a bottle. After a short speech as the initiator of the project, Kay then aimed at the plane with the champagne.

"So where can I hit?" She swung the bottle back. "The propeller hub might be a good target."

"Hell no!" Jack shouted. "You'd break the constant speed system!"

"The wing, then?" Kay said, closing one eye for better aim.

"No, no, no! I don't want dents on the leading edge. Try the main float."

Kay pouted. "I'm not going to kneel with my rear up in the air when I christen a plane! Give me a target!"

Jack produced a plank and placed it on the wing. "Try that—I don't think you have to hit the plane itself as long as the bottle breaks."

Kay swung the bottle back as if to deliver a tennis serve. "I dub thee…" she shouted, "*MISS TUMORA!*" and with that, she smashed the bottle on the plank. A torrent of white foam exploded on the wing, on her, on Jack who was holding the plank, and on everyone on the pier near enough. With great ceremony, Jack then removed the engine cowling plate which was to be adorned with the name, and presented it to the painter. All this was met with much cheering, and Wilma's delicacies were consumed in copious amounts until late into the night.

Kay was awakened by the flicker of a storm light. The wick of the little petroleum lamp gave out a dim, rich yellow glow, and Jack's shadow danced on the wall and ceiling as he held out his hand to Kay. "Come on, we don't have too much time," he said, and ushered Kay to put on some clothes. She dressed and followed Jack out to the porch, only to see his black form wend its way down the path that led away from the huts of the hotel and the village, to a part of the island Kay had never visited. She hurried to get close to him, which to her was the only safe place in the dark forest.

It was a long trek along the path even in daylight, so in the all-absorbing darkness of the moonless, if starry, night, it took a good while. She mis-stepped many a time and almost sprained her ankle, but Jack kept telling her all would be revealed soon and would be worth the effort. Still, by the time they reached a small clearing at the far end of Porsanger, she was pretty well miffed.

Then Jack asked her to peek out into the waterway, but having followed the swiveling lamp and chased the meager light on the ground, she still could not see a thing.

Only after Jack had turned down the lamp, nearly extinguishing its flickering little life, could she see that *Miss Tumora* was moored close to the shore. Now she understood why Martin had taxied the plane out of the harbor in the afternoon; she had assumed it was part of the flight training Jack was starting to give him. He must have taxied all the way around the promontory behind which Porsanger opened into the island. She couldn't figure out why, no matter how hard she thought about it, so she asked Jack what it was all about.

"Shh," he said. "It's a gift from *Miss Tumora* to you."

Jack hushed her protests and carried her down to the shoreline. Stripping to the waist, he carried her to the main float of the plane and asked her to get in. Kay could not understand why, because surely flying was out of the question—not even the opening of the inlet was visible in the dim starlight, and a fine mist moved over the little riffles of the sea. Still, she climbed aboard, sat in her customary seat behind the pilot's seat, and strapped herself in. Putting on the headgear she saw Jack climb aboard and settle in his seat. Putting on his headphones, he began the start routine.

As soon as the first tentative signs of life emerged from the engine, Kay saw gasoline flames leap out of barrels arranged along the shorelines of Porsanger. Eight in all, these formed a visual runway for *Miss Tumora* to follow out of the inlet and into the sky, and they also fixed a horizon for Kay. Up front, the last pair of barrels seemed frighteningly close to each other. With the engine idling, Jack checked all the instruments, and then he advanced the throttle.

Miss Tumora started to accelerate along the path between the barrels, and when Kay looked out of the bottom windows of the plane, she saw white foam on top of the pitch-black water. The contrast was dizzying, as was the mad rush of the float on the water, until it detached itself from the sea and lifted up, up, ever higher. Kay looked out of the side windows to see a person standing behind every barrel, the swirling light giving them all a surreal form.

When the barrels ended and the plane began its ascent into the darkness, Kay lost all sense of direction and horizon. She knew she was in capable hands with Jack flying on instruments, but she still had no idea where they were going, and the lack of reference points made her mildly nauseous. When they reached a height of five thousand feet, Kay finally understood: Jack was flying into the sunrise. Already the eastern horizon showed hints of the coming spectacle, with multicolored bands of light arching over the sea. Jack aimed the plane directly at the brightest part of the arc and climbed still higher.

After only a few minutes, the sun broke through the cover of the water. A blinding flash of yellow light streamed into the plane and it felt to Kay as if it physically struck her with its majesty. Jack pointed the nose of the plane down, so that only a very narrow but very bright slice of the sun was visible. All of this—the light, the noise, the unearthly feelings of flying— combined in Kay's heart into a mystical experience, and when Jack tried to reach her on the intercom, it took him a few tries to pull her back to the real world. What he had to say, though, was very real to Kay.

"Kay, will you marry me?" he shouted into the intercom.

Kay didn't get the message the first time, but when Jack repeated the question, she smiled. "Yes, Jack, yes!"

To celebrate the sought-after answer, Jack put the plane into a series of oscillations which felt like a sideways porch swing to Kay. She laughed, feeling very much alive and exhilarated.

By now, the sun had appeared fully over the horizon and the interior of the plane was getting hotter by the minute. Jack turned them around, back from over the sea towards the island chain, and they watched as the sunlight kissed each island, bringing out the blue and green of the sea and the land. By the time they were above Florida again, it was morning, and while buzzing Tulagi they saw the kaleidoscope of color already on display at the market. Jack set the plane down against the light southwesterly wind and taxied to the moorings. Martin appeared out of nowhere, which led Kay to believe this had been a detailed plan to pop the question.

"May I be the first to congratulate you both?" Martin asked as he helped Kay jump off the wing to the pier.

"Yes, you may," Kay said and kissed him on the cheek. Jack tied the main float to the rope and climbed to the pier too, receiving a hug from a beaming Martin.

Apparently word had gotten out regarding the significance of the flight, because the path to the main lodge was lined by people who wished to congratulate the happy couple. It was a new experience for Jack to be the center of attention, but he made do, and of course Kay took the brunt of the well-wishers.

It was late in the evening already when they were finally again alone together, and they made the most of that, too.

24

Jack awoke to a cool draft from the open door. His instinctive move to touch Kay beside him on the bed came to nothing, as she was not there. A steady rain beat down on the roof, and looking out the doorway he could see only the nearest palms. Everything beyond that was shrouded in an opaque mist of varying shades of gray, whose wisps seemed alive as the wind drove them among the trees.

He lay back on his bed and closed his eyes, feeling the blood rush in the veins of his temples. The pulsating, hissing noise in his ears was a familiar sign for him. It was going to be one of those days.

For some time now, he had felt a chill seeping in between Kay and himself. It was like swimming in the ocean, at first coursing through only the warm and caressing surface waters, but now, an undercurrent from deep cold waters was rising up from the depths below and forcing its way between them. He had said nothing to Kay, but he was sure of what he felt.

Her behavior had changed slowly in the course of four months, in barely perceptible increments, in one direction. Where nothing before had been a problem between them, now one by one simple things became questions, questions evolved into issues, and issues matured into arguments— heated, pitched, vicious arguments. Jack had thought long and hard whether to bring this up with her, to see whether he was right or wrong, but his timidity once again prevented him from seeking a confrontation.

Jack knew well enough that talking about the latent problems with their relationship might be a good short-term solution, but he was also sure the undercurrent would not pass that simply. Like so many times before, he felt his life was following a predetermined course like a gramophone needle travels in the groove, but with alternating turns left and right.

Life with Kay sometimes made him feel like living inside a pinball machine, but he had ceased to enjoy the adventure any more. This time he wasn't sure he'd have the strength left to pull himself up again, if his fears were about to become reality, and the needle would come to the final cracking groove, permanently down in a never-ending one-click circle.

He stood up beside his bed, stretched out, put on his shorts and sandals and stepped out into the drizzle. The rain felt invigorating on his bare chest. Avoiding the small snakes of water which had appeared in the path, he made his way down the hill by stepping from one solid patch of earth to the next. He had a hunch he would find Kay down at the pier, and when the gray mists gave way to a flashing fifty-yard gaze, he saw her sitting at the pier next to the mooring rope of *Miss Tumora*.

Jack sat down beside her, and she looked at him for a second without seeing him. Then she resumed her empty stare at the sea. There wasn't even a horizon to see, the rain and mists covering everything. It was as if they sat in a space without anything but the pier defining it as a space at all, and everything else beyond the dome of rain which encircled them did not exist. The pier itself seemed to be half of a pier, unconnected to the earth. The sea was calm, with only a random wave causing the anchored plane to nod slightly, sideways and down, like a benevolent drunk acknowledging a disapproving lady passing him by.

"There's a flight out tomorrow," Kay said in a voice devoid of emotion, like a recording on a wax cylinder. "I'll take it."

Jack leaned back on his extended arms to miss seeing her face. "I know."

Kay still did not look at him. "I thought you'd be angry."

Jack raised his face to catch more rain. Its motion on his stubbly beard felt like a little massage, tickling, teasing, but most of all reminding him that at least on the outside, he was still alive. Inside, he already felt dead. "No, Kay. I can't be angry for that. It's your life; you have to decide what you want to do with it."

"I'm so sorry. I thought this would be the thing for me to do, to come here and live with you ... but I was wrong. I mean, the time we had here together was wonderful, and you are wonderful, but still I'm just avoiding living my own life. Marrying you—I can't even tell you how hard this is for me to say—but marrying you now would just be wrong." She hid her face in her hands and bent forward until her hands lay on her thighs. "I have no idea what I should do, but I know I have to go away. I'm fooling you and fooling myself if I stay."

Jack wanted to touch her, but knew it would not be right. "There's no reason for feeling like that. You're a brave woman, and you'll survive no matter what."

Kay put her head on his shoulder. "Oh, Jack ... always the stalwart. I'm relieved about the way you're taking it. It's been so bad for me the last few weeks. I tried to understand myself, to understand what I wanted and felt, and I tried so hard to make it work, but I just can't get it right. I thought that coming over here to live with you, I'd finally edge Don out of my heart for good, or at least put him on the back burner, but ... I just can't. And you're wonderful, Jack! You're a fantastic man in your own right, but … you just aren't Don, and you can't turn into him. Nor should you. And since I can't lose him, I have no room for you in my heart. No room for a tenant like you, one who'd deserve it whole, not just a corner."

She raised her face to let the cool rain flow over her delicate features, and then rubbed her hands over her cheeks, as if to hope the water would dilute the painful words she had to say. "There's a part of me that's almost jealous of you, invading Don's space in my heart, and though I know he's dead and shouldn't take up any space, he should be just a memory, I can't push him out. Every time I try to let you in a little more, and a little deeper into me, this jealous bit of me puts up a fight for every square inch, or however you measure hearts."

Jack was silent. Not from a want for words, a want for feelings, but from a desire not to interfere and to make things worse. "I know," was all he could say.

She had more to say. "Maybe I can make him small enough in my heart someday, somewhere else. Some other time, I hope, sooner or later. But I know I can't lose him altogether. He'll always be there, and so will you."

Jack knew the implication. His lease wouldn't outlast Don's.

Kay snuggled her head against his shoulder, and to Jack, it felt like a knife's edge. "But every time I look at the sky here in Tulagi, I know I'm looking at the same sky which took him from me. I lost not just a husband here, I lost my meaning in life, and it's not for me to find it here anymore. In the clouds, not these gray and misty raining ones, but the pure, white towering ones, I see the same Pearly Gates he passed through as he went away from me, so I can't even enjoy the sun and clouds here anymore. And this rain... I thought I liked the rain, but this is ridiculous." Kay began to weep.

Instinctively Jack tried to console her, to hold her, but she pulled away from him. Her silent crying cut Jack's heart into razor-thin slices. And yet his feelings were turning into a vacuum, into nothingness, and all he wanted was to get out of there.

"I'll take you over tomorrow," he said, to enable them to leave that void of a place. "Let's get you packed." He stood up and offered his hand to her. When she took it, it hurt Jack to touch her, for the finality of the situation hit him hard. She got up, and together they walked off the pier and up the slippery path to the main lodge.

Never had there been a more painful twenty-four hours in Jack's life; at no time had he felt more alone. Preparing for the last dinner with Kay and for the other hotel guests, which were numerous by chance, made Jack think he knew what lobsters felt like before being cooked. Trying to be sociable with the guests, who of course had no clue what was going on was no relief; every time he happened to catch her eye the pain renewed itself, like ocean waves battering bulwarks. The guests divined something was amiss, and the atmosphere of the dinner became first moody and then downright dismal. Everyone retired after dessert, not wanting to stay around for drinks and cigarettes as usual.

In the morning the rain had not let up at all, and the same colorless wall of steady drizzle fell from an all-encompassing cloud. Flying Kay over to Guadalcanal was not an option, so Jack asked one of the fishermen to take her over in his speedboat. Kay waved once from the boat, in a small circular motion with the palm upturned, in the royal fashion. Then she sat down in the boat and looked forward, not glancing around once.

Jack didn't stay to watch the boat grow smaller as it sped away on the calm sea, but walked uphill with a definite gait, as if there were some urgent matter to be resolved at the main lodge.

Martin closely watched Jack's progress from the market, and when Wilma burst into tears when selecting sweet potatoes, he held her and soothed her.

From then on, Martin took on a twenty-four-hour watch on Jack. He was worried for him because he could no longer see the fire in his eyes. Jack did go about his work, flying the guests, entertaining them in the evening by the campfire with his tales, but his heart was no longer in it. He even attempted to get going on constructing their largest hut, but lost interest in it after the groundwork was done, and instead of working his grief off, he was more often seen on the porch of the main lodge, sipping whiskey from a too-large glass.

On a gorgeous morning about four months after Kay's departure, Jack was starting up *Miss Tumora*. His guests, a party of three adventure seekers from Australia, were leaving the island, and Jack had agreed to take them along to Guadalcanal on a final sightseeing flight. The passengers were already strapped in and discussing the ensuing trip, excitement plain on their faces. Dutifully Jack had planned a full one-hour trip around all the best views in the area. Uncharacteristically, *Miss Tumora* was reluctant to start; instead of the usual amount of coughing and puffing with associated belches of smoke, there was more exhaust than ever, loud bangs and false starts, and Jack had to use all his experience to coax the Pratt & Whitney to life. Once the engine did start, it ran smoothly and revved like usual. Despite the rough start, Jack deemed it fit to fly.

Takeoff was normal and soon Jack forgot all about the

starting hassle. His showboating flight to Guadalcanal was over in only an hour, and then he ran a few errands. On his way back to the plane he remembered that he'd wanted to test *Miss Tumora* at high speed, because he'd installed a new type of spark plug in the engine with Martin the previous week, and had not had time to give it a high-performance test.

He took off out of the harbor straight towards Savo Island, and then climbed in a left-hand turn to two thousand feet. From there he opened up in a shallow dive and felt some of the exhilaration he used to feel when flying fast fighters. Of course, *Miss Tumora* was no fighter, but she could still whip up a nice speed in a power dive. Jack then decided to climb to test the higher altitude performance of the plane. With the engine still at full speed, he settled to a comfortable climb at eight hundred feet per minute. The engine performed flawlessly, never missing a beat, as the plane hit first five thousand feet, then ten.

At ten thousand, Jack put on his oxygen mask and opened the valve on his supply bottle. He never went this high with customers, even though he'd installed two oxygen masks for the four seats in the cabin behind him. He felt it was unnecessary to risk anything going wrong and stayed below seven thousand at all times, except when flying alone. Out in the Solomons, oxygen supplies were hard to replenish.

Oxygen flowed through the regulator and gave his mouth a slightly sweet taste. Jack swiveled the plane around fast and hard on its longitudinal axis to test the controls at this height. He took deep breaths as the plucky plane pushed ever upwards, through eleven, then twelve thousand feet. The service ceiling of the seaplane was rated at 13,000 feet, but Jack had frequently managed to coax it up to 18,000 feet or even higher.

Now he decided to look for *Miss Tumora's* absolute ceiling. With a very light hand on the stick he invited the plane upwards in small increments, sensing its responses to each little jump. The altimeter seemed reluctant to wind its hands any further, but Jack knew all the tricks for luring it on. In twenty minutes' time, at seventeen thousand eight hundred feet up, Jack looked out the windscreen and saw nothing but the rich blue expanse of the Pacific ahead, and to his right and to the rear, the Solomons chain of lush, green splotches of land.

Jack became aware of a curious idea brushing him furtively, like a feather in the mind, as if it didn't want to be noticed fully. Gradually it became clearer and formed itself into a real memory. When he knew what it was, he knew he felt exactly the same as the day he'd beaten Jamie Schwinn and his friends tossed him in the air; every time he gave the stick a tiny yank with his fingertips he again saw the Nebraska sky, its fierce sun exposing the world to his slow-motion mind, the tatters of clouds dotting the blue abyss. Every yank, every jump a few feet up became longer and higher than the previous one, just as the last tosses had been as long as life itself.

He tried to adjust the throttle a little, to get just a hint of more power for a few more feet of altitude, but his hand felt numb. He looked at his hand and it didn't seem to belong to him anymore. He looked at his hand for a while, and then his slow-working brain hammered out an explanation. Jack slid his hand down his oxygen tube, up to the bottle, and when he got to the tube connector, he felt the faint but definite flow of oxygen rushing out of it. For weeks he had been trying to remember to fix the oxygen bottle holder. It was loose and the bottle sometimes fell out of the holder in tight turns. Apparently it had moved and the oxygen tube connector had jarred against the plane wall, causing a leak in the system. He had not been receiving any oxygen from it for the past few minutes.

Dimwitted, Jack tried to think out his options. He knew he should have just pushed the plane over in a dive for richer oxygen levels below ten thousand feet, which he could reach in a few seconds. Somehow, another competing idea grew in his oxygen-depleted brain. He was already at nearly 18,000 feet; why shouldn't he try to reach 20,000 when he was here already? Or 25,000?

"Hell, let's make it 30,000 feet! I know what it feels like to fly there!" he shouted against the roar of the engine, giggling like a little child.

His roving, dull gaze chanced upon a cumulus cloud, a blossom of white on a sky of cobalt, and Jack thought that inside the towering cloud, he saw the biggest Pearly Gates ever. "Whoa! Lemme fly to that ... peaaaa-rllly gate..." he sang to himself, "...to the gaaaa-tes of my ... paaaals ... and I shall not shrink." He felt an urge, a passion to reach the gate and be free of everything. He felt immensely tired and wanted to sleep, but not before he had flown through that gate in the sky. His dull mind was able to tell him that he could not fly into the cloud, the winds inside it would tear his plane apart, but steadfast he pushed on at the precarious height he'd reached.

By the time his vision began to fade, he finally realized he had to descend or die, so his last conscious move was to push the stick forward and hope he would reach safe altitudes in time. Just before the dive, he whispered, "Sorry, old lady, looks like we'll miss tomorrow." *Miss Tumora* tilted over her left wingtip and began a circling dive through the thin air at an ever-increasing speed.

Back on the island, Martin opened the door of the main lodge. He wanted to have a look at the reservation book; lately, guests had arrived on every ferry, and the proprietors' memory became insufficient as a method for keeping records. As usual, Jack's desk was a cormorant's nest, so Martin had to dig into mounds of paper. In a while he came by the book, but on its opened pages there was another book, the *Rubaiyat*. It too was open, at the Rubai 43:

So when that Angel of that darker Drink
At last shall find you at the River-Brink
And, offering his Cup, invite your Soul
Forth to your Lips to quaff—you shall not shrink.

Martin shivered when he read the lines. It was probably no accident the book was open at that poem, considering Jack's disposition of the past few months. Martin's thoughts were interrupted by a bustle from the path leading down to the harbor. As he bounced up to the door, the focus of the commotion reached the lodge. It was Peter the fisherman, looking distraught. "I... saw... Jack fly real, real fast... southwest... he... climbed and I saw him... go up, up, up. And then he fell!" he gasped.

Martin was aghast. "What do you mean *fell*?"

"He fell, *Miss Tumora*... the plane came spinning down! Spinning! Down!"

Martin started downhill. "Did you actually see him hit the sea?" he shouted behind him as he raced down the footpath.

Peter followed him. "No, he was too far! But he fell from the sky, I saw, I know!" he called ahead.

Martin pushed people out of his path, not heeding their protests, in fact not hearing them at all or understanding what was happening. He had to get down to the harbor and organize a search for Jack and *Miss Tumora*. When he finally reached the harbor, word of Jack's plight had already pervaded the little community, and everyone with anything bigger than a canoe was there offering to join the search. Fighting off panic, Martin boarded the fastest boat on the island, a surplus US Navy patrol craft which had been converted for fishing, and told the other boats to first follow his boat and then fan out when they reached the southern end of Florida Island.

As the boat trundled on as best it could, its speed diminished by years of non-regulation maintenance but still making adequate progress, Martin stayed at the bow scanning the sea ahead. Though no wind was blowing, the sea was now in large swells, which complicated matters. As the boat reached the tip of the island, Martin pointed out to the pilot to press on straight ahead. The roof of the boat had five teenage kids as lookouts, shading their eyes from the sunlight and anxious to find the plane they had come to take as a permanent fixture of their village. Martin kept running from the port side of the boat to the bow and to the starboard side, hoping to cover the entire expanse of ocean ahead of them. Behind them he could see other boats as they began to widen the search.

After an hour and a half, one of the lookouts on the roof shouted that he could see the plane. Rushing up to the bow Martin climbed on it, and when the boat broached a big wave, he saw *Miss Tumora*. She was leaning starboard on its semi-sunken main float, the struts holding the starboard wing float all bent and partially loose from the wing, like an invalid on a broken crutch.

From the approaching boat it looked as if the plane was well on her way to going under. Horrified, Martin could not see any movement in the cockpit. Eventually he reached the plane, and he was within distance to climb on the wing. Treading carefully on the slippery main spar of the wing, he hurried up to the cockpit.

Jack was unconscious. His head had hit the side of the cockpit while the unpiloted plane descended, and there was blood all over the instrument panel and seat. Hastening to find out whether he was alive, Martin opened the lock and slammed the hatchback, then pressed the tips of his fingers to Jack's jugular vein. A faint pulse made his heart jump with joy, and he shouted the good news to the anxious friends on the boat. It still remained to get him out of the plane and into the boat without causing any more harm to Jack, so he asked one of the bigger boys to climb on the wing and come to his aid.

Martin clambered inside the plane, and together he and the boy were able to pull Jack back onto his seat, to unbuckle his seat belt, and with Martin standing on the floor, to push and pull him out of the cockpit and onto the wing. His head wound was still oozing blood, which trickled onto the wing into flower-shaped drops and was swept away by sprays of water, its deep red merging into pink as it approached the trailing edge.

Carefully they dragged him across the wing and lowered him into the boat, into the hands of the waiting boatmen. At that moment another boat appeared at the scene and started to prepare *Miss Tumora* for tow.

Peter turned his boat around and sped southwest. Martin sat on the floor, holding Jack's head steady, and one of the boys pinned his body to the floor. He was unconscious and pale from the blood loss, but somehow Martin thought Jack was not in danger of his life. It was much too long a ride back to the island, and only after Jack had been delivered to the mission infirmary did Martin allow himself to shift down from high gear.

Two days later Jack regained consciousness. When his eyes began to register something other than vague reddish blobs, he saw Martin reading a book by his bedside. "Say, Martin... tell me. Is *Miss Tumora* all right?"

Martin shook his head. "No, Jack, *Miss Tumora* is never flying again. We towed her back here so she can be used for spare parts, but she almost sank under tow. The fuselage is broken behind the cockpit, the main float leaks, the side floats are bent out of all whack ... she is in sad shape, pal. Bill Peet came over yesterday with someone from the airline to have a look, and they said it's impossible to fix." Martin inserted his bookmark with far too much precision into his book, closed it and set it on the floor by his seat.

Jack turned to face the whitewashed wall, on which small cracks in the chalk paint ran crisscrossing, like a roadmap for anthills. "So I didn't even die well enough," he said in a subdued voice.

Martin moved over to his bed and sat down on it.

"Look, Jack, don't start out on that self-pity thing. It won't make you any better and it certainly won't bring your plane back, so don't waste time on that. Instead, start thinking how you're going to get that other plane over here. You have a hotel three-quarters full of people who want to have a flight as advertised, and some of them won't be happy if they don't get to fly."

Jack lay down and closed his eyes, a tear of distilled pain rushing to the pillow. "I don't care. I can't think of anything like that now. Just leave me alone."

Martin thought it best too, at the moment, and left the room without looking back.

391

Within a few days Jack was fit enough to return to the hotel. He still had mild dizzy spells, and he'd not even dared to think about the other plane, as the doctor at the mission would have grounded him anyway. He tried to get back into routines, but none of the tasks of running the hotel held any appeal for him. In fact, he was so absent and vacant that Martin got more and more irritated with him. Jack would stare at the sky when people talked to him, or wander off to nowhere in particular. Even the guests couldn't manage to have any kind of conversation with him, which was a major change.

One evening two weeks after the crash, Jack sat on the pier where *Miss Tumora* used to bob in the waves. It was getting chilly and he had a sweater beside him on the pier. Somewhere down the line of his life he had learned to do a bowline around himself, and he now did so idly, untied it again, not looking at it but out to sea instead.

Martin saw him sitting there and decided to bite the bullet. He went down to sit with him, but getting his attention was not that easy. "We'll get you a new plane. Lucky you bought two."

Jack tied yet another bowline. "No, I don't think so."

Martin winced. "All it takes is for you to make a little trip to Sydney. It'll do you good just to change the scenery for a while. Take all the time you want, I can arrange with Bill Peet for any flights the guests may want in the meantime. His plane works well enough and seats four."

Jack looked at Martin, who felt a chill in his spine when the empty stare hit home. "I don't think I'll come back if I leave for Sydney. Frankly, Martin, I have no clue what to do. I just don't have any life left in me." And his hands again formed the bowline around his waist.

Martin decided to play his last card. "Look, Jack, why can't you see what you have here? You have a hotel, and friends, and customers, and everything you could ever need."

Jack sighed. "I know, it's just that I've got a need for something that isn't here. You know what I mean."

Martin turned to leave. "All I ask is that you think it over before going anywhere. You just won't have it better anywhere else than you have it here." He hung his head low and went away.

Jack stared at his back but had no words to say, not even thoughts. Under his sweater he had his friend Mr. Daniel, and he began conversing with the bottle. The stars came out with tropical rapidity, and by the time the backbone of the Milky Way was supporting all the brilliant stars, Jack was feeling no pain, physiologically speaking. Nevertheless he was very disappointed in his friend's ability to numb the stinging memory of his past happiness. Drowsy and dimwitted he sat on the pier, his thoughts running a slow and dull circular path, with no exit. Somewhere down the course through the bottle he thought he should beware of falling into the sea, but his next thought was, so what?

His whiskey vigil went on until midnight. By the time Martin came looking for him, he was skunk drunk. Martin felt both annoyed and sorry as he sat down by Jack.

Noticing his arrival, Jack began slurring out a theory. "Know what, Martin … I have it all sorted out. Luck and Happiness, they're evil twins. I used to know Luck real well in the war, and I thought I knew Happiness too, but y'know what, Martin? They're evil, both of them. Plain evil."

Martin was no big friend of drunken babbling, but decided to humor Jack in case it would help get him back on track. "Evil, huh?"

"Evil. Mark my words. Take Luck, for example. She sat on my wing when I flew in combat. She flew with all the pilots. You couldn't see her direct, but outta the corner of your eye, she'd be sitting on your wing. Sometimes she did shomer... somm... you know, flips. Stood on her hands, Don told me he saw her do that." Jack fumbled for the bottle, but Martin had already moved it behind his back and away from Jack's reach.

Jack was so inebriated, he didn't even mind. "Annnnd you know what happened to the guys when Luck left? They died. They were blown off the sky. Or even better, they would be up on a checkout ride on a plane that's just been fixed. Everything's all right, plane's fine, no prob... until Lady Luck goes in the tail and finds the cable they missed when they checked the plane, and she takes a pair of pliers and snips the two strands of cable that remain. Then she goes to the wing and waves you goodbye... royal fasshion, palm up, in a circular moshon... and you spin in and buy the farm."

Martin closed the bottle with the cap he found on the pier. "And that's the way it goes?" he said, amused by the thought of a personified Lady Luck riding on wings.

"That's the gawdawful truth, pal. And know why I know they're sisters? Eeeevil sisters?" Jack asked.

"Tell me."

"They work exacthltly the same way. Think about it. Luck rides with you until she gets bored, then takes off and you die. Happiness hangs around until you're absolutely hooked and thinking everything will go on just like that, and poof! She's gone, just like Luck off the wing, she goes away, and you're dead just as well. See the link, ehh? Dead... at least I am."

Scratching his ear, Martin tried to think of something suitable to say. "Well, now... I don't know about that. I've had some luck in my life, and seen a piece of happiness too, but I haven't thought of it at all that way."

"I can feel it," Jack affirmed. "Just as if I'd seen Lady Luck drop off my wing, I've seen Happiness fly away. Crashed and burned, that's what I am."

"But you know what?" Martin asked, with his arm around his friend. "I don't think Happiness has left you like that. I'd rather think she's gone hiding from you and is waiting for you to find her. Like hide-and-seek."

"Hide-and-seek? Damn, pal, I'm way too old to play hide-and-seek!"

"The hell you are. But seriously, Happiness is in what you do here, and what you have, and what you can do. It's not attached to any person, and no one can just give it to you. Besides, it's probably the same for her, for Kay—happiness appeared different to her and she didn't recognize it and thought it wasn't what she wanted, and that's why she left. Nothing you could have done would have given her that happiness she was looking for. Know why?"

"Tell me." Jack looked at him without any focus in his eyes. "Not that I don't know, but stab me one more time."

"She came over here to look for Don. She knew he was dead, but she still wanted to find him. You were her last link to him, and she tried hard to make it work. But her happiness had died the moment Luck slipped Don's wing, and somewhere down the line it hit her. To stay here wouldn't have brought her happiness—nothing would have done that for her here. That's why *she* left, Jack, but *your* case is different. Your Luck stayed with you all through the war, don't you see? Her sister doesn't have to be any more evil than that. She hasn't left you. I'm sure of it."

"Yeah, but look at *Miss Tumora* now. Luck left me fer sure, and that's why I crashed and wrecked my baby."

"No, Jack, she didn't leave you. You're still alive, so at worst she turned her back on you for just a while."

"Same thing. I'm dead inside, dead as a rock."

Martin held him tighter, and when the sobs came, first as barely audible little sighs, and turning up the volume, in massive, convulsive movements, he let him weep. "Hush, now… let it all out," he said, and knew nothing more was needed.

When Jack finally went from crying to sleeping, with the occasional full-lung breaths, Martin nudged him up from the pier and half-carried, half-dragged Jack to his lodge.

Then he closed the door and sat down on the sun chair on the porch and fell asleep himself, without a second thought.

25

Jack's life became a sorry succession of non-events. Guests arrived and left, most of them not terribly worried about the absence of the flights, although some had come to Tulagi Hotel specifically for that purpose. Some wondered about the proprietor's curious lack of interest in anything, for when asked about just any issue, he would start to answer, but then after a few words his sentences would gradually collapse into a string of disjointed words. Often he'd wander off. It was a matter of acute embarrassment to Martin, who as co-owner tried to take up some of his partner's slack, but Jack's behavior made the guests uncomfortable. Business began to decline.

It was during yet another heated exchange, or rather, another tirade which Martin delivered to his disinterested partner, that there was a knock on the door of the main lodge. Martin went to the door and opened it so hard as to almost rip it off the hinges.

On the porch stood a wraith of a man. "Yes?" Martin asked him.

After a long pause, the man said in a barely audible voice: "Is this Jack McGuire's hotel?"

Jack glanced sideways to the doorway, but could not recognize the man. "It is … for a while still at least." Having said this, he returned to his admiration of the color of the whiskey in his glass against the warm-hued light of the fireplace.

The stranger made a faint move with his hand to indicate

to Martin he would like to enter the hut. Martin moved aside, and the man stepped into the light in the hut. Jack took another look, then sprang to his feet.

"Doc Mendel? Is that you?" Jack stepped closer to the man, who held out his hand. Jack shook it, recognizing Doc's secret handshake in which he held out two fingers against the wrist of the other person as if to check his pulse.

Though the handshake was the same, Jack could no longer feel the steely grip, and the hand he shook trembled.

"I can't say you look great, but it's good to see you," Jack said to his old friend. Indeed, Jack was almost frightened to see how he looked. Sunken eyes lolled about inside rims of black lids, a razor must have last visited his face weeks ago, and of the muscular frame of wartime, only a shadow was to be found now. *Haggard in the extreme*, Jack thought, and he wondered what had happened.

Doc let go of his hand. "Thanks a lot, Jack, though you don't look so hot yourself."

Indicating a lounge chair, Jack asked Doc to have a seat. The physician sat down and looked at the bottle of whiskey with the eyes of a hungry rat. Martin got him a glass, poured a drink and handed it over to him. It disappeared in one gulp, and Doc asked for more with a motion of the hand.

Martin poured a thick one this time, and it lasted for two gulps. "Maybe you'd like something to eat," Martin suggested. "I'll go and ask for some." He went out the door, handing the bottle to Jack on his way out.

Jack stood up and walked over to the fireplace. Leaning against the mantelpiece, he assessed his guest. "It's been a while since we met last, Doc. What brings you to these parts?"

Doc Mendel looked him in the eye. "Would you believe it if I said I'm looking for a job? Anything goes."

Jack had some difficulty believing this and said as much.

Doc tried again: "Okay. I need a job, and not having found anything in Australia I decided to come over here and try you."

Jack still looked non-committal, so Doc decided to call the shots. "So I'm on the run from Australian authorities. Does *that* get me a job with you?" Doc Mendel leaned back into the plush chair, and the way most of him vanished emphasized his wiry frame.

Hearing about his old friend's fall from grace was a blow to Jack. He loped over to the other lounge chair and sat in it. "That's not at all what I expected," Jack said softly.

Doc looked around him all tensed up, then relaxed again.

"No, you're right. I didn't plan to go this way. All I wanted after the war was to get back to my hospital and my practice, and to carry on with what I'd set up back home." He looked Jack in the eye. "Didn't think I was asking too much."

"I can say that too, to a degree," Jack commented, "but it seems to me you went pretty far down the rocky road."

Doc's eyes glinted in the dim firelight as he threw a glance around Jack's lodge.

"This set-up looks great, Jack. It looks to me like you've made the grade. My plans already went all to hell even before the war ended. I never told this to anybody, but at the time all you Gentiles were receiving Christmas mail back in '44, I got some too. It was a manila envelope, way bigger than everyone else's letters. Pretty thick one, too, because besides the divorce papers, it contained the accountant's paperwork for divvying up the house and all our stuff. Apparently my wife had finally gotten fed up with my absence from home, and it also explained why I hadn't received any letters from my daughters all through the war. They'd been indoctrinated against me, and against my return to them after the war. When I was discharged in October '45, I was already in Pearl Harbor on my way back, when I started thinking, where was I going exactly?"

Doc leaned back further into the cushions, probably the first soft chair in a long time for him. "So I jumped off the transport at Pearl and found me a westbound ship, landing in Sydney with just my two bags—one sailor's and one doctor's—ready to take on Australia. First thing off the boat, I went to a Sydney suburb to meet a lady I had visited on R&R—which was not a good idea, since her husband had returned from Africa right before me. So I not only managed to have my dreams flushed down the head, but I also wrecked *her* post-war life."

The worn-out man counted his fingers to make sure he got his chronology straight. "I went further down. Finding a job at a hospital in Canberra was easy, but holding on to it was harder. You see, they decided after three infractions in a year that I couldn't handle my booze, which was sort of petty of them, I think. Melbourne was large enough for me to get another residency without undue attention to my previous employment. There they were even faster to lose me, after just six months, so I had to keep moving. Brisbane went the same way, Sydney too. Five years of sliding downhill."

Doc patted at his clothes to give the impression he had cigarettes somewhere, but Jack offered up his own before he ran out of pockets. Doc grabbed one, lit up and carried on. "Thanks, Jack. By the time I got to Adelaide, booze wasn't enough anymore. I'd gone on to morphine by then, but the ward nurse—who looked like a government horse, by the way—kept close tabs on the bottles. Once again I left town, this time following the railroad all the way to Kalgoorlie.

There I offered my services to a local health station, and for a while things were okay. I tried to wean myself off the morphine, but with the town in the middle of nowhere and nothing better to do, it wasn't at all easy."

He had already sucked up the contents of the cigarette all the way up to the filter, spreading ashes all over himself with his shaky hands. When he tried to do his customary finger-flip with the butt to discard it to the fireplace, he missed badly, and the glowing butt landed in a pile of firewood. Jack got to it before it did any damage, but in the corner of his eye he noted how intensely displeased Doc was with his lost skill.

"So ... when I decided that Kalgoorlie was not where I'd eventually retire to, I collected all the morphine they had in the dispensary and all the money they had in the till. It was the day before payday so I got a hefty wad of cash, and by the time they got wise, I was already long gone eastbound. The ride east was kind of nice, and with a little subterfuge in assorted towns the money lasted until Brisbane, and there I used my last change for a ticket to these islands. And that's why I need a job. Got any?"

Jack was thinking hard about what to tell Doc. Of course an old friend was welcome, but this was a bit beyond hospitality. "I have no work for a doctor, but a jack-of-all-trades might be useful," he said finally.

Doc smiled. "I'm beyond practicing anyway. Being a lumberjack would suit me just fine. An honorable profession, lumberjacking." Doc bummed another cigarette off Jack. His hands shook so violently as to extinguish the match before he got the cigarette burning, and had to try again.

Jack wondered just how fast a cigarette could be humanly smoked. He decided for the time being to set Doc up for the night and to try to nurse him back up to full strength.

Martin came in then with some leftovers in a basket, and he seemed pleased to see that something had piqued Jack's interest, even something like Doc in his present state.

Jack and Doc spent most of the next week talking. They would go on a walk, at a slow clip and not far from the hotel, because Doc tired so fast. Most of the time they walked to the harbor, but sometimes they'd head uphill to Jack's favorite spot. A palm tree had grown tilted at the ledge of a hill, and he'd found it served perfectly as his Leaning Tree.

Doc took an instant liking to the view over the Ironbottom Sound and Guadalcanal behind it, and they sat there in almost meditative silence.

"Do you have a single instance in your life, a perfect moment at some point in time, which you return to over and over again in your memories?" Doc once asked Jack. "Well, I do. It's July 13, 1938, at my house, 1120 Fairview Drive, in San Diego. It's my daughter's birthday. I'm out mowing the lawn, and the girls are playing on the swings I put up for them. My wife is in the kitchen making veal cutlets, and the smell of the grass is forever associated with that grand expectation of a delicious dinner. Somehow I took a snapshot of that moment. I even remember telling myself, 'This is it, pal, you've made it.'" He grinned thinly. "How about you?"

Jack weighed a pebble in his hand, and cast it some distance into a sandpit. "Not really, Doc, I can't say that I do. I haven't saved too many moments, even though Don told me to. He was an expert in collecting moments. When I try to think of great moments in my life, I get this blurry, undefined feeling of a good mood, like you just got a slice of warm apple pie with vanilla ice cream from Mom or something."

"Know what the problem with me is?" Doc asked. "It breaks my heart to have that memory. I yearn for that perfect moment, and it's as good as dead. Whenever I tried to make myself a home somewhere after the war, I would set it up as nice as possible, and then I'd think of that one moment." Doc closed his eyes. "And then it all went to hell. I'd be happy to forget I ever had that moment."

Jack had to think for a while. "Y'know, I thought this was my home. I had it all figured out, and I was happy. Then Kay visited me, and when she left, I became an orphan."

"Ah, it's *the Flying Dutchman* all over again." Doc squinted his left eye to glance at Jack. "Remember my gramophone, the one labeled 'Surgical eqpt' and stashed in with the medical stuff to be carried halfway around the globe? It was no accident I played just that one opera over and over. Before my wife sent me that stack of divorce papers, I could always think of the ending where all is well again and love prevails, and look forward to the third act, but after that, I couldn't listen to the whole recording through. I'd just return to the part where the guy sets out again to sail in despair."

"I've been thinking of leaving," Jack said suddenly as he stared into nothing. "Since Kay went away, I can't really see anything here that's worth keeping, or staying for."

Doc whistled through his front teeth. "You're a stupid bastard, Jack, you know that? You've come all this way, and built yourself this ... thriving hotel, and then you want to leave. To do what? To go look for a broad? You'd be better off chasing feathers in a gale, and be left with more in your hand at the end. Pluck out your eye and have a closer look at your life. So you don't have a wife here—big deal. Take it from me, all this is better than domestic bliss. At least you can come and go as you please, and no one is waving divorce papers at you at Christmastime."

Doc retrieved a cigarette from behind his left ear, and let

Jack light it for him. "Me, I'm the Eternal Jew. No home, and as soon as I try to settle down somewhere, I have to go again. Except now I have to kick the morphine out of my system. I need to go cold turkey. If I can do that, maybe I can try and see some future for myself."

"If we can help you do it, Doc, we will," Jack said resolutely. "What do you need to do it?"

Doc winced. "I dunno ... I've never done it, never seen it done. I read about it in medical school, but now, all I know is I get the creeps and crawls all day if I don't get my fix. My stores are all but out by now, so I might as well try and kick it. Just lock me up in a room for a few days and I should emerge victorious. If I don't, well, then I don't."

Jack promised he and Martin would look after him during the ordeal.

"Good, let's get started then," Doc nodded, and walked to his hut on a definite quest.

Jack called on Martin and Wilma, and sent for the mission doctor for advice. He agreed that there wasn't much anyone could do beyond making sure Doc would stay secure in a hut with nothing in it he could use to harm himself. Wilma was to supply very basic food and ample amounts of juice to be available at all times.

When Doc entered his cabin, he shook Jack's hand with a vague hint of his past strength, more by dint of willpower than physicality. "See you in a week," he said as he entered the hut and closed the window shutters. Martin had organized a round-the-clock watch on the door. For food supplies, a part of the door was sawn off to slide a tray through.

It was absolute hell for all involved. For days on end Doc, for all practical purposes, was delirious; crying, cursing, alternately talking to himself and then staying so silent for hours that Jack had to bang the wall in the hope of hearing some sign of life in response. During the second night he wanted a log delivered to his cabin along with a large hammer. Jack produced the requested items and while he wondered what Doc wanted to do, he soon got the point—Doc was chipping the wood with the hammer with all his strength. A hell of a banging went on all through the night, but in the morning there was a stash of wood chunks and chips pushed out from the food hole. Jack ventured so far as to ask, "Would you like another one?"

To which the reply was quick: "Yes."

Eight days later Doc asked for his release. Jack fetched the mission doctor to make sure Doc was okay when he emerged from the hut, and aside from hurting eyes and a desperate need for a bath, he was not in too bad shape. He enjoyed a long shower and a swim, and more than anything he enjoyed Wilma's sumptuous dinner that night. Jack refrained from offering him any alcohol, so when they retired to the porch to admire the starry sky, they had tall glasses of orange juice on hand. After a long sip and a silence, he spoke.

"Haven't felt this good in ages, Jack. Absolutely ages." Though Doc still looked tired and gaunt, his eyes had recovered some of their glint from the past.

Jack smiled at his friend and toasted him with his juice. "I'm glad you pulled through, not that I ever doubted it. Way back on these islands, in a different time, you were our strength, and we never thought you'd let us down. And you never did. No matter how shot up we were, we could count on you to patch us up again. I'm happy I could help *you* this time." Jack looked south and located the Southern Cross, his favorite constellation.

Doc grimaced. "You have no idea, Jack … there were

times when I almost shot myself. There really were times when I felt I couldn't take one more flyboy who would bleed all over my floor, ask me to save him and then die on me. The enemy raids were the worst, of course; you pilots mostly just died in the air, but after some bombings we took, that was so bad. Lost limbs, wounds everywhere, no time to even assess the guys before we had to rush in and start trying to figure which hole to stick a finger in first."

Jack looked out to follow a bright parakeet with his gaze, and when the bird went into the canopy, he sighed. "Too many went that way, Doc. Too many went our way, too, screaming into the mike as they burned out of the sky, or just plain disappeared in a fireball. Still, the ones I wonder most about are the ones who just didn't come back and no one saw them go in the heat of battle. Crew chiefs were like old dogs those days, sitting and facing the evening though they knew the plane would be dead at least. The ones who came back from the jungle, the coastwatcher specials, they just made the real losses worse." Jack's heart felt like a sponge, and his next thoughts squeezed all the remaining emotion out of him.

He spoke quietly: "I miss Nebraska. I never thought I'd miss Nebraska, but I do. I miss the cool summer breeze, and apples off the tree. But most I miss the snow. Here they have no word for it even. Maybe I should go back, call it a day here and see what I could have over there."

Doc Mendel patted Jack on the arm with his old doctor's touch as he answered. "Know what? I'm sorry to be the bearer of bad news, but here's the lowdown. You don't miss the air. Air is cool here in the morning too, and up where you go to meet your lost friends, it's cool too. Apples—they have apples here too, bigger and crunchier than anything that the soil in Nebraska could ever produce. But as for the snow ... you don't miss the snow. You miss the footprints in the snow, the ones you made, and the ones of your brother right beside yours as you walked with your sled from the hill homeward and saw the smoke from the house. But the snow that had the prints melted away a long time ago, and the new snow is white and cold and glistening just like the old, but it just isn't the same snow, and the prints, they're not there anymore."

Doc laced his fingers behind his head. "I miss the grass I mowed that day back in '38, but it's no more, and no grass that has grown since is the same, even on the same back yard. You just have to let go of the footprints, pal, they only exist in your memories now, and looking at where they used to be will only turn the knife. I should let the grass go, but I can't. Pot and Kettle—we ought to go into business under that name, eh?"

Jack wiped his eyebrow with his arm. "It's just that I miss Kay so much, Doc. I was sure I had her for my entire life, and now she's gone. Maybe she'll turn out to be my defining moment in life, but right now she's not even a memory yet."

"There will come a day, Jack, when she's no longer your first thought in the morning but the second. Then, sometime later, she'll be your stinging pain fifteen minutes after you wake up, and one day, you'll get all the way to lunch without remembering her. And the day will finally come when she's in your head only at five in the afternoon without filling it entirely, but there'll never be a day when you go to sleep without her. Sorry about that, but hey, I've lived it. It'll hurt, I guarantee."

Jack couldn't speak. The lump in his throat was just too big. He stood up, squeezed Doc on the shoulder and went to his cabin. Doc remained on the porch until he fell asleep in the chair, the almost empty glass still in his hand.

Next week, on a fishing trip to a nearby stream, Jack told Doc of Don's theory of life as a bag of stones being cast in the lake, and how the flight of the stone equaled the wait for any event and then the event itself was just a plunge through the surface.

Doc nodded. "I like that idea a lot. It's a good analogy for life, for sure. Actually there's a special bag of stones for every man, and the stones in that bag are smooth to the touch, perfectly-formed and rounded to perfection. It's the bag of women. And these stones are cast for skips." Doc wet his whistle so he could keep on talking.

"When you toss those stones, you just hope they'd skip on forever, and never plunge in. The first skip is so high and so long you think your stone will never fall, but after a while there's a first bounce off the water. The next skip is long enough to make you forget the bounce, but then there's the next one, and the next, always with a shorter skip in between."

Doc leaned back and closed his eyes. "Some people have gravity-defying skips, like my grandparents. They were in love with each other all the way until death did them part, and to me at least it looked like they never bounced. With my wife, well, the first bounces were long and high and made me believe I was also out of Sir Isaac Newton's grasp, but looking back, I've got to admit there were many hard bounces, and every one of them bled energy off the flight."

He opened one lid and peered at Jack out of his deep-set, dark-rimmed eye. "I'll tell you I threw some other stones at the same time, a nurse at the hospital and the wife of a pal of mine. But hey, as a kid, you always tried to have more than one stone skipping at once, right? I just extended the idea."

Jack tried to echo the sentiment. "With Kay, I never thought it would come to such a sudden plunge, but I remember how some of the best skipping stones just failed to bounce."

Doc nodded. "Yeah, sometimes when the stone looked perfect, it'd plunge after just a couple short skips. And then, even after many skips, there's the final touchdown, all the energy is spent, you go through the surface, and all that remains is the slow descent down to the bottom. Damn it, that's just how it goes." No fish were caught that day, but they cared little. Sunshine and good company, not to mention Wilma's lunch bag special, was more than sufficient.

For two weeks, Doc seemed to be getting better and better. He participated in the chores of the hotel and even began to help plan the rebuilding of the plantation's main lodge. Still, Jack was surprised to see the mission doctor one morning. "Hello, Jack," Dr. Ullrich said. "Have you seen Doc Mendel today?"

Jack had to say no, as he had been busy all morning fighting with Martin.

"It's just that someone broke into my medicine cabinet during the night and stole all my morphine. I was curious to see whether he knew anything about it."

"Thank you for telling me," Jack said, the pit of his stomach starting to ache. "I'll start looking for him straight away."

Dr. Ullrich turned to leave and said he'd send people out too.

As he went out of the door, Jack had to lean on his fists on the table. His head whirred and he felt nauseous. Martin passed the hut and Jack motioned to him through the window to come in. Jack told him: "Doc's in trouble. Chances are he broke into the mission's supply of morphine. We need to find him *now*."

Martin dropped whatever task he had on his mind. "I'll go

gather people for the search. You start uphill, and we'll go along the coast and towards Tulagi." He darted off, and before long, Jack received a party of five maybe ten-year-old kids to help him. He issued them some instructions in pidgin and they scattered into the bush beyond the plantation. Jack had one idea himself where Doc might have gone.

As he approached a hilltop, he was met by a giggling kid who said he had found Doc, and he grabbed Jack's finger to lead him to the spot. When they reached a hillock from which they could see the lone palm at the highest spot of the hill, Jack saw Doc Mendel.

He appeared to be sleeping, and that was why the kid found it so funny, someone sleeping in bright sunlight. Jack placed his palms against each other and then placed his hands under his cheek, to tell the kid Doc should be left sleeping. Jack reached into his pocket and found a penny, with which the kid disappeared downhill like a ferret. Jack went to Doc and sat down by him.

He took the dead man in his arms and closed his eyes. On the ground next to him was a syringe and a bottle of morphine with just a single drop left in it. Jack loosened the rubber hose from the emaciated arm of his friend and laid it in a coil on the ground. The palm tree, against which Doc had leaned as he took his final fix, shadowed them from the fierce sun. The view from this solitary hill allowed the viewer to soak in the lush forest, the deep-hued sea, and the islands in it all at once, and Jack thought Doc had chosen the perfect spot for dying.

After a long while Jack heard Martin lead a party uphill. The kid had gone to tell all his friends of the funny sleeping man, so Martin had dismissed the search party and gone up the hill with four men and a stretcher. When he found Jack and Doc, Jack had already done his crying, and he lifted Doc onto the stretcher. As the men began to carry the body down to the mission, Martin and Jack collected Doc's belongings, along with the bottle and hose and syringe. On the ground, under a small stone, were two envelopes, one addressed to Jack, the other to Doc's ex-wife, with an address in San Francisco on it. Jack pocketed the envelopes and followed a silent Martin down the hill.

Later, Jack opened his envelope. Sitting on the porch with his legs on the railing, he sighed deeply and then straightened the triple-folded paper to read his letter. It was written in Doc's sketchy doctor's handwriting:

I came back here to build me a hut to keep out the rain and find myself a quiet little spot for fishing. You tried to help me do just that, Jack, and I appreciate your effort. But Life no longer has a hook on the line it's offering me, and I long for the deep waters to escape the nets. Sorry Jack, thank you, and goodbye.

PS Just for the record: my full name is Nathan Benjamin Mendel. Not one of my friends asked for it or used it since 1942. I would like to be buried with the name showing. As for religious rites, I ask for none, but do as you please.

Jack said, under his breath, "Bon voyage, Nathan Mendel, wherever you are."

In the evening he went to the mission, where the doctor had already drafted a death certificate. In the morning they buried Doc's body close to the Leaning Tree, in a spot where the view was perfect. Jack went over to Guadalcanal and rummaged around in the junkyard to find a shot-through propeller blade, on which he wrote Doc's name, nickname, and date of death. He didn't know the date of birth, and in any case he deemed it unnecessary. The mission priests wondered about the suitability of the blade as a tombstone, but Jack merely said, "He was an aviator at heart, even if he never flew." He mailed the remaining letter to Doc's wife, along with a copy of the death certificate, from the big island on the next day.

And on the day after that, he packed.

Martin thought he had to try one last time to turn Jack's head around. With Jack tucking his last remaining clothes into a worn suitcase, Martin stood at his shoulder. "So where will you go? Nebraska? San Francisco? Sydney?"

Jack looked at him blandly. "Eh, somewhere. I'll let you know when I find a spot. I've got no clue, but I guess it's Sydney first and then I'll move on. I'll mail you."

Martin saw no reason to keep calm any more. "Jack, look at yourself. It took a World War for you to find this place and make it your home. What's it going to take next time?" Without waiting for an answer, he left the hut disgusted, angry, and at a loss for words.

Jack opened his mouth and shut it slowly, because even if he could've answered Martin's question, he couldn't have said it out loud. Internally, he was caving in; outwardly, he seemed just a tired man in search of solace. He closed the suitcase and locked it with its tiny key. Looking around him, wondering whether it was the last time he'd see his lodge, Jack prepared himself to leave, but from the doorway he returned to the fireplace. He picked up the enameled matchbox cover and placed it in the breast pocket of his leather flight jacket.

The last Martin saw of Jack was when he was on a boat

which was just casting off from the market pier. Martin rushed downhill to see him one last time, but he was nearly too late. Jack stood at the bow, looking out towards Guadalcanal, but when he turned and saw Martin, he waved once, in the royal fashion, palm upturned and a circular motion of the wrist. Martin burst into tears, but he was too far to see Jack crying.

To Jack's surprise, he had a mate for the flight to Sydney. As soon as Jack was seated on the plane, Bill Peet settled himself down in the aisle seat. "Hello, mate! Fancy meeting you here. I'm off to Woollongong to see me old mum. I go every year. Usually I go a bit later in the season, but she's not feeling too well so I decided to hop on this one instead. Great to have you for company!"

Jack could not be so unfriendly to Bill as to wish him a nice trip on another plane, but he couldn't bring himself to much small talk either. The flight was therefore a long monologue of Bill's. Bill did, however, manage to squeeze it out of Jack that while he was flying away from the Solomons, he had no idea where to go next.

Upon landing in Sydney, Jack tried to get through his goodbyes with Bill as fast as possible. No such luck, as Bill said, "Look, since you've no idea where you're going, don't try to tell me you know. We're going to Rose Bay. I know a great fish restaurant there, and I'll buy you lunch. After that, you're rid of me—but for this meal, mate, you do have the time."

Grudgingly, Jack agreed to the arrangement.

The taxi ride from the airport to the harbor was just as silent as the long flight over, at least on Jack's part. Bill chattered on about just about everything, but nothing could pique Jack's interest. At Rose Bay, Bill paid for the taxi and they got off with their luggage.

413

Jack decided to go for one last tug on the leash. "Look, Bill, it's been great knowing you, but I sort of just want to be on my way. After lunch, I just have to find a place to stay for a day or two and think it all out, so I get an idea of where I want to go eventually."

Bill set down his luggage and put his hands on Jack's shoulders. "I know it's been rough on you for a while, matey. I mean, it sure ain't easy to be dropped like that, I know. Happened to me a couple times, even if not by someone as great as Kay, but by my standards, nice ladies just as well. Hurt like hell. The first couple of times, at least. But you *do* get by, eventually."

Jack smiled. "I know you mean well, Bill, but really, I just need some time by myself to get my thoughts straightened out. There's no avoiding it right now."

Bill saw pleading was not going to help. "My final deal to you. Here's two envelopes, one from Martin, one from Reverend Miller. What if you go out on a walk somewhere and see if that'd clear you up? If you get a chance, take a look at these two envelopes. I have no idea what's in 'em, but I guess they both have something to show you. Then, come back to me and we'll talk it over while having a great lunch right here. Eh? Isn't that a plan? I'll take your luggage and keep it for you, till you get back. No strings attached, except the free lunch—it does exist after all, I'll show you."

Jack took the envelopes and put them in his shirt pocket. He was raring to go, but Bill's sincere attempts disheartened him. "Okay, okay, okay. I'll go for a walk, with these envelopes, which I hereby commit to safekeeping in my breast pocket, like so, and go somewhere. You don't happen to have a map, do you?"

"You don't need a map, just walk that way for half an

hour, then turn ninety, and head where your nose points. Repeat in reverse, and you'll be back here in two hours. If you can walk and look at the envelopes at the same time, fine, otherwise, stop at some point and check 'em out."

Jack started down a road leading away from Bill, hoping it'd lead him away from his past life. "See you in two hours," he shouted over his shoulder. Soon the road met with New South Head Road, and Jack decided to take a left turn here. He walked with nary a coherent thought in his mind, only muddled questions begging for answers. He looked out to Rose Bay, but its beauty was lost to him entirely. His walking was not at all his usual springy gait with a definite push from the ball of the foot, but a heel-to-toe chain-gang shuffle.

After some time the road began to wind up a hill, built upon a ledge and lined with a low stone wall. Jack dragged himself up the hill, oblivious to the surroundings, entirely taken up with his dark thoughts running amok in a circle. Passers-by wondered about his brooding demeanor. He did not acknowledge anyone, unaware of everything in his vicinity.

Gradually the road was getting steep and he felt his weight increase with every step, proving the law of gravitational potential energy. That energy, while stored within his mass, had no effect on his depleted mind. He felt short of breath by the time he came to a hairpin turn in the road, and he had to stop.

A bunch of boys on bicycles freewheeled down the hill, racing to see who had the most nerve. Exchanging the leader every few seconds, with the chickens braking every now and then and the brazen ones pedaling for still more speed, they zoomed down the hill above the hairpin. What they could not see was a truck lumbering uphill, the driver gearing down as the speed he had collected on the level road had begun to bleed off. He was closing from downhill when Jack saw the bicyclists on the road.

Jack's benumbed brain was alerted to the situation by the blaring of the truck's horn, and the shrill screams of the boys as they scattered any which way to avoid a collision with the truck, still roaring uphill. Jack's fighter pilot instincts, quick neck, and his well-honed peripheral vision saved him, as he saw one cyclist approach from the right, and the bulky black form of the truck move on him from the left as he threw his head around. He jumped over the stone wall with a fast bound, just in time to see the truck hit the wall and the cyclist fly over him.

Maybe it was the sudden change from mindless brooding to an imminent threat on his life, but in the air he felt weightless. The slope down from the road was steep enough for him to fall several yards before smashing into the ground. He hit it shoulder first, and on the next bounce, he was certainly not weightless. He felt his weight to be immense, and the Earth, rushing towards him again with its bushes and gravel and assorted trash, was the one gravitating towards him. The second bounce, which he took on his left side, jolted him back to reality, with all mass returned to its respective owner. By now, he was very interested in stopping his descent, with his brain in survival mode for the first time since the war.

A few more yards of tumbling ensued, but now he managed to grab a bush. His grip slipped and the friction burned his palm, but he slowed down enough to decelerate further by spreading his legs and grasping at passing bushes. When he was almost confident he would come to a stop soon, a sudden drop in the ledge threw him in the air once more, and when the final impact of his fall hit him in the chest, forcing all the

416

air out of him, he passed out. His final sensation before losing consciousness was a sharp pain across his sternum.

When he came to, he was lying on his stomach, in grass, facing downhill, with the skin on his hands and face burning and bleeding. His knees hurt. The slope was still steep enough to cause him to slide down, so he slowly turned himself to face uphill. The sharp pain on his chest was pulsating, and he checked to see if any bones were broken. Doing that, he hit upon an object in his breast pocket. Slowly, wheezing with pain, he sat up, dug his heels in the ground, and opened his jacket and shirt. Then he put his hand in his pocket to see what caused the pain.

The matchbox cover had taken the brunt of the impact. It had been edgewise when he hit the ground, and had given him an impression on the chest. A red welt marked the spot where the box had been at the moment he hit the ground, and as Jack touched it, the pain radiated again. He looked at the only item he had brought from his childhood home, which had followed him through the years in Tulagi, then spent some time in Kay's possession in Boston, and returned to be part of his current aching existence.

When he found the envelopes in his shirt pocket while fumbling to see if he had cracked ribs, he wondered for a second whether he wanted to see what was inside them. This feeling passed soon, and he took them out. Neither had any text on them, and the contents seemed identical too—just two photographs. Both envelopes were nearly perforated from being between his chest and the matchbox cover when he hit the ground. Jack took the one on the top in his hand, put the other one back in his pocket, and opened it.

Inside it was a picture of three schoolchildren from the mission school, with Jack and Reverend Miller acting as bookends. Jack had once agreed to a plan of the Reverend's in which Jack would give the top three students a sightseeing flight. All semester long, the students toiled to win this stunning prize, and the three winners, one boy and two girls, were beside themselves with joy when the results were finally announced. Jack studied the radiant looks of satisfaction in their eyes and smiled, remembering how the kids had looked during the flight itself when Jack saw them in the rearview mirror. The picture was but a faint reflection of that delight.

Jack stuck the picture back into its mauled envelope and took out the other one. He was pretty sure he knew its contents, and he was right. Martin had picked the best picture from Gula Island, the one into which Kay had injected all her beauty and presence. Jack looked at that picture for a long while, studying her features with his eyes and remembering in his heart just how lovely she'd looked, stretched out there on the blanket. His only conscious thought was one of redemption—just as he did not number the bullets he fired in the war, he did not cast the shadows in pictures. They were for information only, not to act upon, not to avoid, and especially not to fear.

When he finally put away the photograph, he shook his head and felt his transitory thoughts giving way to one overwhelmingly powerful one. He finally came to understand he could not run any more. There was no new place for him waiting to be found, to be called home. Home was not just a place, and happiness was not just a person. Home was a set of thoughts interconnected with a place, bound to each other like yarn in a loom.

The matchbox cover was his home; it had been someone's possession in Sweden, reminding that person of a place she loved, then it had traveled to the middle of nowhere in Nebraska, and there it had been given new significance. Now, it was Jack's sole remaining link with his childhood home in Nebraska and his last home in the Solomons. It assumed a whole new purpose in his heart.

Jack looked out at the sea and felt a dizzying need to get back to his island, where the snow would still have his footprints. He still had stones to cast, ones that would cross the paths of many other such arcs in the air, and their crisscrossing ripples would become the property of them all. And, he had Don's word on ripples: they were his to keep when all else would fade away. The pain stinging in his sternum reminded him that he was still alive and able to collect more, as soon as he let go of his dark thoughts and concentrated on the light.

Looking left and right to see where to go—down was not an option and upward the scramble would be too hard—he decided to go left on a level route through the bushes. It took him some time to meet up with the road again, and he started towards the bay, scarcely noticing the ambulance and police car which rushed uphill to the collision site. He could not walk fast with the bruises he'd received in the fall, but every step confirmed his determination for returning to Halavo Bay. He fumbled about for his sunglasses, and found that the hard case had indeed saved them from being crushed. Wearing them he was able to look into the sun-splendored Rose Bay and note how beautiful it was, but also how it would always be second in beauty to his own bay.

He met Bill Peet on the terrace of a restaurant, close to the place where he'd left him. Bill was enjoying a large beer and a cigar, having propped his legs up on a rope railing. He looked happy enough for starters, but Jack's appearance widened his smile even further. "Does this mean I can't sell off your suitcase? And what happened to you, mate? Looks like you were

419

hit by a lorry!"

Through his pain Jack forced a smile. "Yep, it sure does. I need my luggage, and you're absolutely right about the lorry. Actually I'd like to have my suitcase now so I can return to the airport and see if any planes are headed back up."

"Excellent." Bill had a sip of his beer, which had glimmering condensation drops on the outside, giving it a dewy appearance. "But let's have the free lunch first, okay? I have a table there in the back so we can chat a bit. Shake some of that dust off your clothes, will ya? I know the manager here and he has a reputation to maintain."

Jack tried again to resist, as now his urge for returning was prohibiting any delays, but Bill would have nothing of it. "Listen, bloke, you haven't eaten anything in donkey's years. You'll pass out and die, and I'd hate that. Just follow me, will you?" Bill stood up, stretched, and went in. Suddenly realizing that he was starving, Jack followed Bill in.

The restaurant was practically built right over the sea. Little dinghies were tied to buoys all around it, standing in for the yachts that were out sailing. Some large sailboats, looking like massive slow metronomes, floated nearby. Bill took Jack to a table at the back with a gorgeous view over the bay, and shoved a menu into his hands. "Pick anything on a plate, mate, you deserve it. I recommend the lobster."

Jack had a look and wanted to order all of the courses at once, but settled on steamed mussels as appetizers and the lobster for his main course. Bill opted for the same and ordered a bottle of white wine.

When the bottle arrived and was opened with all the traditional fanfare, Bill took his glass in his hand and motioned for Jack to take his. "What shall we drink to? I mean, what did you decide to do?"

Jack was silent for a moment. "Let's just say that I saw the light. All I want now is to get back to Halavo Bay and get everything going just as it was until just recently." He took out the envelopes and showed Bill their contents. "These helped, too," he said with a smile.

"I'll drink to that," Bill toasted him, and took a sip. "You know, Jack, that Martin, the good Reverend, and myself, we've been working on you for a while now, but damn, you're one thick-skulled Yankee. You really thought you could go on a walkabout and hit upon something better than what you already had. Judging by your sorry clothes it took a little fall from grace to find out the hard way, eh?"

Jack looked out to the bay, knowing that to his right, beyond the horizon, lay the Solomons and home. "You're absolutely right. I can't tell you what made me so messed up, but it's all clear now. I know just what to do, and how. First thing to do is to get the second Kingfisher assembled and fly it over to the Islands. Do you know of anyone who could help me do that?"

"All in due course, mate, all in due course. Ah, speaking of courses…" Bill said, inhaling the scent of the mussels a waitress brought. "No more talk, not until I have had some food. Dive in!" he urged Jack.

Delicious was not the word for the mussels, and the lobster which followed was profoundly gratifying. Jack ate in silence, all the time thinking of all the food Wilma had cooked for him back in Tulagi, and how good everything tasted when it was eaten at his own hotel. When the lobster had disappeared, Bill ordered coffee and cognac, and even though Jack was not well-experienced with the drink, he savored it with pleasure.

When Jack felt it was the right time to resume conversation, and he opened his mouth to do so, Bill asked the waiter for binoculars. Jack was surprised at this, but said nothing. The waiter soon returned with a pair of 10x50 field glasses, and Bill started scanning the bay from the beach out to the sea.

"Aha!" he exclaimed after a few moments, and handed over the binoculars to Jack. "Look out there, right of the fourth sailboat from the pier," and he lay back in his deep rattan chair with obvious pleasure. Jack focused the view on the pier's end, then counted four boats to the right. When he hit on the floatplane, he couldn't believe his eyes.

"Someone has a Kingfisher down here?" he asked.

"You do, mate, you do. It's the plane you had in crates down here."

Jack was all mixed up. "But it's taxiing this way?"

"So it is. Wonder why? Well, I have a few friends in the business. So when I called them up and asked if they'd like to build me a plane, they jumped at it. You see, for the pros, it only takes a few evenings after office hours to put something like that together, bit like a kid's jigsaw puzzle for them. It's been thoroughly tested—they insisted on breaking it in—and unlike your previous rogue plane, this one sports a registration marking on the fuselage. We got you VH-JMG and it only took some strings to pull. The blokes flew her in just now. I figgered you'd be about ready for her by now."

The realization of what Bill had done was slowly dawning on Jack, but he had no words for his feelings.

"So, instead of trying to hop a ride on a cargo plane, you can hop in your own plane and fly back home. You know the route, but just to be safe, my mates supplied your plane with the latest maps, and behind your seat in the cockpit, you'll find the six jerry cans for extra fuel. Just remember to fill 'em up when you get to Port Moresby."

Jack put away the binoculars. "I'm in your debt for the rest of my life, Bill Peet."

After sipping some more cognac, Bill said, "There's nothing you owe anyone, mate. All it took was a little conniving and conspiring, and of course some cloak-and-dagger intrigue to keep the secret from you and let you come to the conclusion all by yourself. Sorry it took a nasty fall for you to finally come around, but in a week you won't remember what happened."

Jack touched his reddened forearm absentmindedly, and looked out to the bay. "Would you mind if I went to the plane and started on my way home today?"

Bill put on his mischievous smile. "Frankly, I'd be surprised if you didn't. The manager will lend us his speedboat so we can get there right after you're done with your coffee."

Jack's coffee was left to cool by itself. The men descended to a pier built under the restaurant via a stairway from the terrace. Bill had the keys to a Chris Craft Deluxe Runabout which duly impressed Jack. Bill sped and slalomed like a maniac amidst the dinghies until he reached open water, and then he really opened it up. The boat glided along the bay and Jack let the slipstream blow his head clear.

In no time Bill had throttled back and run a circle around the slowly-advancing Kingfisher. Jack felt his throat tightening for all the work his friends had done for him, all the more so when he saw the name on the cowling: *Miss Tumora II*. Bill allowed the boat to descend into the water and guided her alongside the main float from behind.

Jack climbed on the boat's deck, clambered up to the wing, then kneeled down to pick up his suitcase and leather jacket. He greeted and thanked the men, one of whom was on the wing and the other jumping from the cockpit, leaving the engine idling. They hopped down to the boat and took their seats for the ride back.

"Well, this is it!" Jack shouted down to Bill over the noise of the two growling engines.

Bill saluted him and pushed his boat away from the main float. "See you up in Tulagi!" he shouted as Jack climbed into his plane.

Everything felt new and yet it all was as it should be. All gauges read good as Jack scanned them while strapping himself in. He checked to see that Bill was clear of the plane, then looked forward to see his course unobstructed and pushed forward the throttle. With a satisfying roar, the engine responded, and Jack was planing in moments. Remembering something as the main float began to plane, he aborted the take-off, much to the chagrin of Bill and the men in the boat, who'd been racing him. Looking anxious, Bill guided his boat alongside Jack's plane again.

Jack was fumbling in his pockets for chewing gum. Finding a weary packet of PK, he ripped it open and began to chew with renewed vigor. By now Bill had to be thinking whether it was safe to let him fly after the fall, but when Jack had the gum in a malleable form, he held up one of the envelopes for Bill to see. Now he could understand: Jack was merely sticking Kay's picture onto the instrument panel for company on the long flight. What he couldn't see was that Jack had pasted the matchbox cover above the compass.

It would lead him home.

Acknowledgments

This book started out as a one-man project, but whereas the early years were marked by solitude, the last year was a time of collaboration. First, Tim Wright pointed me to Authonomy, the HarperCollins website, and there I met the people who made *Tulagi Hotel* a reality: SJ Hecksher-Marquis and Jason Horger of Diiarts. Without their determination and trust in this book, I'd still be submitting it to agents and publishers. Jason gets a medal for bravery as he edited the book on his own initiative.

At Authonomy, *Tulagi Hotel* found a set of friends, all of whom it is not possible to mention here; however, I must note Kimberly Menozzi, Greta van der Rol, S. Richard Betterton, Tashya Michelle Paul, Alice Gray, Jeff Blackmer, Loretta Proctor, Susanne O'Leary, and Ola Saltin, who expressed their support early on and never forgot to bump any shameless plug I wrote on the site. Dan Holloway was instrumental in making me believe my writing was up to par. Here in Finland, Graham Hill was the first to read *Tulagi Hotel* in its entirety and he offered many valuable comments, as did Pasi Virta and Timo Lampikoski.

I received technical support from many people, and first I must mention Wells Norris. This retired Navy pilot picked up my request for help in 1998 and we exchanged emails for about two years. What little Wells did not know, he dug up from his friends, and thus helped immensely in the construction of the factual base of this book.

My old friend, Juha Heikkinen, produced the cover for the Pfoxmoor and Diiarts editions with his usual skill. Peter

Flahavin sent me thousands of wartime and current photographs from the region. My co-operation with Diane Nelson and Sessha Batto of Pfoxmoor proved to be a most enjoyable one. Robyn Charnock provided the permission to use the authentic Burns Philp letter in the original cover art (now included in the book's front pages). Peter Morin offered valuable period information on Boston. David Chudoba delivered many keen comments on technical, factual and stylistic issues, and last but not least, Barrett Tillman, the eminent historian, read a version of this book and volunteered detailed comments. I am deeply humbled by his kind support to a fledgling author.

I remain ever grateful to all these people, and many more for all the help I've received, and firmly believe the interaction made this book so much better. And finally, the support of my wife Leena-Mari and sons Ossi and Paavo through all these years was essential for bringing this work to a close—I thank them for their patience.

About the Author

Heikki Hietala is a Senior Lecturer at Haaga-Helia University of Applied Sciences. He holds an M.A. in English Philology from the University of Jyvaskyla, Finland, and has worked in IT and localization for more than 20 years.

Heikki is also a keen writer of short stories, some of which have appeared in anthologies, e-zines and literary websites. All of his writing is in English, though his native language is Finnish.

Tulagi Hotel began as a single idea and then went through 12 years of intensive research and background work. It has its roots in the author's deep interest in military history and popular culture.

Heikki is a keen fan of British comedy and an avid Monty Python aficionado.

Catch Heikki online at:

www.tulagihotel.com

THE CYCLIST

A World War II Drama
by Fredrik Nath

"The story is brilliantly executed... Nath's biggest success is the sustained atmospheric tension that he creates somewhat effortlessly."
-LittleInterpretations.com

"A haunting and bittersweet novel that stays with you long after the final chapter—always the sign of a really well-written and praiseworthy story. It would also make an excellent screenplay."
-Historical Novels Review—Editor's Choice, Feb 2011

http://novels.fingerpress.co.uk/the-cyclist.html

FAREWELL BERGERAC

A Wartime Tale of Love, Loss and Redemption
by Fredrik Nath

François Dufy, alcoholic and alone, is dragged into the war effort when he rescues a young Jewish girl from the Nazi Security Police.

Then the British drop supplies and a beautiful SOE agent whom Dufy falls in love with. But as the invaders hunt down the partisans in the deep, crisp woodland, nothing works out as Dufy had hoped.

http://novels.fingerpress.co.uk/
farewell-bergerac.html

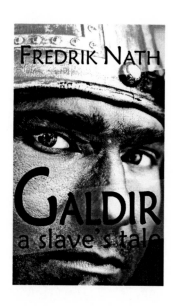

GALDIR: A SLAVE'S TALE

Barbarian Warlord Saga, Volume I
by Fredrik Nath

"Highly commended"
-Yeovil Literary Prize

A tale of love, brutal battles and conflict, in which a mystical prophecy winds its way through an epic saga of struggle against Rome.

**http://novels.fingerpress.co.uk/
galdir-a-slaves-tale.html**

MAGIC AND GRACE

A Novel of Florida, Love, Zen,
and the Ghost of John Keats
by Chad Hautmann

"Quirky and funny and heartfelt and rich"
-Ft. Myers News-Press

"A compulsively readable mixture of fast-paced plot, likable
protagonist, and subtly deep theme"
-Magdalena Ball, CompulsiveReader.com

"Highly entertaining, often thoughtful, and strategically
humorous"
-Ft. Myers & Southwest Florida Magazine

http://novels.fingerpress.co.uk/
magic-and-grace.html

Lightning Source UK Ltd.
Milton Keynes UK
UKOW042331100613

212044UK00003B/653/P